Louise Fuller was once a tomboy who hated pink and always wanted to be the Prince—not the Princess! Now she enjoys creating heroines who aren't pretty push-overs but strong, believable women. Before writing for Mills & Boon she studied literature and philosophy at university, and worked as a reporter on her local newspaper. She lives in Tunbridge Wells with her impossibly handsome husband Patrick and their six children.

Growing up near the beach, **Annie West** spent lots of time observing tall, burnished lifeguards—early research! Now she spends her days fantasising about gorgeous men and their love-lives. Annie has been a reader all her life. She also loves travel, long walks, good company and great food. You can contact her at annie@annie-west.com or via PO Box 1041, Warners Bay, NSW 2282, Australia.

THEIR DUBAI MARRIAGE MAKEOVER

LOUISE FULLER

RECLAIMING HIS RUNAWAY CINDERELLA

ANNIE WEST

MILLS & BOON

First published in Great Britain 2022
by Mills & Boon, an imprint of HarperCollins*Publishers* Ltd,
1 London Bridge Street, London, SE1 9GF

www.harpercollins.co.uk

HarperCollins*Publishers*
1st Floor, Watermarque Building,
Ringsend Road, Dublin 4, Ireland

Their Dubai Marriage Makeover © 2022 Louise Fuller

Reclaiming His Runaway Cinderella © 2022 Annie West

ISBN: 978-0-263-30102-1

10/22

MIX
Paper from
responsible sources
FSC® C007454

This book is produced from independently certified FSC™ paper
to ensure responsible forest management.
For more information visit www.harpercollins.co.uk/green.

Printed and Bound in Spain using 100% Renewable Electricity
at CPI Black Print, Barcelona

THEIR DUBAI MARRIAGE MAKEOVER

LOUISE FULLER

MILLS & BOON

To my mother-in-law, Ann Fuller.

11th May 1935–25th February 2022.

With love.

CHAPTER ONE

FLOPPING BACK AGAINST the scratchy hospital pillow, Delphi gritted her teeth. How much longer was she going to have to sit here?

She had no idea how long she had been waiting. Hospitals were like casinos. The longer you stayed, the harder it was to keep track of time. Annoyingly, her phone had run out of juice soon after she'd arrived, but Carole, the nurse who'd iced her bruised wrist, had looked at her as if she had grown horns when she'd asked if she could charge it.

Breathe, she told herself firmly.

Forcing her shoulders to relax, she inhaled in through her nose slowly, held her breath, counting to seven, and then exhaled through her mouth. She was supposed to make a whooshing sound, like a child blowing out the candles on a birthday cake, but she didn't want to think about her birthday right now. If she did, then she would think about Dan and her brothers and the ranch—

A wave of homesickness rolled through her, and she sat up straight, ignoring the jolt to her wrist. Carole had left the orange floral curtains slightly open and she stared through the gap.

It was the Fourth of July. She would have thought today of all days the hospital would be like a ghost town. That everyone would be meeting up with family and friends to eat charred burgers and their great-grandma's special potato salad.

But there were so many people milling around it might as well be that casino she'd thought about.

When she'd mentioned this to Dr Kelly, the doctor who had examined her, he'd rolled his eyes.

'It might be all burgers and potato salad for you, young lady, but this is the ER's busiest twenty-four hours of the year. You name it. We get it. Food poisoning. Dehydration. Sunstroke. Firework-related injuries,' he'd listed grumpily as he'd peered into her eyes with his ophthalmoscope. 'And, of course, my favourite.' He'd scowled at her. 'Drink-driving accidents.'

'I didn't drink anything,' she'd protested. 'Nothing alcoholic, anyway.'

Which was true. Nor had she eaten at the barbecue either. Maybe if she had she wouldn't be here. It was low blood sugar that had made her sway forward like that, only nobody had listened to her. Then, of course, she'd had to go and wince when they took her pulse.

The corners of her mouth twisted. If only she had eaten something—a mouthful of potato salad, a slice of watermelon. But she hadn't been hungry. Truthfully, she hadn't had much of an appetite for weeks now—

Her thoughts shunted into one another, just as the pickup had shunted her hours earlier, and in one of those strange distortions of time that kept happening on and off when she wasn't policing her brain she was back in London, reliving those few fraught seconds when she had finally accepted the truth. That happy endings happened to other people. *Not to her.*

She hadn't realised at the time, but that was the moment her marriage—that uncharacteristically optimistic...no, make that *reckless* leap of faith into the unknown—had ended not with a bang, or even a whimper, but a *tut*.

A lump built in her throat, so that it hurt to breathe.

It had been such a tiny sound—the smallest click of tongue against teeth. But it was the smallness of it that had hurt the most. As if that was all she was worthy of. As if that was all he had to give her.

Only she didn't want to think about that now. Actually, she didn't want to think about him—her beautiful, cool-headed, cold-hearted husband—ever.

But, just as in their marriage, what she wanted was irrelevant.

Omar was always there—inside her head. A near-constant presence, jolting her awake from her dreams. Sliding into her thoughts with the same smoothness with which he had once slid into her eager, twitching body.

Heart accelerating, she stared through the gap in the curtains to where he stood on the other side of the ER, his dark head bent over the coffee machine, broad shoulders flexing beneath his blue shirt. She stilled instinctively as the dark head turned towards her. But of course it wasn't Omar. It was just her mind playing tricks on her.

He was miles away, chasing down a deal. He probably hadn't even paused to give a thought to his wife—his soon-to-be ex-wife. Her shoulders stiffened and she felt a twinge of pain—not in her wrist, which was the only part of her injured in the shunt, but in her heart.

It wasn't fair. Over the years she had trained herself to tread lightly through life, not to get attached to anywhere or anyone, and in the past it had never been a problem for her to walk away and keep on walking.

But it had hurt unbearably to leave Omar. As much as if she had cut off an arm. Or a hand. Her gaze dropped to the bare finger on her left hand. The only reason she had managed to do so was because to have stayed would have been an act of wilful self-destruction.

Except it was not that straightforward. As she knew only too well from her parents' very public and much-hyped affair and even more hyped tragic deaths, such acts were like black holes, swallowing those closest and sucking them into the darkness.

Like her father, and Dan, her brothers… She knew how hurt they would be when they found out that her marriage was over.

Angrily, she blanked her mind.

This was her fault. It should be her pain. And, however much it hurt, she was better off right now facing it alone.

And clearly Omar thought so too.

In the days following her leaving she had half thought, half hoped he would come after her. But Omar was no needy man-child like her biological father, Dylan. On the contrary, Omar Al Majid was emphatically, arrogantly male, from the top of his sculpted head to the soles of his handmade shoes and every place in between.

They'd married less than a year ago in Las Vegas. For the briefest, sweetest time he had been her man, and her love for him had been shocking in its intensity. Everything else had retreated. He had been everything.

But almost immediately there had been warning signs. The cut short honeymoon. His laptop always open, its screen glowing day or night because he worked all hours.

Work came first.

Maybe she should have said more, but to have done so would have been to admit how much she loved him, and she still found it hard to be open about her emotions. Like opening Pandora's box, she was both tempted and terrified at the same time. And Omar had always apologised so profusely for the long hours and the working weekends.

Her mouth twisted. He'd had a whole repertoire of apologies.

But after London she'd finally accepted that nothing— certainly no apology—would change the facts. She and Omar had been a real fairy tale—the original, old-fashioned kind, where the Little Mermaid didn't win the heart of her prince but was discarded and turned into sea foam.

She'd had to leave, and the next and the only logical step had been to make things official—which was why she'd filed for divorce a week ago...

Her head snapped up.

Two, maybe three voices, all female, were screaming obscenities. There was a crash of something metallic, followed by the hurried thud of footsteps, and then the curtains parted with a flourish, as if it was the opening night of a Broadway show.

'Hi, Delphi.' It was Carole, frowning over her shoulder as the screaming got louder. 'Sorry about that. Just some Fourth of July family fireworks. How's everything feeling?'

'A bit sore, but basically okay.' As if to test the truth of her words, Delphi moved her wrist from side to side. It hurt a little, but now it was more of a dull ache. 'What time is it?'

'Nearly two.' The nurse smiled. 'Now, as you know, things might be a little painful for a day or two.'

Running her good hand through her short, pinkish blonde pixie cut, Delphi nodded. As the X-rays had shown, it wasn't the first time she'd injured her arm. 'But it's best if you try and keep doing what you normally do. It will speed up the recovery and—'

'So can I leave now?'

Watching the other woman's smile stiffen, she felt like a jerk—and not for the first time. She wished she had her brothers' easy charm. But she wasn't a people person. It was one of the reasons she had chosen a career working with horses. But this was an ER, so obviously there were lots of people here, and people made her nervous.

Her gaze rested on Carole's face. Logically, she knew it was highly improbable that some nurse at a small hospital in rural Idaho would connect her with that little girl whose face had once been all over the internet. But it was hard to change her behaviour. Difficult to take people at face value. She had learned the hard way that kind words and a smile could distract from all manner of hidden agendas.

Her pulse fluttered. She could still remember the first time Omar had smiled at her. Not just the way it had lit up his face and turned him into a living flame, but also her panicky moth-like response. She had been stunned, dis-orientated, mesmerised. Torn between wanting to keep on staring at his fascinating curving mouth and a need to turn and run.

She glanced through the gap in the curtains to where the phantom Omar had stood by the coffee machine. It would have been better to run. It was always better—*safer*—to run. And if running wasn't possible, then the next best thing was to keep people at arm's length.

'Yes, you're good to go,' said Carole.

Delphi nodded. 'Thanks.'

Carole gave her the practised smile of a busy nurse. 'You're welcome. Any other questions?'

'Just one.'

Delphi shifted cautiously forward. As her feet touched the floor she stood up, swaying slightly in her high-heeled sandals, the hem of her dress flaring around her ankles.

Earlier, standing at the side of the road, staring at the crumpled back of her car, her first thought, as always, had been to avoid any drama. Drama might lead someone to put two and two together and make four, and before she could blink there would be a whole pack of paparazzi slavering on her doorstep with their long lenses and shouted questions.

That was why she had called her housemate Ashley on the way to the hospital and left a message telling her not to worry, and that she would make her own way back.

Only now she could do without having to wait around for a bus back to Creech Falls.

If this had happened nine months ago she would simply have rung home. Thanks to Omar, that wasn't possible. If she rang home she would have to explain why she was living on her own in Idaho and not in New York with her husband, and it had been agonising enough to admit to herself that her marriage was over.

To admit it to her family would be an entirely new level of pain.

Her heart squeezed with homesickness again, and with love, too, for the man who had adopted her and raised her as his own.

Dan Howard was the best man she knew. He was her pole star, and her brothers, Ed, Scott and Will, made up the compass points that kept her steady and safe. Telling them the truth was going to break their hearts, but particularly her adoptive father's. It was Dan who had introduced Omar to the family. Dan who had encouraged her to trust her instincts and her feelings. To let those feelings show rather than keep them buried.

Her eyes followed the headache-inducing pattern of the curtains from top to bottom. He would be devastated when he found out the truth. That the man he had welcomed as a son had let his adopted daughter down when she'd needed him most. And she would have to break that news to him soon. But not until the bruise around her heart had faded and she could think—no, say Omar's name out loud without stumbling over the syllables. Then at least she might have a chance of persuading Dan that she hadn't been crushed by her selfish, single-minded husband's betrayal.

And, more importantly, convince him that none of this was his fault.

She turned to Carole. 'Do you know if I can pick up a bus to Creech Falls from out front?'

'You can. But you don't need to.' The nurse looked up at her. 'You're getting a lift.'

She was? Delphi frowned. Ashley must have ignored her message. Her throat tightened and she felt a rush of affection for her housemate.

'She didn't need to do that,' she mumbled.

'*She* didn't.' Carole's smile softened as the curtain parted and a man stepped through the gap, his broad, muscular body blocking out the noise and light of the ER.

Every muscle in her body froze. For a few mindless seconds everything including her heartbeat stopped, just as if someone had pressed a pause button. And then, just as swiftly, it began beating double-time.

No, she thought, with a quickening of shock, her eyes still on Carole, feeling herself swaying on her stupid skinny heels. Then, *no*, again, this time more firmly and with a rising panic.

Only some unseen force was turning her head.

And there he was.

Not a mirage or a figment of her imagination but real. Flesh and blood. Bone and muscle. Her husband, Omar Al Majid, in a suit that must have been crafted in some workshop with the sole purpose of advertising the spectacular body that lay beneath.

She stared at him, numb, speechless. A vice was clamping around her ribs. It was all she could do to keep standing upright. She felt weak at the knees. That was the phrase people used, and up until last year she would never have taken it literally. But now here she was, for the second time in her life, shaking inside, her limbs quivering just as they had that very first time she'd seen him at the Amersham Polo Club.

The Amersham was her local club. She had been riding since she was old enough to sit on a horse, and playing polo for almost as long, and Sunday was always match day. Spectators came to enjoy the sunshine and the drama on the field.

She played with her brothers and father. They were a good team and that day they had won their morning match easily. After lunch, she had swapped with Scott and it had been then, standing at the sidelines with the whickering ponies, that she had seen Omar.

Not that she'd known him as Omar then. She hadn't known his name. He was just a man. An opponent in a dark blue jersey and white breeches. But she hadn't been able to take her eyes off him. And when finally, he'd dismounted his eyes had found hers, just as if he had known exactly where she was.

Feeling his gaze now, she looked up at him, her pulse accelerating. She hadn't been entirely sure when or *if* this moment would ever happen. But she had, of course, acted it out in her head multiple times. What she would say. How Omar would react. Only that didn't stop it being a shock.

But not as much of a shock as the fierce, quivering heat flooding her veins and spilling over her skin, so that for a moment she forgot Carole. Forgot the ache in her arm and the ache in her heart. She forgot everything. She just stood there, drowning in need for him, drinking him in…

Only it was ridiculous to feel that way. To feel anything other than anger for the man standing in front of her. The man who had taken her trust—*no*, demanded it—then casually tossed it in her face. A man who had promised to have her back, to be by her side, only to leave her alone in their penthouse apartment like some forgotten princess in a tower. He might have promised to love and cherish and honour her, but Omar was wedded to his business.

For a split second, her eyes flicked to the man standing in front of her. Over the last six weeks she had been asking herself the same question over and over. Why him? Out of all the men on the planet, why had she given her heart to Omar Al Majid?

Seeing him again, the answer was obvious.

She let her gaze rest on his face.

Typically, overhead fluorescent lighting was harsh and unflattering. Bleaching out colour and warmth and high-lighting every tiny flaw and imperfection. But Omar had no flaws or imperfections. Not visible ones, anyway. His beauty was astonishing. Every feature, every angle and line of his face was clean, precise, faceted like a gemstone— and, as with any priceless, glittering jewel, it was impossible to drag your gaze away from it.

Carole clearly felt the same way, she thought, aware suddenly of the nurse's rapt expression. Holding her breath, hating him, hating herself more, she met his gaze.

'Omar.'

'Delphi.'

He spoke softly, but there was a hard gleam in his brown eyes, a tension in the way he was holding his lean muscular body that made her breathing become shallow and her skin grow warm.

'I came as soon as I heard.'

The familiarity of his voice, or rather the dizzying rush of adrenaline it produced, prodded at her already jangling nerves so that for a few moments she didn't take in his actual words, just the smoothness of the syllables. Then she stiffened. What did he mean as soon as he'd heard? Heard how? From whom?

The curtains quivered as a doctor in a white coat strode past, his head lowered over a clipboard.

What had she been thinking? She should never have come here. And she wouldn't have done so. Only the driver of the pick-up—Pete? Was that his name?—had been so upset about hitting her car it had just seemed easier to go along with his insistence.

But, as Dan often said, nothing good came easy.

'How kind,' she said coolly. 'But you really didn't have to go to so much trouble.'

'It was no trouble.'

His mouth—that beautiful mouth that had kissed every centimetre of her body—slanted at one corner like a *fathah* accent.

'I was in San Francisco closing a deal, so it was merely a slight diversion.'

Pain scraped across her skin. *No change there, then*, she thought, a pulse of misery and anger beating in her throat. During the entire time she had known him Omar had always been closing a deal somewhere. It just so happened that today the deal was happening in San Francisco.

'A bit like our marriage,' she said, tilting her chin.

She felt her pulse jerk as his eyes narrowed under the veil of dark lashes, but he didn't react. Instead, he turned his head fractionally to look at Carole. 'Could you give us a moment?'

It was phrased as a question, and if any other man had spoken those exact same words it would have been treated as such. But despite the mildness of his tone there was no mistaking it for anything but an order.

That was how Omar spoke. Who he was.

Omar Al Majid was the son of one of the richest self-made men in the Middle East. His father Rashid's personal wealth was immense, rivalling that of the emirs and sheikhs who ruled the desert lands of the Persian Gulf. In Omar's world—a world which was outside the experience of most normal people—his word was law, his wishes instantly and always satisfied.

Catching sight of the nurse's expression, Delphi felt her pulse start to beat unevenly. It was the same look she had seen countless times on the faces of all those people who'd used to sidle up to her parents in shops and restaurants to ask for selfies or autographs.

It was a mixture of glazed, mute reverence and stunned disbelief that they were in the presence of some near-mythical being. Her stomach twisted. But then, as now, they'd only seen the glittering golden body, not the feet of clay.

'Of course.' The nurse blushed a little and, still staring dazedly up at Omar, disappeared through the curtains.

Now they were alone, his gaze flicked back to her face, and instantly the anger and frustration she had been holding tightly inside for so long surged up inside her. 'What exactly are you doing here, Omar?' she said stiffly.

He was silent for what seemed an eternity, and then he said calmly, 'I would have thought that was obvious.'

There was that same dangerous softness in his voice as before.

'You're hurt, and I'm your husband.'

A shiver ran through her body as he took a step closer.

'Clearly my place is here, by your side.'

Her chin jerked up. 'If you wanted to be by my side, you're about six weeks too late.' The memory of that rainy May morning swelled inside her, and with it an ache that no amount of painkillers could ever numb. 'I needed you then. In fact, I needed you during the nine months of our marriage. I don't need you now.'

Her words were provocative, deliberately so, but Omar didn't so much as blink. He just stood there, watching her in silence, calmly, assessingly.

'You really want to do this now?' he said finally, one smooth, dark eyebrow arching towards the strip lights. 'Here?'

How could he say that so calmly? Stand there with such serenity? But it shouldn't be that much of a surprise. Omar was the master of any social situation—including, it would appear, meeting his estranged wife in an ER at a rural hospital in the middle of Idaho.

'Do what?' Lifting her chin, trying to stay calm or at least look it, she forced herself to hold her gaze steady on his beautiful dark eyes. 'There's nothing left to do. We're done, remember? Finished. Over. Or did you not get the paperwork from my lawyer?'

He frowned. 'It must have got lost.'

She banked down her anger. 'Then I suggest you find it. Or do you think that rocking up here will make me change my mind?'

He did. Even before he spoke she could see it in his eyes. That assumption, so alien to her, that what he wanted to happen would happen.

'We made promises,' he said finally.

Or have you forgotten? She heard his question even though he hadn't asked it, and the tension in her stomach wound tighter. She hadn't forgotten their wedding, but it was easier to remember it when she couldn't see him.

'The kind of promises that mean something…'

He paused, and she thought he was going to say something else, admit that he had let her down, and then a phone rang close by—his phone, she realised a half-second later, and this time there was no pause. She watched in silence, with a pain like hot wire stabbing at her heart, misery and exhaustion swamping her fury as, without missing a beat, he fished it from his pocket and answered it.

'Yeah, that's right… No, send me a transcript and I'll give you a call back with my thoughts.' He ended the call. 'Where was I?'

She gritted her teeth. 'Here. Talking about promises that mean something. But I'm guessing your head is in some boardroom in San Francisco.'

Omar stood for a moment, just looking at her. His face was unreadable, but she could sense his impatience.

'I had to leave a very important meeting to come and find you.' He shook his head. 'But, unlike you, I honour my commitments. Although, given your recent behaviour, it's clear that concept might be beyond you.'

'If you feel that way, I'm surprised you're here. But please don't stay on my account. I'm sure you can find your way out.'

'As usual, you're choosing to misunderstand my intentions. I'm here to help you honour your commitments. Some things can't be left behind. Some things matter too much.'

Was he for real? Delphi stared at him, the hypocrisy of his words making her breathing jerk. Throughout their nine-month marriage, Omar had made it devastatingly clear exactly how important she was to him. Even now, here in the hospital, he was still taking business calls. If they were at home now he would be heading towards his office and she would already be forgotten, swallowed up by the ceaseless hunger of his ambition.

Suddenly it was difficult to look at him, much less speak, and she stared past his shoulder into the crowded ER. 'Yeah, they're really special. It only took you six whole weeks to *rush* to my side.'

His expression didn't alter but his gaze sharpened. 'You're a hard person to find.'

'Apparently not hard enough,' she said tightly. 'And apparently, I'm also not very good at making myself understood. So let me make this completely clear. I don't want anything from you. Except a divorce.'

Silence.

Even the bustle beyond the curtains seemed to still.

Her nerves tightened into a hard knot inside her stomach as he took a step closer.

His fingers cupped her chin. 'But this isn't just about what *you* want, Delphi. The state of matrimony is a partnership. Or it's supposed to be. Only you've spent most of our marriage acting as if you're being corralled against your will.'

She was suddenly aware of the pounding of her heart. In other words it was her fault, not his, that their marriage had faltered.

'Then you'll be glad to be shot of me,' she snapped, jerking her face free of his hand. 'Now, if you wouldn't mind getting out of the way—'

She waited, but he didn't move.

'I do mind.'

His spine straightened, lifting his shoulders and expanding his chest so that his body filled the space between them.

'I just don't know why you do. I'm simply offering you a lift in an air-conditioned limousine. How could you possibly object to that?'

She glared at him. He made it sound as if she was some diva, turning down a too-small dressing room. But he wasn't the good guy here.

'Easily,' she snapped. Frankly, she'd rather crawl over broken glass than get in a car with Omar. 'I'm happy to take the bus.'

His gaze didn't move from hers. 'They're running a

weekend service today. You could be sitting around waiting for hours.'

She stared at him, her skin prickling. 'Oh? And I suppose you know that from your other life as a bus driver?'

'Carole told me.'

His mouth shifted into a shape that made her shiver inside.

'So why not make things easy for yourself?' he asked.

Because nothing good comes easy, she thought again, her heart lurching sideways like a train coming off the rails as his dark eyes locked with hers.

'Because my dad told me never to get into a car with a stranger,' she said hoarsely.

He stared down at her, that mouth of his curving at one corner. 'You're still my wife...' his voice thickened around the word '...my responsibility.'

A wave of misery rose up inside her, blocking her throat. She had so wanted that to be true, and for a time, bathed in the solar intensity of his focus, she had believed it was. She had believed them to be in love—the head-over-heels, truly, madly, deeply kind of love that was as rare and bright as a comet.

But she knew now that what he loved was the chase, and by presenting him with a challenge worthy of some mythical Greek hero she had fuelled his competitive instinct, that same need to win, to call the shots that he displayed both in the boardroom and on the polo field.

And it was why he was here now. She had told him she wanted a divorce, so naturally he had to throw an obstacle in her way.

'I'm not your anything,' she said quickly. 'And, like I told you before, I don't need your help. If I want a lift I can call my housemate, Ashley.'

'Unfortunately not.' He stared down at her through

thick dark lashes, his expression unreadable. 'You see, she went to visit her mother. But after she picked up your message she was worried about you. Apparently, you sounded "shaken".'

The pattern of the curtains blurred a little. Ashley had been worried. If things had been different—if Omar had kept his promises—then she might have told him the truth. She might have shared her stomach-churning panic and fear in those few half-seconds when the car had jolted forward.

But he'd let her down so often and so painfully she doubted she would ever trust anyone, again.

'Is there a point to this?' she asked coolly, and saw his expression harden.

'She sent Travis—I think that was his name—to your house to check your passport. See if there was a family member she could get hold of.'

She felt a spike of adrenaline as Omar's mouth did one of those almost-smiles.

'And guess what? I was listed as your next of kin.'

It was a historical mistake to add to the long list of mistakes she'd already made. An oversight. She had meant to cross out his name but forgotten to do so.

'I could call Dan,' he said softly.

She felt as if she might throw up. Her eyes darted to his face.

'Why? So you can play at being the hero?' She shook her head violently. 'That's not going to happen.'

'But you do want to get out of here, don't you?' Without waiting for a reply, he said smoothly, 'Then let me give you a lift.'

Delphi swallowed. Through the curtains she saw a man limp past on crutches, his foot mummified in bandages, face puffy with bruises. He winced as he moved, but she knew he was leaving the hospital and found herself envying his freedom.

Her heart felt as if it was going to burst through her ribs. She absolutely didn't want to go anywhere with Omar. She certainly didn't want him coming into the untidy little house she shared with Ashley. But she could tell from the set of his shoulders that he wasn't going anywhere without a fight.

Since London the fight had drained out of her, and it was getting harder and harder to balance on her heels. She pressed her leg against the bed to steady herself against a shivering head-rush. Omar was right about one thing. She wanted, *needed* to get out of here—now.

'Okay,' she said curtly. 'You can drive me home. But then I want you gone.'

Not wanting to see the triumph on his face, she turned. The strip-light flickered and the room spun out of focus and her eyes slid sideways, like marbles on a polished floor.

'Delphi?'

His hand closed around her uninjured arm, close to her elbow, guiding her backwards swiftly and purposefully to the bed.

'Here. Sit down.'

She did, shaking off his hand, then choking back a sound that was a mixture of frustration and anger as Omar crouched down in front of her.

He was much too close. Close enough that, had she wanted to, she could have reached out and traced the enviable swell of his biceps beneath the crisp shirt, or pressed her hand against the superbly muscled chest.

'I'm fine,' she muttered, closing her eyes, fighting the urge to lean into his strength. But it was so hard. Hard, too, not to be soothed by the fact that he was there…right there in front of her. Solid. Strong. Steadfast.

Just remember the last time you let your body do the thinking, she told herself. *As for believing in handsome heroes and happy-ever-afters...*

'I'm fine,' she said again, as much for her benefit as his.

'Of course you are.'

In another lifetime, when the vows he'd made were true, that edge to his voice might have been anxiety, but now it was most likely irritation.

'And you were going to go home on your own.'

She sensed rather than saw him shake his head.

'Stay still. I'll get the nurse.'

'No, I just need a moment. And maybe some water.' She let her head tip forward, opening her eyes, focusing on his shoes. 'Could you get me some? There's a water machine somewhere. It'll be quicker than asking someone.'

There was an infinitesimal pause and then her shoulders slumped with relief as he straightened. Slowly she looked up and their eyes met. She held her breath as his dark gaze reached inside her, considering her request and his response.

'Just don't move,' he ordered. 'I'll be right back.'

She wanted to tell him not to bother, but instead she watched, her pulse skipping as he strode away.

Five minutes later Omar snapped back the curtain, a bottle of water in his hand.

'Here. Drink this. I've—'

He stopped mid-sentence, his pupils flaring with shock and incredulity.

The bed was empty.

Delphi was gone.

CHAPTER TWO

OMAR LIFTED A hand and pressed two fingers against his right temple, where his head was starting to pound. His brain, usually so quick and decisive, was struggling to accept what his eyes were showing him.

But maybe he was jumping the gun and she had simply gone outside to get some fresh air.

Turning, he flicked the curtain aside and stalked back across the ER, his eyes scanning the room *Terminator*-style, looking for a flash of rose-pink among all the blue scrubs.

But with every step he took he knew he was wasting his time. Like the horses she worked with, running away was Delphi's default response to any kind of confrontation or threat. Especially when she was angry, and she was still angry with him. Still blamed him for what had happened in London. Hence the divorce papers.

He rubbed his fingers against his forehead, trying to relieve the pressure.

Except nothing had actually happened. Okay, it had been upsetting that the paparazzi were hanging around, and frustrating that she hadn't been able to visit her parents' graves, but her reaction had felt—*still* felt—disproportionate. Unreasonable. Unfair.

He'd known Delphi was angry with him for not going to England with her, but he had apologised multiple times.

In fact, he seemed to have spent half his married life apologising to Delphi.

And how would it have changed anything even if he had gone with her?

What was more, she had never once admitted the part *she'd* played. If she had stuck to the original plan he would have been by her side. But she had changed her mind not once but twice about going to London, and by then he'd been offered a meeting with Bob Maclean, owner of the biggest cable network in North America.

A meeting like that was not something he could just postpone, and he had tried to explain that to Delphi. But nothing he'd said had consoled her. She had simply blocked each attempt he'd made, silently retreating further and further into herself, so that once again she had become that guarded young woman he had met at the polo a year ago.

His jaw tightened. With hindsight he should have refused to accept her silence. When she had frozen him out in London he should have sat her down and made her talk. Or just taken her to bed and kept her there until the ice had melted.

Maybe if he had they would be in a different place now.

Or maybe they wouldn't, he thought as he strode towards the exit.

He was well past the point of thinking their marriage could be fixed. Although, as he'd walked into the hospital, a part of him had wondered if she'd had time to think and perhaps regret her actions.

She hadn't, of course.

Delphi was the most stubborn person he had ever met. And the hardest to pin down.

Apart from Rashid Al Majid.

The doors slid open, and as he walked purposefully into the warm Idaho sunlight he glanced upwards at a sky that was the same faded blue as his father's eyes. Eyes that were always tracking away from him, seeking something brighter, bigger, shinier—

His shoulders tensed. With sixteen older half-siblings, it was almost impossible for him to offer anything new, anything special or stand-out that might snag Rashid's attention. But that hadn't stopped him from trying. On the contrary, he had spent most of his life striving to form a bond with his elusive, uncompromising father by building something he could call his own, something that had nothing to do with his family.

Two birds, one stone. Twin goals. Inseparable and inexorable. Consummate and constant.

But as for marriage…

He had considered it. It had always been more of an assumption that he would marry at some point than an ambition.

Until he'd met Delphi.

And then it had become an obsession. Getting her to trust him had become the plan that had driven everything else from his mind. It had taken the best part of three months to succeed, but he'd done it.

The band of silver on his left hand glinted in the sunlight.

Or rather he'd thought he had. Only apparently, according to Delphi's ridiculously high and ever-upward-moving bar, he had failed.

Failed.

The word scraped against his skin, drawing blood.

Except this wasn't *his* failure. He had gone above and beyond what any other man would have done to prove himself worthy. He had accepted her past unquestioningly, even though it had raised eyebrows among the more conservative members of his family. And not once had he considered walking away.

But one tiny mistake on his part—more of a misstep,

really—and Delphi had bailed on him, on their marriage. Just packed her bags and left. Exactly as her mother had done to Dan.

Only instead of taking fourteen years, it had taken her just shy of nine months.

Eyes narrowing, he stared at the Delphi-free queue of people waiting to be picked up.

At first, he'd thought she just needed time to cool off, and he'd assumed that she would go home to Bedford—to the ranch. But she hadn't. As he'd found out when Dan had called the next day and it had become obvious that Delphi was not with her family and nor had she told them about the row.

He felt a flicker of exasperation. That was all he'd thought it was then. *A row.* Although 'row' made it sound as if they had shouted at each other, when in reality Delphi had said so little it hardly constituted a conversation, let alone an argument.

It hadn't occurred to him that he was witnessing the last gasp of their marriage.

His mouth twisted. For most of their relationship Delphi had made him feel as if he was cross-examining her in the witness box. Everything had to be coaxed out of her, and even then she held things back. But she had been ruthless about ending things between them. Having made her decision unilaterally, she had left.

Walking into their empty apartment, he had felt stricken, shocked, and her absence had been made all the more devastating by the sudden rush of memories it had provoked of coming home as a child to find his father gone.

But as the days had passed and it had become clear that Delphi was gone for good, his shock and misery had been consumed by a black, all-consuming rage that she could just walk away and move on with her life without him.

Not that he would have had her back. He was done with it. With her. With her stubborn refusal to talk, to share herself with him. What was the point of being married to someone who felt like that?

No, divorce was the only option. His one regret was that he couldn't serve her with the papers first.

But he was not done with his errant wife just yet.

Glancing again at the queue of people, he felt his stomach twist. It was pure coincidence that he had been so close geographically when that cowboy had called him and told him Delphi was in hospital. Pure chance he had even picked up the call.

It had been an unknown number. Ordinarily he would have let it ring out, go to messages, but something—some sixth sense, maybe—had moved him to answer.

The knot in his stomach tightened painfully. It was impossible to give a name to the tangle of emotions he'd felt as he'd walked into the hospital just under an hour ago and seen Delphi sitting on the bed talking to some doctor. Exasperation. Disbelief. Relief that he had finally found her and that her injuries were minor.

Only now she was gone again. And his relief was long gone too, swallowed up by a hot, pulsing fury that she had done it again. She had walked out of his life. Sneaked off when his back was turned.

His jaw clenched.

But surely someone must have seen something? he thought irritably, glancing over to where a man on crutches was now joining the end of the queue. In that dress and those heels Delphi was hardly invisible. Remembering how the fabric had flared over the curves of her bottom, he felt heat pulse across his skin, accompanied by a little drumroll of jealousy.

She never wore dresses or heels. So why was she now? And where was her wedding ring?

The pale indentation on her finger had taunted him. Had she already found someone else? Was running away from the promises she'd made not the only thing she had in common with her mother?

He pictured a man holding Delphi's ringless hand, wrapping his arm around her waist as he pulled her closer. Had she replaced him already?

A rush of fury—male, possessive, visceral—pushed everything else from his mind, so all that remained was a savage, mindless urge to find whoever he was and batter him into the ground.

Was that why she was so eager to get a divorce?

Back inside the hospital, he had lied to Delphi. He had, of course, seen the papers sent by her lawyers, but even just thinking about them made the pounding inside his skull ramp up a notch. And not just because it stung, imagining himself being so easily and swiftly replaced.

Being the first person in his family to get divorced was not what he'd had in mind when he'd dreamed of doing something unique…something that would grab his father's attention. But he was done with trying to make his marriage work. He couldn't—not on his own. And he was on his own. It had just taken her leaving for him to realise that.

He wanted this divorce as much as she did—maybe even more. But right now, she was still his wife, and she had one more task to perform before he dismissed her, and she became nothing more than a faint crease pressed into a single page of his life.

Jaw clenching, he walked to the beginning of the meandering queue.

'Excuse me…' He smiled stiffly at a woman with her foot in a cast. 'I'm looking for my wife. I was supposed to meet her out here. I don't suppose you've seen her. She's about so high.' He raised his hand to just below his shoulder. 'Short pinkish blonde hair. Wearing a white dress.'

The woman nodded. 'She went that way,' she said, pointing over Omar's shoulder, and then she frowned. 'But she didn't look like she was waiting for nobody. In fact, she seemed in kind of a hurry.'

Of course she was, Omar thought, striding swiftly away from the hospital.

'That way' turned out to be on to a Main Street straight out of a theme park. There were a couple of banks and some small, shabby-looking shops, all closed for the holiday, and a barber's, also closed. In both the two restaurants staff were wiping down the tables. He scanned the street. Everywhere was either shut or closing up for the day.

Every place except one.

Dark eyes narrowing, Omar crossed the road.

Sliding into a booth in the corner of the Iron Mule Tavern, Delphi breathed out shakily. She had virtually sprinted away from the hospital, and now her lungs were burning and the ache in her wrist had returned.

She hadn't planned to run. Or maybe she had subconsciously. Because that had been the first thought that had popped into her head when Omar strode away.

Run. Run as fast as you can.

And she had. Blindly, unthinkingly, like an animal seeking a place to hide from a predator. And now, thankfully, she was safe. She could stop running, relax. Celebrate, even. Her own personal day of independence. Except she didn't feel much like celebrating.

Clearly she had come to the right place, she thought, glancing across the room to where a barmaid was standing listlessly behind a sticky-looking counter. Opposite her sat six men, all old, hunched over their glasses, eyes glued to the television mounted on the wall. None of them had even looked over when she'd walked in, which was just the way she liked it.

'What can I get you?'

The barmaid had made her way over and was standing next to the table, a bored expression on her face.

'Vodka, please,' Delphi said quickly.

Behind them, the door to the bar banged open and she jerked round, her body humming with panic. But it was just another old man, with sparse straw-coloured hair and vein-hatched cheeks.

She swallowed. 'Make it a double.'

The barmaid nodded, still bored.

Watching her walk away, Delphi leaned back against the faux leather, her body buckling. She needed something a lot stronger than water to blunt the emotions raging inside her. And not just because of Omar's sudden unwelcome reappearance in her life.

Throat tightening, she moved her hand protectively to her wrist. It was such a stupid thing to have let happen, and it shouldn't have happened. Like everybody else in her family she was a careful driver, never taking risks or cutting corners. Because, like them, she understood the consequences could be devastating.

Fatal.

Her breath caught as it always did when she thought about the accident.

To her, Ianthe Reynolds and Dylan Wright had just been Mummy and Daddy. But to the rest of the world the peroxide blonde actress and the pouting up-and-coming pop star had been an 'it' couple. Their affair had been chronicled with voyeuristic frenzy in the tabloids, starting when Ianthe had left Dan Howard, her husband of fourteen years, for her much younger lover, and ending when the car Ianthe had been driving had spun off the road, killing them both.

And just like that Delphi had become an orphan.

She was four years old.

It would be wrong to say that she could remember those first few hours after the crash. Mostly what she remembered was just a blur of people coming in and out of the house. And lights…lots of flashing lights.

The door to the bar banged open again. This time she didn't turn her head. She couldn't look away from the lights in her memory. Red and blue for the police. Then, later, white for the *paparazzi*, who had joined the TV camera crews treading on the fragile heads of the tulips she and her father had planted in December. She could still hear their voices, seeping through the walls and echoing down the pipes…still picture their faces flushed with greedy excitement.

A shiver ran over her skin and she felt an almost imperceptible change in air pressure, like the tremble of debris at the mouth of a subway tunnel before a train arrived. And then—

'There you are, darling.'

She jumped as a bottle of water was slammed down onto the table.

'Sorry it took so long. I didn't realise we were playing hide and seek. *Again.*'

Delphi felt her stomach drop. Her heart squeezed as if she was having a seizure. Looking as out of place in the dusty bar as a peacock in a pigeon loft, Omar Al Majid was staring down at her, his beautiful sexy mouth set in a grim line.

'But I suppose I should have guessed. It *is* your favourite game.'

Her pulse scuttled. He had been angry before, but now

she could almost see the fury and frustration shimmering around his body like a heat haze in the desert. But he could be as angry as he liked. It wouldn't change anything. Certainly not the past. Or the future. And after what had happened in London she knew they had no future.

Her fingers moved to her stomach and she felt something pinch inside her—that same pang of regret and loss that punctuated her day like a clock marking the hours.

She lifted her chin and met his gaze. 'I don't play games. Don't sit down,' she snapped.

But it was too late. Omar had already dropped into the seat opposite her, stretching out his long legs so that she would have to climb over him to make her escape.

'No, you just sneak away when no one's around.'

He pushed the bottle of water towards her across the table. She stopped it with her hand.

'I didn't sneak anywhere. I didn't want to see you.'

'Or you send them on a fool's errand,' he continued, ignoring her remark.

'If the cap fits…' she said coolly.

A muscle twitched in his cheek, and he jerked his hand away from the bottle.

She felt a flicker of triumph, but it was swiftly extinguished as he leaned back in his seat and her eyes felt suddenly as if they were on the end of a fishing hook, reeled in inexorably by the tightening of fabric around smooth, toned muscle.

He looked good in a suit. Good out of one too, she conceded, her breath quickening as, against her will, she found herself remembering every centimetre of his superb body in glorious detail.

As if he could read her thoughts, Omar looked at her across the sticky table.

'It doesn't.' His gaze was steady and unwavering. 'You

see, you don't fool me, Delphi. How could you? I mean, you can't even fool yourself.'

Suddenly she was fighting the wild beating of her heart. 'I don't know what you're talking about,' she said stiffly, her fingers thick and clumsy around the neck of the bottle.

But she did. She could feel it now, one beat behind her pulse. A longing that had nothing to do with logic. A need that was like an itch beneath the skin. Impossible to scratch no matter how much you twisted and squirmed.

A slow smile tugged at the corners of his mouth and the table seemed to shrink. Around them the bar lost shape, the hunched drinkers and the barmaid blurring into one another so that there was just her and him. Omar Al Majid, the man with eyes that could hold her fast in a hurricane.

'Sure you do.' He dismissed her statement with a careless lift of his broad shoulders. 'You just have trouble admitting it. You always have. That's why you ran away, and why you're hiding in some downtown bar in a two-bit town. But there are some truths you can't run from.'

She shivered all the way through, the air leaving her body as he leaned forward. And she wanted to run then— run from the dark heat in his gaze and from the memory of his body flexing beneath hers as he held her waist and thrust up into her—

Breathing in sharply, she pressed her legs together beneath the table, trying to deny the pulse beating between her thighs. How could she feel like this? After everything he had done and failed to do, it was crazy of her body to behave this way—not to say treacherous.

Then again, what did all this heat and twitchiness amount to? It was just sex. Bodies. Biology.

Legally, Omar might still be her husband, but their marriage was null and void. Anything else was just wishful thinking on her part. A stupid, irrational hope that she could outrun her past, outrun the twisting helix of her DNA. Only how could you ever outrun something that was a part of you?

And it was all immaterial now, anyway. She was over him. *Clearly.* Why else would she file for divorce? It was so she could be free of him…free to get on with her life.

'I'm not running. I'm sitting down, waiting for my drink to arrive so I can celebrate my imminent independence from you. But why wait?' She snatched up the bottle of water and twisted off the top. 'Here's to single life.'

The cold water burned her throat as his beautiful eyes narrowed. 'I know what you're trying to do, Delphi. I wonder, though, do you?'

She could feel her pulse thudding beneath the thin fabric of her dress. 'It's really not that complicated, Omar. I'm trying to get you to leave.'

He stared across the table, that mouth of his curving into a smile that sliced through her skin. 'Exactly. You're needling me because there's nowhere left to run, nowhere left to hide, and you're scared.'

'I'm not scared of you.'

She spoke quickly—too quickly.

'No, you're scared of *us*. You're scared of what "us" means, and how it makes you feel. How *I* make you feel.' His eyes shifted pointedly to the dull white of her knuckles, where her hand was clamped to the bottle. 'It's what's always scared you, right from the start. And I know that when it gets too much you do what you did six weeks ago… what you're doing now. Instead of talking to me, you push me away. You run. You retreat. You overreact.'

Overreact.

Delphi stared at him in silence, the word knocking the breath from her lungs. Back in the hospital, when he had stepped into the cubicle, she had actually thought things might be different. *He* might be different. But nothing had changed. Instead of understanding that her actions had originated out of a need to survive, he saw only a challenge.

But this wasn't about her pushing him away. It was about self-preservation. It was about her trusting him, and him letting her down. Repeatedly. Day in, day out. Every day a little piece of her had been chipped away. That was why she had left. Because if she'd stayed there would have been nothing left of her.

Only he had no idea of what he'd done. Actually, he didn't think he had done anything. As far as Omar was concerned, she was the one at fault. She was the one who had reacted—*overreacted*.

Still blindsided by the injustice of that word, she shook her head. 'And that's why you think I left? Because I'm scared of how being with you makes me feel?' She resisted the impulse to slap his stupidly handsome face. He really was the most monumentally arrogant and selfish man on the planet. 'Do you know what your problem is, Omar?'

He raised an eyebrow questioningly, as if he hadn't until now considered the possibility that he might possess one. Probably he hadn't. For men like Omar, other people were always to blame.

'You're so busy building your empire, so obsessed with whatever deal it is you're making, you don't ever stop and take a look at yourself. At who *you* are. And how *you* behave.'

'How I behave?' A muscle tightened in his jaw. 'I'm not the one who walked out on our marriage without so much as a word of explanation.'

She felt her pulse jerk. Would explaining have changed anything? Perhaps in that moment, yes. Omar would have been devastated to know that she had been pregnant and lost the baby.

There was a heavy feeling at the back of her eyes as she remembered her breathless shock, the hot, wet stickiness of her blood. Yes, he would have been devastated—but then what? People didn't change—not really, and not for very long. The miscarriage had simply made her face up to the fact that she came and would always come second to his work.

The part of her that had still been hoping for a happy ending had slipped away in that bathroom too. Lying on the cold tiles, she had accepted that there was something wrong with her. Something that meant that a happy ending would always be out of reach.

So Omar was right. There were some truths you couldn't hide from. They were just talking about different truths.

'We shared a bed and a ceremony,' she said flatly. 'But it takes more than a ring and piece of paper to make a marriage.'

Omar stared down at Delphi's bare fingers, anger and outrage rippling over his skin in waves. Did she really, seriously think *she* could lecture *him* about what made a marriage?

With an effort of will, he held his breath, hung on to his temper. He would deal with the ring later…

'It's not just a piece of paper. It's a legally binding contract.'

She held his gaze. 'So is divorce.'

He gritted his teeth, wanting to shake her. She had no idea what he'd been through these past weeks. Nor, apparently, did she care, he thought, his gaze searching and failing to find any evidence of remorse in her clear brown eyes. But if she thought she could just toss their marriage away like a broken toy, she was going to be in for a nasty surprise.

Almost as nasty as coming home and finding your wife gone.

'Marriage isn't just about the individual and the personal, Delphi. You have obligations to meet, liabilities owed.'

She gave a bitter laugh. 'Trust you to see marriage as a balance sheet.'

Her words stung. And what had she seen it as? A gamble? A chance to reinvent herself. A trap? He didn't like the tightness in the chest those thoughts provoked.

'But you didn't, did you?' he said slowly. 'Trust me, I mean.'

She stilled like a small animal trapped in the beam of a poacher's torch. For a moment she looked young, even younger than she was, vulnerable, almost fragile, and remembering the accident he felt a stab of guilt. But then his mood hardened as her expression hardened into a scowl.

'Wisely, as it turned out,' she said.

'Here you go.'

Their heads snapped round as one.

The barmaid was back.

He watched, his pulse drumming irritably, as she slid a glass onto the table. Opposite him, Delphi sat stiffly, angled off the seat, one foot arched upwards like a sprinter. Preparing to run again, he thought. Although those spike-heeled sandals were hardly designed for running. More for showcasing her legs.

Not that he needed reminding. He knew every inch of them intimately. A beat of heat skimmed over his skin. And how it felt when she wrapped them around his hips...

Delphi leaned forward, shoulders braced, and then her chin tilted upwards, and he realised that he had been wrong. She wasn't poised to run. She was waiting to dismiss him. Just like his father had done so many times in his life.

As if on cue, his phone vibrated in his pocket. He reached for it automatically, his pulse accelerating as he scrolled down to read the email. He felt a tick of satisfaction. It was a good deal. He would talk to the lawyers, tie up the loose ends, and then maybe call Rashid.

Sliding his phone back into his jacket, he looked up to find Delphi staring at him, her face still and set.

'What is that?' he asked as she picked up the glass.

'Vodka,' she said crisply.

He held her gaze. 'I don't think drinking alcohol after an accident is a good idea.'

She shrugged. 'Your time would be better spent getting used to the idea that what you think, say or do is no longer any of my concern.'

There was a short, hard pause, and then she downed her drink in one.

Tamping down a sharp, unprecedented urge to haul her across the table and prove her wrong by pressing her body against his and his mouth to hers, he switched his gaze across the room to the TV screen, where two wrestlers in figure-hugging shorts and lace-up boots were throwing each other around a ring to the cheers of an enthusiastic crowd.

He stared at the screen, his teeth on edge, body taut. It was a performance, of course. But the effort it took to plan those moves and the skill required to execute them with panache was real in the same way that his parents' marriage was real. Rashid and Maryam hadn't married for love, but they had worked their way to affection and understanding. Theirs was a commitment based on pragmatism. A strategic, choreographed performance by two invested participants.

He respected that, but he had never wanted it for him-

self. Until this moment, when it seemed infinitely prefer-
able to this impasse of a marriage he shared with Delphi.

He studied her profile: the small straight nose, the high
arched cheekbones, the soft mouth. Back at the hospital
he'd wanted to give her a chance to do the right thing, but
she had thrown it back in his face. So now they would do
things his way.

'My time would be better spent anywhere but here.' He
got to his feet. 'Let's go.'

Her eyes narrowed. 'For the last time, I'm not going
anywhere with you.'

'You will. Either on your own two feet or over my shoulder. You choose.'

She gave him an icy, disbelieving glare. 'You wouldn't
dare.'

'Try me,' he said coolly.

He was calling her bluff. But, as the daughter of Ianthe
Reynolds and Dylan Wright, he knew she'd blink first. She
hated fuss, drama, scenes of any kind, and he felt a stab
of satisfaction as Delphi got to her feet and sidestepped
past him.

Outside, he lifted his hand in an imperious gesture. Instantly an SUV appeared round the corner and pulled up
alongside the kerb.

'You've stopped fighting me,' he said as he joined her in
the back seat and the car began to move smoothly forward.

'I don't need to fight you anymore.' She shifted sideways, pressing her body against the door. 'It will only take
thirty minutes to get back home. And then you'll be out of
my life for good. Back to San Francisco, or wherever your
next mega deal is taking place.'

'I'm not going to San Francisco.'

He stretched his legs, dragging out the moment, wanting to prolong the sensation of having her right where he wanted her. Just like he had in bed.

'I'm going to Dubai. And if you want a divorce—a nice, quick, uncomplicated divorce…' He paused, his eyes finding hers. 'Then you will be coming with me. As my wife.'

There was a small, stunned pause. In the subdued light of the car he could see her fighting to stay calm.

'If you think that's going to happen then maybe we should go back to the hospital and get *you* examined by a doctor.'

Her voice was steady, but the tick of fury beneath it tugged at his senses. She was close to losing control.

'What part of *I want a divorce* don't you understand, Omar?'

'What part of *We're still married* don't you?' he shot back. 'And we *are* still married, Delphi.' Reaching over, he caught her hand, turning it knuckle-side up. 'With or without a ring. For better *and* worse.'

Her nostrils flared as she struggled to pull her hand away. 'You can say that again.' Twisting her fingers, she made a sound of frustration. 'Why are you doing this? I know you have to win, but I'm not one of your business deals.'

'Indeed you are not.' His eyes meshed with hers. 'In comparison to our marriage, any business deal would be a walk in the park.'

'Then why can't you just let me leave?'

He gritted his teeth, his body tensing, on edge. 'Because you, my sweet, selfish wife, made promises. One of which was to attend my father's ninetieth birthday party.'

That got to her, he thought as her eyes widened.

He released his grip. 'Perhaps in your quest for independence that slipped your mind. But it hasn't slipped mine.'

And he was prepared to exploit the chemistry she was so desperate to deny one last time to get what he wanted.

When the car stopped, he got out. Seconds later, as he had known he would, he heard a door slam. The click of heels.

'What you're asking is impossible.'

He turned. Delphi was standing in front of him. A light breeze tugged at her dress so that it clung to her legs, and he felt a current of hunger curl beneath his anger.

'For you to attend an event as my wife?' He frowned. 'How so? It's not something you haven't done before.'

He saw her hands ball into fists.

'Being a wife isn't just a title It's what you feel about a person. I don't feel that way about you.'

Her face was back to that carefully schooled mask he knew so well.

'I'm not an actress. You can't just snap your fingers and ask me to perform.'

Later he would wonder if it was that click of her fingers or the cool, maddening indifference of her expression that made him step forward. But in that moment, he had no conscious thought. He was just pure need.

'I'm not asking.'

In one seamless movement he grabbed her shoulders and yanked her against him. He fitted his mouth to hers, claiming her as he had done a thousand times before and would have done a thousand times more if she hadn't walked out on their marriage.

He felt her tense, her hands pressing into his chest, pushing, and then not pushing but pulling him closer.

He heard her breathing quicken and felt a spike of satisfaction as she leaned into him, her fingers clutching at his jacket.

She might be able to hide everything else, but in his

arms she couldn't hide the need she felt. A need that mirrored and matched his own.

Hunger and heat swamped him. It burned everything in its path, consuming the past, melting the present.

Her lips were soft and urgent, her tongue was in his mouth, his in hers, their hands were in each other's hair, tugging, teasing, not tender but frantic, unthinking, ungovernable, astonishingly carnal.

It was not enough.

Behind him, across the fields came a distant flurry of thunder. No, not thunder. Fireworks.

He dragged his mouth from hers. She stepped backwards, stumbling a little, her hands clenching. She looked like he felt. Shaking inside, shaken by the burst of heat that was still roaring through him.

He forced himself to meet her gaze. 'See,' he said softly. 'I didn't even need to click my fingers.'

Her pupils flared. 'I don't have my passport.'

'But I do.' He reached into his jacket and pulled it out. 'I had one of my people pick it up this morning. So, if there's nothing more, I suggest we get going. We're on a tight schedule as it is.'

And, ignoring both the flames still crackling through his body and her pale, trembling face, he turned and walked across the runway to the waiting plane.

CHAPTER THREE

EXACTLY FOURTEEN HOURS and nine minutes after it took off from the runway in Idaho, Omar's Gulfstream jet landed in Dubai with an almost imperceptible shudder.

As it taxied smoothly up the runway, Delphi gazed out of the window at a sky that was darkening as she watched. She wasn't a nervous flyer, but her fingers trembled against the magazine she had been pretending to read for the last hour of the flight.

Obviously she had known this moment was going to happen. The plane couldn't keep circling the skies for ever. But now it was here, and the real-time consequences of what she had agreed to back in the States were no longer a distant possibility but an unavoidable certainty.

Not that there was any paperwork, she thought. It was more of a non-verbal agreement.

Remembering those few febrile half-seconds when she and Omar had kissed, she felt her face grow warm. Except it had been less a kiss and more a forced admission of a need that shouldn't still exist, yet inexplicably did.

Glancing down the cabin to where Omar was sitting, his dark head bent over the screen of his laptop, she felt her pulse stumble. In his arms, time had not just stopped, but reversed. Everything had turned to air—her anger, his frustration, all of it—and there had been just the two of them in the moment, tearing at each other's clothes.

It had been fierce and thorough. A rolling and impossible longing and a banked, devastating desire.

And then he had pulled away, and it had been like jerking awake from a vivid dream to find yourself asleep in front of the TV. One moment he'd been kissing her, all seductive heat and wild longing, the next he'd been discussing their flight schedule.

It had been in that moment, with his dark eyes moving restlessly across the sun-soaked Idaho fields and the aftershocks of his kiss still pounding through her body like a herd of stampeding mustang, that she'd understood why Omar had kissed her and why he had stopped.

Whatever it had felt like, it had had nothing to do with desire and everything to do with winning. Like a sniper choosing a rifle, he had weaponised their unfinished physical attraction for one another, recognising it as the simplest, most expedient way for him to silence her opposition. Figuratively and literally.

As if he sensed the path of her thoughts, Omar looked up from across the cabin, and with agonising slowness she turned to stare out of the window. Other than a few stiffly polite conversations when the cabin crew were present, they had barely spoken during the flight, and she was dreading having to play the role of his wife more convincingly at the party.

She swallowed—tried to, anyway. Only her throat was suddenly dry, tight.

Her hands gripped the armrests. Maybe she could just refuse to get off the plane. Like a kind of reverse hostage. Only she knew she wouldn't. And not only because Omar would probably just hoist her over his shoulder and carry her off, kicking and screaming. The truth was that even though she had only met Rashid once before, she felt bad about forgetting his birthday party. It wasn't his fault that his son had let her down. Or that his birthday had coincided with their marriage imploding.

She glanced furtively over to where Omar was talking to the air stewards.

What were they thinking? Did they wonder why she was sitting at the other end of the plane from her husband?

Her gaze shifted minutely to his open laptop. Not if they had spent any amount of time with their boss, she thought. They would know that work came before everything, including his wife.

Her eyes rested on his back. He had changed clothes during the flight. Now, instead of a suit, he was wearing faded blue jeans and a black T-shirt, just like most of the men who worked at the stables.

Although it was highly improbable that anyone would ever confuse Omar with a groom. You could put an ordinary general-purpose saddle on a thoroughbred, but it wouldn't stop it being a racehorse, and even in the most casual of clothing Omar radiated an aura of power and the kind of absolute self-assurance that made waiters scuttle across restaurants and women blush and bite their lip.

She bit her own lip, then released it quickly, shoulders tensing against the leather upholstery. It made no sense to look down on the rest of the population for reacting that way. Not when she was just as susceptible as everyone else, leaning into him like a moth helplessly pulled to the light.

At least she wasn't kidding herself anymore that it was some fairy tale fantasy of love. And it *had* been a fairy tale, thinking that she could fall in love and be loved and have her happy ever after.

Some happy-ever-after! They hadn't even made it to their first wedding anniversary.

Watching him sleep, the morning after their wedding, she had felt her love for him like a superpower. It had crackled beneath her skin like electricity, and she had wanted to drag him back to the chapel and make new promises, to go into battle for him, for their marriage.

But months of always coming second to his work had taken its toll. After London, it had been as if some internal energy grid had shut down. She had waited until he went to work one day, packed a small bag, and left.

She leaned her head back against the seat. Occasionally, when she could longer fight it and the pain threatened to overwhelm her, she told herself that having your heart broken was a rite of passage and that it was a 'good' pain.

Her gaze snagged on Omar's flawless profile.

It wasn't!

She glanced away. But there was no point in thinking about any of that. She couldn't change the past. All she could do was learn from her mistakes. At least that way she could make those mistakes have some value. Her heart began beating a little faster. Although she wasn't entirely sure how coming to Dubai as Omar's wife fitted in with that philosophy...

'Everything okay?'

Her pulse skipped like a startled rabbit. Omar was standing beside her with the light behind him, his eyes soft and almost black.

No, she thought, and briefly revisited the idea of refusing to leave.

But instead, she undid her seatbelt and got to her feet. 'Yes.' She nodded.

'Good,' he said coolly.

He stared down at her. For a moment she thought he was going to take her hand, or perhaps her arm, and she was suddenly and acutely conscious of the rise and fall of her breath. But he didn't move.

She felt her belly clench, the muscles quivering. He didn't need to. He never had. Just being close to him made her feel hot and tight and restless, as if she had been out in the sun too long.

'Shall we get this over and done with?' she said abruptly.

She got to her feet and, stepping outside, stared dazedly at the glowing orange sun sinking beneath the horizon. Right about now in Creech Falls she would have been rubbing sleep from her eyes and rolling out of bed, and her body was still working on Pacific Standard Time. But that wasn't what made her steady herself against the handrail.

It had been hot in Idaho, but this was like stepping into a solid wall of heat. It was a tangible force that pushed back against her body, then swallowed her up. She could already feel her light cotton blouse sticking to her skin.

'It gets a lot hotter during the day. You'll need to take care outside.'

Omar was standing beside her. In the final flickering rays of the sun he looked like a bronze statue of some desert warrior king, not sweating, but shimmering in the heat.

Instantly, she felt hotter and stickier, and grumpier. 'Sweet of you to worry,' she said, focusing her temper on his handsome face. 'But I don't think it will be a problem. I'm sure they'll have sun canopies at the hotel.'

Omar had told her that she would be staying at the Lulua and, having looked it up on the flight, she knew that all the jaw-droppingly expensive suites there came with their own private terrace and infinity pool, so there would be no reason to leave.

He stared at her in silence meditatively. Then, 'If you say so.' He gestured to the steps. 'After you.'

On the runway below a limousine was parked between three SUVs, all with blacked-out windows. Four men wearing dark suits and traditional *ghutras* stood next to the driver's door of each car. Two other men, each roughly the size of a professional wrestler, waited on either side of the limousine, scanning the empty runway with thousand-yard stares.

She stilled, her body stiffening like an animal sensing a trap. She had grown up surrounded by wealth, but security at her father's estate had been low-key. In New York, Omar preferred a more obvious presence. But this felt almost theatrically excessive.

'My father sent them,' Omar said quietly. 'I know it feels a little over the top, but it's just how he likes things done.'

Which, roughly translated, meant that the wishes of Rashid Al Majid would prevail one way or another. *Like father like son*, she thought as they walked across the runway to the waiting cars.

Thankfully, the limousine was blissfully cool after the furnace heat outside. Omar leaned forward and said something in Arabic to the driver, and even though her nerves were still jangling with jet lag and panic she found herself admiring the way he could switch so effortlessly between languages. After a summer living and working at a polo stud in Argentina she could speak some Spanish, but nowhere near as well as Omar. And he spoke other languages too. For business reasons, he'd told her.

Her mouth thinned. What other reason could there be?

Most people worked to live. Omar lived to work. It consumed him. Even when he wasn't working, which wasn't often, some part of him was always thinking about work. No doubt in his dreams, he pursued CEOs across desk-strewn office landscapes in the same way the dogs on the ranch chased imaginary rabbits in their sleep.

Her dreams were different. Confused and confusing so that when she woke, she felt more anxious, less certain. She thought back to when she'd been deciding whether to go and visit her parents' graves. It had been her first visit to England since their funerals, and in the past she had always found a reason to stay away. It hadn't been hard: there were so many. And it had been the same this time—only then she'd discovered she was pregnant, and it had seemed like a sign. A chance to reconcile the past with a future she had never imagined having.

A flash of headlights on the side of the carriageway made her blink. She hadn't told Omar she was pregnant. He had been away on business but it had still been a big decision to visit the graves. Omar had known that, and he had told her repeatedly that he would support her, be by her side. He had asked her to trust him—no, *demanded* that she trust him, and she had. Idiot that she was, she had believed he would be there for her.

But when it had come to it, his work came first. It always came first. She was just a diversion.

It had been the end of the beginning.

What had followed was the beginning of the end.

'That's the Burj Khalifa.'

Omar's voice cut across the quiet murmur of the engine and the less quiet clamour of her thoughts and she glanced out of the window. She wasn't generally that bothered about buildings. There was so much in the natural world to astonish. But now she stared in stunned silence at the illuminated needle-thin spire of metal that seemed to pierce the dark blue sky, almost touching the stars.

'Wow,' she said softly. 'It's like something out of *Brave New World*.'

Omar's dark eyes rested on her face. 'I suppose there is something courageous about taking on the desert.'

That was one word for it.

Tilting her head, she stared up at the Burj, not really seeing the glittering tower anymore. Instead, the lit-up windows reminded her of the keyboard on Omar's laptop when she used to wake in bed and find him working in the darkness.

He wasn't a builder, or an architect, but his goal was just as concrete. And she had no doubt that he would succeed in creating the biggest media empire in the world. With both a ruthless singularity of purpose and a relentless ambition that relegated everything outside of work to the outer edges of his life, how could he fail?

Not that she cared any more.

After this weekend, Omar's obsession would no longer have anything to do with her. What mattered now was getting through the next twenty-four hours.

So don't make everything about your soon-to-be ex-husband, she told herself. *Keep things polite and impersonal. Most important of all, stay away from the past.*

She cleared her throat. 'It's difficult to believe this was all desert.'

'The desert is still here.' His eyes flickered past her to the window. 'Outside the city it stretches for hundreds of thousands of miles. Up until two hundred years ago all of this...' he gestured to the gleaming skyscrapers '...was covered with sand. The tribes that moved into the region stuck to the coast. They fished and traded with their neighbours, and then they started diving for pearls.'

She was interested despite herself. 'Pearls?'

He nodded. 'Saltwater pearls. But they found something even more valuable. They found gold.'

She felt the limo starting to slow. Seconds later, it

stopped, but before she had a chance to process the moment of arrival the car door had opened, and she was stepping out into the hot night air.

'This way.'

Omar was beside her now and, flanked by the two blank-faced bodyguards she had seen at the airport, they made their way to a discreet entrance with a uniformed doorman. Then there was more blissful cool as she followed Omar through a stunning marble foyer into a lift.

The doors closed and her pulse dipped as she suddenly realised that the bodyguards had melted away. For the first time since he had walked into the hospital in Idaho, they were alone. And even though she couldn't see his eyes, she knew that Omar had registered it too.

She felt a flicker of heat, low in her belly. They were standing so close it would take no effort to lean into the space between them and press her mouth against his. To pull his hard, muscle-bound body against hers and feel his heat radiate through the thin cotton of her dress.

From the corner of her eye she saw him turn towards her and her pulse accelerated. Her face felt as if it was on fire. She needed to step away, but she didn't dare move.

Polite and impersonal, she reminded herself quickly and, staring straight ahead, said, 'I didn't know they'd found gold here.'

Did he sense the tension behind her remark? Could he hear the pounding of her heart, the hum of her blood? It was impossible to say. Knowing Omar...probably. It was not a comforting thought.

'I was talking about black gold. Oil. People here got very rich, very quickly, and now it's a city of superlatives.' He reached up and pressed his palm against a screen. Instantly the lift started to move. 'The biggest, the tallest, the fastest—'

No wonder, then, that he called it home, she thought.

The powerful muscles of his arm were capturing her gaze and holding it as her heartbeat tripped over itself. Omar was the flesh-and-blood embodiment of all superlatives. Darkest eyes. Softest mouth. Most passionate lover...

She could still remember that first time they'd kissed at her father's ranch. How much she'd wanted it. How much she'd feared it. Could remember the slowing of her pulse and how his lips had moved over hers, deliberately, thoroughly, and how she had melted into him, her head spinning, her breath fluttering in her throat.

It was dangerous, the effect he had on her. When he was close her brain seemed to short-circuit, Her sense of self-preservation got swamped by his beauty, his assurance, his unfiltered masculinity.

And nothing had changed, she thought, remembering their last kiss—the one that had happened twenty-four hours ago in a field in Idaho.

Her belly clenched and, feeling his eyes on her face, she jerked her gaze away, hating herself, despising the effect even the memory of his mouth had on her body. Hating, too, how, lost in the heat of desire, she had forgotten the most important superlative of all.

The biggest betrayal.

And its aftermath.

All those hours on her own, curled up on the floor of the bathroom, losing the baby she had only just learned was growing inside her.

Her hand moved jerkily to touch her stomach.

She still didn't know what had prompted her to take a pregnancy test. Had she not done so, she would probably have thought it was just a late period that was heavier than usual. In some ways, she wished she hadn't ever known. But then she would never have had those few precious days of shock and wonder and hope. Or the chance to say goodbye.

Her breath felt thin and light. Afterwards, she wished she had told Omar about the pregnancy, but it had been too late by then. Too complicated. Too devastating. Too irrelevant. Anything she'd planned to say had been swallowed up by her anger and hurt.

Besides, it had all been over—so what would have been the point of saying anything? And she hadn't wanted the footnote to their marriage to be just another meaningless apology.

She felt a twinge of guilt. Maybe she should have told him... But there was no point thinking about that now. This time tomorrow he would be out of her life for good. Better to concentrate her energies on surviving the ordeal ahead.

The lift stopped and the doors opened onto another beautiful marble interior. Lined up waiting for them were four women, all wearing neat black uniforms, and a tall man in a dark suit.

'*As-salam alaykum.*' Stepping forward, the man inclined his head.

'*Wa'alaykum as-salam.*' Delphi smiled stiffly, glancing round the beautiful empty foyer.

'Samir, this is my wife, Sayeda Delphi.' Omar turned towards her. 'Samir is in charge of the household staff.'

'Welcome home, sir...madam. I hope you had a restful flight.'

Delphi froze. *Home!* The word punched a hole in her composure. What did he mean by that? Had she misheard him or was it some kind of language mix-up?

Something of what she was feeling must have shown in her face, because in the next moment Omar had fired off a round of Arabic, and Samir had inclined his head again, then turned and retreated, accompanied by the women.

'What's going on?' She turned to Omar, her eyes narrowing. 'You said I was staying at a hotel.'

He strode past her without answering, the movement of his body illuminating his path just as if he was some mythical god. For a moment she hesitated, but where was she going to go? She swore softly and then, gritting her teeth, she followed him inside, panic swelling against her breastbone as an expanse of pale walls and richly coloured furnishings in Pharaoh hues of blue, yellow, white and black led into a huge open-plan living area.

Omar stopped and turned to face her.

'No, I said you would be staying at the Lulua, and you are.'

She stared at him, hating him, fighting the desire just to look at him in wonder. Despite the long flight, and the heat and the tension between them, he looked cool and relaxed. Now she was fighting a different desire: to take off her espadrilles and throw them at his head.

'There are two parts to the complex. The hotel next door.' His eyes locked with hers. 'And the private apartments.'

Private. The word shivered across her skin, and she stared at him mutely. Warning bells were ringing so loudly in her head that she was surprised the fire service hadn't turned up.

'And where will you be staying?' she asked slowly.

He smiled then. It was a smile that might spread across the face of the villain in a film. The sort of smile that denoted mockery or madness, and usually pre-empted a nasty surprise for the heroine or hero. So even before he replied she knew what his answer would be.

'Why, here, of course.'

Tipping back his head, he stretched out his shoulders, just as if he was still her husband, returning home after a long working day. Only that had never happened, she thought savagely, because after the first week of married life she had given up waiting for him and gone to bed alone.

'There's no "of course" about it,' she said.

Her voice sounded breathless and high, but for once she didn't care that she was revealing her feelings. 'Private' plus Omar equalled a bad idea, she thought, her skin shrivelling with panic and with something else—something she wasn't even going to acknowledge, much less give a name to.

She watched his forehead crease.

'Why are you making this into such a big deal? It's a tri-plex apartment. Our paths will hardly cross. It's quiet and private. There's a gym, a sauna and a pool. There's even a cinema room.'

'I don't care about the facilities,' she snapped. 'This isn't what I agreed to.'

She had thought she would be staying at a hotel. Hotels were neutral spaces populated by strangers. Any space she shared alone with Omar was never going to be neutral.

His dark eyes hadn't moved from her face. 'What you agreed to, Delphi, is that while you're here in Dubai there is no "I". There's only "we". And *we* will be staying in *our* apartment—together.'

She stared at him mutinously. 'I'd rather stay at the hotel.' She didn't want to share this apartment with him and be reminded of the apartment she had lived in when she had believed herself loved. The apartment she had left behind. She needed time alone to steel herself for the or-deal to come.

'The hotel is fully booked.'

'Then I'll stay at another hotel.'

A muscle flickered along his jawline. 'That's not possible.'

Her eyes found his. 'Don't be ridiculous, Omar. They can't all be fully booked.'

'I wouldn't imagine so, no.' His tone was cool and hard. 'But it's not appropriate.'

She stared at him, trying to breathe normally, stunned by his response. 'For a woman to stay in a hotel on her own?' The intensity of his focus was making her skin prickle.

'In this situation, you're not just a woman. You're my wife, and the daughter-in-law of Rashid Al Majid—so, *yes*, it would be inappropriate for you to stay at a hotel on your own. Besides, why would you want to when we have a perfectly good apartment of our own?'

Did he have no understanding of what it was doing to her, being here with him? And what was it going to be like, having to pretend to his entire family that they were still in love?

She looked up at him, disbelief vying with fury. 'You really want me to answer that?'

'Obviously,' he said, breaking the taut silence. 'That's what husbands and wives do. They have conversations. Discussions. But, as we both know, I'd have better luck squeezing blood from a stone than getting you to answer a question about yourself.'

Her eyes widened. 'That's not true. Or fair.'

'Fair?'

His voice scraped against her skin like the heat-charged air.

'You walked out on our marriage. No note. No forwarding address. Tell me, how does that equate to being *fair*?'

The injustice of his words almost knocked her off her feet. It hadn't been about fairness…just survival. And she wanted to throw the truth in his face. But where would hurling accusations at him take her? She felt her stomach lurch. She knew where. It would take her back to a place she never wanted to revisit. Back to the past…back to her parents' last row.

She took a deep breath, bit back the comment she wanted to make, and made herself speak calmly. 'I didn't come here to talk about our marriage, Omar. I came here to go to your father's birthday party.'

'You mean the party you forgot about?'

She hated him then. Hated how he twisted everything. In Omar's world he was never wrong. *She* was wrong for not opening up more to him. *She* was to blame for not simply accepting that his work took priority over everything else in his life. For not accepting his apologies and forgiving him. And now she was at fault for not remembering his father's party.

Her heart was beating out of time. 'At least I only forgot a party. You forgot you had a wife.'

'Not this again.'

Her pupils flared. 'Yes, this again.'

He stared at her for a long moment, and she sensed that he was battling to control his temper.

'If you're talking about my working hours, you knew who I was when you married me. I don't just have some little nine to five office job. I run a global business. I'm responsible for thousands of people. So, *yes*, I work late, and I travel often. And if you're talking about London, I didn't forget you, Delphi. *You* changed the plan. *Twice.* And I understood why that happened—why you needed the time and space to get things straight in your head. But you didn't extend to me the same courtesy. You refused to understand why I couldn't just ditch my plans. You didn't even try. You just did what you always do: deflected everything I said and threw up more barriers between us.'

She could feel his frustration, his bafflement that he hadn't been able to stop that from happening. But it wasn't the same, she thought, replaying the twisting, conflicted process of her thoughts at that time. She had been confused and scared about going back to England. It was her birth-place, but it was also the scene of so much pain and loss. And then she had found out she was pregnant, and that had added in an extra layer of complication, a sudden and un-expected hope, clear and bright like a flame.

Only the last thing she needed right now was to think about that. She was suddenly furious with herself for pick-ing at a scar that needed to be left well alone.

'There was nothing to understand,' she said flatly. 'It was just another business meeting.'

He shook his head. 'It was a once-in-a-lifetime busi-ness meeting. If I hadn't had that conversation with Bob Maclean, he would have had it with someone else. And I would have missed my chance.'

Her hands curled into fists, her nails scoring the palms. He was impossible. Impossibly stubborn and self-righteous and blinkered. How could she have let him kiss her again? Worse, how could she have liked it so much?

She took a breath. 'Which would have been annoying, but I'm sure you would have got over it.'

His dark gaze tore into her. 'It wasn't just about me. I was doing it for us. For our future.'

Something in his words made her stomach curl in on it-self. 'We don't have a future. We just have a brief, unhappy past and a truly dysfunctional present.'

'Because you expected marriage to be one long hon-eymoon.'

Surprise, surprise—that was her fault too.

'Not based on personal experience. How long did we get in Maui? Two days?'

'Three,' he said curtly. 'And I apologised for that at the time. Just like I apologised for not coming to London with you. I don't know what else I could have done.'

And that was the problem, Delphi thought, staring at

Omar's handsome, arrogant face. With his tailored suits and Harvard business degree he thought he was such a modern male. But his attitude to relationships might have come straight out of a nineteen-fifties soap opera. For him, an apology was the beginning and the end of his input. That was his part over and done with. Her job was to accept the apology and move on. If she didn't, then *she* was the problem.

A heaviness was creeping over her. Like the flu…only not the flu. It was more a sense of sadness and defeat, like before. She felt empty, fragile. *Lonely.*

But that was one of the consequences of thinking you could trust someone with your happiness. Because you loved them, and you thought they loved you, you gave them power, expecting and believing and hoping they would use it to protect you and cherish you and heal you.

Instead, they hurt you.

And she knew that.

She'd known it when her parents died, and her aunts had fought over her like hyenas with a bone…only the bone had been her trust fund. Later, girls at school and their mothers had seemed so caring and concerned for her—until she'd read about herself online, with quotes from the same 'concerned' but anonymous family friends.

It was why she'd held herself apart for so long. Why she worked with horses and not humans. But then she had met Omar and it had been impossible to keep her distance. She had allowed herself to trust him, to need him…

But never again.

She felt that same flatness she had felt after returning from London. Not tiredness, exactly, just a desire to curl up and hide beneath a duvet. There was no point in any of this. He would never understand what he had done. What he had destroyed.

'Fine. You win,' she said quickly. 'I'll stay here with you.'

His face relaxed a little. But she could already sense him regrouping, planning his strategy for the next battle.

'Good. Because it might have escaped your attention, but you are being treated with all the respect and consideration afforded to my wife. Which, by the way, is more than you deserve. So perhaps for the remainder of your stay you could try not to make a drama out of every little thing that doesn't quite meet with your approval.'

She could barely swallow. Heart hammering, she stared at him. 'Are you being serious?'

'I could ask you the same question.' His expression was hard and uncompromising. 'You know, up until six weeks ago we were sharing more than a living space…we were sharing a bed. Or have you forgotten about that too?'

No, she hadn't.

His words, and more specifically the memories they evoked, rippled through the taut air and through her. Her body felt suddenly tight and yet loose, hot and cold at the same time, as she tried not to remember Omar's mouth devouring hers, and the tangle of their limbs as they fought to get past not just clothes but skin and flesh. Tried too to forget how often they had failed to undress or lie down or even make it to the bed.

Shaking inside, she blanked her mind, and looked him straight in the eye. 'Well, I'm not going to be sharing a bed with you tonight. Or any other night for that matter.'

There was a long, quivering silence, and the already strained tension in the foyer cranked up several notches.

'Oh, believe me, that won't be a problem.'

He spoke calmly, but she could sense the anger fizzing beneath his smooth, tanned skin.

'Do you honestly think I want you in my bed, in my life, after the way you've acted? I didn't come and find you in that hospital or follow you to that seedy little bar to rekindle our relationship, Delphi. I don't want to fix what you smashed into pieces. In case I didn't make it clear enough before, you're here now for one reason and one reason only. For my father, my family.' His lip curled slowly and deliberately, like a dog confronted by a stranger. 'And when this is over, we're done.'

Floored by the hostility in his voice, she took a step back. It hurt more than it should. More than she wanted it to. But she would never let it show. She was done with sharing secrets with this man.

'Finally, we agree on something.' Her heart was aching so much that she felt as if she was about to double over. 'Now, if there's nothing more, I suggest you tell me where my room is.'

CHAPTER FOUR

SHE WAS IMPOSSIBLE. Utterly impossible.

Walking into his bedroom—the master bedroom, the bedroom he should be sharing with his wife—Omar let loose a torrent of expletives. With an effort of superhuman willpower, he just managed to resist the temptation to slam the door. Although, frankly, he'd had more than enough provocation to tear down the apartment with his bare hands. In fact, he was feeling so thwarted, so infuriated with Delphi, he could probably raze the entire city back to the sand it had come from.

He took a breath, tried to steady his heart rate.

Outside a moon hung in the darkening sky and drawn perhaps by its uncomplicated serenity, he snatched up the remote control by his bed and watched it, his mouth taut, his shoulders straining against his T-shirt as the door to the balcony slid open silently.

Taking a deep, calming breath, he stalked into the darkness. The air was still hot, much hotter than the apartment, but he didn't care. He needed distance from Delphi.

He had bought this apartment off-plan nearly three years ago and stayed here maybe seven or eight times. He had never once taken time to stand and stare at the view. Now, though, he was grateful for it. The endless merging darkness of the sea and sky was serene, tranquil, calming, and with Delphi throwing obstacles in the way of each and every suggestion he made he was going to need all the help he could get to stay calm.

His mouth twisted. *Easier to say than do.*

Six weeks ago, when he'd returned home from work to find Delphi gone, he had been blinded, speechless, numb with shock, and then furious that she had given up on their marriage. Stealing away as if he was some one-night stand instead of the husband she had promised to love until death parted them.

His shoulders were suddenly rigid with tension.

Her leaving had done more than break his heart. The shock of walking into the empty, echoing apartment had raised memories he'd worked hard to forget. Literally. Until he'd met Delphi, his homes had simply been assets, accruing value. All his energies, all his time, had been spent working. He'd lost count of how many all-nighters he'd pulled. But what did a little physical exhaustion matter if it helped achieve his goal of having something of his own that would finally catch the eye of his father?

And if Delphi had been the wife she'd promised to be then his dreams would have been her dreams too. But instead of supporting him unconditionally she had acted like a sulky child. Retreating into silence whenever he had to work late or take a phone call over supper.

In the days and nights that had followed her leaving, his hurt pride had stoked his anger and he'd feverishly and repeatedly imagined the moment when he finally caught up with her and could angrily demand an explanation.

But then he'd remembered his father's party and ensuring that Delphi was by his side had become his new priority. He knew he could track her down. All he'd needed was time or luck.

He'd got lucky.

Hanging up on the cowboy who'd called to tell him Delphi was in hospital, he'd promised himself that he would stay cool and detached. Unfortunately that resolution had been broken the moment he'd stepped between those curtains. Delphi had looked up at him and he'd seen the same old wariness and intransigence in her brown eyes.

But her stubbornness had simply made him determined to win.

And he had won.

She was here in Dubai.

Only now it was starting to feel less like a victory and more like an act of unparalleled foolishness on his part to have brought her here. His mouth twisted. The same foolishness that had driven him to arrogantly pursue her when even her own family had warned him of the challenge of doing so.

'I like you, Omar,' her adoptive father, Dan, had said to him. 'You're smart, and hard-working, and I'm guessing you don't usually have too much trouble attracting women.'

No, he didn't. Of course he hadn't gone so far as to actually agree out loud with Dan, but nor had he denied it. Why would he? Ever since he was a teenager women had thrown themselves at him.

Until Delphi.

'I'm not interested in other women, Dan,' he'd said, with the complacent arrogance of a man who took it for granted that he could win any woman he wanted. 'I'm interested in your daughter.'

'And I know my daughter.' Dan had smiled wryly. 'She doesn't trust easily. You won't get reins on her unless she feels safe.'

An understatement, he thought, his fingers curling around the rail, tightening against the still-warm metal. Delphi was ice-cool and aloof with outsiders. An expert at keeping people at arm's length and her emotions in check. Never before in his life had he worked so hard, committed so much time and energy and effort into trying to understand anyone.

It had taken three months to break through the barriers she had built against the world, and when finally she had stopped running, stopped deflecting, and opened up a little to him, it had been easy to see why she found it so hard to trust. Her parents' lives and deaths had marked her out as a target for all kinds of unscrupulous people. If Dan hadn't stepped in, who knew what would have happened to her?

Only the trouble was nobody was more aware of that fact than Delphi. It was why she was so hard to pin down. Why persuading her to trust him had been a Herculean task.

But he had done it.

Watching her with her horses, he'd seen how she let them make choices, let them set the pace. He'd seen her patience as she'd waited for them to come to her. And he had done the same. He had watched, waited, held his breath…

Sliding that ring on to her finger in Vegas, he'd thought—hoped—he'd done enough.

Some hope.

She'd been so insecure, so certain that he would let her down. It had been almost as if she was waiting for it to happen…looking for it to happen. Maybe that was what their marriage had been about? Not love. Not him. But proving herself right.

Why else would she refuse to give him—give *them*—a second chance? She had deemed him deficient, unnecessary, and cut him out of her life with the ruthless, dispassionate precision of a surgeon removing a ruptured appendix.

His fingers twitched against the warm metal.

Not completely dispassionate, he thought, remembering how she had softened against him back in Idaho.

In the weeks after she'd left, he had imagined a life without her. He had told himself that she was a burden, an impossible weight to carry. But in those few shimmering, electric moments, he had forgotten all that. Suddenly there had been no barriers between them, physical or otherwise. Her body had fitted against him seamlessly, as it had so many times before, and he would have held her close like that until the end of time if those actual real-life fireworks hadn't broken the spell.

He ran his hand over his face, wishing he could as easily erase the memory of Delphi's mouth on his.

But it was going to stay a memory, he told himself grimly. Once upon a time he might have believed he was strong and sane enough for both of them—not anymore. He was done with trying to make sense of what went on inside that beautiful head of hers.

Bracing himself against the ache in his groin, he stared up at the moon. Here in Dubai, and in most of the Arab world, the moon was an important symbol. There were lots of documented reasons for that. His favourite was the story his mother had used to tell him when he was a child, of how, to avoid the heat of the day, his ancestors had used to travel by night along the desert trade routes, and therefore their navigation had been dependent upon the position of the moon and stars.

If only the moon could guide him through the next twenty-four hours… Truthfully, it couldn't make a bigger mess of things than he and Delphi had, he thought sourly, yanking off his T-shirt as he walked back into the bedroom.

Staring out of the window at the blue-black sky, Delphi felt her stomach tighten. Although she wasn't quite sure why, given that this was the third time in as many days that she had found herself sitting reluctantly in the back of an oversized car with her estranged husband. This time, they were en route to her father-in-law's residence in the exclusive Emirates Hills suburb of the city.

Then again, she *was* just about to meet Omar's entire family for the first time.

And the last.

And if that wasn't enough of a reason to make the butterflies in her stomach go into a tailspin, Omar was wearing a black *kandura*—the traditional robe worn by men throughout the Gulf States.

She glanced over to where he was sitting, his long legs stretched out casually, his dark-eyed profile fixed on the phone in his hand. Her pulse twitched. He looked good in a suit; in a *kandura* he looked sublime. There was something about the austere collarless robe which emphasised the raw, uncompromising masculine beauty of the man wearing it.

Her eyes snagged on the phone in his hand. Pity about his choice of accessory. Of course you could take the man out of the boardroom, but you couldn't stop him doing business. Not if that man was Omar Al Majid, anyway.

As if sensing her focus, Omar looked up and across the car. Suddenly finding herself the object of his hard, steady gaze, she felt her skin begin to sting. She swallowed, her mouth dry and tight. Only he had this way of skewering her with his eyes—but how? And why did he still have the power to reach inside her and make her body hum with nervous energy?

It was a strangely intimate moment in a day during which he had barely spoken to her. Waking mid-morning, she had showered and dressed, but it had been Samir who greeted her. And Samir who had shown her around the apartment, which was as large and well-appointed as Omar had told her it was.

Of Omar there had been no sign. Her mouth thinned. Actually, that wasn't quite true. There had been the usual familiar laptop left open on a table with a bowl of dates and a cup of strong, black coffee cooling beside it, but the man himself was, according to Samir, tied up on important calls.

No change there, then. Not that it was any of her business any more. She was just here to show her face at the party.

Suddenly she was trembling inside, and in an effort to calm herself she smoothed out an imaginary crease in her skirt.

Maha, the stylist Omar had provided, had chosen it for her. She had arrived after lunch, with rails full of beautiful dresses in every colour imaginable, and Delphi was intensely grateful that it hadn't been left to her to choose. Dressing up was not her thing. Day to day, she lived in jeans, T-shirts, and boots. She'd had to borrow a dress and those unbelievably painful sandals from Ashley to go to the barbecue. Even on her wedding day she had kept it low-key, choosing to wear a cream cashmere sweater with a pair of matching tailored shorts.

She glanced down, her heart bumping against her ribs. This dress, though, was anything but low-key.

Made of sunset-gold iridescent sequins, it was a one-of-a-kind couture piece—two pieces, actually. A bandeau top with a tulle overlay and fitted sleeves, and a shamelessly over-the-top full skirt.

'Don't you think it's a bit much?' she had asked Maha.

Maha had shaken her head vigorously, her glossy ponytail flicking from side to side like a cheerleader's hair at a football match. 'Just because we have a modest dress code it doesn't mean you need to be invisible.' She smiled. 'I know you're worried because it's your father-in-law's birthday party, and he is a very important man. But people here are proud about who they are and what they've achieved. Trust me—if all eyes are on you, that is a good thing.'

In other words, go big or go home.

'Going big' was not something that came naturally to her. When she was a child, Ianthe and Dylan had used her as an accessory, taking her to movie premieres and concerts and once, famously—and to the disapproval of parents all over the world—to a nightclub.

As far as she was concerned, all eyes being on her was very bad. She hated the flashing cameras, the strangers calling out her name and telling her to smile. At least she wouldn't have to worry about that at the party. The Al Majid name didn't just open doors: it closed them. There would be no press or curious members of the public craning their necks to see what the orphaned daughter of Ianthe Reynolds and Dylan Wright looked like now.

Just one unfeeling, infuriatingly arrogant husband, she thought, glancing over at Omar.

'Something to say, Delphi?' he said softly.

Plenty, she thought, but it would be wasted on him. After all, in less than twenty-four hours he would be out of her life for good.

Keeping that fact at the front of her mind, she shrugged. 'I was just thinking it's a shame you didn't leave your phone at home. But then I suppose that would mean you'd be off-grid, and you've never let anything, including our marriage, get in the way of work before. Why should your father's ninetieth birthday be any different?'

A cool shiver ran down her spine as he gave her a long, steady look. 'I was replying to a message from my sister Jalila. She texted me to say how much she is looking forward to finally meeting you.'

She felt her body tense. There was an edge to his voice—

probably because she'd called him out for always being on his phone—but it felt like an attack. As if it was her fault that she and Jalila had never met. But Omar had never encouraged her to meet his family.

She had met his parents briefly in New York, a month after their wedding. What she'd noticed most about his mother, Maryam, was how much younger she was than her husband. And as for Rashid... Like his son, he was a master at controlling social situations, so it was hard to say for sure, but she'd got the impression that Rashid was either bored or distracted, maybe both. Either way, they hadn't stayed long.

And, despite his having sixteen of them, she had never met any of his half-siblings. For some reason she still didn't understand it had just never happened. But then she was so close to her own family she hadn't given it much thought.

She felt a sharp pang of homesickness, like she had in the hospital. Her brothers Ed, Scott and Will had welcomed Omar into their homes and into their hearts, and they had encouraged her to let down her guard, to stop shielding herself from her feelings.

Her heart thudded. Thinking about telling them that her marriage was over made her feel sick. It was even worse when she thought about Dan. Even though he had done nothing but love and support her, she knew he would blame himself and that she was going to break his heart.

Just as her mother, Ianthe, had done.

'I need you to do something.'

Omar's voice cut across her thoughts and she stared at him warily. 'You've dragged me halfway around the globe to spare your blushes, so I think I'm already doing enough, don't you?'

Immediately she wished she hadn't said anything. His

expression was like stone, but there was a glitter in his dark eyes that made her breath catch.

'Out of the two of us, Delphi, I'm not the one prone to blushing.'

He paused and she saw something in his eyes that darted though her, hot and unchecked like the lick of a flame.

'But perhaps you need me to refresh your memory.'

For a moment she couldn't breathe, couldn't think of any kind of comeback. She was swamped by the slow, heavy pounding of her heart. It was true. Omar knew exactly how to make her skin grow warm, in public and in private, with his eyes, his hands, his tongue...

She swallowed. 'I don't require any reminders. That's why I want a divorce.'

He stared at her steadily. 'And, as I told you before, until that happens, you're still my wife. So tonight, for reasons I shouldn't have to explain, you will need to wear a ring.'

There was a short, stiff silence, and then he held out his hand. Heart hammering, she stared down at the fine silver band. It looked so similar to the one Omar had given her in Vegas she might have thought it was that very ring. Only she knew the original was tucked into the pocket of her toiletries bag.

Don't, she warned herself.

But it was too late, she was already there in the Little Chapel of Love, with Omar beside her, tall and handsome and serious, his dark eyes holding her steady, holding her safe.

And yet she hadn't believed it was happening, that she was really there, exchanging vows with this shockingly beautiful man. She'd had to keep touching him, her hand trembling against his chest and his arm, even after he'd slid the ring on her finger, needing to make sure that he was real and that she wasn't dreaming.

Beneath her ribs, her heart began beating unevenly. She had been wrong. For her, happy endings could only ever be a dream; that was something she'd known since waking to find herself an orphan at the age of four. Only back in Vegas, lost in the velvet-soft focus of his gaze she hadn't wanted to believe it was true.

She did now.

Her pulse jerked as beside her, jaw tightening, Omar leaned forward. 'Here, let me.'

'No. I'll do it,' she snapped.

She wouldn't let him take the memory of that day and turn it into something ugly. It was all she had left, and it wasn't going to be ruined along with everything else.

Ignoring the tenderness in her chest, she picked up the ring and slid it onto her finger. It fitted perfectly—obviously—but that only rubbed more salt into the wound. It should be too big or too small, she thought dully.

The car was slowing and, turning towards the window again, she caught a glimpse of wide marble steps flanked by men in dark suits. And then the limousine stopped. Her heart was racing; she could taste the adrenaline in her mouth. Parties, people, crowds…they were so not her thing.

If only she could stay here in the car. Just drop Omar off and then go back to the apartment—better still the airport. But if she did that then she wouldn't get her divorce. Or at least not quickly or easily. And slow and difficult would just mean more pain for everyone.

All she had to do was get through the next few hours and it would be over. She would have kept her side of the bargain and she could get the hell out of Dodge. Or, in her case, Dubai.

'This way, darling.'

Omar was standing beside her, his hand outstretched. She blinked, the sudden casual intimacy of his words knocking the air out of her lungs, and then held out her hand and let him lead her through the gleaming white hallway.

Her first thought was how unlike her own family home it was. The ranch house was large and sprawling, but really it was five thousand square feet of dimly lit log cabin with stone fireplaces and worn leather sofas.

This was a real-life palace. With each step she took, polished metal and crystal chandeliers jostled with huge modern canvases and centuries-old artefacts to grab her attention. Clearly Maha had been right, she thought, remembering what the stylist had said to her. People here were proud about who they were and what they had achieved.

'You're very quiet.' Omar glanced over at her. 'Are you plotting your escape? Or my demise?'

She bit into her lip to stop it from curving into a smile. She had forgotten that side to him. The side that could make her smile and laugh. Unlike both her parents, smiling had never come naturally to her. But making her laugh was one of the ways Omar had broken down her barriers. It was why he was the first, the only man she had given her heart to.

Her eyes paused on his arresting face beneath the *ghutra*. Although other things had played a part too...

She swallowed and looked away. The sound of voices was filtering through the walls. And music. Soft, lilting, rhythmic. It reminded her of Vegas and Omar teaching her the *dabke*, a traditional Arabic wedding dance, in their room as the sun rose on the first day of their married life. They'd danced and laughed and ended up back in bed.

Now they were walking towards two huge bronze doors and, focusing her attention on what lay on the other side, she pushed back against the wave of nostalgia rising inside her.

'Both. But I would need two hands.'

Her words fluttered between them, foolish and unthinking, like moths bashing into glass.

'Not always,' he said slowly. 'Sometimes you managed perfectly well without the use of either.'

Their eyes locked and she stared at him, the air leaving her body. There was no point pretending that she didn't understand what he was talking about. She could see it as clearly as if she was there, feel it as if it was happening… their bodies twisting against the sheets and then his hand catching her wrists to stretch them above her head as he thrust deeper and deeper, until she was arching against him, mindless and moaning.

She shivered all the way through, hating herself, hating the fact that even now she could feel this way.

'Things change. I've changed.'

The music was getting louder. At the margins of her vision, she sensed rather than saw two men step forward, and then the doors swung open and her footsteps and her breathing faltered.

They had arrived at the party.

But she barely registered the huge, high-ceilinged room, or the guests turning to look at them. Drawing a jagged breath, she tugged her hand away, but he simply tightened his grip.

'If you're planning on making a scene, I'd advise against it,' he said quietly.

Heart pounding fiercely, she looked over at the man filling the space beside her. 'I'm perfectly in control of my emotions, thank you.'

The corner of his mouth curled, but there was no humour in his dark eyes. 'Then clearly you haven't changed at all. Perhaps if you had our marriage might have had a chance.'

She blinked as a camera flashed to her left.

'It's okay,' Omar murmured. 'It's a private photographer. My father likes to have a record of family events.'

'Omar!' A tall man with a close-cut greying beard

stepped forward, his dark eyes widening with happiness. 'I heard you'd arrived, little brother.'

Omar smiled. 'Hamdan.' The two men embraced. 'It's good to see you too.'

Watching him, Delphi felt her stomach tighten. Nobody would know that she was here under duress, obligation. But she could sense Omar's tension. It was there in the rigidity of his body and the tightness in his jaw even as he smiled.

'Not as good as it is to see you. Don't leave it so long next time.' Hamdan squeezed Omar's shoulder, then turned, his face growing serious. 'And you must be Delphi.' He inclined his head. 'I am Hamdan, Omar's eldest brother. Welcome, finally, to Dubai.'

She knew all the children of his father's first wives were older than Omar, but Hamdan was much older—old enough to be his father or hers.

Hiding her surprise, Delphi smiled. 'Thank you. It's lovely to meet you.'

Over the next few hours she repeated that sentence more times than she could count, as one by one Omar's siblings came up to greet him and welcome her, only varying it once when Omar led her through the crowded room to meet his parents.

Then she said, 'It's lovely to see you again.'

As the only one of Rashid's children not living in the Middle East, she had thought that Omar might be treated like the prodigal son by his father. But although Rashid's greeting was affectionate, his blue gaze moved on with surprising speed.

Still, gazing round the room, it was impossible for her not to feel a twinge of guilt as her eyes leapfrogged Hamdan to each of Omar's siblings in turn. Marriage and family were clearly important to the Al Majids. Only now, just like her mother had done before her, she was going to blow everything apart. Shatter the bedrock of their lives by divorcing their son and brother.

Heart pumping, she glanced sideways at Omar. Was he thinking the same thing? Was that why his hand felt so rigid? Her chest squeezed tight, the pain suddenly too big for her body. It made no sense, given the current state of their relationship, but she couldn't bear to think that he was suffering.

'Excuse me, Delphi.' It was Hamdan, his handsome face apologetic. 'Would it be all right if I just borrowed Omar for a couple of moments?'

She nodded, her smile aching as Omar followed his brother through the guests, emotions she had managed to contain for weeks now clawing at her, overwhelming her. Why had she ever agreed to do this?

A flash caught her eye from the other side of the room, where the photographer was now taking pictures of Omar's father and his wives. Her hands clenched. She knew it was all perfectly legitimate, but it was making her nervous. Maybe she could find somewhere quiet to sit out the rest of the party. She turned, hoping she might slide discreetly away—

'Delphi!'

A beautiful woman in an exquisite flute-sleeved robe the colour of ripe pomegranates was standing in front of her.

'Sorry, I didn't mean to startle you. I just wanted to say hi, and that I love your dress. You look beautiful. You *are* beautiful.'

'Thank you.' Delphi smiled. She wasn't good at small talk, but somehow this woman made it easy for her to say, 'I love the colour of yours. It's an amazing party, isn't it?'

The woman nodded. 'What's amazing is that Baba agreed to cut short a business trip to be here. Oh, I'm Jalila, by the way—Omar's sister.'

So 'Baba' must be Rashid. But surely he wasn't still working? Delphi felt her stomach clench, but there was no time to pursue that thought.

'I'm the one you haven't met.' Jalila laughed. 'Although, to be fair, you might not have noticed there are so many of us.'

Delph screwed up her face. 'I have to admit I did lose count after I got to double figures.' She smiled at Jalila. All of Omar's siblings were good-looking, and they shared his dark hair and eyes, but with her flawless skin and fine bone structure Jalila was the one who most resembled him.

'It's fine, honestly.' Leaning towards her, Jalila lowered her voice. 'Just tell me, though, did Hamdan introduce everyone in age order or alphabetically?'

Delphi hesitated. 'I think it might have been age order.'

Jalila rolled her eyes. 'He does that because otherwise Aisha and Ahmad would come before him. Brothers—honestly.'

Now Delphi laughed. 'I know what you mean. I have three, and I love them, but they can be a real pain.'

'Think yourself lucky. I have nine.' Jalila smiled then, almost shyly. 'But you got my favourite one, and I'm really glad about that.'

Delphi frowned. 'You are?'

Jalila nodded slowly. 'Honestly, none of us ever imagined Omar would tie the knot, and if he did we thought it would all be planned out, with a mile-long agenda. But it was so romantic…getting married on impulse like that. That's how I know he must be crazy about you.'

Wordless, Delphi stared at Omar's sister. Her hands were shaking, and she was fighting so many crazy and contradictory thoughts and feelings that her head was spinning. And some of those conflicting emotions must have shown on her face because the next moment Jalila took hold of Delphi's hands.

'Sorry, I didn't mean to be so forward. I know we've only just met, but I'm so happy Omar's found love. I know he's rich and gorgeous…' she screwed up her face as if the opposite were true '…but I also know how intense he can be, how fixated he is on proving himself.'

Proving himself? Delphi stared at her in confusion. Proving what? To whom? Her eyes flickered across the room to where Omar stood out from the crowd, and not just because he was taller than most of the other men in the room. His face was a wonder—all dark shadows and gold highlights—and his smile made him look as if he was posing for a photograph. Not the kind of man who needed to prove himself to anyone.

Jalila squeezed her hands. 'Sometimes he can be his own worst enemy, but I can tell you *get* him. And I see how my brother looks at you and I know there's nothing he wouldn't do for you. All you have to do is ask.'

Suddenly it was a struggle for Delphi to keep smiling.

Once upon a time Omar had said almost those exact words to her, and she had believed him. That was why she'd asked him to be there when she went to visit her parents' graves. Only he had let her down. Time and time again he had left her on her own. London had simply been one time too many.

'So, the magicians are circulating now.' Hamdan looked at the schedule on his phone. 'Then the aerial acrobats will start their show before the fireworks begin at midnight.'

Omar nodded, because that was what was expected of him. Frankly, he'd had more than enough fireworks over the last forty-eight hours to last a lifetime—but they were expected too.

Mohammad, his second-eldest brother, frowned. 'Unless Father decides he wants to retire early, in which case—'

Omar stood in silence, watching his brothers' talk. Despite the age gap, and their having different mothers, he loved his siblings, but being surrounded by his entire family always had the same effect on him. He felt swamped, unremarkable, irrelevant.

And probably that would never change. Because despite being thirty years old, and the CEO of a global media business, he was still the little brother. A postscript in a nappy. A last-minute addendum to an already over-long agenda.

And who bothered reading those?

Except him, of course.

He glanced over to where Rashid stood with his wives, his blue eyes moving restlessly around the room. It would take more than aerial acrobats and magicians to hold his father's attention.

Only his mother and Jalila had even come close to treating Omar as a person in his own right. Glancing across the room, he narrowed his gaze on his favourite sister with pinpoint accuracy and felt a flicker of irritation as he realised that he only knew where she was because she was talking to Delphi.

A second flicker followed, as he was forced to admit it wasn't a one-off and that he had known his wife's exact location in every second that had passed since Hamdan had towed him away from her side.

Not that he'd looked. On the contrary, his neck was aching with the effort of *not* looking. Now, though, he had an excuse, and he watched Delphi smile, then laugh with his sister, his shoulders alternately tensing then relaxing. Seeing her so at ease with Jalila was both baffling and oddly satisfying. But he was also jealous that his sister had so effortlessly done in minutes what it had taken him weeks to achieve.

Aware suddenly of a silence behind him, he turned to find his two eldest brothers watching him in amusement.

Mohammad nudged him in the ribs. 'Are we boring you, little brother?'

'Not at all—' he began.

'Go.' Hamdan grinned and gave him a little push. 'Go and talk to your beautiful wife. We can manage without you.'

But of course they could, he thought, as he made his way across the room. Throughout his life he had been extraneous to requirements. A small boy running after his much older siblings, crying and shouting, 'Wait for me!' Or tugging at the sleeve of his father's robe in a fruitless attempt to gain his attention.

It was why he had wanted to set up his business far away from his family. Here, as an Al Majid, he would have been given a high-ranking job for life, no questions asked. But he needed more. He needed something for himself. Something of his own. Something unique and beautiful and shimmering that would make his family, and in particular his father, sit up and take notice.

His eyes locked on his wife, and he felt hunger punch through his chest. In that dress, Delphi ticked all those boxes and more. In a room filled with beautiful, wealthy people and priceless objects she shone the brightest.

Breath catching, he let his gaze skim over the glittering iridescent fabric. But it wasn't just the sequins and tulle that made it hard for him not to look over and even harder to look away. She might not see it, and she certainly didn't exploit it, but as well as Ianthe's wild-honey-coloured eyes and Dylan's famous pout, Delphi had inherited her parents' ability to light up a room.

In a world where people fought tooth and nail for their fifteen minutes of fame, she was an enigma. The child of two celebrities and yet she shunned the spotlight. A beautiful young woman whose strength was her vulnerability.

And she was always vulnerable. Even now, dressed like a goddess, he could almost see her trembling inside. And outside, he thought, as Jalila took hold of his wife's shaking hands.

'You two seem to be getting along very well.'

'Finally!' Jalila turned, her forehead creasing into a mock frown as Omar kissed her on both cheeks. 'Don't bother coming to say hello, will you?'

'I tried. You were with Khalid.'

Her face softened. 'Have you seen him yet?' As he shook his head, she clutched at his arm and gave a squeal of excitement. 'Thank goodness! I'm just going to go and get him. So don't go anywhere. Either of you. Please,' she added, before turning to scamper away.

Beside him, he felt Delph stiffen. 'She won't be long.'

'It's fine. I don't mind waiting. I like her.'

He felt his stomach clench, and a quickening of his pulse as she gave him a small, tight smile. It reminded him of the first time they'd met, and he found himself responding just as he had then. Only why? It was over. Except it didn't feel over when she was standing this close...

'You look beautiful, by the way,' he said abruptly. 'I wanted to say so earlier. But I was angry.'

Was? He frowned. Was he not angry now?

Confused, he pushed the thought away. 'What I'm trying to say is that I know you don't like getting dressed up, so thank you.'

He felt the back of his neck tingle as her eyes found his. 'I was worried I'd be overdressed, but—'

They both glanced across the room at the guests in their jewel-coloured robes and glittering gold accessories.

'Looks like you have one less thing to worry about,' he said softly. Their eyes met again. 'Now you just have to get shot of your monumentally arrogant and selfish husband.'

She blinked. 'You weren't always arrogant and selfish.'

The air around them seemed to snap to attention. He stared at her, not moving a muscle, scared to move. 'Do you mean that?' There was a note in his voice he didn't quite recognise.

The pulse in her throat jerked against her pale skin.

'Sorry I took so long.'

He swore silently as Jalila returned. 'Fahad was showing him off to the aunties, but he needs to go to sleep now, otherwise he'll be up all night—only I wanted you to meet him first.'

Omar's heart twitched as she held out the baby.

'Khalid, this is your uncle Omar. Omar, this is your nephew.'

He settled the baby in the crook of his arm and gazed down into his huge brown eyes. 'He's beautiful, Lila.' Throat tightening, he thumbed a feathery dark curl away from Khalid's doeskin cheek and kissed his forehead. Tiny, beautiful, and mesmerizingly perfect.

'Yes, he is. Actually, he reminds me of you.' Jalila bit her lip. 'Baba thinks so too. He even got Auntie Maryam to find a photo of you at the same age.'

Batting away the twist of pleasure her words produced, Omar said quickly, 'How old is he now?'

'Six weeks. Talking of photos—yes, please. My son and my brother.'

It was the photographer. As the camera flashed, Omar caught a glimpse of Delphi's face. She looked like a deer in the headlights, all huge panicky eyes and jerky pulse.

'That's enough.' He dispatched the photographer with a jerk of his head.

'Oh, goodie.'

A waiter had materialised at his shoulder and Jalila leaned forward and snatched up a glass of orange juice.

'He's so hungry it makes me thirsty all the time. Would you like one, Delphi? Or you can have champagne. Honestly, nobody will mind.'

'No. No, thank you.'

Delphi's voice, or rather the brittle *keep-away-from-me* edge to it, jolted him out of his baby-fixated trance and he looked up in surprise. She'd seemed to be getting on with Jalila so well.

But his sister hadn't registered the change. 'It's no trouble, really. Let me—'

'I said no.' Delphi's voice rose and snapped like a sail in the wind. 'I don't want champagne. I don't want a drink. I just need some air.'

She stumbled backwards. Behind her, a magician made a dove appear out of a scrunched-up handkerchief with a theatrical flourish. Distracted, Omar glanced over and felt his body tense. Inside his head a thought, a possibility, was starting to take shape…hazy at first, then growing clearer.

'Delphi.' He reached for her but was hampered by the baby. And, swerving his outstretched hand, she sidestepped past him.

Jalila's dark eyes brimmed with tears. 'I'm sorry…' A flush was creeping over her cheeks.

'It's fine. She's still upset from the accident. Here, take Khalid.' Heart hammering, he handed the baby to his sister. 'It'll be okay.'

'She looked so pale.'

He'd have to take Jalila's word for it, he thought as he wove through the guests. He hadn't been looking at Delphi's face. He'd been too busy watching the way her hand had moved to curve protectively over her belly.

The corridor was empty.

He turned, caught a glimpse of gold.

'Delphi!'

Like Cinderella fleeing the ball, she gathered up her skirts and ran. But no woman wearing a floor-length dress and heels could outrun a man. Particularly not a man like him, who had a burning question that needed answering.

He caught her arm as she reached the gardens, his hand clamping around her waist, stopping her in her tracks.

'Let go of me.'

He tightened his grip. 'Not until you tell me the truth. Are you pregnant?'

She squirmed against him, but her strength was no match for his.

Capturing her chin, he tilted her face up to his. 'Tell me.'

Her eyes were as huge and dark as the baby's, her face pale with shock and pain as she jerked free.

'No. I'm not.' She sounded as if it hurt her to speak. 'But I was. I had a miscarriage.'

CHAPTER FIVE

OMAR STARED DOWN at Delphi. The confusion of anger and tension that had been driving him forward since she'd walked out of their home six weeks ago had dissolved, and in its place was—

Nothing.

No reply. No response. No reaction.

It was as if her words had hollowed him out, stolen not just the breath from his body but his understanding of the world, and in its place was the static rush of the ocean, like the sound when you held up a shell to your ear.

Only this rush was so big and so loud it was a roar, swallowing him whole.

He was in shock, obviously. That was why he couldn't swallow or speak. And why, despite the warmth of the evening, he felt as though his body was encased in ice.

Shock on top of shock—because just a few moments earlier he had assumed she was pregnant.

All the evidence had suggested that. Her sudden tension when he held Khalid. Her refusal to drink alcohol. The way she had touched her stomach.

Only he was wrong, and the opposite was true.

His gaze dropped to where Delphi stood now, in that astonishing glittering gown, her hand clutching the sequinned fabric, her lips parted as if she was having to take in extra breaths through her mouth.

She had been pregnant but had lost the baby. Not *the* baby, he corrected himself. *Their* baby—*his* baby. And now his heart was thumping violently against his ribs, so that even though the flagstones beneath him were literally made of rock, it felt as though he was standing in the epi-centre of an earthquake.

'You were pregnant.'

He didn't know why but he needed to hear the words in his own voice to make it real. She nodded, her face taut, her gaze steady and unblinking, but beneath the stillness he could see she was fighting to hold something in, or back, or together.

'But you lost the baby. *Our* baby.'

From inside the house, he could hear the faint but clear clink of glasses and the hum of conversation. It all sounded so reassuringly normal—only how could anything be nor-mal when there was this terrible, unalterable truth?

Delphi nodded again. Only this time as she did so her hand slipped away from the front of her dress.

It was such a small gesture, but there was a hopeless-ness and a hurt in it that wrenched at something inside him. He reached out unthinkingly and took her hand, because surely this was the moment when she would bring down her drawbridge and let him in? When finally, she would choose to share her loss and pain?

She was standing in front of him, straight-backed, body braced, and then she made a small choking sound and swayed forward, just as she had in the hospital.

He pulled her against him, his arms curving around her as her body crumpled. And then, so suddenly that he al-most lost his balance, she was pushing against his chest, pushing him away.

'No!' Her chin jerked up. 'Don't touch me. Don't you touch me. I don't need your sympathy.'

He stared at her, a hot lava of primaeval emotions coursing through his veins.

She didn't need it, and more importantly nor was she offering any in return. His heart was beating slow and hard. Not only had she just tossed a grenade into his life and blown everything up, but she was also willing to let him stagger alone and maimed around an unrecognisable landscape.

He stared at her, his breath quickening, almost as shocked by the uncompromising and unexpected ferocity of her rejection as he was by the discovery that he had been, briefly at least, an expectant father.

The muscles in his shoulders locked painfully. In the past when Delphi had clammed up, he hadn't liked it, but he knew that she had trusted people before and been hurt, and that was why she found it so hard to lower her guard and let people in—even him.

But this was different.

This wasn't just about her. Her feelings, her needs, her wishes, her past. This was about him too. How could she keep something like that a secret from him?

He thought back to when she'd swayed forward, and he had caught her. For those few half-seconds, just like in the hospital, he'd forgotten his fury and his pain. He'd simply been relieved to have found his wife…to have found her. His Delphi.

His chest was tight, his lungs on fire. Only that implied she had been his to lose—and she had never been his. All of this proved it. Proved that he had never known what was going on in her head…never known her.

'I had a miscarriage.'

The words still burning in his brain, he stared at the woman standing in front of him, seeing a stranger.

'When did it happen?' he asked.

There was the briefest of silences, so that her answer almost overlapped his question. 'In London.'

He stared at her, with a terrible dropping feeling in his chest. How could that be? He had arrived at the London apartment late in the evening on the day she'd been to visit her parents' graves. Delphi had been quiet, but he had thought she was still angry with him for not cancelling his meeting and going with her. He had kissed her, apologised again for not being there, and asked her about her day. That was when she had told him about seeing the paparazzi and deciding not to go to the graves.

At no point had she told him that she had miscarried their baby.

'And you didn't think to mention it?' He held her gaze, shock curdling in his stomach. 'I didn't even know you were having a baby.'

Were. Past tense. Anger and misery rushed through him again. She had always been secretive, but surely this hadn't been only her secret to keep.

'How many weeks were you?'

'Eight. But I didn't realise. There was so much going on…'

Eight weeks. Two months. So, the baby would have been roughly the shape and size of a bean. For a second he couldn't feel himself breathing. *Little bean.* That was what Jalila had called Khalid when she was pregnant.

'So, when *did* you realise?'

'At about seven weeks.'

He felt like he was floating away from the confines of his body. 'I'm your husband, Delphi. You should have told me.'

She drew in a quick, unsteady breath. 'I was going to.'

'You were *going* to?' he repeated.

His chest was still warm from holding Khalid in his arms, and that hurt most of all. Knowing that he would never feel their baby's warmth or kiss its forehead.

He took a step back from her, no longer needing sympathy but space. If he hadn't asked if she was pregnant, would he have ever known about their lost baby's momentary tiny, fluttering existence? The only reason he did now was because he had made it impossible for her not to tell him.

What would have happened if he hadn't tracked Delphi down and forced her to come to Dubai?

The answer to that question tore at his insides.

'You expect me to believe you? Actually, you don't need to answer that.' A muscle flickered in his jaw. 'You don't care if I believe you or not, right?'

He scarcely recognised his own voice, but he didn't care. Nor did he believe her. Delphi had never told him anything willingly in her life. Everything had to be prised out of her. Why should this be any different?

Her eyes were huge and dark in the moonlight. 'Of course I care. But it's complicated.'

It's complicated.

He gritted his teeth. It was one of her stock get-out-of-jail-free responses to any difficult conversation—'difficult' being anything that trespassed into the personal. But personal meant relating only to one individual; this was about *him* too.

'No, it's simple, Delphi. You were pregnant with our baby, and you didn't tell me. And then you lost our baby, and you didn't tell me that either.'

The starkness of his words appeared to shock her—shock them both. But so much of his life had been spent trying to matter, and this was one occasion when he should automatically have done so—only she hadn't deemed him important enough to tell him anything.

She still didn't.

He watched her take a small step backwards, her eyes darting past his, planning her next escape route.

'Look, I know this is a shock…' she said.

Had it been a shock for her too? Not the miscarriage… the pregnancy?

Somewhere in another part of his brain he could picture Delphi in the bathroom of his New York apartment, staring down at a pregnancy test. He saw her confusion, her disbelief. And then what? Happiness? Relief? *Panic?*

He didn't know. And not knowing was like a hammerblow to the head. But, seriously, what did he know? He'd had no idea she'd even been trying for a baby. Or maybe she hadn't. Delphi might have promised to love and cherish and honour him, but she had always disguised her feelings—held herself apart, held her past close.

Only now it appeared she had lied to him about the present too.

'But it needn't have been a shock.' He gritted his teeth. 'You could have told me about it when it happened.'

'Actually, I couldn't.' Her voice sharpened. 'Because you weren't there.'

Not here…not there…not old enough…not ready for the responsibility. He'd heard it, or some version of it, so many times before.

'So you decided to punish me by letting me find out now, here, in my father's home, at his birthday party?'

'You know that's not what happened.' Her face was flushed with anger. 'You know I'd never do that.'

'How? I don't know anything about you. You've kept things hidden from me our entire marriage…lied to my face. I have no idea what you're capable of.'

'Maybe if you'd been around a little more you would know,' she said shakily. 'Look, I didn't choose any of this. It was your decision to come after me and demand answers. Your decision to come to the hospital and then that bar. Your decision to blackmail me into coming to this party.'

He couldn't keep the sneer from his voice. 'And I thought you were here because you wanted to do the right thing.'

'I did. I do. I'm doing all this for Rashid...for your father.'

'You mean our lost baby's grandfather?'

There was a fraction of a pause as her eyes widened. He waited for a reaction, but it didn't come. Instead, ducking her chin, she moved again to step past him.

'Where do you think you're going?' he asked quietly, blocking her. 'You're not leaving until we're finished talking.'

But she had already turned and was walking away. Not waiting for him, ignoring him. Literally giving him the cold shoulder.

Blinking the red haze from his eyes, he caught up with her in four strides, stepping in front of her. 'I am so done with chasing after you, Delphi.'

'Then stop doing it,' she hissed. 'Look, I did what you asked. I came to Dubai as your wife, and I came to your father's party. That's it. I'm done.

'I'm not done. We need to talk.'

'And you think this is the right time and place to do that?'

He glanced past her shoulder to where a group of guests had wandered out into the gardens and were now gazing admiringly at the fountains. It wasn't. But, knowing Delphi as he did, it was unlikely there ever would be a right time or place.

He clenched his fists as a burst of music, inappropriately

loud and celebratory, filled the warm evening air. The fireworks were next on the schedule. Soon the gardens would
be filled with guests.

'No, I suppose I don't. And you're right. You have done
what I asked. So perhaps now is a good time to end this
farce.'

There was a moment when her face relaxed. It was so
brief that if he'd blinked, he would have missed it, but it
was enough to make up his mind. Before she could react,
his hand caught her elbow, and he began to frogmarch her
along the path.

'What are you doing?'

Once again, she was trying to shake free of his grip,
but he didn't release her. 'You want to leave. We're leaving,' he said shortly.

He had to get her out of here fast before the guests out-
numbered the palm trees. Before he lost his temper in a
way that would rival the upcoming pyrotechnic display.

'But the house is that way. Aren't we going to say goodbye to your parents?'

'You're here to avert gossip, Delphi, remember. Not create more. I'm the host's son and you are my wife. If we leave
early, people will notice and talk.'

'I don't mind leaving alone,' she said quickly.

'Oh, I know. It's one of your major talents.'

'I just meant I can take the car back to the apartment.'

The static was back in his chest. 'You think you can
run from this? You think you can just get on a plane and
leave it all behind?'

Her eyes widened again, and there was a trace of uncertainty in her face. Suddenly he was fighting to stand still
where he was. She was so close. All he had to do was take
one step forward and kiss her…let his mouth, his hands,

his body persuade her to close the gap between them as he had done so many times before.

'That's not what I said.'

'Good.'

Because this time she was going nowhere until he got some answers.

He glanced past her to where a sleek black helicopter sat squatly on its concrete apron on the lawn. Two members of his father's security team were standing beside it and, jerking his head in greeting, he barked out his instructions in Arabic.

Delphi turned, her face stiffening with shock, as one of the men leapt forward and yanked open the doors.

'After you.' Omar propelled her forward.

'No.' It was a flat, unequivocal negative. 'I don't want to.'

'You have to. We can't use the car.' He spoke with such certainty that he saw her flinch. 'For exactly the same reason that we're not going to go back and say goodbye to my parents. And we're not going to the apartment either,' he added. 'Because, as you so rightly pointed out, you and I need to talk.'

'I didn't say that. You did,' she protested, but he kept on speaking.

'And for that to happen we need somewhere quiet and private.'

Although in this instance for 'quiet and private' read 'isolated and secure'.

'Somewhere we can talk without interruption,' he continued.

Somewhere he could get answers to all the questions and conjecture swirling inside his head.

'Jalila is already worried that she's upset you. When she realises we've left the party I wouldn't put it past her to come to the Lulua. Besides, why does it matter either way where we go? It's just a few hours of your life.'

A pulse of anger beat over his skin as he thought back to that moment at the party when the shifting, disconnected pattern of dots inside his head had taken shape and he had uncovered a life-changing truth about himself.

'Surely you can give me that?' he said.

She stared at him, pale in the moonlight, as beautiful and as unreachable as the moon. 'I am not going to get into some random helicopter with you,' she said, sounding out each syllable as if she was talking to a child.

He held her gaze. 'You will, Delphi. One way or another. But it will be easier if you co-operate.'

'I have already co-operated.'

'Then you know how easy it is.'

She stared at him, and the hostility and despair in her eyes almost stopped him. But then he reminded himself that this woman had deceived him. She owed him the truth. And this time he was going to get it from her.

Gazing down at the tops of the palm trees as the helicopter rose up into the night sky, Delphi took a small, panicky breath. The smell of the leather upholstery reminded her so much of the tack room at the ranch that she felt almost faint.

Not that the man sitting beside her cared.

She turned to look at the dark-eyed, astonishingly handsome stranger who was also her husband. Her very angry, single-minded husband.

'Where are we going?'

He didn't turn to look at her. 'It's a place in the hills. About twenty minutes from here.'

She didn't know what to say to that. Right now, she felt as if she had said everything that could be said. Only it wasn't enough for Omar.

How could it be?

A pang of guilt pinched inside her chest. Whatever he might have accused her of, she hadn't planned on telling him about the miscarriage today, at his father's birthday party, surrounded by his family and friends. But then Jalila had brought over Khalid, and it had brought it all back, and the walls she had carefully built around herself to contain the hurt and pain had fallen away like petals on the wind.

Watching Omar hold the baby, seeing his fierce, brooding focus on Khalid's sweet face, had almost made her double over. Was that what their baby would have looked like too? The answer to that question had made it impossible for her to stand there another moment, and so she had done what she always did when things hurt and scared her.

She had run.

And, because he was Omar, he couldn't *not* follow. And, because he was Omar, by the time he'd caught up with her, he'd already known what question to ask.

The one she had decided nearly seven weeks ago never to answer.

And she knew that was unfair, and selfish and wrong, but the moment when it would have been possible had passed nearly seven weeks ago, in that gleaming anonymous bathroom in London. Then she had wanted him so badly it had hurt almost as much as the cramps.

Afterwards, she had thought she had no words for what had happened. No words to express the aching sense of loss and despair, the bruising emptiness.

Her throat tightened.

But in the end, all it had taken was four. *'I had a miscarriage.'*

It was the first time she had said it out loud, and it had been a shock saying it, hearing it. Maybe that was why she was still reeling inside. That and watching Omar's face lose colour and stiffen with shock and pain.

She could still see his expression now; he had looked shattered.

Closing her eyes, Delphi leaned back in her seat. She didn't want to think about Omar's pain. It was more than she could manage when she still hadn't come to terms with her own.

For weeks now the terrible dark memory of that day had been there, keening and scrabbling at the back of her mind to be let in. But she had kept it at bay—taking on extra work at the stables, watching reruns of familiar shows on TV late into the night so she was in a near-permanent state of physical exhaustion.

Now, though, the frantic, terrifying thing was loose, and she felt her legs start to shake just as they had in London.

It had started off as a stomachache. She'd put it down to too much adrenaline. And, arriving at the graveyard, she had felt the ache fade, swept away by a prickling rush of excitement that finally she had made it.

Over the years she had seen pictures of her parents' graves in magazines and on the internet. Their headstones weren't the first to be covered with lipstick kisses—Oscar Wilde and Marilyn Monroe were just two of the celebrities whose graves had received the same treatment. But none were as smothered in kisses as those of her parents'.

Their fans still loved them almost as much as she did, and she had waited so long to make this pilgrimage. But her excitement had been short-lived. Walking into the cemetery, she had expected to see perhaps a few particularly devoted followers. What she hadn't anticipated was spotting a pack of paparazzi lounging beneath a huge yew tree, their cameras dangling over their shoulders like avant-garde handbags…

Behind her eyelids she caught a flicker of light, and then, opening her eyes, she flinched as a volley of flashes momentarily blinded her.

Fireworks.

Heart pounding, she watched them bloom in the darkness.

Was it a cosmic joke or just coincidence that as her world was imploding, the wider world kept sending up fireworks?

If Omar noticed the fireworks he gave no indication. He sat relaxed in the pilot's seat, but his dark eyes were moving endlessly over the dials and buttons on the panel in front of him as he made minute recalibrations of height and speed.

There would be no talking now, she knew.

It was one of the things that had first attracted her to him. How he was one hundred percent in the moment. Whatever he was doing—be it driving, riding a horse, flying a helicopter—he had an incredible, unparalleled intensity of focus.

Her heartbeat slowed to a crawl. Once upon a time he had given *her* that same intensity of focus. Only then they'd got married and it had been as if he'd done enough. As if by giving her a ring and his name he thought he had proved himself once and for all. And then that focus, that glorious feeling of sunlight heating her skin, had stopped.

Her breathing sounded as if she'd been running.

Except in bed.

Then he had never faltered. And nor had she. It had been the one place she hadn't questioned herself. How could she have when together they'd been so perfect? Like dancers moving instinctively, each had known exactly, intuitively, what the other wanted, what the other needed, demanded, craved. A flickering tongue. A whisper-soft caress. Hard, urgent kisses.

It had been heat and light, havoc and passion, sensation,

and sensual overload. But in the end, it hadn't been enough. *Obviously.* Marriages couldn't survive on sex alone.

'We're here.'

Omar's voice was soft, but she still jumped about a mile. Glancing out of the cockpit, she felt the hairs on the nape of her neck rise slowly.

Where was 'here'?

Panic exploding inside her like popcorn, she squinted through the glass. When Omar had told her they were going to a place in the hills, she had assumed he was talking about another of the exclusive suburbs that edged the glittering high-rise city centre, but there was nothing suburban about the view through her window.

There were lights, and the moon was huge and dazzlingly white, so it wasn't dark. But aside from the castellated outline of a pale stone building there was nothing to see but a seemingly never-ending range of stark, jagged peaks.

'You said we were going to a place in the hills,' she said slowly.

'I may have misled you.' There was a faint glitter of moonlight in his eyes. 'But I didn't think it would be a big deal. It's not as if the truth matters to you.'

A tiny shiver rippled through the helicopter. They had landed. Beside her, Omar flicked a switch and silence filled the cabin. Then he was out of his seat and, almost before she had undone her belt, opening her door and half pulling, half lifting her out of the cockpit.

'I can manage.' She pushed his hand away, watching his face harden as her stiletto heels slipped sideways on the smooth flagstones.

'Of course you can. Perish the thought that you might actually need me for anything.'

She *had* needed him. He had made it his mission for

her to need and trust him. But she wouldn't make the same mistake twice.

Biting back the comment she wanted to make, she adjusted her feet. Regaining her balance, she let her eyes skate past him. They were standing in a vast courtyard surrounded by high walls. 'Who owns this place?'

'I do. It used to be a fortress.' He left a pause. 'But for now, it's going to be your home.'

She shook her head. 'My home is in Idaho.'

His face stayed blank, but his eyes narrowed just a fraction. 'If you say so. But we didn't talk in Idaho any more than we talked in New York. Perhaps we'll have more luck here.'

Without waiting for her to reply, he turned, and she watched him walk away, her heart suddenly going at ninety miles an hour. And then she hurried after him, almost tripping in her haste to keep up with him as he strode through a doorway.

'This is insane, Omar. This is not how people behave.'

Couldn't he see that rehashing the past wasn't going to change anything? It would just scrape against a wound that was barely healed.

They were walking upstairs now, and she had to pick up her skirts to keep up with him.

'Firstly, I'm not "people". I'm your husband. And talking to your partner is not generally considered a sign of insanity.'

She followed him into a room, and he stopped so abruptly she almost cannoned into him as he spun round, fatigue and frustration etched into his handsome features.

'Maybe if you accepted that…maybe if you hadn't turned every conversation into a masterclass of deflection and dissimulation… I wouldn't have found out by chance what I should have been told by right.'

She stared at him. His words froze in the air between them like bullets in those Gun Fu films her brothers loved so much.

'And that's what this is really about, isn't it? Not me. Not our marriage. Not the truth. This is about you not being in control, not having the last word. So, actually, it's all about you.'

The look of fury in his eyes almost slammed her against the wall.

'No, that's one thing our marriage has *never* been about, Delphi. You have only ever let me into your life grudgingly.'

The word felt like a serrated blade, scraping against her skin.

'And you bumped me down your agenda for work.'

'Don't blame my work for your deceit.'

Something inside her snapped. '*You* deceived *me*. You made me think that we were a team…a partnership. Before you, I managed my life on my own and I was fine with that. I didn't want or need anyone. But you kept on pushing me to trust you, to talk to you. You made me need you. And then you were never there. You told me that I only ever had to ask for help, but when I did you let me down.'

'And I'm sorry for that.'

'You have every possible apology at your fingertips. The conditional, the phantom, the déjà vu, the *get-off-my-back*. All equally meaningless.'

'Oh, but running away when things get hard is straight out of the marriage playbook?'

Hard. The word punched the breath out of her lungs. 'This is getting us nowhere.'

'Because you're giving up.'

'And you won't—or can't let me. Because you've obsessed with winning. And if something or someone—*like me*—challenges you, then it just cements that desire to win.' Her voice was rising, and she let it. 'That's why you married me and why you came to the hospital. That's why you've dragged me out here, to the middle of nowhere. But you've wasted your time and mine bringing me here, because I will never have anything to say to you.'

There was a taut silence. 'You think?' he said finally. '"Never" might be beyond even you.' He stared down at her, the overhead lights carving shadows beneath his cheekbones. 'And if you're thinking about running away—don't. There's no point. It's a twenty-eight-hour hike across the dunes to the city.'

She could feel her heart banging high and hard somewhere beneath her ribs. 'Sounds like a dream compared to spending another minute with you.'

His eyes narrowed, but he didn't rise to her words. Instead, he seemed to expand the space, and anger and panic and misery and exhaustion reared inside her like the four horsemen of the apocalypse, and she slammed her open palms against his chest.

'Get out. Go on. *Get out.*'

She breathed in sharply as his hands caught her wrists, and for what felt like several lifetimes she struggled against him as he stood staring down at her, deliberate and unflinching. Then, without saying a word, he let go of her, turned, and stalked out of the room, closing the door softly behind him.

Heart still pounding, she waited for the click of a key, but he didn't lock the door.

But then he didn't need to.

Suddenly, as if she had been running too fast, her legs started to shake. She sat down on the bed, staring blindly around the room. Large and square with pale walls and whisper-light muslin curtains, its only colour came from a huge Persian rug.

It was beautiful.

A quick, violent tremor rippled through her as she remembered Omar saying this place had been a fortress. Now it was a prison—the most beautiful, elegant prison in the world. And she was locked in here with her pain, trapped with her anger, and her misery, and a man who hated her almost as much as she hated herself.

Stalking away from Delphi's beautiful, pale, defiant face, Omar walked straight past his own room. There was no point going to bed. He wasn't going to sleep. He needed space…he needed air—

He needed to go back in time.

Back to before he had decided to take up Dan's invitation to play polo at the Amersham. Back to when Delphi Wright Howard had been just a name in the ether.

Breathing out unsteadily, he ran lightly up a narrow staircase and pushed open a door. His heartbeat juddering through his bones, he stared up into the inky blackness of the sky, his brain automatically joining up the stars to form constellations.

If only it was as easy to make sense of his wife.

But she was out of reach as Orion's belt.

What if she'd stayed pregnant? What then?

He thought back to the small, warm weight of Khalid in his arms, then switched effortlessly to an image of Delphi, gazing down not at Khalid but at another dark-eyed, soft-skinned baby.

It was too much to bear. It was easier to focus on how she had left him in the dark. To fix on the anger and pain of being the last to know when he should have been the first.

He glanced up at the sky, his chest aching. The moon was still watching him, just as it had been back in the city.

'Thanks for the help,' he muttered.

But he couldn't blame the moon. Delphi was a force of nature in her own right.

And he was an Emirati, he thought with a stab of pride. His people had conquered nature to build a city that was the envy of the world. Surely he could conquer one woman?

Feeling calmer, he made his way back downstairs. The building was still and quiet, but as he walked past Delphi's closed bedroom door his footsteps faltered. He thought he had heard a noise…faint like the whispering sand on the dunes.

It must be the wind.

He thought back to the still, night air, his chest tightening.

It wasn't the wind.

He opened the door, his breath knotting in his throat as the shadows darted across the room. On the bed, still in her beautiful dress, Delphi was moaning in her sleep, her face creased in distress, her hands clutching the bedspread.

CHAPTER SIX

'THREE... FOUR... FIVE...'

Delphi ran lightly through the ranch house. She felt happy and free and excited. Hide and seek was her favourite game.

Ed would find Scott first. Her middle brother was too laid-back to bother hiding properly. Will was way better, but she was the best.

And the smallest.

Except she wasn't small anymore. She stared down confusedly at her body in a glittering golden gown. When did that happen?

'Six... Seven... Eight...'

The hairs on the back of her neck rose. Behind her, Ed's voice was fading. Across the room, the familiar stone fireplace was collapsing, the walls dissolving to mist, and now she was in an overgrown graveyard, standing in front of a lipstick-covered headstone.

Heart drumming against her ribs, she forced down a scream and stumbled backwards, staring wildly in every direction. Her skin was burning as if she had caught the sun, but the mist was chillingly cold. She could hear other voices now, different, unfamiliar, rising and falling, drawing nearer on every side. They sounded harsh; they sounded hungry, and she knew she had to get away.

Run, she told herself. As fast as you can.

Only it wasn't her speaking, but Dan.

'Nine... Ten... Here, I come. Ready or not...' the voice chanted, close by now.

Whimpering, she spun away, slipping sideways, brambles clawing at her dress, but she couldn't run because she was holding a baby: she was holding Khalid.

She stared down into his liquid, dark eyes, waves of hot slippery panic surging over her skin. Around her, the mist was closing in, growing brighter, sharpening into a flash of light, then another, and another.

'Ianthe, this way—'

'Over here, Dylan—'

The voices were getting louder...the light was dizzying, swallowing her up.

She felt her grip loosen, felt Khalid start to slip from her fingers. She opened her mouth, and the sound of screaming filled her head...

'Delphi! Delphi, it's okay.'

Another voice, this time close by.

Her eyes snapped open, and she jerked upright, gasping, breathless, arms flailing, snatching for the baby. But he wasn't there.

'Khalid... Khalid...' She croaked his name, her body rigid, shuddering with fear and panic, and then a hand touched her arm and she lashed out wildly.

'Delphi, it's okay. You're okay.'

Omar was leaning over her, the outline of his body blurred in the moonlight filtering through the half-closed curtains. After the dizzying blaze of lights in her dream the soft darkness felt surreal and, inching up the bed, she stared past him, her heart still pounding, trying to make sense of her surroundings, and then she remembered.

'What are you doing?' She tried to clear her throat from the last of her panic. 'Why are you here?'

'I was walking past your door, and I heard you.' He hesitated just for a second. 'I heard a noise. I just wanted to check that you were okay.'

Okay? She let out a shaky breath, somewhere between a choke and sob. She had lost their baby. Her heart was broken. And her marriage was over. She doubted anything would ever be okay again.

'I'm fine,' she lied.

Actually, she felt exhausted, and horribly cold that she was having to hold herself rigid not to shake. But then she was still wearing her dress and evening sandals.

'You didn't sound fine.'

'It's nothing. I just had a dream.'

His face was in shadow, but she could sense his uncertainty—and something else. Something that felt horribly like concern. Only she couldn't let herself think like that. Couldn't let herself believe that Omar cared about her.

She thought back to the moment in the garden when he had reached out and touched her hand, and she had weakened, leaning into him, and just like that she had got used to the feel of his body against hers, to his solidity and his gentleness. She could have stayed there in his arms for ever, letting his heat and strength envelop her.

But it was dangerous to think like that. Or rather it was dangerous to stop thinking and let her body make the decisions.

She felt his gaze on her face. 'It sounded more like a nightmare to me,' he said quietly.

Remembering the mist and the gravestone, she felt her hands start to shake, and she flattened them against the mattress to steady herself. It had been so long since she'd had that nightmare and she'd forgotten the horror of it, the horror of the aftermath too.

'It's nothing,' she said again, trying to sound normal… casual, even. Only it didn't feel like nothing, and suddenly she wanted him to hold her more than she had ever wanted anything in life.

And so, of course, she had to make him leave.

'Really, it's nothing. You don't need to worry about me. Honestly. Just go and get some sleep.'

He stared at her in silence, his face unreadable, and then without a word, he turned and walked out of the room. She let out a shuddering breath. Without Omar there she didn't have to hold back anymore, and her body started to shiver uncontrollably.

She had opened the window earlier and now she thought about shutting it—only that would mean moving and she wasn't sure her legs were working. Instead, she drew her knees to her chest and hugged them, lowering her face so as not to have to look into the unfamiliar corners of the room.

She should have been relieved that he was gone, but instead she wanted to turn and weep into her pillow. She shouldn't have let him go. She should have asked him to stay. She should have tried to talk to him—

Tears filled her eyes.

No, it was better this way.

But if that was true, then why did it hurt so much? Why had having him there made her feel so much want and need and hope?

'Here.'

She glanced up. Omar was holding out a glass with a measure of clear golden liquid. His dark eyes rested on her face and her breath caught. He was still so much a part of her, and she wondered helplessly if that feeling would ever gentle. Would the ache of losing him ever stop?

'It's brandy.' He paused. 'I know you said you didn't want a drink earlier, but it might help now.'

She had been about to refuse, only his face in the moonlight looked soft, younger, as he must have looked when he was little, and she felt something twist inside her as she imagined how their child might have looked had he been a boy.

Forcing her mind away from that devastating train of thought, she took the glass. 'Thank you.'

Brandy wasn't something she would usually drink, but it was what people drank on TV and in films when they were in shock, so maybe it would help her stop feeling so cold.

'You're shaking.' Frowning, he reached down and touched her arm, then her cheek. 'You're freezing.'

His skin felt blissfully warm, and she had to stop herself from rubbing her face against his fingers like a cat. But it was the gentleness in his voice that made her want to take his hand and wrap it round her waist like a bandage.

Not wanting him to feel that need in her, she got to her feet. 'I should probably get changed.'

She just about managed to totter into the bathroom. But once she had closed the door, the energy that had propelled her there evaporated. Even the thought of getting undressed seemed almost unimaginably complicated, and her fingers were so numb she couldn't even feel the buttons, much less tackle the thin leather straps of her sandals.

But finally, after a few false starts, she managed to undress herself.

It was only then, standing naked apart from a pair of flesh-coloured panties, that she remembered she didn't have anything to change into.

There was a knock at the door.

'Would these be of any use?'

She opened it a crack. Omar was holding out a pile of clothes. Men's clothes—presumably his.

'They'll be a little big, but they should be warm.'

They *were* big. She had to roll up the legs and the waistband of the loose cotton trousers several times, and the T-shirt looked more like a mini dress. But they were soft and warm.

Omar was sitting on the bed as she came into the room, and he watched in silence as she carefully laid her dress on the armchair by the window. As she turned, he stood up, and she felt her stomach lurch.

She had half expected him to still be there when she finally walked back into the bedroom. What she hadn't expected was the fierce, chaotic rush of relief, and for a few half-seconds she fought the same urge as earlier, to step into the circle of his arms and let him hold her close as he had in the garden.

But she couldn't just hand herself over to him again. It had been so hard to trust him the first time and leaving him had been brutal. She wasn't about to start up that whole cycle again. Only the flipside of that was that she couldn't expect him to comfort her either.

The bed was still warm from where he had been sitting and she wriggled under the covers. In a moment she would tell him to go, but it wouldn't matter if he stayed for a few moments longer, she told herself. Just until the nightmare faded a bit more.

'Here.'

He handed her the brandy again. Her fingers brushed against his as she took the glass, and she felt the contact like an electric current. Only how could such an impersonal touch make her feel like that?

The answer to that question made her panic so much that she wanted to bolt down the brandy in one frantic gulp. But she didn't. They were over. Her mind was straight about that, and she didn't need alcohol un-straightening it.

'Are you not having one?' she asked.

He shook his head. 'I'm not the one who had a nightmare.'

Except he had, in a way, she thought, remembering his shocked expression when she'd told him about the miscarriage. He just hadn't been asleep.

'I'm sorry about the party. I'll write to your parents…tell them it was my fault we left early.' She gave him a small, tight smile. 'They're going to hate me soon enough anyway. Your whole family will.'

And it shouldn't matter, but it did. She thought about Jalila taking her hands. She had been so open and welcoming. They might have been friends—like sisters, even. But now that was ruined too, before it had even started.

His eyes rested on her face. 'Why would they hate you?'

'Because I'm divorcing their son, their brother, their uncle.'

Picturing Khalid in his arms was almost enough to unloose the emotion trapped inside her, and she took a shaky sip of the brandy. It was smooth and rich and complex—a bit like the man who had handed it to her, she thought, glancing up at Omar.

While she'd been in the bathroom he had switched on a lamp by the bed and its light was spilling across the room, chasing away the dark shadows in the corners. And now that there was more light, she could see his face clearly.

Her heart began beating faster. His dark eyes looked smudged, and there was a tension in his shoulders as if he was holding some invisible weight.

'You look tired,' she said quietly. Actually, he looked exhausted.

'There's been a lot going on.'

'You mean work.'

There had been a hint of bitterness in her voice, and she knew from the tiny, defensive flash in his eyes that he had heard it. But there was no trace of anger or pent-up frustration in his tone when he replied. Instead, there was a rough edge that hurt, high up between her ribs.

'Work. Planning the party. But mostly trying to find you.'

His beautiful face was taut.

'I don't know which was worse. Being told you were in hospital. That you'd been in a car accident. Or finding out about the baby.'

She thought back to the moment when she'd told him about the pregnancy and the miscarriage. They hadn't been touching, but she had still felt the physical impact of those two statements on Omar. Now the pain in his eyes knifed through her.

'And then hearing you cry out like that—'

He broke off and walked towards the window, his head tilting up towards the moon, hovering serenely in the blue-black darkness.

Delphi stared at his profile. She didn't know what to do…what to say. Normally, she was the one who retreated into herself, and the more questions Omar asked the deeper she retreated, the longer her silences. But now, for the first time in her life, she was the one wanting to break the stillness in the room.

'It was just a bad dream. I used to have them when I was younger, sometimes.'

His face turned towards her. 'After the crash, you mean?'

She nodded slowly. 'Yes, but they didn't start immediately—more like six months later. Apparently, it's very common with very young children who lose a parent.' She drew in a breath. 'Parents... The grief counsellor said it was my way of coming to terms with what had happened.'

Her legs were trembling again.

'I used to get really panicky about going to bed. Dan tried loads of different things. A nightlight...warm, milky drinks. But what worked in the end was him sleeping on the floor by my bed.'

Like some faithful hound. She could see Dan's face. Outwardly calm, reassuring, unfazed. But beneath the patient, soothing smile he'd been exhausted. Shattered by grief and regret and the need to do his best for her even though she wasn't his child.

'He did that every night,' she said quietly. 'Even though it went on for quite a long time...maybe a year. Always the same dream.'

There was another silence.

'Apart from tonight?'

His voice was so low she might have missed his question. She stared at him, her heart beating unevenly. 'Why do you say that?'

He hesitated, as if he was debating something. Then, 'You were shouting Khalid's name. But you obviously hadn't met him until this evening, so you must have been having a different nightmare.'

His words fluttered up towards the moon like moths.

'It started off the same.' She swallowed, reluctant to go back to the beginning, knowing what was to follow. 'I'm playing hide and seek with my brothers. It was my favourite game. I was always the best at hiding.'

She half expected Omar to make some facetious remark, but he said nothing.

'I'm in the ranch house. Only then the house collapses and there's this mist...' She shivered. 'It's cold, and then I realise I'm in a graveyard. I can't hear Ed counting any more, but there are other voices. And then the mist gets brighter and brighter, and I know it's the men with the cameras. The men who camped outside my parents' house for days…'

Gazing down at Delphi, Omar felt sick to his stomach. His heart felt as if it was going to break through his ribs. So intensely it took his breath away, he wanted to reach out and touch her small, stiff body, to pull her close until that pain in her face melted away.

She had never talked about the days following her parents' accident, and even now she was only doing so obliquely, by telling him about her dream. But he knew how much she feared the paparazzi, and the efforts she had made her whole life to avoid coming to their attention.

A beat of anger pulsed across his skin. He hated it that they still cornered her when she was at her most vulnerable. Asleep, and trapped in a nightmare from which there was no escape.

'What happens next?' he said quietly.

'That's when I start running.'

His chest tightened. A year before they'd met, two years ago now, Delphi had gone to Wyoming to help tag the wild horses. He could still remember her face, that mix of envy and empathy, as she'd told him about the trip. About how some of the mustangs had refused to be caught. How they would keep running, their pounding hooves filling the air with dust.

Delphi had been running since she was four years old. In one way or another she hadn't ever stopped running. First from the paparazzi. From her scandalous past and her fear of being hurt. Then from him and the wreck of their marriage.

'And I try to run,' she went on. 'Only I can't because I'm holding Khalid, and I'm scared I'll trip.'

Omar stared down at her, his pulse jerking. When she had been in the bathroom he had switched on the light, sensing that it would comfort her. Now, though, the air in the room had gone dark with the sadness and pain of her past.

Her mouth trembled. 'And then the mist starts to swallow me up and I can't see my hands.'

He saw the flash of pain in her eyes, the panic.

'I can't feel them. And then I let go of Khalid. I let go of him—'

She made a small, wordless noise and pressed her hand not against her mouth, but in front of her stomach, just as she had back in the garden, and he moved then, crossing the room in three strides, putting his arms around her and pulling her close.

Her head was on his shoulder, and she was sobbing, and he didn't try to stop her. He knew she was crying for another baby. A baby that she would never press close to her beating heart.

His chest tightened. He had wanted this for so long. Wanted her to confide in him…wanted her to need him and only him. And now he had what he wanted. Only he felt no satisfaction or triumph. Instead, he felt suddenly and savagely angry with himself. What kind of man would want his wife to be so diminished and desperate?

His own eyes burning, he stroked her hair, speaking softly in Arabic, saying the words his mother had used whenever he'd fallen and hurt his knee. The same words she had spoken whenever his father had left early one morning without saying goodbye.

He felt her breathe out shakily and he shifted backwards on the bed, taking her with him, tucking the covers over her trembling body. Still stroking her hair, he said softly, 'You didn't let go of our baby, Delphi. If there was anything you could have done to hold on to it, you would have done.'

She was shaking her head. 'I should never have gone back to England.'

He could feel her fighting for control, fighting to stay calm. It had caught him off guard, her deciding to go. He'd known England wasn't a happy place for her—and not just because it was where her childhood had ended. After her parents' deaths, Dylan Wright's sisters had each tried to get custody of their niece, arguing that, unlike Dan, they were blood relatives. Dan had won, but it had been a long, vitriolic battle, played out in the tabloid press, and the media attention had got worse and worse.

The final straw had come when stories about Delphi had appeared online. It had been clear that the 'sources close to the family' quoted were people she had trusted. It was then that Dan had moved her to the ranch house.

Dan, the cuckolded husband, and substitute father had upended his world to make his wife's daughter feel safe. No wonder Delphi trusted him.

'Your father thought it was a good idea,' he said quietly.

She looked up at him, her eyes wide with shock. 'How do you know that?'

'I called him. When I got back from Sydney. After you changed your mind again about going.' He hesitated. Then, 'I was worried. You were distracted. Preoccupied.' *Like his father.* As always, that had been his first thought. 'I told him I thought you should forget about going, but Dan said you needed to go.'

His chest felt tight. *'She's scared of what she's going to feel,'* Dan had told him. *'And when she's scared, she pushes things and people away. And she's been pushing the past away forever.'* There had been sadness in the older man's voice. *'I want to help her, only I can't—because I'm part of the problem, part of that past. But you...you're her future. So go with her, help her face the past and let her live the life she deserves.'*

A wave of self-loathing rose up inside him. Because he hadn't gone with her, had he? He had gone to meet Bob Maclean.

'I know he wanted me to go. He tried so many times to make it happen,' Delphi said in a small, bruised voice. 'One year, we got all the way to the airport.'

The twist to the corner of her mouth told him that was as far as they'd got.

His throat was dry. 'So what was different about this time?'

She bit down on the inside of her lip. 'You.' Her beautiful brown eyes flicked to his face, then away. 'And then the pregnancy.' Her breathing was suddenly unsteady again. 'I really was going to tell you, but when I found out you were in Sydney, and I wanted to do it face to face. So I decided to wait.'

She glanced up at him, and in the light from the bedside lamp she looked soft-edged...like a painting.

'Only the whole time I kept thinking about going to London. It was just there, in the back of my mind. And then I realised why. I realised that I wanted to tell them too. My parents, I mean. I wanted us all to be there together. But then everything went wrong.'

Her words fell into silence.

'You said you couldn't come. I should have told you then, only I was angry with you, so I didn't. The whole flight over I felt odd, and then when I reached the graveyard it got worse. I thought it was just nerves and excitement.'

Hearing the echo of that excitement in her voice, Omar

felt his heart squeeze tight. He knew all about that jittery anticipation; that mix of hope and tension. His father's absences and returns had governed his life like the rising and setting of the sun. He could still remember all the days and sometimes weeks when Rashid had been away on business or staying at his other homes.

Everything around him had felt flimsy and make-shift…like scenery on a stage. His mother had always been breathless and on edge, like an actor waiting in the wings for her cue. And he had been a small, fearful boy, sitting like some sentinel by the window overlooking the driveway, scared both that Rashid would never return or, worse, that when he did, he would look right straight through his youngest child without even seeing him.

He felt a rush of shame. At least he had a father and a mother.

He stared down at Delphi's small, tense body. 'You'd waited so long to go there,' he said gently.

There was no excitement in her face now. Just pain. 'Long enough to realise that maybe another day would be a better idea. It's not like it was some tradition I had to keep. I mean, I'd managed to miss the anniversary of their deaths every other year.'

His eyes didn't leave her face, but he barely heard her words. Instead, that static was roaring in his ears again, and something that had been fluttering like moths' wings at the edges of the mind was suddenly there centre-stage, clear and sharp in the spotlight. She had lost their baby on the same date she had lost her parents all those years ago.

He made himself speak. 'You couldn't have known the paparazzi would be there.'

Her face was paper-white. 'Couldn't I? They'd never left my parents alone in life—why should it have been any different when they were dead?'

She glanced past him to where a thin straight line of

light was quivering along the horizon. It was the dawn of a new day—but not for Delphi. She was still reliving those hours alone in London.

'The cramping started on my way back to the apartment. When I got there, I went to the bathroom, and that's when I realised I was bleeding. I should have gone to the hospital, but I was too scared to move. And I thought if I stayed still the bleeding would stop.'

His hands tightened in her hair. He didn't want to think about her bleeding, in pain, scared. *Alone.* Would the outcome have been different if he'd been there? Probably not. He knew that miscarriage was common...

And that's relevant, how?

The question was an angry roar inside his head. He was her husband. She had needed his support, needed him to be there. Instead, he'd been chasing another deal.

He thought back to the meeting with Maclean. Or rather the meetings, plural. Hours and hours spent picking through the contract with his lawyers while he'd been fighting jet lag and a need for Delphi that had crept into every fibre of his being, so that simple activities like brushing his teeth and getting dressed had felt impossible.

And what did he have to show for it? Another cable network in Australia.

But what if he had been there with Delphi?

Would it have been different?

It was the second time he'd asked himself that question, and he wanted the answer to be definite. He needed it to be no, but he wasn't sure it was. He didn't know if he would ever be sure.

Only he couldn't deal with that now. Right now, Delphi needed him, and this time he wasn't going to let her down.

'You did the right thing.'

She looked up at him. Her eyes were puffy, her cheeks

tearstained. 'Did I? I just keep going over all the things I could have done.'

The static was roaring in the ears again.

'You can't think like that. Miscarriages happen for all kinds of reasons.'

She was shaking her head. 'I know. But I was so sure it was going to be okay. Everything's always been so difficult for me. School. Making friends. Even you.' Her voice shook a little. 'But this was so easy. I was just pregnant. No fuss. No drama. And I thought that must mean something. But it was the same. I couldn't make it work.'

In the dimly lit room, her body was made of shadows.

'I'm so tired of having to fight for everything… I can't do it any more…'

The ache in her voice rolled over him like one of the sandstorms that swept in from the desert, and he heard it then. Not just grief, but defeat, and finally he understood that she had lost more than their baby in London. What little faith she'd ever had in him, and in the world and in herself, had been torn from her.

His arms tightened around her, and guilt swelled inside his chest, crushing his lungs so that it was difficult to take a breath.

'And you don't have to. You're not alone, Delphi. I'm right here, and I'm not going anywhere.'

He held her close, cradling her against his body, stroking her hair, wishing he had more than words to prove what he was saying.

He didn't know how long they stayed locked together. Maybe they would have stayed there all night but somewhere in the night an owl screeched and she shifted away from him, blinking as if she had woken from a trance.

Staring up at Omar, Delphi felt her heart flutter. She knew that to stay any longer in the half-circle of his arm was a risk not worth taking, but already she missed his hand caressing her hair, gentle as the wings of a hummingbird.

'You should probably go and get some sleep. Goodness knows what time it is…'

'Is that what you want?' he asked.

His eyes were fixed on hers, dark and velvet-soft, shimmering with something that made her breath catch and her heart feel suddenly too big for her chest. She had supposed that talking would unravel the last threads binding them together. But how could 'we' become 'I' when he was holding her so close? Suddenly she was acutely aware of the thin layers of fabric that was all there was between her skin and his.

'Do you want me to leave?'

She felt her body tense in objection. But her body was not to be trusted. She was not to be trusted. 'I want… I want…' She paused, took a breath, tried again. 'I want…'

There was a beat of silence.

Her heart was speeding now, and she knew she should push him away, but she was hypnotised by the sudden harshness of his breathing. Around them the lights were blurring and the air in the room was changing, blooming, starting to press in on them, weighty with the feelings they had both pushed aside—feelings she refused to name but that were impossible to ignore, impossible to deny.

'I want it too,' he said hoarsely.

A minute went by, and then another. And then, reaching up, she touched his cheek, tracing the line of his mouth with her thumb, fear and desire and anticipation chasing through her restless body. Somewhere in the back of her mind a drum was beating out a panicky, percussive message in Morse code.

Stop this. Stop this now.

But it was too late. Her heart was beating louder. Running wild and free like a mustang across the sagebrush grasslands.

She wanted him. Wanted the kiss. And now she leaned into him and brushed her lips against his. Her belly clenched with desire as their warm breath mingled, and then their mouths met blindly, fiercely. Any thoughts she had of stopping were forgotten, all doubts and memories and pain dropping away as the taste of him went straight to her head and there was nothing but his solid body and his warm breath.

She felt his hand move to her cheek, the callused thumb stroking the soft skin there. This was right, she thought, feeling the heat beneath the light caress. This was what mattered.

Heat flared inside her as his fingers slid from her cheek, down over her collarbone to cup her breast. A galaxy of tiny stars exploded inside her head as his fingertips grazed the nipple. She twitched, muscles tightening. Heat was flooding her limbs, dissolving her body, and she felt the kiss change, felt him change.

Lips parting, her breath quickening, she could feel his heart, feel his pulse beating into her body. His mouth was moving against hers, shaping her desire, and then he shifted her weight, tipping her forward, and she felt the hard press of his erection against her pelvis.

He took a quick breath, like a gasp, and she arched helplessly into his groin, breasts aching, a shivery pleasure dancing through her veins as he forced her head up, deepening the kiss, sliding his hands beneath her top to find hot, bare skin. Touching, teasing, tormenting…

Closing her eyes, she rested her forehead against his. Oh, how she had missed him…missed this. This was what she needed. He was what she needed. Only Omar could do this. Only he could feed the hunger and soothe this tenderness in her chest, soothe this ache that felt like a huge, dark bruise swallowing up her heart.

'*Delphi*… Stop, we have to stop…'

Her eyes opened. The carousel was slowing. Omar's hands were on her shoulders, his thumbs gripping her collarbone.

Breath snagged in her chest and something like a sob rose in her throat. She was fighting him, trying to pull him closer, her mouth seeking his, her body not fully under her control, and she realised with shock that her face was wet with tears.

'Shh…' he said soothingly. His hands were gentle, but he was holding her firmly. 'You've been so brave, so strong. Let me take care of you.' As her body went limp, he clasped her face, thumbs stroking the tears from her cheeks. 'It's okay.'

He tipped her gently off his lap onto the bed and she lay down, feeling suddenly, brutally tired.

'It's okay,' he said again, tucking the covers around her body and lying down next to her.

His hand was moving gently through her hair, like the breeze through the woods that surrounded the ranch house.

'You're not alone, Delphi. I'm right here, and I'm not going anywhere. You can sleep now.'

Sometime later, Delphi stirred. She felt warm and safe, just as she had as a child but as her eyes fluttered open, she saw not Dan but Omar sprawled in the armchair, her dress clutched in his arms, his head resting awkwardly in the crook of his arm.

She knew she was dreaming, but it was still calming to see him there, and for a moment she watched the rise and fall of his chest, feeling the rhythm of his breath inside her own body. And then her eyes closed again, and sleep pulled her back under.

CHAPTER SEVEN

PUSHING OPEN THE WINDOWS, Delphi took a step back from the punch of heat. It felt as if the air was on fire. She had woken late, and it had taken her a moment or two to orientate herself, then another longer moment to process everything that had happened in the hours following the party. Coming here to the mountains, fighting with Omar again, that twisted nightmare involving Khalid and her parents, and then, finally, talking to him about the miscarriage.

Raising an arm to shield her face, she breathed out shakily. It was a conversation she had never expected to have with him. Like so many other conversations in her life, she had let the weight of it carry it down to the depths of her mind. Only somehow, last night, it had come bubbling up to the surface.

Her face trembled in the sunlight. She hadn't cried since those few terrible hours when she'd realised she was losing their baby—but then she wasn't a crier. She never had been. She had learned early on that tears had no power to change the things you didn't like.

But last night she had cried—sobbed, in fact, in Omar's arms. For her parents. Her marriage. The baby she would never hold. For the failures of her life. For the failure she was.

Only after she had stopped crying things had changed.

The pain had still been there, but distant, softer, so that it no longer hurt to swallow or breathe—almost as if some of the jagged edges inside her had been rubbed smooth.

And it wasn't just about her talking.

Omar had listened.

Instead of pushing her for answers, or boxing her in like before, he had given her space, let her set the pace. It had still been hard for her to get the words out, but for the first time in their relationship she hadn't felt like an item on his agenda to be ticked off, or a challenge to be overcome and conquered.

He had treated her in a different way, and because he'd been different—quieter, less intense—things had taken a different path and she had finally managed to open up to him. Not just about the dates and the places. She had shared her feelings. And it had been painful and exhausting and terrifying to relive those hours, but somehow not to have done so would have been a worse option, and that was a first too.

And after all the talk and the tears she had slept deeply.

But not dreamlessly.

She glanced back into the room at the armchair. Last night, in her dreams, Omar had slept in that chair, his muscular body contorted into the velvet upholstery, her dress hugged tight in his arms. And when not keeping watch on her he had slipped into bed beside her, pulling her against him, their bodies blurring as her hands had splayed over his shoulders, his hands parting her thighs, his tongue dipping inside her with tortuous precision—

All dreams.

Only it was hard to remember that when she could almost feel of him holding her against him as if nothing had ever gone wrong between them. Feel them both moving as one, to touch, to kiss, to pull closer, kiss deeper. His mouth, her mouth, his hands, her fingers…all seeking the same goal with the same urgency.

And it didn't matter that it was nonsense for it to have still been like that between them. In her dream she had felt him lose control, heard that sharp intake of breath when he'd tipped her into his lap against the hard ridge of his erection. And her body had responded instantly, instinctively. Softening and flowing towards him. The barriers she had created between them melting like winter ice in spring sunshine.

Only as much as it had felt right, it had been wrong. Because there had been loss and loneliness and sadness mixed in with the lust. Not that she had noticed or cared. She'd been racing towards the edge of the abyss…

It had been Omar who had pulled back from the brink—pulled them both back from the brink. She should be grateful for that. And part of her was.

She glanced down at the 'wedding ring' Omar had given her in the car on the way to the party.

Why, then, did she feel as if her heart was breaking all over again?

At some point while she'd slept her suitcase had been delivered to her room, and she dressed in the dress she had been wearing in Idaho and a pair of flat sandals. It felt strange, putting it back on.

She glanced down at the fluttering fabric as she left the bedroom. Was it really only three days since she'd been at that Fourth of July barbecue?

Now, that was the kind of simple yes/no question she could answer.

The other question—the one about her heart—required not just thought but a mental agility that was a stretch for her right now. She knew she had hurt Omar, and even though he had hurt her, by continually failing to put her first, she cared that he was hurt. And she knew he cared that she was hurt too.

'You're not alone, Delphi. I'm right here, and I'm not going anywhere.'

It would be so easy to believe Omar meant what he'd said, to let his words catch fire inside her. But she knew that it was the kind of thing people said in the moment before they had sex. The kind of thing estranged couples said before make-up sex.

Except they hadn't had sex.

Her footsteps faltered. Was this the right way?

Arriving last night, it had been dark, and she had been too furious to take in her surroundings, but none of this felt familiar. She walked a little bit further and then stopped, pressing her hand against the wall to steady herself. There was a door only half open, but thanks to the beautiful, antique cot she could see she knew that she was looking at a nursery.

Her heart pounding inside her head, she stepped into the room. It was a tiny oasis of palest green, with a canopy of exotic hand-painted flowers trailing from the ceiling that looked just like the ones outside their honeymoon suite in Maui. Her eyes tracked slowly around the room. There was a photograph of Las Vegas and another of some grazing horses—no, not just some horses...

She took a step closer, her breath catching.

They were *her* horses: Embla and The Pigeon.

She turned slowly on the spot. Last night, Omar had made it sound as if this fort was a new acquisition. Or maybe she had just heard it that way. But it couldn't be, she thought, as her gaze moved from a lamp with a Statue-of-Liberty-shaped base to the Roman blinds decorated with pictures of caravans of camels. Every detail had been carefully chosen as a reminder of the places that were unique and special to the two of them.

Eyes burning, she dug her fingers into the back of a pink velvet sofa.

For so long she had thought Omar indifferent, but now, standing here, thinking about him creating this for her... for the child he'd imagined them having one day...she felt the thread that had come loose inside her last night begin to unravel a little more.

The thread unravelled again as she made her way through the rooms downstairs. Despite having only arrived last night, she felt strangely at home in a way that she never had in the slick, modern interior of their New York apartment. Maybe because this was more like the Bedford ranch house in feel, with huge, faded rugs, exposed stone walls and comfortable linen-covered sofas.

Outside on a terrace, breakfast—or perhaps brunch—was set out beneath a huge cream canopy. She sat down, realising as she did so that for the first time in weeks, she felt hungry. Ravenous, in fact. And that wasn't the only change. It seemed easier to breathe than it had been yesterday. But maybe that was just the mountain air.

The food was delicious.

Puffy melt-in-the-mouth flatbreads with fennel, cardamom and saffron. Scrambled eggs cooked with vermicelli rice, caramelised onions, raisins and rose water—and, of course, dates and coffee.

But she was too distracted by the view to fully concentrate on what she was eating. In the dark, the mountains had been simply shapes. Now, though, they rose grey-brown, majestic, and implacable, and so huge that the fort looked like a child's toy. It was impossible not to be impressed. The garden, too, was impressive—not just in scale but in its lush greenness. All palm trees quivering in the heat and verdant lawns broken up by narrow, vibrantly coloured tiled pools.

It was like an oasis, she thought—and instantly she was back upstairs in that pale jewel of a nursery.

She could have sat there for what remained of the morning, trying to make sense of that tiny green room, and maybe she would have done if she hadn't heard the sound of something so irresistibly familiar that her limbs were moving of their own accord, and she was pushing back her chair to investigate.

Heart pounding, she followed the sound to a dark oak door. Walking through it, she pressed her hand against the wall to steady herself. She had found the stables. Her breath caught and, feeling a buzz of excitement and impatience, she walked towards where horses were peering over their half-doors, whickering and stamping.

'Hello, my beauty,' she said softly to the grey in the nearest stall.

The horse responded, leaning forward to rest its face against hers, and, closing her eyes, she breathed in the smell of straw and leather and sweat.

'I thought I might find you here.'

Her eyes snapped open. Omar was standing at the entrance to the stables, watching her intently, his muscular shoulder wedged against the door frame. She hadn't actually allowed herself to think about this moment, but after her febrile X-rated dreams it was a shock to see him looking calm, composed, and fully clothed in worn-in white twill jeans, jodhpur boots and the faded blue and yellow Howard Harriers polo shirt, worn by her father's polo team.

That gave her a jolt, and she wondered momentarily why he was wearing that particular shirt. There were any number of possible answers to that question, all equally unnerving, but luckily, he chose that moment to walk towards her, and all thought was drowned out by the sound of her heart hammering like a blacksmith shoeing a horse.

'I'm sorry. I shouldn't have just let myself in.'

'I'm glad you did.' He inclined his head towards the mare. 'Her name's Alima. It means wise.'

She watched him stroke the horse's neck, his fingers moving slowly and steadily over the silky coat and felt her pulse jumping haphazardly like a startled frog. Omar had a great sense of touch, and it was far too easy to remember those strong, firm hands caressing her body, effortlessly making her soft and hot, making her melt inside.

'And is she?' she asked, turning away, hoping that nothing of what she was thinking had shown on her face. 'Wise, I mean?'

'She is. But she's also young, and she doesn't trust very easily. Her last owner messed up her head, so you get one chance and then she tries to buck you off. And if that fails, she bolts.'

She glanced up at him sharply, sensing something beneath his words, but his face was smooth and unreadable.

'That's a pity.' It was none of her business, but she couldn't stop herself from asking, 'And what's her current owner doing about that?'

His eyes didn't leave her face. 'Honestly? He's struggling a little.'

Fine lines fanned out from the corners of his eyes, and she felt a click of connection between them. Trying to ignore it, she said, 'Any particular reason?'

'I think she requires a sensitivity and lightness of touch that's beyond him.'

Her nipples tightened against her dress as he reached past her and picked up the head collar hanging from a hook outside the loose box. They were standing far too close, and she had a sudden, sharp flashback to the moment last night when she'd leaned in and brushed her mouth against his.

'How old is she?'

'Two,' he said softly.

She watched, dry-mouthed, as his hand slid up and over Alima's beautiful muzzle. Above the scent of horse sweat and hay, she caught a whisper of his scent—that mix of skin and salt and sage that made all the air leave her body.

He unbolted the stable door and led Alima out onto the flagstones, and as he walked the horse in small circles she saw instantly what he meant. There was a tension in the way the mare was moving, an uncertainty in her step that made Delphi's fingers itch to smooth the twitches from the horse's quivering flank.

'Any thoughts?'

Glancing up, she met Omar's gaze. She felt that feverish embrace swell up in her again—not just as a memory but tangible, so that she could feel his mouth, his hands, on her skin.

Flushed with panicky heat, she opened her mouth, fully intending to tell him that she would email him the name of several equine therapists who might help, and that now she wanted to leave.

Only instead she found herself saying, 'Do you have any boots I can borrow?'

There was a sand school next to the stables and, watching Alima trotting alongside the post and rail fencing, she forgot about Omar, forgot about leaving the fort. All her attention was focused on the little horse.

She was a beautiful animal, but her her tail was clamped in tight. A bird suddenly screamed high up in the sky and Alima shot forward, her eyes rolling white, but Delphi kept her moving, waiting until the horse's movements softened, and then she let Alima come to a standstill.

'There you go, little one,' she murmured, letting the horse sniff her hand.

Breathing softly, she waited until Alima gave a whicker of consent, and then she moved her hand slowly to the horse's neck, working her way along the mare's body. As she moved, she kept talking…nothing that mattered or made any sense, just talking softly.

Watching Delphi lean into the horse, Omar felt his heart slow. Last night, just for a few hours, it was as if the past seven weeks had never happened. She had fallen asleep in his arms, the way they'd always slept.

Asleep, it was the one time when she would relax her guard and let him get close to her.

Aside from when they made love.

Jaw clenching, he pushed that thought away, just as he had pushed Delphi away on the bed. He wasn't ready to go there yet. Instead, he thought back to her face, pale in the lamplight, and the tremor in her voice as she'd told him what he wanted to know. What he'd thought he wanted to know.

His fingers tightened against the railing. He hated picturing her curled up on that cold bathroom floor in London. But it was the exhaustion in her voice that still haunted him.

Waking at dawn in the armchair, with the daylight pressing redly against his eyelids, he'd had a stiff neck and a head full of questions, the answers to which should have been irrelevant at this point in their relationship.

Like why, having eased himself away from her body to go and shut out the sound of that screeching owl, had he not gone back to his own bed? She'd been sound asleep. It would have been the perfect moment to leave.

He glanced over to where Delphi was standing beside

the small grey mare, his eyes following the soft, seamless movement of her hand.

But he hadn't. *He hadn't been able to.*

The idea of leaving her had made some kind of earth-quake happen inside him, so that he'd had to sit down in the armchair to steady himself.

But why had he felt like that? Their relationship was over. They were getting a divorce. There was nothing left between them.

Liar, he thought, and before he could divert the direction of his thoughts he was back at the kiss he had been trying so hard not to think about. His heart thudded inside his chest. He could keep telling himself it had been just a kiss, but he knew it had been so much more than that.

Last night he had wanted her so badly his hunger had felt like a physical ambush. Truthfully, they had both wanted it—had both been waiting for it to happen since that mo-ment on the field in Idaho when he'd pulled her into his arms. Having failed so spectacularly to do so in his mar-riage, he had wanted to prove a point—to pin Delphi down not just metaphorically, but literally.

With his mouth.

But, unlike in Idaho, last night there had been no point to prove. It had been simply an acceptance, an acknowl-edgment, an admission of a mutual need that was stron-ger than both of them. A surrender to that need to kiss and touch and caress and press against one another that was ever-present, circling them constantly, whipping at their senses and nudging them closer, like the rope Delphi had lightly flicked into the sand to make Alima move.

And she'd tasted so good. Hot and honey-sweet. And the taste of her had gone straight to his head.

In those few febrile heartbeats nothing had mattered except the sweep of her tongue against his and the fierce hunger raging through his body. Five more seconds, maybe ten, and he would have stripped them both naked and slid deep inside her.

That he had not done so, but instead had taken her arms and held her away from him, still stunned him now.

But, looking down into her face, he'd known he had no choice. Emotions—big emotions that neither of them knew what to do with—had been roaring inside both of them. He'd known in that moment that Delphi was vulnerable and that he couldn't exploit that vulnerability.

Remembering how she had fought him, how she had kept trying to pull him closer and how, shockingly, her cheeks had been wet with tears, he felt his chest suddenly tight, as if his ribs were in a vice.

He understood her longing to disappear, to displace those big, unmanageable feelings with something else. Something all-consuming like sex. For hadn't he felt that way himself? But instead of sex, for him it had been work. Empire-building. His need to catch his father's magpie gaze chasing him around the globe.

Not that there was any need to tell Delphi that. She needed support from him—not some two-bit excuse for the behaviour that had left her feeling so diminished and abandoned.

He stared across the sand school. Delphi was wearing that dress, the one from Idaho, paired with jodhpur boots. With her tousled short hair, she looked nothing like the woman sheathed in gold who last night had shone brightest in a room full of beautiful people.

A pulse of guilt beat through his veins. She'd looked like a child playing dress-up. And in some ways she was still a child. A scared, confused little girl, orphaned before she understood the meaning of the word, and then left in a terrifying state of limbo while a judge decided her fate.

And, yes, Dan had got custody of her in the end, but like with Alima the damage had been done, he thought, his gaze moving between Delphi and the small grey mare.

For a moment he battled to keep his breathing steady. And now there was more damage. A lost baby. A broken marriage. A husband who'd made promises he had failed to keep. He knew that sex would have briefly blotted out the pain, but what about afterwards?

That was the reason he had stopped them going further.

That and the fact that, whatever he told himself, told *her*, he wasn't ready for it to be their last time.

Ducking between the rails, he made his way towards her. 'So, what do you think?'

She turned, and the look on her face was almost too much to bear.

'I'm guessing her last owner was giving her mixed messages and punishing her when she got confused. When any horse gets confused, particularly one this young, it panics and tries to save itself. Hence the bolting and the bucking.'

She moved out of sight behind the horse, and he shifted position, moving just casually enough that it wouldn't seem as if he was following her. But he was.

'Do you think she can get past this? Can she learn to trust again?'

He watched the pulse hammering against the delicate skin of Delphi's throat.

'That's up to you.' Her voice was scratchy when she answered, and her fingers twitched against Alima's shoulder as if she couldn't control them. 'She won't hold on to the bad if you don't.'

The breeze was lifting the sand around her feet now. Reaching out, he rested his hand on the mare's shoulder, a hair's breadth from hers. 'And what about us? Could we do the same?' he asked softly. 'Follow her example?'

A bird swooped over their heads into the eaves of the barn and Alima jerked her head. He swore silently as Delphi moved her hand to soothe the horse.

'I don't know,' she said at last.

Her voice was bruised-sounding, as it had been last night, and as Alima shifted to nuzzle the side of Delphi's face he wondered if the mare had heard it too.

'But I do.' He ran his hands over Alima's smooth neck. It was that or place them on Delphi's shoulders, and he sensed it might be better to wait a moment before taking that next step. 'Look, I know I took things for granted before.' He took a breath, his mind a swirl of guilt and grief. 'And what happened in London was terrible. But what we have is too special to just throw away.'

She bit into her lip. 'Divorce isn't about throwing things away, Omar. It's about acceptance and change.'

'And so is marriage,' he countered. 'Maybe it took all this for me to realise that, but now that I have, I can change. I am changing. I was trying to change. That's why I bought this place.'

She stared at him in silence, and he felt a flicker of panic. After last night he had thought that something had shifted between them, but now he could feel the past hanging over them like a mourning veil. He needed to make her understand that things would be different. That he could be different.

'I used to come up here with my older brothers to ride and climb and swim in the *wadis*.' It was here that he had felt closest to them, for they too had been dwarfed by the mountains. 'I'd been looking for somewhere to buy for some time, and then I saw this and it was perfect.'

There was a small silence; he made himself wait.

'Perfect for what?' she said finally.

'For us. For you. The Lulua is fine for overnight stays,

but I wanted to give you a place where we could come, and it would be just the two of us and the mountains and the sky.'

More than just the two of them.

After years when the future had been a blank spot in his mind's eye, blotted out by the weight of expectation in the present, he had planned for a family.

'It was supposed to be a surprise. I was going to bring you here on our wedding anniversary. Only then you left.' His eyes found hers. 'I understand why. I didn't then, but I do now. I know I wasn't there for you. I should have been, but I wasn't. I let you down. I made assumptions.'

'Assumptions?'

The sound of her voice made his heart skip a beat. 'I guess I thought it would be easy to get you to trust me. I knew you'd been hurt in the past, but you trust Dan and your brothers. And I've watched you walk into a schooling ring with horses that were dangerous, and you trusted them not to hurt you.'

'Because they didn't,' she said quietly.

'I know. And I know I did. I messed up. But I thought, after last night... I thought there was a chance. I thought maybe we could... That we might try again. Try and fix things.'

Last year he had given a TED talk, speaking fluently for nearly twenty minutes on the importance of perseverance. In comparison, this was the least eloquent speech he had ever given. But for some reason he couldn't find the right words, so he held out his hand instead, just as he had watched Delphi do so many times when she worked with a head shy horse.

Heart beating unsteadily, he watched her face, silently willing her to take his hand, and finally, just when he had given up hope, she did.

His fingers tightened around hers.

'I've learnt from my mistakes. I made bad decisions, wrong choices, and I'm going to make better ones.'

'I made bad decisions too.' She bit into her lip. 'I was too scared to let you in, so I pushed you away instead.'

'And I deserved it. I'm not surprised you left me.' He hesitated, and then, reaching out, he stroked her cheek. 'I've missed you so much, and from now on things are going to be different. I'm going to change.'

Suddenly he tensed, his chin jerking up like Alima's had moments earlier—except it wasn't the shadow of a bird making his nerve-endings quiver but the sound of his phone. Glancing down, he felt his heart begin to race. It was Rashid.

'What are you doing?' asked Delphi.

He had pulled his hand free of hers and now it froze in mid-air. What *was* he doing? For the first time, probably ever, he and Delphi were talking. But, having seen the caller ID, he couldn't not answer any more than Delphi could ignore a barn full of horses. Besides, it would only take a few minutes.

'I need to take this. It's my father. I spoke to my father about settingup a meeting for me with Ali Al-Hadhri.' He saw Delphi was staring at him blankly. 'He's an intermediary for several key media conglomerates in the Middle East—'

'When?' She cut him off. 'When did you speak to your father?'

He frowned. 'This morning.'

The look on her face felt like a punch to the head.

'That's what you were thinking about this morning?' Her voice was thin and brittle. 'A business meeting?'

Clenching his jaw, he shook his head. 'That's not what I said. My father called me. He suggested the meeting.'

'And you didn't think to say that you had more pressing things to discuss? With me?'

She was staring at him as if what he was saying made no sense, and a part of him knew that it didn't. But the sound of his phone was tugging at his senses like a dog on a leash, so that it was impossible for him to think about anything but answering it.

'I don't have a choice, Delphi. You don't mess around with men like Ali Al-Hadhri. All I need is five minutes...'

He turned away from her angry, pinched face.

As predicted, the call took five minutes. Hanging up, he glanced at his watch. Four, in fact. Although judging by Delphi's narrow-eyed gaze that was four minutes too long. But it was done now.

He held up his hands in a gesture of apology. 'Okay, I admit that was bad timing, but that call was a one-off. It won't happen again—'

'Are you listening to yourself? How is this you changing?' Shaking her head, she gave a bitter laugh. 'You know, when you said you could change, I thought about last night and I believed you. I thought about this fort, and why you bought it and, idiot that I am, I let myself think that you meant what you said. That what we have is special. Only then you took that phone call. We were in the middle of a conversation about getting back together and you broke off to set up a business meeting.'

'It was four minutes, Delphi. And it was important.'

'More important than our marriage. That wasn't a question, by the way. I know that compared with business I am nothing to you. And I know that nothing I do or say will ever change that. Because you can't change. You won't stop until you have the biggest media empire in the world. And even that won't be enough. You'll probably have to go into space and see if you can set up a cable network on Mars. Omar Al Majid—media master of the universe.'

'You think that's why I work? For status and power?'

Of course she did. She couldn't know that he was driven by something more basic, more fundamental. The need of a child for his father.

So tell her, he told herself. *Tell her the truth.*

Except he had never admitted that to anyone. To the wider world, even to his closest family, it was something he held close. Only Jalila had ever sensed the root of his obsession with work.

Delphi's eyes were like fierce dark flames.

'Yes—yes, I do. I think you have to be on top of the podium, and that's what this is really about. Not me…not us.'

With an effort, he kept calm. 'I'm trying to save our marriage, Delphi.'

Her mouth trembled. 'No, what you're doing is telling someone who got bitten by a shark not to worry about going back into the water.'

He took a step closer. 'Aren't you the one who told me that sharks are the most misunderstood animals in the oceans…possibly the planet?'

She stared at him; he saw that her whole body was trembling now.

'Try telling that to someone who's been bitten by one. Look, I know this is hard for you to accept, but you can't win this one. There's nothing to save. You just proved that by answering that phone call.'

'You can't give up on nine…nearly ten months of marriage because of one four-minute phone call,' he protested.

'I'm not. I'm walking away from something that doesn't work. We don't work together, Omar. We don't want the same things. We can't be what each other needs. You just don't want to admit it. You don't want to admit that we failed because you don't know what it feels like to fail, to not be good enough.'

Something serrated scraped inside him at the flatness in her voice and he felt a flicker of panic. Or was it another emotion? He seemed to be spilling over with them right now.

'How can you say that after last night?'

'I'm saying it *because* of last night. Standing at the edge of an abyss is not the sign of a happy marriage, Omar.'

Her face was pale, and he could see the walls that had tumbled last night were back up—just as high and wide as before. 'Me coming here was never about saving our marriage. You wanted me to talk to you, and that's what happened, and now we're done.'

'That's not all that happened. You cried, and I held you, and if I hadn't stopped it, we would have made love.'

'And what if we had?' Her brown eyes were wide with frustration now. 'Do you think that would have changed anything? It's just chemistry, Omar. Or nostalgia. It's meaningless.'

She turned swiftly away and began leading the horse towards the gate. He swore under his breath and stalked after her. Using her arm and her momentum, he drew her in hard and fast against his body. He watched the anger in her eyes darken, saw her pulse accelerate in her neck.

'You think this is meaningless?' He felt the wind on his neck, but he didn't care. He only cared about proving her wrong. His hand slid over her collarbone and he felt her breath shiver. 'That you can get this anywhere? With any man?'

He felt a pang of jealousy—the same as he'd felt when he had seen her first wearing that dress.

'No, I don't.' She pulled away. 'But it's not enough.'

Her voice sounded like the sand blowing across their feet. 'There has to be more.'

'We have more. We ride. We eat. We laugh. We talk.'

'We talked once.'

A gust of wind blew across the sand school. 'It's a start.'

Delphi shook her head. 'No, it's the end, Omar...'

Her voice petered out and she stared past him, her forehead creasing into a triangle of confusion.

'What?' He frowned.

'Where have the mountains gone?'

Now he was confused. He turned—and felt his stomach turn to stone. She was right: the mountains had disappeared. In their place was a huge, rolling russet-coloured cloud, as wide as the horizon, filling the sky.

'It's a *haboob*. A dust storm.' He turned back to Delphi as another gust of wind swirled across the sand. 'Take Alima inside. Close the barn doors. Then go back through to the house and stay there.'

Gazing up at the quivering sky, Delphi felt her heart slow. She had thought a dust storm was just a strong wind. But this looked more like a tidal wave or some monstrous creature.

Behind her, Omar was shouting orders in Arabic at the men now moving swiftly across the yard, picking up stray buckets and bolting gates.

Talking soothingly to Alima, she led the horse back into the barn and into her stall. Against the gale, it took all her strength to pull the huge barn doors across, and incredibly the wind was getting stronger and louder by the second. Outside the air was growing hazy. The men were starting to lose their shape.

Her heart gave a lurch. *Where was Omar?*

Without thinking, she ran back outside.

It was like stepping into another world. Actually, it felt like the end of the world. The noise was deafening, and the air was churning with dust and debris. Choking, she staggered forward, lifting her arms to shield her mouth and eyes. Not that she could see anything.

She felt a flicker of panic. The barn had vanished. There was just swirling sand and the screaming wind tearing at her skin.

She turned, trying to get some sense of direction, but in zero visibility the five yards back to the barn might as well have been five hundred miles. She was dizzy, disorientated. And then a driving gust of wind made her stagger and she fell forward, coughing.

'What are you doing?'

A hand caught her elbow and hauled her upright. It was Omar.

'I told you to go back through to the house.'

Bent almost double against the wind, he was propelling her forward now, and she felt a sharp relief as the barn loomed into view.

'Get inside!' Omar shouted.

As she nodded, something dark and blurred spun through the air and slammed into his side. He grunted in pain.

'You can't go back out in that!' She clutched at his arm, frantic with fear, as he turned towards the storm.

'I'll be fine. Go into the house.' His eyes were narrowed against the wind and he was having to shout above the noise.

She shook her head. 'No, I want to stay with the horses.'

She had never heard him swear, but he swore then— using a word that Dan had sent her thirteen-year-old self to her bedroom for saying.

'I can be with them.'

He pushed her back into the barn, but as he turned to step back outside, she clung onto his arm. 'I want to stay with you.'

The words came easily, just as if they'd been waiting to be spoken, but he didn't react, and she thought they had been lost on the wind. And then he was pulling the doors shut.

The noise dropped a notch and her hand tightened on his arm. 'Did everyone get inside?'

He nodded. 'They know the drill. Better still, they follow it.' A muscle beat in his jaw as he stared down at her, eyes accusing. 'What the hell were you thinking, going out there in that?'

'I didn't know where you were. I couldn't see you.'

His expression was unreadable. 'I thought you didn't want to see me.' Their eyes met and then he looked away. 'I'm going to check on the horses.'

Heart hammering, Delphi stared after him. Outside the wind had settled into a kind of rasping howl, and most of the horses were stamping and moving uneasily. Only Alima seemed unperturbed.

Omar shook his head. 'Brave as well as wise,' he murmured.

He reached out to stroke the mare's velvety muzzle and Delphi felt her spine turn to ice. On the front of his shirt, which should be yellow, a patch of red was spreading out like spilt wine.

'You're hurt.'

Looking down, he frowned. 'It's nothing. It's just a scratch.'

'You're bleeding. That's not nothing.'

There was a first aid kit on the wall next to an empty stall. A defibrillator hung beside it. As he tugged his shirt over his head, she felt a thud of shock. There was a graze along his abdomen—not deep, but ragged and oozing dark blood.

'It looks worse than it is.'

Trying not to fall into the gap in her mind where all the bad things were buried, she cleaned the wound and applied a sterile dressing. But as she pressed the edges against his smooth golden skin, she couldn't stop imagining what might have happened. What she knew could happen. And the possibility of that seemed enormous, rising up and crashing over her, sweeping everything away.

'What if it had hit your head?'

'It's okay.'

The concentrated gentleness in his voice made her hands start to shake. 'I couldn't see anything.' Her heart was pounding inside her chest. 'I couldn't see you.'

He pulled her into his arms. 'I know.'

Tears clogged her throat, and she pressed her hands against his chest, his shoulders, his beautiful undamaged face, needing to feel him, to check he was okay. 'No, you don't understand. I can always see you. Even in the dark… even with my eyes shut. Only I couldn't then.'

He stared down at her, his eyes burning black in the dim light.

'But I could see you.'

Everything stopped.

The wind outside paused, and the world hung motionless.

She held his gaze, and her breath, and then their mouths met blindly, greedily, urgently, and she melted into him.

CHAPTER EIGHT

OMAR LEANED FORWARD, backing her against the stable wall, one arm moving to brace himself against the wood, his tongue parting her lips to deepen the kiss. It was as if he had lit a fuse, and she felt a tingling heat sear through her straight to her belly.

She moaned as his lips moved across hers, teeth catching her lower lip, and then he tipped back her head and he was kissing her neck, his mouth pressing against the pulse beating wildly beneath her ear.

Shivering inside, she arched against him, her nipples hardening as they brushed against his smooth bare skin, and she shuddered at the sensation, nerves, need, anticipation swamping her.

His fingers had found the zip of her dress and he was working it down her back, pushing the fabric away from her shoulders. A shiver of anticipation rippled over her skin as it fluttered to the floor, but Omar did nothing. He just gazed down at her simple white underwear, breathing deeply, a dark flush fanning across his beautiful cheekbones.

Everything about him was beautiful, she thought, her head spinning as she looked up at him. He murmured some words in Arabic, a language she could neither speak nor understand. But she didn't need to do either to know what he was saying. His eyes made it clear, and she felt heat flood her limbs as his dark gaze slid down her body.

Her eyes never leaving his face, she slowly toed off her boots, then reached behind her back to undo her bra, letting it, too, slip to the floor. Heart thudding, she touched his chest. His skin was incredibly warm. She could feel his heart beating beneath her fingertips, and lower down it was as if his hand was already stroking her belly…smoothing her hips. Cupping the slick heat between her thighs.

She shivered, her breasts aching, body tense. Damp. *Yes*, she thought.

And then her breath caught as he reached for her, scooping her into his arms and carrying her into the empty stall. He kicked the door closed behind them and set her down firmly on a pile of hay.

Dragging in a breath, she pulled him to his knees—not gently. She wanted him…wanted to be completely his—physically, at least—and she clasped his face, kissing him fiercely, her hands reaching for the button of his jeans.

As her fingers slid beneath the waistband Omar groaned against her mouth, and then he was batting her hands away and holding her still, a storm of passion in his dark eyes.

'Are you sure this is what you want?'

His voice was hoarse, as if the sand had chafed his throat, and she could feel the effort it was taking him to hold back.

'I've never been surer of anything.'

She pressed her hand against the hard outline of his erection and that was all it took to accelerate him. He slid his hands beneath her panties, drawing them down her thighs and lowering his weight against her. His mouth found hers. His lips and tongue were urgent, his body hot and hard, his hands cupping her breasts, stroking, shaping them.

Heat was lapping over her body like waves curling onto

the shore's edge and hollowing out the sand, and she sucked in a sharp breath as his mouth closed over one taut nipple, licking, nipping, teasing the swollen tip, before switching to the other.

Curling her arms around his neck, she pressed up against him, her body so sensitive now that she wanted to tear off her own skin.

He made a rough sound in his throat, and she felt his palm slide over her abdomen to brush the wet curls at the V between her thighs. Then he parted her legs and she jerked, body twitching, as his fingers flexed inside her, then stilled. Helplessly, she lifted her body, wanting more, wanting the ache pounding through her to be answered.

'Omar…'

She whimpered his name, the muscles inside her clenching with frustration, and then his callused thumb began moving in slow circles that made her tremble inside. Moaning softly, she moved her hand to his groin, and she felt him tense as she pulled him free of his trousers, her fingers curling unsteadily around him. She had forgotten what it felt like to hold that length of smooth, polished flesh in her hand. The power and the thickness of him.

He grunted and jerked backwards. 'Wait,' he commanded.

She watched him strip off his remaining clothes, and then he was lowering himself down onto her body, lifting the hair from her neck to kiss and suck her throat. Heart hammering, she raised her hips and stroked the blunt head of his erection against her clitoris, moving it back and forth.

Omar gripped her hand, his ragged breathing vibrating against her skin. 'I don't have protection.'

She felt a momentary flicker of indecision. But she wanted him, without barriers of any sort, and so, shaking with need, she pulled him closer, cupping him in her hand.

She felt his body tense and his control snap, and he gripped her hips and pushed inside her.

A moan of pleasure escaped her lips. The waves inside her were getting bigger, sucking her back further. This was what she wanted. *He* was what she wanted. Her fingers bit into his shoulders as he began to move against her, thrusting deeper, then withdrawing to thrust again more deeply still. The waves were moving faster and faster, feeling hotter, so that she was panting now. And just when she thought she couldn't take any more those waves crashed over her, embracing her, and her back curved upwards, her body gripping his tightly.

As she shuddered against him, she felt his lips brush against hers and he groaned out her name and thrust upwards, surging inside her.

They lay together, panting shakily, their bodies hot and damp with sweat, muscles twitching.

Outside, the storm raged on. Not that she noticed. Lost in the white heat of their passion, there was only her and Omar. Truthfully, the *haboob* could have peeled off the barn roof like the lid of a sardine tin and neither of them would have noticed.

She felt Omar shift his weight and then he rolled sideways, taking her with him, still inside her. *Still hard.*

Her heart skipped a beat. Her body felt wonderful, as if all the tension of the last few days had been ironed out of her, but her head was spinning. What had she been thinking? Having sex without protection was not just stupid but reckless.

Only it didn't feel reckless. It felt right.

More than right.

After weeks and weeks of feeling broken and scared, she felt complete. Safe. *Happy.*

Just like she had in Vegas, when Omar had slid the ring

on her finger. When they'd run hand in hand through the hotel corridors to their ludicrously over-the-top honeymoon suite, she had got so close to believing in happy endings, so close to believing in the two of them, in the possibility of their future together.

And now, lying here, wrapped in his arms, their bodies fused, it was so tempting to let herself believe the same.

But she hadn't known then what she knew now. That even if somehow, they could put the past behind them a future was no longer possible.

What had happened in London had changed everything. Or maybe it wasn't that it had changed everything so much as shown her what was real and possible and what was just fantasy.

Her heart began to beat faster. She knew everything there was to know about fantasies. Ianthe and Dylan had been a Romeo and Juliet for the social media age. Two photogenic lovers: unfiltered in life, undivided in death. Tens of thousands of words had been written about their tempestuous relationship, and their most devoted fans might still want to believe their affair had been a real-life fairy tale.

But as far as she was aware there were no stories about Sleeping Beauty sleeping off a hangover, or Prince Charming being too stoned to go to the ball.

The wind was drumming against the roof, but not loudly enough to drown out the pounding of her heart.

As for their tempestuous relationship: with hindsight it was clear that her parents' arguments had been inspired not by passion but by alcohol and insecurity. Their rows had been frequent and explosive, but the next day it had always been as if all of it—the shouting and the screaming and the door-slamming—had never happened.

No wonder she found it so difficult to talk. To express her feelings. To say what she wanted. What she needed.

'Where have you gone?'

Omar's voice broke into her thoughts and, twisting round in his arms, she tilted her head back and met his eyes.

'I'm right here,' she said quietly.

The tension had left his body and it suited him. Relaxed, he looked even more sexy than normal, with his limbs resting negligently against the hay and his eyes dark and drowsy. Skin prickling, she reached up to touch his face, needing, as always, to check that he was real.

As if reading her thoughts, he pulled her closer, and her breath caught as his fingers moved lightly over her hip to caress her bottom.

'And so am I.'

Her heart thudded. Unlike her, Omar always knew what to say and how to say it. It was how he had got under her skin all those months ago, so that the barriers she'd built against the world softened and melted. But nothing had changed, she told herself. Not really. Whatever her body was saying. Which was lucky, she thought a moment later, as he shifted position so that her breasts brushed against his chest, and she felt her hips lift towards him without her consent.

'Can I get you anything? I'm not sure I can offer much, but there's a fridge in the office.'

The lazy softness in his eyes reached out to her, and she felt fingers of heat tiptoe over her skin 'Some water would be great. I'm just so thirsty suddenly,' she lied.

'Okay.'

She had wanted him to move and put himself out of temptation's reach, but as he got to his feet, she felt the loss of his sleek, hard body like the amputation of a limb. Then, to add insult to injury, she had to watch him walk away, and her mouth felt as if it had been sandpapered—which served her right for lying.

Don't look, she told herself.

But it was impossible not to. Not to savour his gorgeousness. Except for his silver wedding ring he was naked, and with his rippling muscles and smooth golden skin he was as gloriously, unashamedly male as the stallions in the neighbouring stalls.

And he was still aroused.

She squirmed against the hay, her insides liquid and hot. *As was she.*

'Here.'

Omar was back. He handed her a glass of water, and she took it, trying not to look at his body as he sat down beside her. The water was ice-cold and she drank it thirstily, wishing it could satisfy all her needs.

'Is there anything else you want?' he asked, pulling her close.

Yes, she thought, imagining his hands on her belly, and on her hips, and between her thighs. But it would be greedy and stupid, as well as irresponsible, to let anything happen again. And yet the idea that this was their last time together made her feel so miserable that her skin could barely hold it in.

'What is it?'

Omar touched her wrist, and there was a tension in his hand that made her look up at his face. He was staring down at her, his eyes moving over her, through her, as if he was seeking something.

'I didn't hurt you, did I?' he said finally.

She frowned. 'Hurt me?'

His gaze held hers. 'I should have checked everything was okay. After the miscarriage, I mean. But I didn't think... I wasn't thinking.'

That made two of them, she thought. Why else had she

not stopped when he'd told her he had no condoms? There was no good answer to that question, so she pushed it away.

'Everything's fine; you didn't hurt me.'

Above them, the sand sounded as if it was scouring the roof.

'Except I did, didn't I?' His voice sounded scoured too, and taut, as if it was an effort to get the words out. 'I hurt you, and I'm so sorry for that, Delphi. I am so very sorry.'

She stared at him; her pulse suddenly featherlight. Omar had apologised so many times in their marriage, but usually the 'I'm sorry' had been followed by some conditional clause that largely exonerated him from whatever had upset her. Because, of course, the real problem was her inability to trust and confide in him.

So now she waited for the 'if' or 'but' to follow his apology. But he didn't say anything like that. Instead, he bent his head. 'I'm sorry,' he said again. 'I should have been there for you, and I wasn't. I let you down.'

With the barn doors closed and the air outside dark with sand there was not much light in the stable, but there was enough for her to see the strain in his face. And the remorse.

Her heart beat in the darkness. She hated it that he was hurting, even though he'd hurt her. 'And I should have told you I was pregnant.'

He shook his head. 'I'm not just talking about the baby. Last night, when I was watching you sleep, I kept thinking about all those business trips I took. All those times I was late home or didn't come to bed. It never occurred to me how hard that was for you.'

Delphi swallowed. Her throat felt tight, and her stomach lurched a little as she remembered all those long evenings and weekends alone.

New York was only an hour away to the family ranch house in Bedford, but it had been harder than she'd thought to live in the city. Hard and terrifying to leave her father and her brothers and the home that had been her sanctuary for so many years.

'It was all right at the beginning…' When she'd thought his long working hours were necessary. When Omar had made them sound temporary. 'But then it wasn't.'

His dark eyes met hers.

'I know. And I know you probably don't believe me, but it was never meant to be like that. I just wanted to take care of you, and I told myself that was what I was doing… that I was being a good husband even though I was hardly ever there. I knew you were homesick and lonely, but I was too thoughtless to admit that I was the one making you feel that way.'

'I *was* homesick and lonely…' It had been more than that. Over time, it had felt as if she was losing her substance. 'And scared.'

'Of me?'

The shock in his voice wrenched at something inside her.

'No, not of you. Of having made the wrong decision.'

Again.

She thought back to Vegas, remembering the intensity in his voice as he spoke his vows, the feeling of her blood pounding round her body. She had been full of love, full of hope.

Afterwards, in the weeks when she should have been honeymooning with Omar, she had felt both lonely and fraudulent. As if she was exercising squatter's rights not just on the coolly beautiful Manhattan apartment, but on the idea that she could be happily married to a man she loved.

'I thought our marriage was your priority…that I was your priority. That's what it felt like before the wedding. Then everything changed on our honeymoon. I thought that once you made that deal it would go back to how it was.

Only it didn't. It just got worse. You were always at work, or away on business, and even when you were there you were working. I suppose it just ground me down.'

She felt his spine go rigid, but for the first time in their relationship he didn't attempt to defend himself.

'And then, after London, I was just so tired. I couldn't do it anymore. I couldn't keep telling myself that it would work when I knew that you wanted something more or different. So I left.'

The white-hot pain of leaving him had been offset by one tiny, frail hope.

'I thought you'd come after me,' she whispered.

She heard him take a breath.

'I thought you'd come back,' he said. 'So I waited. And then I was so angry with you for not staying and fighting for our marriage that I thought I'd make *you* wait.' His mouth twisted. 'Only you'd been fighting for months, and I didn't know because I wasn't there. I was never there when you needed me.'

Her throat clenched as she remembered something. 'You were there last night. I thought you left, but you stayed, didn't you?'

He nodded. 'There was an owl screeching, so I got up to close the window. When I came back you'd rolled over, so I slept in the chair.'

She stared at him, her heart leaping against her ribs. 'I thought I was dreaming.'

The intensity in his eyes scraped under her skin. 'I couldn't leave you. I couldn't walk away. And I never stopped looking for you either.'

His hands were clenched, and his face had lost colour. Heart thumping, she gazed up at him, thinking back to the complicated series of choices and omissions that had brought them to this point.

Could she walk away?

But she knew the question that needed asking was not *could* she, but *should* she? And the answer to that hadn't changed. Because deep down she knew that he couldn't be who he wanted her to be, and he wasn't what she needed.

That admission knocked the air from her lungs, and suddenly she was desperate to stop thinking and feeling. Eyes stinging, she pressed her finger against his mouth, quietening him.

'We both made mistakes.'

But she wasn't going to make yet another one by thinking that this quivering, mind-melting, incessant pull between them was something more than it was. More than it had already failed to be. More than it was capable of being.

They had reached the end, and there was no point reading anything into the fact that they were here, together, naked in this stall. What was happening in this little bubble was not real life. It was understandable, excusable. *Human.* A reaction to the hostility of what was happening outside. Two people trapped in a storm, hunkering down together, bodies surrendering to their lingering sexual longing for one another...

So make it about what it was, she told herself. *Make it about sex. And passion. And heat. And need.*

Pulse leaping, she placed her hand against the hard muscles of his stomach and glanced up at the roof. 'How long will the storm last?'

He followed her gaze. 'It's difficult to say. I could go and take a look outside in a bit.'

'There's no rush.' Her fingers walked down the vertical line of fine dark hair arrowing across his stomach. 'We have shelter and water.'

Something flickered in his dark eyes. 'And you think that's enough?'

There was a second's silence and then his hand moved to her hip, and she felt a rush of hunger flare inside her.

'It could be a long night.'

Her gaze roamed over his beautiful naked body. 'I think we can probably think of a way to pass the time,' she said softly.

Leaning forward, she wrapped her fingers around the smooth length of his erection. She heard him swallow, and then his head dipped, and he was clasping her face and kissing her. She told herself that was what she wanted. She wanted to be kissed. In kissing, she could forget everything—the good, the bad, the ugly and the beautiful.

He pulled her closer and she felt him press against her belly, hard where she was soft and yielding.

Tomorrow she would leave. But first there was this. One last night together in the eye of the storm. She arched into him, her body melting, seeking blindly for the oblivion of his mouth, her heart beating with hunger and relief as, angling his head, he took what she was offering.

Turning his body away from the shower head, Omar closed his eyes and jabbed his fingers through his hair to remove the last traces of shampoo.

It was the morning after the night before.

The storm had lasted until dawn, the raging wind alternating with short pockets of calm. Thankfully, the first rays of sun had woken them early, so that by the time his panicky staff had opened the barn doors he and Delphi had been fully dressed.

Unlike last night.

He felt his body harden.

Their coupling had been like a storm within a storm… their desire as hot and fierce and relentless as the wind. Jolted to the core by a hunger that had circled them for days, they'd touched and teased and tormented one another, changing position, losing themselves in the rhythm of their pounding hearts and hips, pausing to catch their breath or a few minutes' sleep until need drove them on again, only stopping when their aching muscles and chafed skin had forced them to.

His groin twitched and he pressed his hand against the blunt end of his erection as if to stifle it. Delphi had been like quicksilver in his hands, white-hot, her body quivering and arching against his, her soft moans of pleasure sweeping over his skin like tiny dancing flames licking at the logs in a grate.

He hadn't been able to get enough of her. He hadn't been able to taste her deeply enough. His desire had scraped him raw. Her desire had cut him loose and left him spinning, adrift in the dark of the barn.

And now, incredibly, he was aching for her again.

Gritting his teeth, he flicked the shower control to cold and, without flinching, let the freezing water course over his naked body.

Last night had unleashed more than that boiling, twitching hunger. Or perhaps it was more that unleashing it had swept away all the confusing detritus of their marriage, crumbling it into sand. And in that clean, uncluttered landscape it was easy to see that his previous assessment of his role in their marriage had been biased, not to say inaccurate.

He had always considered himself to be a civilised man, a good husband, a perceptive and attentive partner. But this morning, as they'd made their way back to the fort, he had been forced to rethink that assumption, and the truth was that he had behaved badly. Selfishly. Unkindly.

Instead of supporting her, he had hurt and confused her so badly that she had shut down, and he hated it that she'd felt that way—hated knowing that *he* had made her feel that way. For so long he had blamed her past for the obstacles that lay between them. But he had been equally to blame, if not more.

Delphi was right. Work was his obsession—an obsession she could see, anyway. And over time he had let it consume him, and bumped Delphi to the bottom of his agenda.

Remembering how he had taken that call from his father out in the sand school, he felt his face burn with shame. After weeks of separation, and months of being at odds with one another, they had finally been talking openly, honestly, about their marriage. Delphi had been holding his hand. The last thing he should have done was answer his phone, but he had reacted unthinkingly, ruthlessly turning his back on her, driven by a need that outweighed everything in his life—even his wife.

It hadn't started out that way.

Meeting her at the Amersham, he had been smitten, mesmerised, and the fact that she had neither encouraged nor welcomed his attention had only cemented his desire to change her mind. He had dropped everything to pursue her.

She had become his new obsession.

Even now, picturing their wedding, he could feel the relief, the almost orgasmic ecstasy of a marathon runner crossing the finishing line first. But three days later, prompted by a phone call from his father, he'd cut short their honeymoon and flown off to secure yet another in a long line of empire-building deals.

And Delphi had returned home.

Alone.

All the time he'd been promising to be by her side, pressurising her to trust him, telling himself that he was taking care of her, protecting her from the world. But he had been the one hurting her. Jaw clenched, he dipped his head beneath the spray of water. He had spurred her on. But at the same time he'd leaned back and pulled on the reins.

He had confused her, and she had tried to save herself.

Like Alima, she had bucked, and then bolted.

And she would have bolted again yesterday, except the storm had made leaving impossible.

He switched off the shower and leaned forward, watching the water swirl down the plughole.

And now?

There was an ache in his chest that made it hard to catch his breath. The idea of her moving on and making a life without him was agonising. He wanted her to stay more than he had ever wanted anything, but if he wanted that to happen then the conversation he had started out in the sand school would have to be finished.

Only this time he would let nothing get in the way.

Wrapping a towel around his waist, he took a breath and walked back into the bedroom. Delphi was standing on the balcony, and his pulse soared as she turned towards him. She had showered first and was still wearing his bathrobe, the sleeves rolled up, the hem grazing the floor. With her slightly damp hair and bare feet she looked incredibly sexy.

Her gaze rose to meet his, and a faint rose-coloured flush crept across her cheeks. 'I was just looking outside. It's like the storm never happened.'

He glanced past her at the cloudless blue sky. It was a perfect summer's day. There was no reason Delphi couldn't leave. What mattered, though, was giving her a reason to stay. The thought made his heart thump.

'It's hard to believe, isn't it, that something that intense doesn't leave a trace?'

He saw her gaze move to where the towel clung snugly to his hips, and she frowned.

'But it did.'

He followed her gaze, glancing down at where the skin across his abdomen had turned plum-coloured. 'It's just a bruise.'

Without apparently moving, she had drifted closer, and for a few agonising half-seconds he thought she was going to touch the bruise. But then her hands fisted at her sides.

'Last night, you said it was just a scratch.'

'Which only goes to prove what you already knew,' he said.

'What's that?'

Her brown eyes were glittering, but her mouth was soft and vulnerable, and everything inside him slid sideways—just as it had that first time at the Amersham, when she had made an entire polo match, complete with ponies, players, and spectators, disappear.

'That I don't always know what I'm talking about. That I get things wrong. And I *was* wrong, Delphi. About so much. I know that I confused you, and I hurt you, and for a long time—too long, in fact—I didn't even see what I was doing. But I do now, and nothing is more important to me than you.'

Beside his bed, his phone buzzed once.

Watching Delphi's face tense, he took a step closer, as if doing so might reinforce what he was about to say.

'And if you'll give me a second chance, I promise things will be different—*I* will be different. Let me prove to you that you can trust me.'

Now his phone started ringing. They both stared at it and he almost laughed—although nothing about the situation was funny. He wanted to break the tension between them, and the only other way he knew to do that was by kissing her. But if their marriage was going to work it, sex couldn't be the only way they communicated. He had learned that much in the last few days.

Snatching up the phone, he switched it off and tossed it onto the bed.

'You didn't have to do that,' Delphi said stiffly.

'Yes, I did, and I should have done it a long time ago. But now I need to do more than just tell you that I can change. I need to show you. I need to show you that our marriage matters more to me than anything else. That you matter more than anyone else.'

All the time he was speaking she was still there, and that was all that mattered. Keeping her here. But he'd realised that he was telling the truth. For the first time in his whole life, nothing—not even his father's approval—was as important to him as Delphi and their marriage. He wasn't interested in who was calling him or what they wanted.

She was shaking her head, her eyes too bright. 'Don't do that. It's not fair.'

'I don't care about fairness. I care about you.'

'You hurt me.'

His heart contracted. 'I know.'

'And then I hurt you. I don't want us to keep hurting each other.'

'I don't want that either. But if you leave now, do you think the pain will go away?'

'No. But sometimes hope is more painful than loss.'

Her raw admission made his pulse quicken and, cupping her cheeks, he tipped her face up to his, refusing to let her look away. 'But our hope survived the storm.' He stared down at her. 'You're the beat of my heart…the air I breathe. And I know I've been selfish, and I'm still being selfish in asking you to stay. But I don't have a choice. Because I—'

Because I love you.

He stared down at her, his heart pounding, the unfinished sentence booming inside his head, shocked. But why? He had never stopped loving her—even when he'd been furious and hating her for leaving him. But Delphi was so ready to run, and big words like love had always scared her. He couldn't risk scaring her now.

'I need you. Without you, nothing matters. I don't matter.'

Panic had made him careless, and his throat tightened. It was his worst fear—one that he had never admitted to anyone—and the idea that he had just done so to Delphi made his stomach churn.

'Of course you matter,' she said hoarsely.

'Then stay. At least for a few weeks.' His thumbs caressed her face. 'I still owe you a honeymoon, remember?'

'A honeymoon?'

Hearing the longing in her voice, he felt his body tighten. She was so close that he could feel the heat of her, see the pulse beating in her smooth throat, the conflict in her eyes.

'I can take you anywhere. We can go back to Maui.'

She bit her lip. 'I don't want to do that. I want it to be about us. Not fireworks or acrobats. Just the two of us, spending time together. Both of us present, not hiding or distracted.'

Omar nodded slowly. She was right, and it sounded so easy—only he knew he was treading on eggshell-thin ground. They could go anywhere in the world. All it would take was a phone call. But why go anywhere? Why not stay, and spend time together here?

'Then could I show you around the city? I don't mean the malls or the fountains or the Burj. I mean my Dubai. The place where I grew up.'

Her eyes were tired, but he saw a flicker of curiosity, and he took a deep, burning breath as he realised just how scared he'd been up until that moment that she would leave him.

'I'd like that,' she said quietly.

'Then that's what will happen.'

His voice shook a little and he leaned closer, needing to touch her, to check that she was real and that she was still his.

As if sensing his thoughts, she looked up into his face. 'This is just a trial, Omar. I can't… I don't want to make any more promises.'

'I understand. All I want is a second chance.'

Their eyes met. 'Is that all you want?' she asked slowly.

Omar stared down at her, captivated by her question and by the rise and fall of her breasts beneath the robe. He waited a moment, and then he reached out and undid the belt around her waist. Breath bottled in his chest; he slid his hand beneath the soft linen. Her skin was hot and smooth like satin. He touched her breasts, feeling the tips harden beneath his fingers.

She moaned and tipped back her head, exposing more of her throat, and then the robe slid from her shoulders, and she was naked.

Their eyes met, and then she reached out and unhooked the towel from his waist. It joined the robe on the floor. Now they were both naked.

He sucked in a breath, and then he was nudging her backwards, and her hands were pulling him down onto the bed, shaking with eagerness, and then there was only Delphi, and the cool sheets sliding beneath them, and the pure, pulsing beat of their desire.

CHAPTER NINE

TURNING HER HEAD, Delphi breathed in deeply. The air was so different here from the mountains. There it was clear and dizzyingly fresh. But this was different with every breath. There was salt and spice and the fumes from the various boats chugging up and down and across the choppy waters of the Dubai Creek, or the Khor Dubai, as it was known locally.

It was two days since she and Omar had emerged from the barn into the daylight. But they had survived more than one storm. And the second—the one that had taken place in the bedroom—had been infinitely more terrifying and painful.

Honestly, she hadn't believed him when he'd said he wanted to change, that he *could* change. But when it came to it, it didn't matter. She didn't know if it had been the desperation in his voice, or the smudges under his eyes, but she hadn't been able to walk away.

Her heart bumped against her ribs. She still didn't know if she had done the right thing by staying, but she did know that walking away wasn't the solution anymore. It never had been, only she hadn't been able to see that then. She had been too locked into her own fears, too scared to take a risk. But something had changed—she had changed. And he had too.

And now she was sitting in an *abra*, one of the flat-decked wooden boats that ferried people from one side of the creek to the other, with Omar's hand wrapped around hers, breathing in not just the air but the sights and sounds of the waterfront.

There were hundreds of wooden boats tied three deep along the creek, and on the quayside, men were ferrying boxes of shirts and milk powder and cooking oil on their shoulders.

And, as if all that activity wasn't incredible enough, they were alone.

Or at least it felt as if they were alone. The bodyguards were still close by, but Omar had insisted that they blend in. She glanced over to where he was sitting beside her, his gaze tracking the movements of the river traffic. They were supposed to be doing the same, but it would take more than a baseball cap to make Omar Al Majid blend into any crowd.

'What do you think?'

She felt him shift closer and she turned, her heart making a startling leap into her throat as their eyes met.

'I think it's amazing,' she said truthfully. 'It's so busy.'

Omar had been right. This was nothing like the Dubai she had seen on the way to the Lulua. There were no glittering skyscrapers or glossy supercars. Everything was brightly coloured and there was so much to see.

'It's like this day and night. The people who live and work here never stop.'

'So where are we going first?' she asked as he helped her disembark on the Deira side of the creek.'

'The market. Although it's not quite like the farmer's market in Bedford Hills.'

Her chest felt tight, as though it might burst. It had been one of her favourite places to go with him before they'd got married. But those lazy mornings spent browsing hand-made cheese and local honey had been swept aside and forgotten, like everything else.

Or maybe not forgotten, she thought now, as his hand tightened around hers and he led her through the crowded, labyrinthine lanes.

First stop was the cloth market. Every single space was occupied. In some places bolts of vividly coloured textiles were balanced in unsteady piles against the walls, in others they spilled onto the streets. There was barely standing room and the noise was astonishing.

'Is that Arabic?' she asked, as a woman began to shout at a man who was holding up a pair of beautiful, embroidered slippers.

Omar shook his head. 'Urdu. But around ninety per cent of the population is expat, so you'll hear a lot of languages. You get used to it.'

'Is that why you're so good at languages?'

He seemed surprised by the question. 'Not at all. I'm only good because I had so many extra lessons. It's not something that came naturally to me.'

'But you wanted to get better?' It was typical of Omar that even as a child he had seen it as a challenge to overcome. 'And you worked hard to get what you wanted?'

Next to her, Omar was silent, and she sensed a tension that hadn't been there before.

Then he said, 'It was my father who wanted me to get better, so that's what I did on my weekends. I learned German and Mandarin and Spanish and French.'

It didn't sound like much fun. It didn't sound like her weekends on the ranch... 'Wouldn't you have rather been playing with your friends?'

'Of course. All I wanted to do was play football and

polo. But it's been very good for business.' He gave her a small, tight smile. 'Shall we move on?'

Very good for business, she thought, but surely that couldn't have been Rashid's intention.

After the cloth market they made their way to the souks. Omar had been right, Delphi thought, gazing at the crowded stalls. It was nothing like the farmer's markets back in the States.

'This was part of the old Silk Road,' Omar said, leading her through the throngs of shoppers. 'Goods from all over the world have been coming through here for centuries. For a few decades Dubai was Deira.'

As they wandered down one alley after another, Delphi found herself falling under his spell again. She loved the sound of his voice, the strength of it. Most of all, she loved the fact that there was no agenda, no pressure to move on— and she was finding out things about him. Stupid, small things that glowed in her mind like the jewelled necklaces in the gold market.

'What is it?' she asked.

They had stopped to drink coconut water at a stall, and Omar had been gazing down at the green coconut in his hand. Now he looked up at her, smiling, and the sudden softness in his face pierced her heart.

'I used to come here with Hamdan when I was very young,' he told her. 'He'd pick me up after school and get the driver to drop us off. I remember being so excited by how they chopped off the end of the coconut with a huge knife.' He shook his head. 'I'd forgotten all about that.'

She smiled. 'Why did Hamdan pick you up from school?'

Omar stared past her into the bustling market. 'He didn't always. But my dad worked away a lot, and when he travels, he likes to have his wives with him. Hamdan was married by the time I was six, so I'd go and stay with him and his wife.'

Delphi stared at him, replaying not only his words, but what Jalila had said at the party. 'You said "when he travels", but he doesn't still travel for work, does he?'

His face stiffened a little. 'Sometimes. He gets a lot out of it.' He pulled her against him. 'Now, can I tempt you with something a little spicier?' he said softly.

As his dark eyes rested on her face she felt her heart start to hammer inside her chest. She was almost desperate to feel his mouth against hers. 'I thought you'd never ask…'

The spice market was huge and open air, but the alleys leading to and from it were so thick with scent she could practically taste it on her tongue. There were bulging sacks of dried black limes, barberries, rose petals and rosemary.

Delphi rubbed some of the familiar needle-like leaves between her fingers. 'I thought this was more of a Mediterranean flavour.'

'They do use it in cooking, but it's also medicinal. My mother uses it for dizziness. Olive leaves… They're supposed to be good for the heart.'

She met his gaze, her own heart hammering. 'And what about all those?' she asked quickly, gesturing to the photo-op-worthy miniature cone-shaped mountains of heaped spices.

'That's sumac, ginger, cinnamon, *ras-el-hanout* and saffron. You have to be careful with saffron,' he added. 'A lot of it is fake. They use dyed cotton or shredded paper. That's why you should drop it in water before you buy. To see if it loses colour. The darkest is the best,' Omar said, pointing past her to a teetering burnt orange mound. 'And the real thing should have a splayed end. Oh, and you have to haggle,' he added. 'It's expected.'

But when he finally paid, she could tell the vendor was delighted. 'I thought you said you had to haggle,' she said.

They were eating lunch at one of the waterfront restaurants, where *leqaimats*—seductively sweet dumplings drizzled with a sticky syrup—had followed a thin pancake filled with buttery tarragon-flavoured scrambled egg topped with shards of black truffle. Now they were sipping coffee.

He shrugged. 'I don't need to win at everything.'

Something stirred in her head. A memory of Jalila taking hold of her hands at Rashid's party and telling her how happy she was to see her brother in love. *'I know he's rich and gorgeous, but I also know how intense he can be, how fixated he is on proving himself.'*

How fixated he is on proving himself: present tense.

At the party, she had been too stressed to mull over Jalila's words, and afterwards there had been so much going on. Now, though, she had time to think. But the more she thought, the less they made sense. What did Omar have to prove now? He was wealthy enough to stop working tomorrow and still live a life of unparalleled luxury. And she had seen first-hand the reverence with which other important and successful people treated him.

'I still want to win. But I know that I have to stop, or it will ruin our future.' His hand tightened around hers. 'It almost destroyed our marriage. It's just hard for me to stop.'

There was a long, weighted silence.

'Why is it hard?' she said quietly.

But in her head she was wondering why she didn't already know the answer to that question. And why she had never thought to ask it before now. But then she had always been too busy resenting Omar, too distracted by her own feelings and thoughts to consider his. She had viewed their life together through the lens of her past, her pain.

But what about his past...his pain?

'It's been so long.' His beautiful mouth twisted. 'I was so young when it started. I don't even think it was conscious. I just slipped into it. It didn't matter when it was just me and my goal. But then I met you, and you made everything disappear. I couldn't stop thinking about you. I knew you'd been hurt but I thought that if I could get you to trust me, then I could take away your pain.'

'You did take away my pain.' She reached out and touched his hand.

He flinched. 'But I caused you pain too.' His voice was hoarse. 'I took you for granted. I told myself that marrying you was enough. That it proved how much I loved you.'

His words made her eyes sting, and she felt a rush of misery. 'It would have proved it to any normal person. But I was so scared of being let down that I couldn't let it mean anything.'

'Of course you were scared. What happened to you as a child was appalling. Of course it was going to affect how you see the world.'

'The world, yes. But you were my husband. I should have talked to you. I should have told you how I was feeling and asked about *your* feelings. Only I didn't try to fix things. It was easier for me to run and hide and blame you.'

'Because I am to blame.' His face was taut. 'I made promises I didn't keep. I said one thing and did another. I didn't plan for it to happen. But then, on our honeymoon, my father called.'

Delphi blinked, but she wasn't remembering that day on the beach in Maui, but her first meeting with Omar's parents in New York. Rashid had been distracted, hardly present, but Omar had been the polar opposite. There had been a tension in him...

'I remember,' she said quietly.

Omar nodded. A muscle was working in his jaw. 'And do you remember me telling you that it was an important deal? I told you it was necessary. I told myself it was a one-off.' He sucked in a breath. 'I was wrong.'

'You made a mistake.' She squeezed his hand. 'Your father must think very highly of you to bother you like that.' She wanted to comfort him, but instead she saw his shoulders brace against an imaginary blow.

'Not really. Mostly he struggles to notice me at all. Although, to be fair, it's not just me. But I suppose I struggle with it the most.'

Glancing up at Omar's face, she felt her heart tumble in her chest. His dark head was bent, and the strain in his voice was visible around his eyes, but she was seeing his face at Rashid's party, and the tension beneath the beautiful smile. The same tension that had held his body taut like a switchblade during his parents' visit to their New York apartment.

'Because you're the youngest?'

It was a hunch, but he nodded.

'Everything I did had been done sixteen times already. Nothing I did mattered. And it was worse when we were all together. My brothers and sisters were always so much bigger and louder and more articulate than me. When I was with them, I felt like I was lost in this crowd. It was like nobody could see me or hear me.'

Tears filled Delphi's eyes. When she was a child that had been her dream. She had longed to be invisible. But never from Dan or her brothers—just the wider world: the gossip-hungry public and the paparazzi who fed that hunger.

She glanced over to where their coffees sat cooling on the table. 'Do they know how you feel?'

He shrugged. 'Jalila does. And Hamdan. They understand. But it wasn't the same for them. Jalila is one of seven, and Hamdan is one of nine. When my dad went away on business, or stayed at the other houses, it didn't matter so much to them. But there was only me and my mother, and when he wasn't there my mum found it hard. That's why she would go away with him on business. Only then it was like I was living in this huge, empty mausoleum. That's why I used to go and stay with Hamdan.'

Her chest squeezed tight. At the margins of her mind, things were falling into place. Like how he hated coming back to an empty apartment.

'It sounds awful.'

She felt his grip on her hand tighten.

'To be honest, it was worse sometimes when he was there. I was so desperate to get his attention, but then there was the pressure to keep him interested. And I never knew when he was going to leave, so I used to follow him around, because I was paranoid he would go without saying good-bye. Which he usually did.'

Delphi felt her stomach clench. And she had done it too—and hurt him by doing it. Only she hadn't known she was hurting him in that way. Hadn't known she was pressing against an old bruise. She had been too wrapped up in her own past even to consider that he had bruises too.

Her face must have shown some of the shock she was feeling, because he gave her a small, tight smile.

'I don't want you to think he's a bad father, or that he doesn't love me. He's not and he does. And it's not all his fault. He's ninety years old, and he's been preposterously rich since he was younger than me. That means he's always the most important person in any room. Maybe not always—I mean, he does know heads of state and kings. But most of the time people treat him like a king, and so he acts like one. He never has to wait for anybody or anything, and if he gets bored then he just moves on to the next thing.'

He stared past her at brightly coloured *dhows*.

'The trick is having the one thing in the room he's curious about…'

And now, finally, she understood the long hours and the late nights. 'That's why you work so hard. To build something that holds your father's attention.'

He nodded. 'He ran a newspaper at university, and he loved it, but other things happened. He got into property and shipping. But he always had a soft spot for news and media, and I suppose I picked up on that. I did a stint at the *Crimson* when I was at Harvard, and I liked it. So when I got offered a chance to buy up a bunch of local news stations across the US, I took it.'

The intensity in his eyes transfigured his face.

'It was probably the first time I'd ever held my father's attention to the end of a conversation.'

She could hear the wonder in his voice. The wonder of a little boy finally managing to balance the obscure, complicated equation of novelty and challenge that held his father's gaze.

'That must have felt amazing,' she said quietly.

She couldn't imagine Dan acting that way. He had always put her first and centre stage. Her brothers too. But there had also been space for her to become her own person.

'It did. I've never done drugs, but I guess it was like a high. And I was hooked. Like you said, I became obsessed. It was all I thought about.'

She stared at him. 'I don't remember you being like that when we met. I don't remember talking about work at all.'

'That's because when I met you it was like being born again. Nothing before you mattered. I was completely smitten. I actually thought I was going mad because you were always in my head. I could always hear your voice, see your face.'

His eyes rested on her face, dark, steady, blinking.

'Normally when I met a woman even before she opened her mouth, I knew who she was. But with you I felt like I was trying to catch a kite by the tail. You were this beautiful wild girl, riding bareback, and every moment I spent with you was a breath of mountain air.'

Delphi stared at him without blinking. Her heart felt as if it was on fire. For so many weeks she had pushed away those memories. Now, though, they broke through like a river bursting its banks.

'I felt the same way. It was as if my whole life up till then had been lived in a gale. I was always fighting just to keep on my feet. And then you came along. It was like the wind dropped and I didn't need to struggle any more, because you were there, and everything was so calm and quiet and safe.'

Omar lifted her hand to his mouth and kissed it softly. 'I'm so sorry I hurt you. It makes me ashamed, thinking about how I behaved when you've gone through so much. So much loss. So much pain. I've lost nothing. I had no right to feel like I did. To do what I did to you.'

'You were lost. That's not nothing.'

Around them, the noise of the creek was fading. The stevedores and the fishermen were just blurred figures, moving as if through water. The cacophony of language and dialects was a faint hum. It was just the two of them now.

His dark eyes rested on her face. 'But then I found you, and I wanted to be everything to you. I wanted to be your everything. Only I knew you were holding things back. Dan told me to be patient. That you weren't the kind of woman I could put reins on. But I didn't listen. I just kept pushing and pushing you... Only then I pushed you too far and you left.'

She breathed out shakily. 'After London, I just gave up.

But I was wrong to leave. I should have stayed and told you how I was feeling. I should have told you that I needed you. That I loved you.'

His dark eyes reached into her, holding her still. 'And what about now? What are your feelings now?'

Tears were running down her face. 'They haven't changed. I still love you.'

More even than she had before, because now she knew the real man she was loving.

'And I love you.'

For a moment, neither of them could speak. Then Omar cleared his throat. 'I want to kiss you so badly, only I'm not sure I could stop at kissing you, and I don't want to end up breaking any public decency laws.'

The huskiness in his voice as much as his words made her pulse leap. 'Maybe we should head back home.'

The corner of his mouth lifted, and his gaze, so full of love, reached inside her. As much a part of her as her love was a part of him.

'There's no maybe about it.'

* * * * *

RECLAIMING
HIS RUNAWAY
CINDERELLA

ANNIE WEST

MILLS & BOON

I'm delighted and amazed to say that
this is my 50th book for Mills & Boon! I hope you enjoy
reading it as much as I had fun writing it.

I'd never have reached 50 books without lots of help,
encouragement and understanding from my family,
who are all fabulous and inspiring, my dear writer
friends (you know who you are), who listen and chivvy,
problem-solve and celebrate, my excellent editor
and you lovely readers, who continue to pick up
my books and share the worlds I create.

Thank you all for making this career
and all these stories possible!

CHAPTER ONE

THE FAMILIAR MUSIC began and behind him Cesare heard a hush descend on the packed church. Not a complete silence, for even over the triumphant swell of music came the sound of hundreds of whispers and the rustle of designer dresses as people turned towards the entrance.

Cesare waited, eyes straight ahead, as if taking in the gilded pomp of the renaissance interior.

But his thoughts were elsewhere. On the events which had culminated in today's ceremony. The circumstances, some predictable, others unforeseen, all compelling. All pushing him to this moment.

A collective sigh gathered behind him, and it felt as if the air in the vast space thickened. The scent from the elaborate floral arrangements grew more intense and the bone-white candles flickered in their silver candelabras.

The priest flicked him a look and Cesare knew it was time to turn.

Finally he swung around, his eyes going unerringly to the figure halfway up the aisle.

Now he understood the sighs.

Ida Montrose looked ethereal, floating down the aisle in a long, gauzy dress that looked held together by wisps of lace.

There was lace too on the veil that covered her face and

draped her shoulders. But through it he saw the golden-red gleam of her hair and the huge pools of her eyes.

He hadn't meant to, but he couldn't stop his gaze dropping. Pausing at the sweet swell of her breasts, barely covered by white lace, down to a waist so narrow his fingers twitched at the thought of spanning it.

The dress clung to her neat hips then fell in folds of transparent fabric and lace that made her look like a cross between a flower fairy and a lingerie model.

Cesare's body responded accordingly. With a thudding pulse of heat that plunged from his chest to his suddenly aching groin.

His lungs stopped as he imagined his hands on her. Big hands ruthlessly parting those insubstantial layers to reveal satiny skin. Eager hands palming her pale body and preparing her for his possession.

Heat shot through him like flames through a petrol-soaked bonfire. Moisture beaded his hairline and nape while a jab of pain told him he was clenching his jaw in the effort of control.

This wouldn't do. He had a solemn ceremony to get through under the watchful gaze of Europe's oldest families and monied elite.

He yanked his gaze away from his bride to the man walking down the aisle beside her. White-haired, wearing a satisfied grin. Fausto Calogero.

It might be years since the man had frequented Rome, but he nodded and smiled as if he knew half the high-born guests, his chest thrust out in pride.

Cesare took a slow breath and schooled his features.

He didn't fool himself that after today he'd be able to ignore the man. But as of today, things would change. Cesare would make sure of that.

The pair paused at the bottom of the steps and Cesare's

attention snapped back to his bride-to-be. She was so close he saw the puff of movement as her breath stirred the veil, and the way the pure white lilies and orange blossom trembled in her hands.

But her chin was high, and he felt her gaze on him.

She wanted this wedding and so did he.

Cesare let his expression ease into a smile of pure anticipation.

Soon he'd have exactly what he wanted.

Ida should be exhausted.

She'd barely slept the night before and today's formalities had gone on for ever.

First, she'd had to run the gauntlet of her grandfather's eagle-eyed inspection. He'd paid for her to be turned out in style and that gave him the right to bark orders at the coterie of dressers, make-up artists, hairstylists and even the poor florists who'd attended her.

It hadn't occurred to Ida to suggest how *she'd* like to look on her wedding day. Or object that the flesh- coloured backing in her diaphanous gown made her look like a raunchy parody of the virginal bride her grandfather had intended.

You didn't argue with Fausto Calogero.

Then there'd been the wedding in one of Rome's most venerated churches, filled to standing with well-heeled, well-connected people she didn't know.

Finally had come the reception. Hours of polite conversation, exquisite food that she'd been too keyed-up to eat and vintage wines she'd never heard of, but which had made her grandfather nod approvingly.

There'd been dancing till her feet ached and photographs till her face ached and stares from people who didn't bother to conceal surprise or dismay that Cesare Brunetti had married *her*.

Yet Ida was too wired to think of sleep.

Because she was in the opulent prestige suite of Rome's most famous and expensive private hotel. And her husband was in the next room. *Waiting for her.*

Ida shivered. Not with cold. And only with a little trepidation.

No, it was excitement that rushed through her like a scouring tide. Anticipation that made her skin tingle and her blood pump faster.

She looked in the mirror and saw the hard points of her nipples jutting against the midnight-blue silk of her new nightie. Her hands shook as she smoothed the whisper-thin fabric from her hips to her thighs.

The sensation was unfamiliar, and not simply because she'd never worn a sexy silk nightdress before. The brush of fabric under her palms made her think of *his* hands on her. Would they be slow and easy or urgent and needy? Her breath quickened, intensifying the unfamiliar, heavy feeling low in her body, like a throbbing ache.

Ida met her eyes in the mirror, and they told the same tale. They were wide and bright, almost feverish with anticipation.

Had she done right to take her hair down? It rippled around her shoulders and even that felt like a caress.

Would Cesare know, just by looking, how she felt?

She frowned and reached for the dark blue silk robe, slipping her arms into it and tying it at her waist. Now her puckered nipples weren't so obvious.

Ida shook her head. What did it matter? As soon as Cesare took her to bed he'd realise how eager she was.

She hoped her inexperience wouldn't mar their first night together. Cesare, scion of an ancient, aristocratic family, blessed with stunning good looks, money, magnetism and an aura of power, could have any woman he wanted. No doubt he'd had plenty, even if he kept his romantic conquests private.

It still astounded her that he wanted *her*.

She wasn't naïve enough to think he loved her. They'd met because he and her grandfather had become business associates and, as he'd explained, he needed a wife.

But he'd chosen *her*. Ida Montrose.

Not one of the uber-sophisticated socialites who'd looked daggers at her during the reception. Not the glamorous princess who'd flown in for the wedding and looked as if she'd like to gobble Cesare up.

To Cesare Ida was convenient. But there was more to it. There was an affinity between them, and Ida *knew* they could build on that to make a success of this marriage.

She'd felt the powerful connection in the way he looked at her. In those rare, devastating smiles. The way he actually listened when she spoke.

There'd even been times, when her grandfather laid down the law about something, when Cesare had caught her eye and she'd felt their connection and shared understanding. She'd felt the impatience he was too well-bred to show, the riposte he was too polite to make.

Cesare…her husband…wasn't cowed by her grandfather. That, above all else, gave her hope for the future and courage to go through with this. He'd chosen her as his bride because he *wanted* her.

As she wanted him.

Now he was hers.

She was nineteen and all her dormant female longings had rushed to the surface the moment she met him.

Life hadn't given her opportunities to date or simply get to know many men. But she was ready to make up for that.

Not because she was desperate for a man. That hadn't been a priority. It was *Cesare* who made her want to explore the sensual delights she knew he'd share with her.

Ida looked down at the rings weighting her left hand. The gold wedding band and the engagement ring with its enormous square-cut diamond solitaire.

She'd work hard at this marriage. She could imagine the pair of them, years from now, easy in each other's company but sharing those glowing, loving looks she still remembered seeing her parents share.

Thinking about that lit a tiny spark of hope deep inside where for so long she'd felt cold and unwanted. Orphaned at eight, she still missed her parents' love.

Her chin firmed and she stood straighter. She slipped off her robe and put it neatly on a nearby chair. Then she breathed deeply and reached for the gilded door handle.

Cesare was in the luxurious sitting room. Not ensconced on a sofa, waiting for her, but on the phone, looking out over the rooftops of Rome.

The sound of his native Italian in that rich voice made her think of dark, molten chocolate and she licked her lips, wondering how he'd taste. That peck in the church had been too quick.

A quiver of arousal ran down her spine and she pressed suddenly clammy hands to her thighs.

Maybe she should have worn the robe after all. For he was still fully dressed, right down to the lovingly tailored formal black jacket that clung to his wide shoulders and tapering back.

She'd never seen Cesare in moulded-to-the-skin jeans or clinging polo shirts, yet she knew that beneath his urbane exterior was a virile man. He oozed masculinity just as he radiated confidence. Without the latter her grandfather would have steamrollered him as he did everyone else.

Ida's gaze dropped to Cesare's long legs, remembering the way his hard thighs had brushed hers when they danced at the reception. She'd seen heat shimmer in his gaze too.

She might be inexperienced, but she wasn't totally naïve. It had been a look of sensual promise and she couldn't wait for him to deliver.

Ida moved closer, bare feet silent on the thick carpet, enjoying the unaccustomed luxury of watching Cesare unobserved.

He swung around, eyes widening for a second, and satisfaction punched low in her abdomen. He'd sensed her approach. And he hadn't been able to hide his response.

She breathed out, relieved, realising he liked what he saw. She'd aimed for sophisticated and sexy with this nightgown that skimmed rather than hugged her figure. Yet despite the fact it covered her from breastbone to knee, she'd never been so naked before anyone.

Cesare ended the call and pocketed his phone, then shoved his hands in his trouser pockets, surveying her with a stern look that made her smile falter on her lips.

'Ida.'

Just that. Yet the way his voice deepened to a low, unfamiliar rumble tickled her senses. Surely that was a good sign?

But he made no move towards her. Nor did he make any move to undress. He hadn't even undone his bow tie.

She swallowed. Was that something she should offer to do? Her fingertips tingled at the thought of touching him. The prospect of peeling back that snowy shirt to reveal his powerful chest jammed her breath in her lungs.

Gathering her courage, she walked closer, feeling the weight of his gaze with every step.

Did he like what he saw? She was suddenly conscious

of how ordinary she was. Her curves weren't bounteous, her height on the small side.

Mentally she shrugged off her doubts. She'd had a lifetime of her grandfather finding fault. She was determined to start her new life without that baggage.

The future was about her and Cesare. That trounced the flutter of nerves in her abdomen and she smiled.

She'd never been so happy.

She stopped before him, and Cesare felt winded. Her incandescent smile reminded him of the rising sun spilling its golden rays over his beloved Tuscan countryside.

Remarkably he felt it too, like a rush of flame igniting in his belly and shooting along his veins. Heat seared his lungs and groin as he looked into her upturned face.

Everything else vanished. The all-important plans that had to be implemented straight away if he was to achieve his goals. Thoughts of Calogero's stranglehold on Cesare's business, and by extension his life, ebbed from his brain as he basked in that dazzling smile and lost himself in Ida's mesmerising pale green eyes.

She might be Calogero's granddaughter, but she had the face of a Botticelli angel and the form of a young Venus. Rose-gold hair falling in waves around pale shoulders. A rosebud mouth. Slender curves and an aura almost of innocence that even now intrigued him.

Innocence!

That dragged him back to reality.

She couldn't be anything like innocent. Not when she'd been a vital part of the old man's scheme. She was the one who had joined the ancient and proud Brunetti family. As her grandfather's heir and now as Cesare's wife, she'd benefited from Calogero's manipulative schemes.

Cesare spun on his heel and strode to the antique side-board.

'I'm having a drink. Do you want one?'

Silence for a second. Then an unexpectedly husky voice made his belly clamp tight. 'Thank you. I'll have what you're having.'

Her voice was pure sexual invitation. That raspy whisper belonged to a lounge singer in some smoky bar, all deca-dent invitation and sultry innuendo.

Cesare swallowed, annoyed to find his pulse racing and his collar too tight. As if he'd never had a woman before. As if he were the nineteen-year-old and she twenty-seven.

As if he didn't know about grasping women.

Or the dangers of letting lust conquer common sense.

Yet, to his amazement, Cesare was in half a mind to dis-pense with the preliminaries and take her now, hard and fast, right where she stood. Or maybe against the window with the lights of Rome at her back where anyone looking up from the piazza could see him debauching her.

The turbulent emotions he'd held in harness all day were close to detonation point.

That realisation steadied his hand as he poured them both a glass of Sangiovese. Cesare hadn't come this far to bend at the first provocation. No matter how tempting.

He'd learned the dangers of losing control. If his dead father had done the same, the family wouldn't be in this predicament.

He swung around, a glass in each hand, to find her still standing in the centre of the room. Did she know the over-head light turned her hair to glorious fire? Or that it re-vealed her pebbled nipples beneath that shimmering slip of nothing?

Undoubtedly. Ida was an expert at managing her appear-ance. Demure dresses in pastel shades before their wedding, emphasising her youth and apparent innocence. And today's bridal dress, a mix of virgin and vamp designed to mess with his head.

Cesare passed her a glass, ignoring the frisson of sensation when their fingers touched. He raised his glass and took a sip, savouring the wine. Its familiarity steadied him. It was from the family vineyard, a reminder of things he'd once taken for granted that were under threat.

Not for much longer, if his plans succeeded.

'Are you coming to bed soon?'

Her soft voice was pure temptation. She looked at him with big eyes and he wondered how often she'd used that look to get what she wanted.

But he, Cesare Brunetti, was not at her beck and call.

'No. I have work to do.'

Her eyebrows wrinkled into a frown. To his annoyance that only made her look cute as well as sexy. He felt a growl of vexation build at the back of his throat.

'But it's our wedding night!'

'And?'

He shouldn't enjoy her look of dismay quite so much. But after the stresses of the past months, it was one tiny pleasure to give in, just a little, to his white-hot anger. She and her grandfather thought they could yank his chain and have him obey like a whipped dog. He'd had no choice about this marriage but, no matter what the temptation, *he* controlled his sex life.

Cesare took another sip of wine, savouring the rich flavour. That was one success at least. Even if the rest of his plans failed, today he'd secured the vineyard and the jobs of all the workers there. As for the rest of the Brunetti holdings—

'And…don't you want…?'

She shook her head as if too shy to speak plainly. The

idea would have amused him if he weren't fed up with pretence.

'Don't I want sex, do you mean?'

Cesare let his gaze travel deliberately down her slender body. He reached her bare feet with their pale pink painted toenails, then trailed his stare back to her face. Her cheeks were flushed and her neck blotchy with heat.

So, she wasn't quite as poised as she appeared.

'I like sex,' he said slowly. 'But I have my standards.'

'Sorry?'

She flinched and a few drops of wine spattered across the gleaming silk she wore.

Cesare thought of what lay beneath the fabric and paused.

Because he *did* want her.

He'd felt the tug of arousal the first day old man Calogero had led her in to meet him, looking like some wide-eyed innocent. He'd felt it again and again at every meeting. Never more so than today when she'd become his in the eyes of the world.

Some primal part of him wanted nothing more than to claim her physically, forgetting the debacle of the last six months as he lost himself inside her.

He resented that she made him so desperate. Which was why he would not, *could* not, give in to that need.

'I don't understand.'

He took in the uptilt of her jaw and the way her mouth flattened and registered that she *still* looked too delectable. What would it take to eradicate the weakness he felt around her?

'Then let me make it absolutely clear.'

He paused, watching her breasts hitch with her indrawn breath, feeling an answering ache in his groin. In the past there'd been no need for sexual abstinence and Cesare had enjoyed his lovers, but a man had his pride.

'I have no interest in bedding a woman like you. A protégé of that twisted criminal who's damaged not just my family but plenty of innocents besides. I wouldn't touch you if you were the last woman in Italy.'

CHAPTER TWO

HE MEANT IT. He really meant it.

Stunned, Ida felt his words stab into soft flesh.

She gripped the wine glass so hard it was a wonder it didn't shatter. Wine slopped over the brim onto her hand, but she didn't look down. She couldn't break Cesare's gaze. It felt as if she was locked into the high beam of that laser-like stare.

Yet it seemed imperative that she keep hold of the glass, so she wrapped her left hand around the frozen knuckles of her right, trying to steady it.

Because it gave her something to think about other than the hatred in her husband's dark brown eyes.

Before this she'd thought his eyes velvety and warm, a welcome contrast to the mean glitter of her grandfather's furious stare. Now Cesare's eyes were so cold she felt ice crackle along her bones and frost her skin. He looked piti-less.

'But I—'

'Don't bother making excuses. It doesn't matter.'

'Of course it matters. We're *married*!'

This was some terrible mistake. They'd promised to build a future together, to—

'Exactly. You got what you wanted. A high-profile husband and the cachet of an aristocratic family name to open doors for your social aspirations.'

Ida shook her head, hair swirling wildly around her face. How could he think that? What about the times, albeit brief, when they'd talked and she'd thought that they shared the beginnings of a real connection?

But when she opened her mouth to object he spoke over her.

'Your grandfather got what he wanted, didn't he? All those years scheming and cheating to bring down the family he hated. To manipulate us and strike a fatal blow that gives him control over our company and us.'

Cesare paused, chest heaving, and Ida felt the fury throb through him. It clogged the air between them.

If she could have moved away she would. Ida knew how dangerous a truly irate man could be. Beneath her, one ankle buckled as if that old injury had resurfaced, and it took everything she had to stand tall. The only parts of her that moved were her thundering heart and shaking hands.

She wouldn't cower. Yet she had a horrible, dizzy feeling, as if the walls pushed in and she might collapse. Cesare made it sound like her grandfather had orchestrated their marriage as part of some vengeful scheme. But that couldn't be true. Her grandfather *was* thrilled about the wedding, and he used people for his own ends, but Cesare was wealthy and powerful. He made his own choices.

'But he wanted more, didn't he?' Cesare snarled. 'It wasn't enough just to ruin the family enterprises, he wanted what he'd never had. A chance to lord it over us. Acceptance in polite society. Entry to the world that draws the line at gangsters, blackmailers and murderers.'

Her gasp was loud in the thick silence.

With an effort Ida finally managed to swallow, though it felt like her throat closed around shards of glass.

'You're exaggerating.'

Her grandfather was awful. No one knew that better than her. But a murderer?

'Which part of the truth don't you like, Ida? That I don't want you in my bed, or that I won't play your grandfather's games and pretend he's honest and respectable?'

She wasn't going to beg for Cesare in her bed.

'I know he's not honest.' He was ruthless and vicious, but he wasn't a murderer. Was he? She frowned. 'But he's not a murderer. And you're mistaken about me.'

'Am I?' Cesare put his glass down and folded his arms. The movement accentuated his height and the breadth of his chest as if he deliberately tried to intimidate her. 'You mean he forced you into this marriage?'

Ida sucked in much-needed air then finally scraped out a response. 'No, he didn't force me.'

Because she'd seen marriage to Cesare as her chance to escape. She'd believed they could build something special together. Because she wanted him and thought he wanted her.

More fool her!

The stabbing pain was worse now, carving through her middle.

She looked into that handsome, severe face, noting the sneering curl to Cesare's sculped mouth and the flare of chiselled nostrils, as if he detected a foul smell. And those eyes... There was no mistaking that expression for anything but distaste.

Suddenly Ida felt ashamed of the hopes and plans she'd woven around this man. Of the tenderness she'd harboured and the budding attraction she'd felt.

More than budding. She had a full-blown crush on the man.

Correction. She'd *had* one. It wouldn't survive this, for

which she was thankful. Imagine pining for a man who looked at you like you were dirt under his polished shoe!

She'd been sucked in by what she realised now had been polite manners and his determination not to reveal his true feelings until the deed was done and they were married.

Because you were naïve.

Because he was the first man since your dad to be gentle and kind to you.

Because you're a late bloomer and you've never had a chance for romance.

'You admit you married me of your own free will?'

Fury spiked and she welcomed it. It was better than the devastating feeling that everything inside her was collapsing into an aching void.

'Are you hard of hearing, Cesare?'

He blinked and she saw his pulse throb, quick and hard in his jaw. He hadn't expected her to challenge him.

A lifetime's training told her she shouldn't have spoken so. Provoking or even inadvertently annoying a man who was bigger and stronger than you was a huge mistake. But as she tensed, ready for his response, she saw him draw a deep breath and lower his shoulders, as if seeking calm.

Ida stared. The way Cesare reined in his anger when she argued back told her he *was* completely different to her grandfather. He was irate but instinct told her he'd use only words as his weapons.

Stupid to feel a burst of admiration at the knowledge.

'So you admit you married by choice. You were greedy for what I had and you didn't. The aristocratic title and connections. And the chance to be a spy for your grandfather in the enemy camp. He thinks he has the upper hand now, but he'll want to know I'm toeing the line at all times, so everything goes just as he wants.'

Ida considered denying it. But that would leave her needing to explain why she *had* agreed to marry a man she barely knew.

She felt like she'd shrivel up and die if Cesare realised she'd acted on sheer romantic dreams and a desperation to escape.

He'd scoff at the first. As for the second, he thought her in cahoots with her grandfather. He'd never believe her protestations. Even if by some miracle he eventually did, he'd never understand.

For despite his talk of her grandfather having the upper hand, Cesare was one of the strongest, most capable and determined people she'd met. He radiated power and self-control. It was one of the first things she'd noticed about him. Along with his looks and charisma. And she'd read about his formidable business acumen, even though he wasn't yet thirty.

He wouldn't understand what it was like to be helpless. How desperate you could be. How much you'd dare.

'Why did *you* marry *me*, Cesare?'

At last she managed to unfreeze her muscles and took a couple of steps to a side table, where she put down the glass. She hoped she looked nonchalant though she felt like a marionette, pulled on jerky strings.

Cesare's stare, less ferocious but no less daunting, had her folding her arms tight around her middle. How she wished she'd worn that robe. Or something much more substantial than silk and naked skin. Every time she moved, the shift of thin material across bare flesh made her skin prickle.

'You're going to play the innocent?'

Ida shrugged. What could she say that he'd believe? 'It's a simple question.'

'This is pointless.' He lifted his glass and took a long swallow as if he needed something to ease his mood.

'You owe me more than insults.' Ida watched him lower his glass, surprise on his features. 'I *married* you today. So you can oblige me by explaining your insinuations.'

Her tone was frosty. It would take years of practice to achieve Cesare's glacial disdain or her grandfather's venomous fury, but it felt good not to leash her feelings as she'd done for so long.

She lifted her chin and ignored the hurried thump of her heart against her breast, warning her to be careful. She'd spent most of her life being careful and look where it had got her.

'Are you going to explain or are you going to drink yourself into a stupor because you're in a bad mood?'

Ida felt her eyes widen as the words escaped. She'd never dared speak like that in her life. But Cesare didn't seem shocked. He merely raised his eyebrows and, holding her gaze, lifted the crystal wine glass to his lips and drank deeply.

It was the strangest feeling, staring back at those dark eyes. Noticing too the way his throat muscles worked.

It felt…intimate. His glittering stare made her hot and edgy. Aware of him at an elemental level as tension corkscrewed low in her body.

Ida blushed. That wasn't just challenging but also sexual. She felt it even though she couldn't explain how she knew it.

Cesare was toying with her. She spun on her heel, ready to leave, when he spoke.

'You know what your grandfather is. You live with him.'

'Actually, I don't. Not usually.'

He frowned. Maybe her grandfather had painted a picture of them as a close-knit family. It was the sort of thing he'd do if it suited him.

'I'm no apologist for him, but this is the first I've heard about blackmail or murder.'

Cesare stared at her for a long moment then gestured to the sofas. 'Let's sit.'

'I'd rather stand.'

This wasn't going to be a cosy chat. It took all her strength to hear him out, pretending she didn't care that he despised her or that she felt defenceless in nothing but navy silk. But she had to know it all.

Cesare scowled. Because he felt guilty over his accusations? More likely he wasn't used to a woman saying no to him.

Cesare Brunetti had the looks and charisma to make women say yes.

Ida raised her eyebrows, pretending to a calm she didn't feel. 'You were going to explain.'

'It's straightforward enough. Fausto Calogero hated my grandfather and vowed revenge on him and my family. Now he's taking that revenge.'

'Why? What did your family do?'

Cesare stiffened, his cheeks hollowing in an expression of pure hauteur. 'Nothing. Except look after the girl your grandfather attacked and call the police.'

'He attacked a girl?'

Ida rubbed her hands up her bare arms as the chill inside her turned arctic.

'He claimed she wanted him but then changed her mind. But she was the one with the black eye. He would have raped her if *my* grandfather hadn't heard her screams. That was when Fausto left Italy, before the authorities could arrest him. He blamed my grandfather, who was from a respected family, for turning the town against him.'

Ida swallowed the sour taste on her tongue. It shouldn't surprise her. It *didn't* surprise her. Yet she felt ashamed. As if her grandfather's crimes tainted her.

Was it true that her marriage was part of a scheme for

vengeance? She'd heard him often enough muttering about getting his own back on enemies in the old country, though he'd built a new life in England.

Ida shifted her weight, the phantom ache from the old ankle injury throbbing in time with her heartbeat, making her reach out to steady herself by gripping the back of a nearby armchair.

'Go on.'

'You know the rest. He's been scheming ever since to build a fortune and bring us down, any way he can. When my father became CEO there were more problems that I've tried to rectify.' Cesare spread his hands in a gesture that opened up those imposing shoulders. 'But Calogero already had his hooks in too deep. There's a liquidity problem. He had the power to destroy the company. Unless I agreed to his terms.'

Ida's hand pressed against her breastbone, holding in her thundering heart. She felt sick. Because, as outlandish as it sounded, she could believe it only too well. Her grandfather was devious and totally ruthless.

'That was the blackmail? Marry me to save the company?'

Cesare narrowed his eyes then shook his head. 'There's no point playing the innocent. He made it clear you're part of this. You know why I married you.'

'To save your family business,' she whispered as the pieces fell into place.

Of course Cesare Brunetti hadn't decided she'd make his ideal wife. That had been foolish naïvety.

What did she have to recommend her? She didn't move in his rarefied circles. She wasn't sophisticated or glamorous. She didn't speak Italian, just a smattering of phrases.

He was powerful and privileged, with the hauteur of a man used to the best of everything.

How had he felt as he'd watched her walk down the aisle on his enemy's arm? The man who threatened the business his family had built and nurtured for generations.

Cesare could probably snap his fingers and have the most gorgeous, talented, interesting women at his beck and call. Why would he want someone who had nothing to recommend her but her eagerness to please?

Ida didn't even have to wonder why her grandfather had lied and said she was a party to the scheme. It was the sort of thing he'd do, to turn the screws and inflame an already dreadful situation. He felt no softness towards her. He didn't even like her.

She doubted Fausto Calogero liked anyone, except maybe Bruno, his head of security. The thought of that brute sent a shudder down her spine.

Cesare returned to the bar, refilling his glass. 'Now that you've stopped pretending—'

'Murder.' Her voice sounded strangled. She swallowed and tried again. 'You said he was a murderer.'

Cesare swung back to her. Something about his expression made her think that for the first time he suspected she didn't know the whole story. It was cold comfort. Nothing could breach the chasm between them now.

'Your grandfather's campaign of revenge wouldn't have worked if he'd just waited, hoping my father would make more bad commercial decisions. He *created* the circumstances that almost ruined us. He had the fire set that burned one of our factories to the ground. Two people died, a security guard who'd been knocked on the head and a manager working late, catching up on paperwork.'

Ida's breath stopped, her fingers clawing the chair's upholstery.

It was one thing to know her grandfather was ruthless and cruel. It was another to hear this.

She had no doubt there was more. Nor did she question Cesare's certainty that her grandfather was behind the arson. It all made a terrible sort of sense as she remembered various cryptic comments she'd overheard.

'Nothing to say? No objections?'

Ida didn't meet his stare. What was the point? She couldn't remember ever feeling so exhausted. So hollow.

Amazing to think that a bare hour ago she'd been excited and optimistic for the future. Her lips twisted in a grimace that matched the wrenching pain deep inside.

'Yet you're doing business with him. You've married his granddaughter.'

He shrugged, those broad shoulders seeming to expand, or maybe it was that her view of the room narrowed. Everything fell away except for this handsome man with a brutally hard expression. Even his perfectly fitted dark suit now looked like a lesson in severity and disdain.

'Doing business with him is necessary if the enterprise my family built over generations is to survive. As for marrying you…' His lips twisted. 'You know that was a condition of the deal. No marriage, no business.'

Cesare paused, his lips turning down as if he too tasted the bitter tang that filled her mouth.

'But you need to know, Ida…' Icy fingers closed around her throat at the sound of her name in that harsh voice. 'I don't take kindly to blackmail. Don't expect me to pander to your whims, or Calogero's.'

Ida met his eyes then, drawn by the sheer depth of hatred in his voice. What she read there stopped any thought of trying, again, to explain that she hadn't been party to her grandfather's schemes. She looked away.

Perhaps, one day, Cesare would hear her out. Not now. Despite the way he leashed his anger, it was clear he was at the edge of his control. She felt his ire in the thickened air like electricity sparking between them.

She sympathised. She'd thought she knew the worst about her grandfather, but these revelations shocked her. She'd learnt to fear the old man. Now she felt ashamed to share his blood.

What else had he done? He'd built a fortune and lived lavishly. Was it all based on criminal activity? No wonder her mother had grabbed the first chance to run away from him. If only Ida had been able to do the same.

She sucked in a breath, trying to calm her rackety pulse. 'What now, Cesare?'

Ida fixed her gaze on the black silk of his bow tie. She couldn't meet his eyes. Not feeling this terrible guilt and horror, the taint of the old man's crimes.

'What now?' Cesare's voice was like that bow tie, smooth and beautiful but severe. 'I don't know what you plan to do but I have calls to make. As for tomorrow…' He paused, and she watched his chest rise on a deep breath as if the prospect of tomorrow was unwelcome. Finally, something they shared! 'Tomorrow we continue the pretence of being a happily married couple.'

'You can't be serious!'

Her gaze shot up, to find him scrutinising her. This time she read nothing in his stare. Not distaste or impatience. Not even anger.

It felt as if he couldn't be bothered wasting his energies on her when he had more important concerns.

'Naturally I'm serious. We agreed to this marriage and now we'll live with it. In public. I have stipulations, of course. Expectations to be met and ground rules you'll need to abide by—'

'Not now,' she whispered, pressing her hand to her churning stomach. 'I'm suddenly very tired.'

Nausea swelled. She'd thought this situation couldn't get worse, but now he asked the impossible. To expect her to act in public as if they had a real marriage while in private they were enemies. To live a pretence of what she'd believed just a short time ago was real...

It was mockery and degradation on top of devastation. Her heart seized up at the very idea.

'Then we'll continue this conversation in the morning.'

Ida swallowed convulsively, forcing back bile at the idea of continuing their discussion. The flesh between her shoulder blades crawled as if an army of spiders danced there.

She turned away, hurrying to her room. But, as in a nightmare, the more urgent her steps the slower she seemed to move.

By the time she finally made it through the open door she almost sobbed her relief. She paused only long enough to snick the lock shut before stumbling to the bathroom.

A scant hour later Ida stood in the centre of the opulent bedroom, checking she hadn't forgotten anything.

Her wedding gown still hung in the wardrobe, as did most of the clothes her grandfather had chosen. There was no point taking more than she could easily carry. She had to travel light, since she'd be hitchhiking.

Stoically she suppressed a jitter of fear at the idea of getting into a car with a stranger. She understood the risks. But the alternative, to stay with a man who despised her, was impossible.

Ida had precious little money. One of her grandfather's methods for keeping her under his thumb had been to ensure she didn't have cash to strike out on her own. Not that it had stopped her trying.

She opened her shoulder bag, checking the contents. Passport. A couple of euro notes, a few pounds, the string of natural pearls her grandfather had produced for her to wear at the wedding. Not because it was an heirloom, precious with family sentiment, but to flaunt his wealth.

Ida's gaze caught on the plain wedding band she wore and the stonking great diamond solitaire beside it. How had she ever imagined Cesare had chosen them as tokens of respect and affection? They were like the pearls. Cold, hard symbols of wealth and ownership.

She'd belonged to a man who'd never cared for her but kept her to use in his obscene scheme. He'd passed her to a man who not only didn't care about her but also actively hated her.

Gritting her teeth, she pulled the rings off and dropped them in her bag, zipping it securely.

She had no idea how much she'd get for the jewellery but selling it was necessary. It would also bring enormous satisfaction.

Ida lifted her other bag off the bed and marched to the door.

CHAPTER THREE

Four years later

CESARE FROWNED AS the limousine turned into a dingy alley. The London downpour was so heavy it should have made everything look cleaner.

Not this place. Even the night failed to soften its squalid edges. Clogged gutters threatened to overflow and, while the road surface glittered slickly, nothing could make these buildings look clean. The neon signs were lurid and the few people on the street reinforced the sleazy atmosphere.

Ida worked *here*?

It didn't make sense. Maybe Calogero *had* told the truth when he said he didn't know where she was. Cesare hadn't believed it.

As the old man's heiress, she had no need to work in this seedy area.

He almost leaned forward to query whether they had the right address, but his staff didn't make such mistakes. Neither his driver nor security staff. Nor the investigators he'd paid handsomely to locate his errant wife.

Wife.

The word sat in the pit of his belly like a lump of cold lead.

In the years since their wedding Ida had never been a

wife. She'd been a resented burden, foisted on him. From the first she'd been a thorn in his side with her almost unconscious sensuality that threatened to seduce him even when he deplored her unscrupulous ways. Only his fury at being forced to marry her had kept him from sleeping with her. Then, with her disappearance four years ago, she'd become a scandal and an embarrassment.

He'd had more important things to do than track her down. Until now.

She was an enemy and an enigma. But only when his investigators reported back had he realised how much of an enigma. Though they'd located her, they hadn't been able to track all her movements through those years. Not surprising when she'd taken a new name not listed on official databases. Yet it was their information about her early life that had astounded him.

Far from growing up in Calogero's London home, after she was orphaned she'd lived most of her life on a remote Scottish island so small it didn't have a regular year-round ferry service. She'd visited London every year, staying with her grandfather for no more than a month each time.

It was bizarre. Almost as bizarre as finding her here.

The car halted. Instantly a woman approached, her red mesh singlet top, vinyl miniskirt and sexualised prowl advertising her profession.

Cesare left it to his bodyguard to send her away while he got out and strode to the club's narrow entrance. The bouncer, taking in his vehicle and his tailoring, stepped smartly aside.

The dark entry smelled of cigarettes, cheap perfume and alcohol. He strode forward, pushing open a heavy door, and sound hit him. Raucous music and male laughter. Surely the investigators had it wrong. Ida couldn't work here.

His mouth tightened as he took in the pale gleam of gyrating female flesh on what passed for a stage. The other women, some topless, some in what passed, barely, for dresses, were entertaining men at tables around the room.

He'd been warned but he hadn't believed it.

Until his gaze alighted on the bar that ran along one wall and he saw a bright head. A gleam of red-gold, a colour he remembered as clearly as if four years' absence were just four hours. An upright posture, like a dancer's.

The sounds dimmed, replaced by a jackhammering that he eventually registered as his pulse.

It couldn't be her, though the slicked-back hair, pulled tight against her scalp, was the same colour as Ida's. This woman, looking down at the glasses she filled with whisky, wore make-up so bright and heavy she looked like a mannequin. She was all pale skin, scarlet lips and exaggerated eyelashes.

Her black leather lace-up bustier left her shoulders and arms bare and revealed plump breasts on the verge of spilling free.

Even in her translucent-seeming bridal gown Ida hadn't looked so obvious.

Cesare swallowed as he recalled her on their wedding night. She'd dressed for him in blue silk and nothing else. He'd carried that memory ever since.

That night he'd wanted to forget his vow to have nothing to do with the woman who'd been forced on him. He'd wanted to take what she offered. That wanting had fuelled his anger to combustible levels and for the first time since adolescence he'd truly lost his temper.

The woman behind the bar had Ida's colouring but wasn't her. She didn't have that understated allure. She was blatantly, smack-in-the-groin sexy, with her shiny Cupid's bow lips, creamy bosom and narrow waist.

If those weren't blatant enough, she wore long, black

gloves past her elbows, that for some reason looked incredibly erotic. As did the black velvet ribbon around her throat.

Was it the contrast of black leather and velvet against soft skin? The thought of his olive-skinned hands touching her pale flesh?

He remembered the contrast when he'd taken Ida's hand in church. Just as he recalled the pillowy softness of her lips beneath his in that perfunctory kiss.

Heat speared his groin, rising to fill his gut in a churn of desperate hunger.

But Cesare didn't do desperate. Especially not for a tarty barmaid in a dive like this. He was turning when the woman lifted her head and smiled at someone at the end of the bar.

Shock smashed his lungs, stealing his air while his belly clenched in response to the unseen blow.

Ida.

The woman behind the bar, a living, breathing invitation to sex in its raunchiest forms, was his wife!

And he wasn't the only one watching her. Half the men in the place were ogling.

Disbelief vied with distaste and a fury so strong he felt it as a physical surge through his body.

Cesare had been taught to control his impulses, to master anger and think clearly, act logically and honourably. Four years ago, he'd let his control slip and regretted it ever since. Yet as he took in the scene before him it was through a hazy red mist.

It was only when pain shot up his wrists that he realised he'd clenched his hands so tight they throbbed.

Dimly he was aware of a familiar presence beside him. Lorenzo, his chief of security. But this wasn't a matter for staff. This was personal.

Ida was pouring a tray of drinks when she sensed someone approach. Someone who stood close.

Her nape prickled. She'd become better at handling importunate customers with a smile and a quip, and by moving quickly out of reach when necessary, but some of the insistent, aggressive ones scared her.

She glanced to the end of the bar but Mike, the shift manager who sometimes looked out for her, had gone.

She fixed on a careful smile. But it bled from her face as she lifted her eyes, then lifted them further.

White noise rushed in her ears. She had that woozy feeling she recalled from years ago when she'd broken her ankle. She'd looked up from the atrium's marble floor to see her grandfather surveying her coolly from halfway up the staircase and wondered for a second if she'd imagined the slap that had sent her tumbling.

Now she wondered if she could be imagining this.

For the eyes that met hers were familiar. Rich, dark brown eyes that didn't look cold but blazed with heat.

Cesare.

She'd never expected to see him again.

It was her grandfather she was hiding from, not her husband.

Despite her shock, she pulled her lips into a grimace of dark amusement. Cesare had made it abundantly clear he'd be happier without her in his life.

Why was he here?

The whisky bottle thudded onto the bar. There was only one reason he'd come. He must be in London on business and wanted some R and R. Ida had learned in her short time here not to be surprised at the wide range of clientele with a taste for the sordid.

She'd imagined Cesare surrounded by high-society women, the sort who looked like they'd been born wearing haute couture. But maybe he had other predilections.

Her voice was tight as the words jerked out. 'Would you like a drink?'

A bubble of hysterical laughter rose. Where had that come from? Treating him like just another customer.

Was there a chance he wouldn't recognise her? It had been years. The lighting was low, her make-up thick and—

'What I *want* is an explanation. But not here.' He jerked his head towards the door. 'Come on.'

'Sorry?'

Her voice rose and she flinched, sensing heads turning their way.

'We can't talk here.' His lips barely moved, and she realised he spoke through gritted teeth. 'It's time to leave.'

'Maddy?' It was Mike, the shift manager. 'Need help?'

Cesare didn't even look his way. 'She doesn't. This is private family business.'

'Family business? Who are you, her brother?'

Cesare glanced past her then, his look pure macho threat. 'No. Her husband.'

Ida gaped, her mind reeling. The last thing she'd expected was for Cesare to seek her out, much less claim her as his wife. He was ashamed of her. He hated her!

'Maddy? Is this true?'

She turned to see Mike frowning. He'd taken her under his wing when she'd come to replace Jo. He'd been kind in his own way, and she was grateful.

'Technically, but—'

'It's true,' Cesare said across her, his soft tone threaded with steel. 'And she needs to leave now.'

'Now wait on!' she gasped. He couldn't come here and make demands.

'Alternatively, I have the resources to make business very, very difficult here.' Cesare used the dulcet tone of a man used to getting what he wanted instantly. A man who wouldn't take no for an answer. Those dark eyes moved back to her, fixing her to the spot. 'Is that what you want? For me to bring down a lifetime's trouble on the head of your friend here?'

Ida had never been afraid of Cesare the way she'd been of her grandfather. Both were powerful, single-minded and used to getting their own way, but she'd always felt there was a line Cesare wouldn't cross. She'd never felt physically threatened by him.

Yet looking into those blazing eyes beneath deceptively heavy lids, she saw a man ready to make good on his threat to make trouble. She had no loyalty to the club. She hated the place. But Mike had been good to her and Jo. He didn't deserve trouble. Plus Jo would return to work here soon and desperately needed the job.

Ida wanted to tell Cesare to go to hell. But if he'd found her here, he'd find her again. Better to discover what he wanted and get it over with. So she shoved down her indignation and shock and turned to Mike.

'It's almost the end of my shift. Could I leave early?'

Ida glanced back at Cesare, noting for the first time the man in the impeccable suit behind him. He was more discreet than her grandfather's bodyguards, but she recognised the type and shivered.

The air was so thick you could cut it with a blade as the men surveyed each other.

Mike broke the silence. 'You're sure, Maddy?'

No, she wasn't. She didn't want to go with Cesare. But the alternative was just as bad. She nodded jerkily.

Why had Cesare come? What did he want?

'Okay. Give me five and I'll get your pay.'

'She doesn't need it,' Cesare said, his voice dripping disdain. 'She—'

'I certainly do need it.' She spoke across him. She

hadn't worked here for weeks to walk out with nothing. 'Thanks, Mike.' She smiled at him, her facial muscles stiff. 'I appreciate it.'

With one last, curious look, he headed for the back room.

Ida reached for the whisky to finish pouring drinks. It gave her an excuse not to look at Cesare.

'Leave it! We'll go now.'

His hand shot out to shackle her wrist and she jerked away. '*Don't* touch me, Cesare!'

She half lifted the bottle as if daring him to try and saw surprise widen those narrowed eyes. Behind him his bodyguard shifted as if ready to intervene.

Ida had never hit anyone in her life. The thought made her feel nauseous. But they weren't to know.

How dared he come in here making demands, treating her like a possession? Disrupting her life after all this time?

A bruised corner of her heart silently keened at the way the sight of him opened up all the pain she'd tried to put behind her. She'd told herself that was in the past. That she was over him and that the pain, shame and distress his revelations had caused were long gone.

Now she knew better.

With a shuddering breath that actually hurt, given the tight lacing of Jo's clothes, she broke eye contact, focusing on the whisky.

By some miracle her hand was steady. As if the roiling nerves inside didn't exist. But then, from the age of eight she'd been perfecting the art of not revealing her feelings when she was upset or afraid.

Except with Cesare. That night in Rome he'd undone her with his words and his contempt. Because that day she'd

actually imagined herself free from all the bad things, free
to start a new life the way she wanted to live it.

'You shouldn't be here.'

His voice was low, rippling over her bare shoulders
and the top of her spine like a wintry breeze, drawing her
flesh tight.

'It's none of your business.'

She didn't bother looking up, just poured the last glass
and slid the tray away, nodding to the waitress who'd come
to collect it.

Ida watched the other woman's gaze trace Cesare's tall
form, snagging on his wide shoulders in his custom-made
suit and that chiselled profile. Finally, after lingering longer than necessary, she lifted the tray and sauntered off
with an exaggerated swing of the hips.

'What I do hasn't been your business for four years,'
Ida added, turning to put the bottle back.

'That's where you're wrong, Ida. You're still very much
my business, whether you want it to be or not.'

She froze, heart hammering against her ribs. Her
skimpy outfit was no protection against his scathing stare.
She could *feel* it, like an ice cube sliding down her spine
and chilling her marrow.

Ida firmed her jaw and lifted her chin. She'd done nothing wrong. She had nothing to be ashamed of.

'Here you are, Maddy.' Mike was at her side, her wages
in his big hand. Relief flooded her. For a moment she'd
imagined leaving without the cash they needed for the rent.
He leaned closer. 'Are you really okay?'

Wordlessly she nodded, his concern touching her.

When she'd first come here Mike, with his brawn and
pugnacious air, had made her nervous but she'd been so
grateful for his presence.

'Fine, thanks. I'm sorry for leaving early.'

He shook his head. 'Don't fret. But tell Jo to be on time next week.'

She nodded. 'Will do. Bye, Mike. Thanks for everything.'

Cesare's eyes narrowed as he watched the interplay between Ida and the burly guy who'd positioned himself as Ida's champion. Against *him*, her husband!

He felt all sorts of wrong inside. Flummoxed by a riot of unfamiliar feelings. Undone by the surge of anger that, for only the second time he could recall, he had trouble harnessing. The last time had been his wedding night, when Ida had sauntered in, ready for sex, and he'd unleashed his pent-up fury at Calogero's machinations.

He'd been so tempted by her, despite what she represented.

Why was it that with this one woman Cesare's control shattered? At other times his words and actions were careful and considered. He prided himself on his cool head, never being led by emotions. He'd not have been able to deal with Calogero otherwise.

He watched her shrug into a long raincoat, belting it tight around that narrow waist, and the answer came to him.

Because this woman gets under your skin as no one ever has.

Because you want her. Desperately. Despite who she is and what she's done. Even now, seeing her in this place.

And you hate that need you can't conquer. Because it makes you weak.

Cesare's mood was sombre as they walked through the now sprinkling rain to the limousine. It darkened when she baulked at the open door.

'We'll go back to my hotel,' he murmured, gesturing for her to get in.

'No! Not there.'

Did the idea of being alone with him bother her so much? Her gaze flicked to the car with its door open and driver waiting impassively, then over Cesare's shoulder to where he guessed Lorenzo stood.

'You'll be perfectly safe.'

Safer than here in this insalubrious neighbourhood. The fact she hesitated, as if fearing for her safety with him, felt like a slap in the face.

'There's an all-night café—'

'Absolutely not. I won't have this discussion in public.'

She opened her mouth as if to argue then snapped it shut. For a moment longer she stared at him from under lowered brows. 'Okay,' she said at last. 'We'll go to mine. It's close.'

Would Joe be there? Cesare had told himself he'd meet Ida briefly and get what he'd come for. Yet now that wasn't enough. His curiosity was aroused. Not least about her man.

'Excellent. I'll look forward to seeing your home.'

Her mouth twisted. She didn't like the idea. Too bad. She wouldn't get rid of him as easily as she'd ditched him four years ago.

He strove to look calm while molten metal poured through his veins. Cesare shouldn't be surprised that she had a lover, yet it felt wrong. He tasted bitterness on his tongue and his hands clenched iron hard.

What sort of man was Joe to let his lover work at a place like that?

Cesare flexed his fingers. He'd soon find out. And on the way he'd try to fathom why it was that, out of all the emotions bombarding him, the strongest felt like jealousy.

He'd never felt possessive of women. He liked their company and enjoyed sex, but he'd never felt strongly enough about one to be jealous. For that he could thank his father, whose disastrous mistakes of judgement served as a horrible warning.

Cesare's nape prickled at the idea he was envious of the man who shared Ida's bed. Until he realised it wasn't personal. It was simply because, though he didn't like her, Ida was still his wife.

His.

Wife.

All those traditional mores around fidelity sprang to the fore, as if within the modern man dwelt the sort of traditional male who'd lived generations before.

But then, as his mother had died when he was a baby and his father had abandoned him to follow a series of ever more unsuitable women, he'd been raised by his grandfather. The old man had instilled a sense of family honour in Cesare, hence his determination to save the family business no matter what the cost.

Could those values really be why he hadn't taken a lover since their farce of a wedding? No, that was just because he'd had other priorities these past four years.

'Are you ready?' he murmured when still she didn't move.

'What is it you want?' she whispered.

Cesare's patience wore thin. After the way she'd run in the night and the huge scandal he'd had to weather, she begrudged him one face-to-face chat?

'We'll discuss it in private. Not on the street.'

With one last, frowning glance, she got in.

The flash of long, slender legs in fishnet tights beneath her drab raincoat was a punch to the belly. Or perhaps to his pride.

He didn't want Ida in his life. Never had. Yet the idea his wife, the woman on whom he'd bestowed the proud Brunetti name, was shacked up with another man and working as a prostitute, or something close, shattered his dignity.

Cesare slid into the seat after her, stretching his legs as she gave her address to his driver.

It was good they wouldn't see each other again after tonight. He didn't like the heated, uncomfortable emotions she stirred.

So it was a surprise when, as they drove through the dark, wet streets of London, he found himself thinking, not of the business he'd come to finalise, but about the one thing pride and common sense dictated was off-limits. How satisfying it would be to strip Ida slowly bare.

He'd remove one item of provocative clothing at a time before losing himself in the soft, slick warmth of her femininity. He'd listen to her gasps as he pleasured her and hear the sound of his name, only his, on her lips, as he took her to screaming climax again and again before finding his own completion.

Cesare's breath atrophied in his lungs and he had to drag in oxygen, his heart hammering, his groin tight as if gripped by a vice.

It was good that his self-control was strong enough to withstand such tawdry temptation.

Wasn't it?

CHAPTER FOUR

HER NEIGHBOURHOOD WAS worse than he'd expected. It wasn't a street where anyone would choose to live.

Cesare recognised the signs from some of the community building work he'd done, part of his grandfather's determination to ensure he didn't grow up as an entitled kid with no idea how the other half lived. It had been hands-on work and had left him with a respect for those who survived the difficult circumstances life threw at them. And a distaste for those who preyed on the vulnerable. The pimps, pushers and stand-over men.

Was Joe Ida's pimp? Ice crackled along his bones at the idea.

She'd been selling drinks, not her body at the club, but in a place like that lines blurred. She dressed as if she were for sale.

His belly cramped down on nausea as he followed her into a cement shell of a foyer then up a couple of flights of bare steps. His nose wrinkled at the smell of the stained walls.

Easier to think about the rundown building than Ida's slim, net-clad legs in those ridiculously high patent leather shoes. Or the possibility that she sold more than drinks at that club.

She stopped outside a dingy door and fumbled with

the key. Did she have cold fingers because of her skimpy clothes? Or was she nervous?

The possibility took Cesare aback.

Earlier Ida had been wary but not afraid. He'd read surprise when she saw him, swiftly followed by indignation and resentment. She was clearly a woman used to standing up for herself. Nothing like the fake innocent she'd played before their wedding.

She pushed the door open but it jammed, a chain rattling across the gap.

'Jo? It's me.'

At the sound of the guy's name a confusing welter of feelings rose. So Joe was in the flat.

Cesare moved closer then wished he hadn't when he caught the fresh scent of hyacinths. As if Ida had been working in a spring garden instead of a strip club.

There was another rattle then the door opened so Ida could slip in. It was already closing when Cesare jammed his foot in the gap.

'It's okay, Jo, he's with me.'

Cesare's half-formed assumptions about her boyfriend died as he shouldered his way in and saw the figure behind the door. A slender woman with a short cap of black hair, wary eyes and a massive bruise fading to yellow all down one side of her face. She looked about sixteen. Until he looked closer and realised she was much older.

Her face was taut with surprise melded with anxiety as her gaze climbed to meet his eyes.

'I mean no harm,' he murmured, instinctively seeking to reassure.

She said nothing but jerked her head once and turned to shut the door. The chain and a bolt had been inexpertly fitted and, by the look of it, recently. Instinct prickled. What had prompted its installation?

'I'm Cesare Brunetti.'

Slowly he held out his hand. The girl looked at it for what seemed an age then slipped her hand in his. 'Jo Randall.'

Jo? Not Joe, as he'd assumed?

Rapidly Cesare recalculated. He'd jumped to conclusions. How many of his assumptions were wrong? The possibility disturbed him.

He strode after Ida, determined to get answers, and almost bumped into her. The flat was tiny and a couple of paces took him halfway across the room.

He surveyed it in a glance. Cramped but with a surprisingly welcoming air, due, he realised, to the clever use of paint and soft furnishings in terracotta and pale citrus that drew attention from the old, mismatched furniture.

But his attention was on Ida, putting her bag on a small table and opening her raincoat. He caught a glimpse of creamy flesh and fishnet stockings and hurriedly lifted his gaze to her face. Her make-up looked even more garish under the overhead light.

She wasn't looking at him. 'What are you doing here, Jo? Did something go wrong at work?' Ida's voice was low as she drew the young woman aside.

Cesare wasn't into eavesdropping. But the space was too small for privacy, though the women spoke in whispers. There was some problem with work, and money.

He took a few steps away, as if inspecting the combined kitchen, living and dining room, taking in the curtain across one end of the room. To partition off a sleeping space?

He frowned. This wasn't how he'd expected Ida to live. She was Calogero's heiress. This only deepened the mystery of her work in a sleazy bar.

Cesare swung around. As if sensing his movement, both women turned to look at him.

He'd waited long enough. They had business to settle, and he chafed to get it over with. But Cesare refused to conduct his business with a stranger listening.

'Ida, we need to talk. Alone.'

Ida glowered as if wishing him anywhere but here, but finally she nodded. He saw her pass the envelope with her wages to Jo.

'Okay. Let's go.'

'Wait.' Jo put a hand on Ida's arm, her gesture and tone urgent. 'Why did he call you Ida?'

Cesare watched emotions flicker across his wife's face, too fast to read.

Finally she shrugged and spread her hands. 'It doesn't matter, Jo.' She paused then went on, as if recognising that her friend deserved more, 'It's my first name. But I haven't used it in ages because I wanted a fresh start. My middle name is Madeline, so I've been Maddy for four years.'

Yet the question was why she'd thought it necessary to hide her identity in London. Who or what was she afraid of?

Him? The idea made Cesare's skin crawl.

But it was hard to believe. He'd been blisteringly furious that night in Rome but, though he'd shocked her with his refusal to sleep with her, he hadn't aimed to frighten her. Nor could she have expected him to seek her out. He'd made it clear he wasn't interested.

Besides, he'd been busy for four years fighting tooth and nail to claw back control of the family's luxury goods company from under Calogero's nose. That had left precious little time for wondering about his missing spouse. The old man had been furious at her disappearance but the legal contract he and Cesare had signed meant he hadn't been able to liquidate the company as he'd threatened. No doubt that infuriated him even more. He'd given up some of his leverage for social gain that hadn't materialised.

'Your name's really Ida?' Her flatmate didn't seem upset at the deceit.

'It doesn't make any difference, Jo.'

'But it *does*. There was a man looking for you.'

'A man?' Ida and Cesare spoke together.

'What man?' Ida took a step nearer her friend, her voice sharp. 'Did he come to the door?'

'No, he was at the entrance to the building, asking if anyone knew an Ida.'

Cesare watched Ida's complexion turn chalky white beneath her make-up and took a step nearer. 'When was this?'

'Yesterday.' Jo looked from Ida to him then back. 'I would have mentioned it if I'd known.'

'You weren't to know.' Ida shook her head. 'But he definitely asked for me by name? You're *sure* it was Ida?'

Jo nodded. 'I'm sure. He waved a photo under my nose, but I didn't really look because he scared me and I wanted to get away. But I did glimpse rose-gold hair like yours.'

She stopped at Ida's quick intake of breath.

'Was he working for you?' Ida spun around. Those light green eyes snared his with an intensity he felt to the soles of his feet. 'Cesare?'

He shook his head. 'No. My investigators located you a while ago, but they had instructions not to approach.'

Because this was business he preferred to conduct in person. He'd only arrived in Britain today, ostensibly for commercial reasons, but the most compelling was to settle things with Ida.

'So if he doesn't work for you…'

He saw her swallow and reach for the back of a chair, fingers gripping so tight they looked bloodless.

'What did he look like, Jo, do you remember?'

'Not nice,' came the immediate answer. 'That's why I remember so well. Short-cropped hair and a nose that had been broken a couple of times. He wore a suit, but he was so bulky his arms were like hams, and he looked like he had no neck.' She paused, her breath hitching. 'He had a voice like the bottom of a gravel pit, and I didn't like the way he looked at me.'

Ida sank onto the spindly chair. The movement was so abrupt Cesare guessed her knees had folded involuntarily.

He moved forward but made room for Jo to crouch before her. 'Maddy? Ida…are you okay?'

Clearly the answer was no. He saw a shudder rack her whole frame. Yet to his surprise Ida nodded, her mouth drawing up in a weak approximation of a smile.

'Of course. I just got a surprise.'

'It's someone you know,' Cesare interjected.

She kept her eyes on her flatmate. 'Just someone from the past I'd rather not run into.'

Which meant, since she hadn't used her real name in four years, that it was someone from before their wedding. An ex-boyfriend? Surely not with that description.

'Time enough to worry about him tomorrow,' she added, her false cheer so jarring that Cesare's hackles rose.

'I haven't seen the guy since,' Jo offered. 'Maybe he's left the area.'

Cesare crossed his arms, taking in the contradiction of Ida's hunched shoulders and fake smile. It was obvious she didn't want anyone prying and discovering her secrets.

It seemed his dear wife had more than one skeleton in her closet.

Technically he didn't need to uncover those secrets. He could finalise what he'd come to do quickly and be gone.

Yet from the first, Ida with her machinations and mysteries had got under his skin like a burr under a saddle. If he intended to eradicate her from his life, he needed to lay those truths completely bare so he could move on.

Maybe this wasn't going to be sorted as quickly as he'd planned.

Ida shifted on the limousine's soft leather seat, her limbs stiff with stress and the effort of fighting a chill that seemed to come from her bones. She wrapped her arms around her torso and folded her legs together.

Too late she'd realised her mistake in leaving the flat in the clothes she'd worn to the club. But she'd been too dazed to think of changing.

She should have demanded they talk in her flat as planned. She didn't like the idea of going to *his* suite, being on *his* territory.

But she'd shied away from reliving her embarrassing history with him before anyone, even a friend like Jo. Ida felt scraped raw whenever she thought of their catastrophic wedding day, her naïvety and Cesare's expression as he'd shredded her tentative hopes. His scorn had been like acid on soft flesh and her even softer heart.

On top of that, the news that her grandfather's henchman was searching for her had scrambled her brain. Jo's description fitted Bruno perfectly. It was hard to think when fear gripped her lungs like a vice.

She swallowed, her throat scratchy as if lined with emery. Bruno.

The man who for years had either looked right through her or, occasionally, directly at her like a starving bulldog slavering over a piece of meat.

No wonder she'd let Cesare lead her to his car without protest. She could only be grateful he'd left his bodyguard to keep an eye on the flat lest Bruno return. Cesare's thoughtfulness in protecting Jo had been unexpected. The flat that had been her refuge now felt flimsy and unsafe. Bruno was looking for her, right at her building, and she was terrified.

Ida shuddered as memories teased her. The way her grandfather had squashed her tentative bid for a little freedom when she was sixteen. He'd threatened to teach her obedience by giving her to Bruno, his hulk of a bodyguard, for a night.

She'd seen Bruno in action with anyone who got too close to Fausto Calogero. The ex-convict was quick and violent. That afternoon he'd leered and licked his lips ostentatiously as he'd stripped her naked with his eyes. Then the two men had laughed as she'd scurried to her room.

You think you're safer with Cesare Brunetti?

The voice in her head goaded and she turned, surveying the figure on the other side of the seat. Even in the gloom he looked imposing as he ignored her, talking on the phone in low, liquid Italian. Her heart gave a little fluttery roll as passing lights defined his handsome, hard profile.

Some things hadn't changed.

She hated the way she still felt vulnerable around him, those old hormonal responses still there under the surface. But surely that was just a sense memory, a remnant of the crush she'd once had on him.

More importantly she *did* feel safe with him.

He might be cold and condescending. They might detest each other. But Cesare Brunetti wasn't like her grandfather or Bruno. He wasn't violent. He wasn't a criminal with no compunction.

What was the worst he could do to her? Give her a stern talking-to?

Ida thought of the way he'd spoken to Jo, reassuring her, taking his time to put her at ease. He'd made it seem easy, which was remarkable given his impressive height and Jo's nervousness after the assault that had left her battered and wary.

Ida closed her eyes and let her head loll against the back of the seat.

She'd told herself for so long that she was free of Cesare. He'd probably instituted divorce proceedings the day she left. He'd certainly washed his hands of her, and she was glad.

Yet from the moment tonight when she'd looked up into dark velvet eyes, she'd realised that was a lie.

In four years she hadn't dated. She'd told herself she was too busy keeping a roof over her head and food in her body, but that unmistakable sensation of heat unfurling as she met Cesare's eyes gave another reason.

However much she disliked the man, she was still attracted to him.

What a nightmare!

Could tonight get any worse?

'We're here.'

That deep voice lassoed her around the middle, pulling tight as if to draw her close. Ida snapped her eyes open and goggled when she saw where they were.

A man in a long uniform coat and tall hat opened the door. 'Ma'am.'

He didn't precisely bow, but his gesture was a mixture of welcome and deference, and she found herself swinging her legs out of the car, grateful she still wore her raincoat over the fishnet tights and ultra-short miniskirt.

'Thank you.'

Then Cesare was beside her. He looped her arm through his and they stepped into a world of hushed luxury.

Ida had never been here, but she'd heard of this iconic hotel. She could only be thankful that at this hour the foyer was empty.

A receptionist greeted them, but Ida kept her head averted, conscious of the image she projected with her laden make-up and hated fishnets.

Ida had never liked the limelight. She wasn't shy but for most of her life she'd felt like she didn't belong.

Her mouth twisted. Here it was the truth. She did *not* belong in one of the country's most exclusive hotels.

Yet Ida refused to let Cesare know how weary and nervous she felt. She stiffened her backbone.

She'd get through the next half-hour, deal with whatever problem Cesare posed and then go home, ditch the make-up and awful clothes, and work out what to do about Bruno.

Ida barely noticed the beautiful furnishings as they reached Cesare's suite and he shut the door behind them. But she did take in the size of the sitting room—it was big enough to fit her flat six times over—and the faint scent of lilies and luxury. For a weak moment she contemplated dropping onto one of the cream lounges and shutting eyes scratchy with exhaustion. It had been a long time since she'd started her dawn cleaning shift.

Instead, she strolled into the room then twisted around to face her companion, ignoring the burn where the borrowed shoes rubbed her heels.

'Okay. We're alone. Why did you come looking for me?'

'I thought that was obvious.'

How could she have forgotten the intensity of that brooding stare? Cesare's eyes bored into hers as if seeking out misdemeanours or weaknesses.

But she'd done him no wrong. She didn't owe him anything and refused to be cowed by that flinty gaze. She shoved her hands deep in her raincoat pockets and raised her eyebrows.

'It's been a long day, Cesare. I'm not in the mood for guessing games. Just tell me. What do you want?'

He crossed the space between them in a couple of deceptively easy strides. Deceptive because his expression told her it was the prowl of a predator.

'To sort out our divorce, of course.'

CHAPTER FIVE

'WE'RE STILL MARRIED?'

Her hand went to her throat and Cesare was torn between the idea she was shocked and knowing she had to be faking.

'Of course we're married. You haven't signed divorce papers, have you?'

She shook her head, her glossy lips opening then closing. Those exaggerated eyelashes fluttered, and he almost thought he saw the movement echoed in the pulse point at her throat, so convincing was her show of surprise.

She was a fine actress. Though in retrospect she'd slightly overdone the role of shy innocent when they'd met.

What role was she playing now? Not the ingenue, given what he'd seen tonight.

Abruptly she sank onto the sofa behind her. It wasn't a graceful movement and made him think she really had been taken by surprise. As when she'd heard someone was searching for her.

Once again, he experienced a sharp pang that felt like concern.

It annoyed him. His concern was for his extended family, his employees and investors. It shouldn't be for this woman who'd been foisted on him, an insult to add to the injury Calogero had done his family.

Cesare turned on his heel and crossed to the bar. He took his time pouring two glasses of Sambuca before returning to where she sat, head bent, arms wrapped around her middle.

'Here.' He pushed the glass into her hand. 'This will warm you.'

Despite his impatience she worried him. This was the second time he'd seen her turn parchment pale, making her heavy make-up appear even more false against the delicate curves of her cheeks and lips.

Cesare took the seat opposite, eyes narrowing as she lifted her face.

'I assumed you'd divorced me four years ago.'

'When you left me high and dry for all the world to gossip about? The bridegroom with no bride.'

That still stung. One more debt to lay at her door. He was a proud man. Having acquaintances and even people he didn't know sniggering up their sleeves at him had been hard to endure.

'You didn't want a bride! You made that clear.'

'There's a difference between not wanting you and having you disappear off the face of the earth. Don't you have any regrets over the scandal you caused? The speculation and rumours? You dropped me into a hell of a mess.'

As if he hadn't been busy enough saving the family company and all those jobs, independent of Calogero. He'd had the fallout of a missing bride with the world agog for stories of Cesare Brunetti and his new wife. His plan had been to maintain the fiction of a happy marriage though in fact it would be in name only. Then he'd divorce her as soon as he could erase Calogero's influence from his life.

Ida sipped her drink then grimaced and shuddered as if she'd never drunk alcohol.

'You should have thought of that before you treated me as a whipping boy for my grandfather.'

He should indeed. He'd made the mistake of letting the anger he'd tamped down for so long finally get the better of him. It was a brief loss of control that he'd lived to regret.

But what intrigued him was that Ida said it to his face. She'd changed from the woman he'd known.

Of course she has. She's stopped pretending butter wouldn't melt in her mouth.

'You knew there was no divorce. There's been no paperwork.'

Ida took another sip. 'I don't know the process.' She lifted one shoulder. 'What? I've never been divorced before.'

'And you're not yet. That's why I'm here.'

'It took you long enough.'

She sounded belligerent, as if *he'd* let *her* down. The gall of the woman!

'I had a few things to keep me busy.' Like turning around the enterprise Calogero had sabotaged and finding ways to create the profits it needed without his nemesis realising Cesare's plan to oust him. 'What's your excuse?'

Her eyes met his in a flash of fire that reminded him of green-tinged clouds that presaged summer thunderstorms in his beloved Tuscany. That green tint was a warning of a dangerous electrical storm to follow.

'It never occurred to me that you'd let the marriage stand. I was sure you'd arrange a divorce or an annulment. The marriage wasn't consummated.'

Cesare's nostrils flared on a sharp inward breath.

He could imagine the gossip if he'd tried to end their union that way. There'd be salacious speculation about why they hadn't slept together. No one would believe it was because he wouldn't touch his pretty little bride. Not when every man at the wedding, and untold others who'd seen the media photos, had been busy imagining themselves in Cesare's position, stripping that diaphanous bridal gown off her slender body.

He lifted his glass and tossed back the fiery aniseed alcohol.

The burn down his throat was the distraction he needed from the well-worn direction of his thoughts. It was too easy imagining himself helping Ida out of her wedding dress or that slinky nightdress that had provoked him, finally, into losing his cool.

Cesare looked at his empty glass, surprised that he'd finished it. Moderation in all things was his motto, learned from his beloved grandfather and reinforced by his father's appalling example.

Cesare always stood strong in the face of provocation and temptation. Even when, in Ida's case, he'd teetered on the brink.

'That's why I'm here. To sort out the divorce.'

The sooner the better. After four years' absence this woman still messed with his head. It was inexplicable.

'Good.' She put down her drink and sat forward. 'Where do I sign?'

Cesare had expected prevarication or pleas. Coaxing or apologies. Not eagerness.

He struggled not to betray his stupefaction. 'You agree to the divorce?'

'Of course.'

For the first time tonight those amazing eyes looked clear and unguarded. Her plush mouth even crooked at the corners. As if it was the best news she could imagine.

Cesare leaned back, surprised.

She was giving him what he wanted. What he *needed*.

Yet he hadn't been prepared for it to be so easy. He'd expected her consent to cost him.

Had he *wanted* her to object? Was her enthusiasm a blow to his pride?

He was accustomed to women trying to persuade him to extend their time together, though admittedly that hadn't been for a while. The last four years he'd had no time for women, devoting his energy to wresting the company free of Calogero's clutches.

Maybe his appeal had diminished in that time?

Though, recalling the way Ida had eaten him up with her eyes earlier, he couldn't believe it.

Four years of abstinence did, however, explain his response to her. He was a healthy man with a healthy interest in a sexy woman. He didn't like or approve of Ida, but he couldn't deny she was sexy. He refused to countenance the idea that he'd been celibate so long because he'd been fixated on her.

She'd opened that shabby raincoat in the warmth of the suite and as she leaned forward he had a view of white breasts that was impossible to ignore. That bustier was cut so low and pushed her bounty so high that it looked like her nipples would burst free of their confinement at any moment.

He had to forcibly drag his gaze up, only to find it snagging on glossy, full red lips that made him think of searing, straight-to-the-groin orgasm.

Heat flared, his body tightening and his throat turning arid.

In one swift movement he rose and made for the bar.

'Another?' he asked over his shoulder, his voice grating.

'No, thanks. One's my limit.'

Cesare bit back the urge to tell her it was too late to play at inexperience. Not when he'd found her pouring shots in a strip club. But why waste energy?

He took his time pouring the drink. When he turned around the raincoat was open a little more, treating him to a view of long legs clad in fishnet stockings.

If asked, he would have said his taste ran to women whose sensuality was more discreet and refined. Tonight, he realised he was as responsive as the next man to pale flesh in black leather and provocative high heels.

His fingers tightened around the glass, but he refused to swallow the drink in one. He didn't need alcohol as a prop. He could easily withstand Ida's obvious attractions.

'I have the papers.'

He pulled them out and dropped them onto the coffee table before her, then took the seat opposite. Only then did he allow himself a tiny sip of his drink. Its warm bite dragged his attention from his heavy groin.

Ida picked up the papers and scanned them, turning page after page. She really was keen to sign, flipping quickly to the end. Cesare reached in his pocket for a pen but paused as she spoke.

'I can't sign these.'

Ah, as he expected. She wouldn't make this easy. Now came the play for a better financial settlement, despite the watertight prenup they'd signed.

Something like relief settled inside him at the realisation he'd had her pegged right.

'I'm sure you can.' With the right incentive. Like knowing he wasn't going to renegotiate. He placed his pen on the low table before her. 'You wanted a divorce. Here's your chance.'

She dropped the papers on the table, her mouth twisting. 'Much as I'd love to oblige you, it's not possible. These are in Italian.'

Cesare watched her sit back, folding her arms and pushing her breasts higher.

He swallowed. Such obvious tactics wouldn't work. 'And that's a problem because?'

'I don't understand Italian.'

Cesare stared. It was true that before the wedding they'd always spoken English. 'But the wedding service was all in Italian.'

She shrugged. 'I practised. My grandfather wanted me word perfect.'

But it wasn't just the church service. 'You had no trouble signing the prenuptial contract. You didn't ask for an English version.'

He and her grandfather had watched her sign the agreement. She'd simply picked up the pen, glanced at the document and signed in her neat, round hand.

'That was different.'

Cesare raised his eyebrows. 'I don't see how.'

Those pale green eyes met his, her look haughty. 'My grandfather and his lawyer had already been through the contract.'

Cesare would never sign anything without reading and understanding it himself. 'You left it to them? They explained it all to you?'

That didn't fit with his memory. There'd been changes made just before the meeting. He'd watched old Calogero read that section carefully before passing it to her to sign. 'Or are you saying you signed it without understanding it?'

Surely that wasn't normal for a gold-digger?

Abruptly she shifted, pulling her coat closer.

'What do you care, Cesare? I signed your all-important prenup, so you're safe. I'm not going to take you to the cleaners with this divorce.' She huffed out a breath. 'But I'm not signing this until it's translated. I could be signing *anything*!' He opened his mouth, but before he could speak she went on. 'I want an English copy, not for someone to read the Italian and explain what it means.'

She thought he was trying to dupe her? That he'd lie about the contents?

His hackles rose. The Brunettis did not do business that way. He was neither a bully nor a criminal like her grandfather.

Which means you respect her right to sign a document she can understand.

'So be it.'

He finished his drink and slammed the glass down, glancing at his watch. It was well into the early hours of the morning.

'It will take some time to get a translation.'

Ida nodded, rising in one supple movement. 'Call me when—'

'No, Ida.' Cesare was beside her in a moment. 'You'll wait here until the translation's made.'

'I beg your pardon?'

Her freezing tone would have done an empress proud.

'You don't think I'm letting you out of my sight before you sign on the dotted line? Not with your record of vanishing without warning.'

Ida's head tipped back as she met his eyes. Even in these teetering heels she didn't come near his height. He was taller, physically stronger and had a brooding air of ruthlessness that made her blood slow in her veins to a heavy, warning beat.

'You really mean it!'

He inclined his head. 'I never say things I don't mean.'

'You know where I live. I'm not going anywhere.'

He shook his head. 'I learned my mistake with you in Rome. I won't make the same mistake twice.'

Ida rubbed her arms through the thin coat. 'That makes no sense. I want a divorce too. I won't disappear.'

'So you say.' His words fell like lead weights in the thickened atmosphere. 'But I'm taking no chances.'

He didn't believe her.

Ida smoothed her coat down, at the same time drawing herself taller. 'You're not the only one who isn't in the habit of saying what they don't mean. I don't lie.' She paused but saw no softening in that sharp stare. 'Anyway, I have to work.'

'You've just finished work.'

She rolled her eyes. 'I have two jobs.' More than two, actually. And though Jo had taken on some of her night cleaning shifts while she'd filled in for Jo at the bar, Ida still worked through the day.

'Tell them you'll be in the next day instead.'

As if! Her work was cash in hand. No sick days or time off. She worked hard and did a good job, but if her clients thought her unreliable they'd get someone else.

'This isn't worth arguing about.' Ida belted her raincoat. 'I can be back here around three in the afternoon. Will that give you time to get the translation?'

'I'm sure it will.' He moved between her and the door. 'But you'll stay here until then.' He cut off her protest. 'There's a spare bedroom and bathroom.'

His phone rang just as she was about to tell him what she thought of that idea. He pulled it from his pocket, frowned at the caller ID and lifted it to his ear.

Indignation rose. He didn't even have the decency to ignore his phone while he made his outrageous demands.

Ida stalked past him, only to slam to a halt as a hand wrapped around her wrist.

Shock filled her.

At that unexpected, unwanted touch.

And at the heat rippling under her skin. A sensation that had less to do with outrage and more to do with awareness.

Something needy stirred. Something she'd told herself she'd imagined from her short time with Cesare. It was wholly feminine, responding even to his harsh, take-charge masculinity. She hated this weakness.

She swung around, lifting her hand, about to break his hold, when she read his expression.

He spoke in Italian, brusque and decisive, then ended the call. 'You know this man?'

He held out the phone and Ida's blood froze at the image there.

Bruno. Her grandfather's enforcer.

Bruno on the street outside her flat, and a second photo of him outside this magnificent hotel.

Her breath stopped.

He knew where she was. Which meant her grandfather did too. She wasn't safe.

Ida swayed and this time Cesare's hold wasn't imprisoning but supportive. Dimly she was aware of him tossing his phone aside and grabbing her elbows as stress took its inevitable toll and her knees gave way.

The world rolled and she found herself floating off the floor, pressed tight against Cesare's hard chest, his powerful arms embracing her.

She caught a hint of that lemon, cedar and man scent she remembered from years ago, and squeezed her eyes shut against an overwhelming barrage of sensations.

When she opened them he was sitting on a sofa and she was across his lap, tucked into his embrace, the thrum of his heart steady beneath her ear.

She felt undone. Tonight had been one shock after another. Her hard-won defences were unravelling, and her strength with them.

She should be pushing free, getting off Cesare's lap and leaving.

But where would she go?

Was Bruno out there, waiting for her?

A shudder racked her and Cesare's arms tightened. Ida told herself she didn't like or trust this man, but it was impossible to regret the comfort of his firm hold.

It felt bizarrely as if he could keep her safe.

He who'd hurt her so badly!

'It's the same man, isn't it?'

She nodded. 'Who took the photos? The man you left behind at the flat?'

'Lorenzo is head of my security team. He saw this guy watch us leave your flat and follow us here. Lorenzo tailed him.'

Cesare paused as if expecting her to explain. But her mind was racing, grappling with the implications.

She'd have to move. Start again.

She couldn't afford to let Bruno catch her. The air thickened, pressing down on her as black spots danced before her eyes.

Her grandfather would be furious at the way she'd deserted her marriage when he'd aimed to build on that to stake a place for himself in the society that had rejected him for so long. His rage would be monumental, and his vengeance didn't bear thinking about.

If she continued to flat-share with Jo she would put her friend at risk too.

Ida put her fingertips to her forehead, her pulse beating so hard at her temples she felt sick.

For four years she'd managed, just, to keep her head above water. She'd stayed safe, found a home and work.

She'd even added to her slim savings in the hopes of eventually moving to the countryside, once she had enough money to start again.

Now her hopes were shattered. With Bruno on her trail, she had to leave immediately and start somewhere new. Where would she go? Where would she be safe?

'Talk to me, Ida.'

It should feel odd, sharing information with this man, but for some reason it didn't. 'He works for my grandfather.'

'I remember his face. Your grandfather's bodyguard.'

'That's part of his role.'

Thug. Stand-over man. Enforcer. Gaoler. Bruno was adaptable.

She shivered and Cesare again tightened his hold. Strange that now his touch didn't feel like imprisonment but protection.

But then, there was nothing like the fear of imminent violence to clarify your priorities. She didn't like Cesare Brunetti but she didn't fear him.

Cesare felt the shivers course through her slender body.

'You're scared.'

Which made the tight tug of material at his crotch an embarrassment. He shouldn't lust after a woman who was shivering with fear, no matter how good she felt against his body.

'He's not a nice man.'

The way she said it made his nape tingle. Beneath her calm tone was an unmistakeable thread of terror.

'Is it him you're scared of or your grandfather?'

Her head tipped back so that her face turned up to his. He saw shimmering ruby lips. Thick make-up and exaggerated lashes that earlier had made her eyes look slumbrous and heavy. Now as he met those pale mint-green eyes he read not defiance or indignation but distress.

His pulse stuttered in shock.

Because his overwhelming impulse was to shelter her.

Closely followed by the urge to settle his mouth over those plush lips and delve deep, to see if she tasted as honey-sweet as he remembered from their kiss in the church.

Had the appalling London weather shorted his brain?

'Does it matter?'

Technically, no. Except something had changed tonight. From the moment Cesare had discovered Ida in that dingy club everything had become complicated. His response to her wasn't what he'd anticipated.

Now he'd discovered another mystery.

There was something between Ida and her grandfather that he needed to understand because bringing down Fausto Calogero was his top priority. Anything concerning the old devil was vital information.

Then there was the mystery of Ida herself. What was she hiding? Why, after what she'd done, did he respond so viscerally to her?

He couldn't in good conscience walk away and leave her terrified. Which all added up to one solution. Outlandish but unavoidable.

'Forget staying here overnight. Or,' he added when she moved as if to stand up, 'coming back at three. Do you have a current passport?'

Those clear eyes widened. But instead of questioning him Ida slowly nodded.

Half an hour ago she'd have protested that she wouldn't go anywhere with him.

'I'll have Lorenzo go to your flat and get it.'

She breathed deep, her soft breast pushing against his chest and messing with his head. But for once he was sure that wasn't intentional. Nor was the nervous way she moistened her lips with the tip of her tongue. Ida was truly terrified.

'There's no need. I always carry my passport with me.'

That, more than anything else he'd seen tonight, proved her desperation. Unless she travelled constantly, which, given her circumstances, wasn't an option, there was only one reason for that. Because she was always prepared for a quick getaway.

That solidified his sudden decision.

'Good. You're coming with me to Italy. Now.'

CHAPTER SIX

IDA WOKE TO the sound of someone moving about in her room.

Heart pounding, she jack-knifed up, wisps of nightmare still fogging her brain.

The fine cotton sheet slid against her skin and she realised she was naked. Instantly she clawed the sheet up around her shoulders.

Her breath sighed out as she realised she wasn't in her cramped flat with its flimsy front door. The noise wasn't her grandfather's henchman breaking in.

Gradually her racing pulse eased.

Instead of seeing a tiny sliver of louring London sky, bright sunshine flooded across the honey-coloured wooden floor and a sumptuous antique carpet of blush roses on a cream background. A trim, grey-haired woman drew the floor-length curtains open.

Ida shaded her eyes. Through the tall windows was a cerulean sky with a single puffy cloud, cotton wool against the vibrant blue.

'I'm sorry to wake you, *signora*. I've brought you a late breakfast.' She nodded to a laden tray on a nearby table. 'Signor Brunetti asked me to wake you so you can freshen up before the lawyer arrives at midday.'

Midday? Ida was usually working at dawn. She *never* slept in.

But last night, or rather this morning, had been remarkable, she realised as impressions crowded her brain.

Cesare's astounding determination to spirit her out of London. The ease with which he'd organised transport in the dead of night. A limousine to the airport, a private flight to Florence then a helicopter to his country home.

Most remarkable of all was the fact that she'd acquiesced! As if she were used to letting someone else take charge. As if every day wasn't about the struggle to be free to make her own decisions.

As if she trusted Cesare Brunetti.

What choice had she had? Faced with either her unwanted husband or Bruno, there'd been no choice.

Besides, there was something powerfully appealing about, just once, having someone else solve her problems, albeit temporarily.

A shiver skated down her spine. It was a weakness she couldn't afford to foster.

Deliberately she shut her mind against thoughts of the other weakness she felt around Cesare Brunetti. The insidious desire that still haunted her.

'Thank you. I shouldn't have slept so long.' She paused, uncomfortable. She wasn't used to servants. The only person who occasionally saw her in bed was Jo if their shifts worked out that way. 'I don't know your name.'

'I'm Dorotea, the housekeeper.' The woman smiled, though her eyes were wary. 'Welcome to Tuscany, Signora Brunetti.'

Signora Brunetti!

Ida snapped her gaping mouth shut.

Why would Cesare reveal her identity? He wanted to end their marriage as soon as possible.

'Thank you, Dorotea. Have we met before?' Ida had never visited this house.

'No, but I recognise you from your wedding photos in the press. Such a beautiful bride! It's a pleasure to welcome you here at last.'

'Thank you very much.'

Ida blushed, realising what had seemed simple and expedient last night brought with it a stack of complications.

She hadn't just escaped Bruno. She'd walked into the role of Cesare's wife.

Had he intended that? What was the real reason he'd helped her?

She recalled his scathing expression the night he'd revealed his true feelings for her. That meant his actions last night had been on the spur of the moment too.

Yet he seemed the sort of man who didn't leave anything to chance.

She pushed her hair off her face, fingers tangling in waves still tacky from the product she'd used to slick down her hair yesterday. After clients at the bar had grabbed at her hair to haul her close, she'd opted for a severe hairstyle there.

Now she regretted she hadn't washed her hair last night. She'd been so weary she'd cleaned off her make-up, stripped off her borrowed clothes and fallen naked into bed.

'Signor Brunetti said your luggage has been delayed but there are clothes in the wardrobe.'

Had she supplied something of her own for Ida to wear?

'Thank you. That's very kind.'

The other woman shook her head. 'Don't thank me. Thank your husband.'

Her husband!

Every cell in her body rejected the idea. After years of separation, she thought of herself as single or as good as.

For four years she'd been Maddy Wickham, a name chosen to hide her should her grandfather search for her.

Yet it wasn't Fausto Calogero on her mind. It was Cesare and why he'd brought her to his home. Was he so desperate for this divorce that he didn't dare let her out of his sight?

She stilled, her hand on the wardrobe door. Had he found someone he wanted to marry? That would explain him taking no chances about getting her signature.

Ida was surprised by the dart of discomfort under her ribs as the idea took root.

She didn't want to be married to him. So why did the thought of him with another woman unsettle her?

She shook her head. She was tired and stressed, imagining things.

Like the way you keep imagining the feel of his arms around you. And how it felt with that gorgeous body pressed up close.

Firming her mouth, she wrenched open the cupboard door, and discovered it wasn't a wardrobe but a room.

Ida paused, dumbfounded as she scanned the bespoke storage running around the large space, the sofa in the centre and the floor-to-ceiling mirror that reflected the image of her wrapped in her plush bath towel.

She blinked. It wasn't the luxury that stole her breath, but the fact it was full of clothes. Clothes in clear plastic as if they'd just come from the cleaners or, she realised as she stepped in and got a proper look, from a couture house.

Dazed, she took in the sight of clothes for every occasion. Shelves that held more shoes than she'd owned in her life, all in her size. Drawers containing underwear of cobweb-fine silk and lace, again in her size.

Icy fingers of warning danced across her scalp and down to her prickling nape.

What had she walked into?

What did Cesare want from her?

Ida breathed deep, tamping down coiling unease. She'd demand answers when she saw him.

But instead of reaching for a pair of jeans or plain tailored trousers, she let her gaze linger on a dress that stood out against the blocks of solid colour. Without intending to she found her hand moving out, lifting the plastic and stroking the fabric.

It was as soft and weightless as she'd suspected. A delicate floral with tiny bunches of dark violets and pale leaves on a creamy background. It had a gathered skirt, a fitted bodice, and a ribbon of dark violet velvet that ran under the bust and up to form narrow shoulder straps.

It was a party dress, delicate and pretty, and it reminded her of the dreams she'd had as a girl. About parties and romance and a bright future.

Ida's hand fell, her mouth compressing. She needed something plain and businesslike. She didn't need...

But suddenly she *did*.

Life had been tough for years, a combination of worry, struggle and drudgery. In London her only clothes were cheap trousers and T-shirts she wore to work, an inadequate coat and a collection of second-hand pullovers she wore at home to counteract the chill when they couldn't afford heating.

Why not wear a pretty dress while she had the chance? Why not do something just because it made her happy?

Ida felt decadently selfish and daring as she reached for the coat hanger.

Cesare sensed her before he saw her. The air grew charged, crackling with unseen energy.

He didn't like it. That elemental awareness of Ida should have ended years ago, when she'd left him high and dry, a groom without a bride, the cynosure of public speculation and gossip.

He swung around and his breath caught.

Just like that.

One look and the oxygen bled from his lungs while fire combusted in his lower body.

How did a woman who made her living dressed as a cheap hooker manage to look like a breath of spring—delicate, lovely and wholesome? And incredibly alluring.

Was she trying to pretend she didn't work in a sex club by dressing as a sweet innocent?

Amazingly, she almost succeeded, except that his body's avid response told its own story. It recognised the starkly sensual woman beneath the flowers and ribbons.

How long since a woman had made him breathless with wanting?

No one since her.

It seemed incredible. He assured himself it was because he'd been too busy to think about women when he'd had the battle of his life saving the family business.

'Ida.' The name ground low from a throat turned tight with hunger. That hunger, inexplicable and unwanted, prompted him to go on. 'You look completely different. You only wear leather after dark?'

It was a cheap shot that made him almost ashamed. Discomfiting her because she got to him should be beneath him. But apart from a hint of heightened colour along her cheekbones, she betrayed no sign of being discomposed as she entered his study.

'That's a work uniform, not my choice.'

Cesare watched the feathery fabric swirl around her bare legs, took in the way that dark ribbon underscored her breasts, and the gleam of her pale, bare shoulders and arms. Ida was even more devastating than he remembered.

Four years ago she'd rocked him to the core, threatening his focus. Now he faced the fact he'd tried to avoid last night, that she still affected him at the most elemental level.

'Since we're talking about clothes…' She stopped before him and he realised that behind her composure lurked something else. Anxiety? 'Whose dress is this? There's a room full of clothes in my size.'

Cesare scowled, remembering. 'They're yours.'

Now he got a reaction. She started and faltered back. 'I don't understand. You weren't expecting me here.'

'On the contrary, I was. Four years ago.'

'Four years…?' She blinked and surveyed him with dilated pupils. 'After the wedding?'

'Of course, after the wedding.' He shoved his hands into his trouser pockets. 'As my wife you'd attract a lot of attention, more so as I head a luxury goods company. It was important you dress the part, showcasing fashion from our designers. I had my people organise a suitable wardrobe.'

Because, though expensive, the clothes she'd worn before had never seemed quite right on her, despite her poise and grace. They'd looked as if she'd chosen them only for their high price tag, not because they suited her.

'Except you disappeared in the night, leaving me to deal with the furore.'

She lifted one eyebrow. 'Don't expect me to apologise. No woman would have stayed after what you said that night.'

Ida tried to make him out to be at fault? It was she and her grandfather who'd blackmailed *him*.

'If you can't face the truth…'

Her eyes flashed and unholy excitement dug its claws into his belly. The devil in him, the one he kept leashed, responded to that spark of fire. Yet instead of following through she looked away.

When that green gaze met his again, he read no emotion there. 'Why did you keep the clothes, Cesare? You surely didn't want me to return and use them.'

Could she really believe that? Pride demanded he disabuse her of that idea.

'Nothing so puerile. I just forgot about them.'

'Forgot?' She stared as if she didn't understand English. 'A whole *room* of designer clothes?'

This time he was sure her amazement was real. It puzzled him. Whatever her circumstances now, she was heir to a fortune. She'd be used to designer clothes and other luxuries.

'I had other things on my mind. My business. Dealing with your grandfather. Quelling the worst rumours about your disappearance, including the ones that painted me as a Bluebeard who'd done away with his wife.'

Ida's head jerked back. 'You're kidding!'

'You know it's true. Even if the reputable news outlets didn't say it, there was enough gossip.'

It had been horrendous. The only positive the fact that through him the Brunetti brand was constantly in the limelight and doing better than ever.

Her wide-eyed stare bored into his. 'I didn't know. I didn't follow the news.'

Cesare frowned. 'It was splashed across social media.'

She shook her head. 'Not that either.'

It was too unlikely to be true, yet despite his reservations Cesare began to wonder. What had she been doing with her time?

'You really kept a room full of designer clothes for me all this time?'

'If I'd thought about it, I'd have got rid of them. But I forgot until I talked to my housekeeper about getting you more suitable clothes than the ones you arrived in.'

'I see.'

Did she? Cesare didn't want her getting the idea he'd been sentimental about what had been not so much a wedding gift as a necessity so she looked the part as his wife.

'Just as well I hadn't disposed of them.'

The idea of her parading around his home in her raunchy clothes set up a flurry of distaste in his belly.

It *was* distaste, he was sure.

Just over half an hour later Cesare returned to his study after seeing his lawyer out.

He still couldn't believe it. He'd been sure Ida would find some last-minute reason not to agree to a divorce. Yet it had gone smoothly. She'd read the papers, asked a few questions, then signed without hesitation.

He was on the way to becoming a free man.

Exultation rose.

It had taken years to manoeuvre Calogero out of the business and soon he hoped to see the old villain behind bars. Now the unwanted wife Cesare had been blackmailed into accepting had agreed to a divorce without a murmur.

Why would she do that? If she ran true to type, as venal as her grandfather, she'd make his life difficult while she tried to negotiate a better pay-out.

Cesare had so many questions that needed answering. Plus any inside information he could get about Calogero could only help his cause.

'How do I get to Florence?'

Ida stood near the window, the light creating a fiery nimbus around her bright hair. Sunshine backlit her, revealing the delectable figure beneath that filmy dress.

Cesare's pulse stalled then sped into overdrive, thundering through his body. He hesitated a second, telling himself it was her unexpected question that threw him, not the desire clawing at him.

He moved into the room. 'Why?'

'To leave, of course. I've signed the papers.'

Ida was full of surprises. Once more she defied expectations. But their business wasn't over.

'Shall we sit and discuss that?' Because he could do without the distraction of seeing her body so lovingly revealed against the light.

After a second, she shrugged and took a chair near the fireplace. Cesare took the one opposite.

'You want to leave?'

She frowned. 'Naturally.'

'And go where? To your flat where your grandfather's man will find you?'

She stiffened. 'That's no concern of yours.'

'It is if you've fallen out with Calogero.'

Or was it his henchman she feared?

Wary eyes held his, but she said nothing.

'Have you, Ida? Have you fallen out with the old man?'

Her lips curved into a crooked smile that snagged something buried deep inside. 'You could say that.'

Then, as quickly as it came, that hint of humour disappeared, leaving her expression strained. Once more Cesare felt that unexpected tug of connection. As he had last night when she'd been scared.

'You could stay here for a short time,' he said slowly, gauging her reaction. 'You'd be safe and I'm guessing you'll need time to plan your next move.'

Instantly a voice sounded in his head.

Remember your father. His poor decisions, his foolishness when in thrall to some woman.

But this was different. Cesare wasn't taken in by Ida. He simply recognised her terror and couldn't ignore it.

Her eyes rounded. 'Why would you do that?'

Because he wasn't an ogre. He didn't like the idea of any woman in fear of a thug.

'Because you're afraid of him.'

Ida said nothing but her stare was eloquent. It was the wary look of a woman who'd seen too much.

Cesare felt a flare of compassion. She'd been part of the scheme to blackmail and control him but, he realised, maybe her own situation had been difficult. He thought of that investigator's report, of a girl orphaned at eight then shuttled between a remote island and Calogero's ostentatious London house.

'But I'm not your responsibility. You hate me.'

Cesare didn't deny it and for reasons Ida refused to examine, that still hurt.

Finally, he spoke. 'You surely didn't expect friendship from a man who was forced with threats to marry you.'

No. But she'd been such an innocent she hadn't realised the situation. She'd imagined Cesare had at least liked her and found her attractive. She smoothed her palms down the delicate fabric of her dress. If he hadn't revealed the truth that night in Rome, if she'd discovered he'd ordered this romantic dream of a dress for her, she might even have tumbled further into—

'No, I don't expect friendship.'

'But things have changed, Ida.'

Her head snapped up and she met that steady dark gaze. 'How?'

'You connived against me, but we could be mutually beneficial to each other now.'

Ida contemplated telling him again that she hadn't been privy to her grandfather's blackmail. That she hadn't been Cesare's enemy. Because it hurt that he should think her to be anything like her grandfather. But he wouldn't believe her. She had no proof, just her word.

'Go on.'

'You've fallen out with your grandfather and so have I. Our interests coincide that far at least. I'll do whatever I can to stop him getting what he wants. If he wants you it will give me great pleasure to deny him that.'

'You're saying you'd keep him away from me just to thwart him?'

Something flashed in Cesare's eyes. An expression she couldn't read, but it made her warier than ever.

'Is that so unlikely?'

It should be. She'd seen Cesare's disdain for her.

Yet last night he'd acted decisively when he understood she was frightened. Surely bringing her all the way to Italy meant there was kindness beneath that steely determination?

Or was he simply another man like her grandfather, determined to win at all costs?

Ida shivered. She couldn't blame Cesare for despising Fausto Calogero. She did too. But she'd seen how the need for revenge blackened a man's soul, eating away any trace of decency.

Yet there was something more. Something she sensed he wasn't telling her.

But what? She didn't know her grandfather's secrets. If Cesare wanted to milk her for information, he'd be disappointed.

She hadn't even seen her grandfather since the wedding, for which she was thankful. The last four years had been a struggle, but in some ways they'd been the happiest of her life, the most free since those halcyon days before the accident when her parents had been alive.

Ida shot to her feet, emotions in such turmoil she couldn't

sit still. Doubts crowded her mind and above all the awareness of Cesare, big and predatory.

And fascinatingly male.

'Ida?' His deep voice grazed her skin, drawing it tight
and, to her horror, making her nipples bud. Heat stroked
through her, down her abdomen to that restless place between her thighs.

'I need time to think.'

She turned away, trying to block him from her thoughts,
but it was impossible. Even with him metres away she was
hyper-aware of him.

That feeling had burst into life last night the moment
she'd looked up to see him before her. But if she was honest the trembling awareness, the desire, had never really
gone away. In four years, even telling herself she detested
him, the kernel of longing had remained.

Suddenly he wasn't metres away. His breath feathered
her hair and down her nape and she felt the heat of his body
behind her. 'There's another reason you should stay, Ida.'

'There is? What is it?' She turned, then realised her mistake when she looked up and his expression stole her breath.

Cesare's hands skimmed her bare arms, creating in-
cendiary trails, up to her shoulders then higher, to cup her
face. It didn't occur to her to object. His touch was gentle,
barely there, yet Ida felt it like an earthquake shuddering
through her.

He moved closer. 'This.'

CHAPTER SEVEN

HIS DARK EYES looked black now, gleaming with sinful invitation.

Ida canted forward, leaning into him. By the time she realised what she'd done he'd moved closer as if about to wrap his arms around her.

No, no, no!

She couldn't. He couldn't. The misery of his rejection on their wedding night told her not to trust him.

Yet her body had its own ideas. Her legs had shifted apart, a lush, melting feeling throbbing at her core.

Cesare wanted her. She saw it in his eyes, as clearly as before she'd read contempt.

That was new. Cesare desiring her.

She'd grown up a lot in the last four years. Had seen something similar in the eyes of other men, especially in the last two weeks, working at the club. But never had such a look made her feel eager.

Ida drew herself tall, fighting the craving for more than that featherlight touch. For the feel of his mouth on hers, not fleetingly like when he'd brushed his lips over hers in the church, but with passion.

The depth of her need horrified her.

After four years! How could he spark such a powerful

response? She'd hoped last night's visceral awareness had been due to shock and would have vanished today.

'You're inviting me to stay for sex?' Her voice choked with throbbing emotion. 'You think because I worked in that club I'm a prostitute, available for—'

Cesare's thumb pressed against her mouth, stopping her words.

'No! This has nothing to do with where you worked. It's about you and me. Nothing else.'

Ida tilted her head back, out of his hold, but for some reason couldn't get her feet to move. Maybe because the way he looked at her made her believe him.

They stood toe to toe, gazes locked, as he lowered his hands to his sides.

'There *is* no you and me. There never was.'

Despite the hopes she'd once harboured.

'Yet the sexual attraction is still there, isn't it, Ida? It hasn't gone.'

She blinked. Had Cesare just implied he'd *desired* her four years ago?

'You feel that thrill in the blood when our eyes lock, don't you?'

To her horror she felt it now. An effervescence running through her whole body, making her more alive than she'd ever been.

'And the quickened breathing like you can't suck in enough air.'

Ida's eyes widened. How did he know? Her chest *did* feel too tight, as if she'd run out of oxygen and her breaths turned rapid and shallow to compensate.

'Are your fingers tingling because you want to reach out and touch me?' His voice dropped low. 'Mine are, Ida. I want to touch you. All over.'

She swallowed and clenched her hands, telling herself she didn't feel the same. Refusing to think of Cesare's long fingers stroking her flesh. Stroking places where no man had ever touched, except him in those restless erotic dreams.

She wanted to tell him to stop but feared her voice would betray how he affected her.

'What else are you feeling, Ida? You're flushed. Did you know that? Flushed with desire. Is your pulse thudding hard and fast, down low in your body?'

Snatching in a sharp breath, she finally found the will-power to move. She stepped back, telling herself his persuasive words were just that, they couldn't actually affect her.

Except they had. Ida felt everything he'd said and more. Her pulse drummed hard and fast, and she felt it at her feminine core. At the juncture of her thighs where moisture bloomed.

She might not have been with a man, but Ida understood what that meant.

Why, oh, why did it have to be Cesare Brunetti of all people who turned her on, ripening her body so that all she could think about was how it would feel to surrender to him?

'You have a marvellous imagination, Cesare.' Her voice was husky, so she swallowed and tried again. 'But if you want sex, you need to look elsewhere.'

He shook his head, his eyes never leaving hers, the knowledge in them holding her captive.

'If only things were so simple.' He drew in a breath and her attention snagged on the rise of those powerful shoulders. 'You complicate my life, Ida. *You're* the one I want. Not some nameless woman. *You.*'

Ida stared, dumbfounded, as that needy being inside her leapt into eager life.

He made it sound like no other woman would do. Surely

that was admitting to weakness. If she'd learned anything from her grandfather it was not to reveal weakness, especially before your enemy.

How did Cesare view her?

'Careful, Cesare, I might be tempted to think you care.'

He laughed. It was over almost as soon as it started but that deep-throated chuckle scythed through taut muscles and every protective bastion, leaving her adrift.

She liked his laugh, she realised in astonishment. So much that she wanted to hear it again.

Don't go there.

'You're not as I remember you, Ida. You've changed.'

'It would be nice to think that was a compliment, but you know, Cesare, I don't care what you think of me. I don't like you.'

Once she'd hung on his words and his rare smiles. She'd imagined a future for them that was full of promise. So when he'd turned on her, throwing her grandfather's crimes at her and judging her guilty too, she'd crumpled. Ida was stronger now.

'Liking isn't necessary for what I'm suggesting.' His mouth lifted in a slow smile that, despite her determination to be unaffected, curled her toes and planted heat deep in her body. 'In fact, the tension between us will add spice. You know I'm not suggesting we embark on a meaningful relationship.'

'Oh, I got *that*.' Her tone was as dismissive as she could make it. 'You want sex. I can see it in your eyes.'

'And I can see in your eyes that you do too.'

His voice was soft, like a velvet ribbon trailing across her shivery skin before wrapping around her insides.

'Looks are deceptive.'

It was a blatant lie, but she'd crawl over broken glass before admitting it. Instead, she shrugged and fought the impulse to take another step away. Cesare would see that for what it was, proof that the force field he radiated made her body spark and tingle.

'Anyway, I'm leaving.'

'That's your prerogative. Where will you go that he won't find you? Your grandfather knows now that you left with me. He'll have people keeping an eye on my homes. People who'll follow you once you're out of my protection.'

It made sickening sense. Of course they'd be looking for her. Ida's hope of disappearing among the tourists of Florence before moving on died. She hadn't thought further than that, apart from knowing that she couldn't return to her flat, or to her cousin in Scotland. Both would be under surveillance.

'What are you suggesting, Cesare?' Her hands found her hips and her stare narrowed. 'That you'll keep me and protect me from my grandfather on condition I give you sex?'

His head snapped back and for the first time since they'd met Ida saw she'd rattled him. It lasted barely a moment, so brief that a second later she wondered if she'd imagined his shock.

But it made her feel better to think he abhorred the idea.

Cesare raised both hands and stepped back.

'Calogero might have given me a master class in ruthlessness, but I don't model myself on him. I'm not a blackmailer or rapist.' His chest rose on a mighty breath and Ida saw she'd actually punctured his arrogant air of assurance. 'I've never forced a woman and I'm not going to start now.'

He paused, staring down at her from under lowered brows as if to make sure his words sank in.

'As for letting you stay here safely while you make your plans, that offer stands, no strings attached.'

Ida saw the truth in his face. It was a genuine offer.

'I... Thank you.'

Once again she realised how much she owed him. He'd spirited her out of London to safety when he could simply have waited for her signature on his papers then left her to manage. Now he offered to extend that protection until she worked out her escape plan.

His generosity puzzled her. And made her feel wobbly. It was easier to deal with this man when she could simply hate him.

'As for pursuing this attraction, we're both adults, and neither of us is under any illusions that this is more than sexual. All I'm saying is that in the middle of this fiasco your grandfather tangled us in, we could take some pleasure for ourselves. Nothing more, nothing less.'

'Because it's convenient?' She hoped her tone sounded sardonic rather than hurt.

'You think any of this is *convenient*?'

His eyes flashed and once again it seemed she'd pushed him into uncharted territory. That was exactly what he did to her. Then his expression shuttered.

'But you're right. The fact we're divorcing only makes it better. No chance of confusion about this meaning more than it does. We can enjoy a short affair and get this,' he gestured wide in a way that looked wholly Italian, 'attraction out of our systems before moving on to separate lives.'

'Like scratching an itch?'

He inclined his head. 'Exactly.'

Perhaps Ida was naïve but the sensations bombarding her when she was with Cesare felt far more complicated than an itch.

What did she know? She'd never had an affair, casual or otherwise.

Maybe he was right. If they had sex maybe her fascination for him might finally fade.

And maybe that was dangerous temptation talking.

'We're in a unique position,' he continued. 'Married and on the brink of divorce but never had a wedding night.' His eyes locked on hers and she had to fight not to shift her weight because parts of her anatomy responded far too emphatically to that stare. 'Maybe that's the problem. We never gave our attraction its natural outlet.'

'A wedding night?' She shook her head, but the movement felt stiff. 'As I recall, you didn't want sex. You were in a foul mood.'

'Can you blame me?'

No. She'd understood his anger. Her grandfather had targeted a proud man and brought him almost to his knees. No wonder Cesare had been furious.

But that was no excuse for attacking her. She'd been a victim of the old man's machinations too. Not that she could prove it, and she knew Cesare wouldn't take her word for it, not after his experiences with her family.

'You behaved appallingly,' she said finally.

She saw he hadn't expected her to call him out on that. But then *he* surprised *her*. 'I did. I'd kept everything under control for so long and suddenly it all came rushing out. I didn't mean to drive you away. Most of my anger was directed at your grandfather.'

Most, not all. And that wasn't a proper apology. Yet it was closer than she'd ever expected to get.

'That's no excuse.'

'True. I pride myself on keeping an even temper and not responding to provocation. But that night...' He shook his head. 'Anger and thwarted sexual attraction are a dangerous mix.'

Thwarted attraction? He'd wanted her that night?

It shouldn't colour her thinking yet the primitive part of Ida yearning for Cesare's touch swelled in triumph. It didn't negate his behaviour, but it was a tiny salve to her pride.

'You think sharing a belated wedding night will help you move on?' She tried to sound cynical but feared her husky voice told a different story.

'Help *us*, Ida. This is mutual. You know it is.'

She looked away, not liking the stirring in her blood. 'It's an interesting idea. I'll give it some thought.'

'Just so we're absolutely clear, I won't ask again.' She felt her eyes widen and turned back to him. 'I won't pressure you. You're not obliged to sleep with me for my protection.' On the words *sleep with me* his eyelids drooped, giving his eyes a lazy, suggestive gleam that made her stomach twist in eager corkscrews. 'The choice of when we get together will be entirely yours.'

When not *if*?

He had the arrogance of the devil. Indignation stirred. As if she'd give herself to a man so self-satisfied!

Something flickered in his expression. Amusement? Impatience?

She was on the point of leaving the room when a thought hit her. Something more important than Cesare's ego and sense of entitlement.

'I'm glad to hear you're willing to wait.' Her tone told him he could wait till hell froze over and she let a smug smile curl her mouth. 'In the meantime, I need to send something to London. Is there a local post office?'

Not that she really wanted to venture out if Bruno or someone like him was lurking in the vicinity.

'Can't you send a text or email?'

'It's not a message, it's a parcel.'

Cesare's eyes narrowed in suspicion. 'You didn't bring any luggage.'

Did he think she'd swiped one of the precious pieces of art from upstairs and hoped to post it under his nose? Ida would have smiled if she weren't tired of his suspicions. Instead she felt it like a blade to her heart.

How could this man do that to her? He'd always made her feel too much.

Her hands found her hips and her chin hiked up. 'I need to send Jo the clothes and shoes I wore last night.'

'Jo, your flatmate?'

Ida nodded. Still he didn't give her the information she needed. Was there a postal outlet here or did she have to organise a courier? That would cost more but Jo needed her gear, something Ida hadn't considered last night when she'd let Cesare usher her onto a flight to Italy. All she'd cared about was escaping Bruno.

'Why?'

Damn the man for being so intractable and curious. For four years he hadn't thought about her and now he seemed determined to dig through her life.

Instinctive reticence warred with Ida's need to do the right thing by her friend.

'They're Jo's clothes, okay? I borrowed them so I could work her shifts at the club, but she needs them back.' Jo was on a tight budget and couldn't spare the cash to replace them, especially that leather bustier.

Ida had the satisfaction of seeing Cesare stare as if for once robbed of words. It didn't last long.

'Why would you want to do that?'

Ida turned away, folding her arms across her body as she stared out at the spectacular view of undulating hills. A line of dark cypress trees marked a road or boundary, and in the distance a small hilltop town looked picturesque and inviting. The scene was a mix of gentle greens and ochres under the clear blue sky and she wished she could absorb some of its glorious tranquillity.

'Jo got mugged.' She shivered, remembering the trip to

the emergency department and the fear that her friend's injuries might be more severe than just bruises. 'She wasn't
well enough to work at first. Even when she improved, she
couldn't work behind the bar because make-up couldn't
hide those bruises.'

'You took her place?' Cesare's tone held a spiky note
she didn't bother to analyse.

'For two weeks. Jo couldn't afford to lose the job. She
goes back next week.'

'I thought you said you had your own job.'

'I do.'

Ida chewed her lip, thinking of the customer base she'd
built up through hard work, and the efforts she and Jo had
made to retain that. Ida had worked all hours between the
bar and her cleaning jobs, trying to juggle everything. Jo
had pitched in when she was well enough, taking over some
of Ida's night shift office-cleaning, which was why Ida
hadn't expected her at home last night.

Yet even if Ida returned to London it would need to be
to a completely different area if she wanted to stay under
the radar. She'd have to give up her clients and start from
scratch.

'Ida?'

Cesare regarded her with a curious look on his face, one
she couldn't identify. 'You were only working there while
your friend was sick?'

It was none of his business, but she was tired of shoring
up the barriers between them.

'For a fortnight. Last night was my last shift and she'll
go back in two days. Do you know how long the mail will
take?'

He stared at her as if puzzling something out. But what
was there to puzzle? He'd made up his mind about her character years before.

Unless he intended to rescind his suggestion for an affair? Maybe the fact she'd worked in the bar *had* prompted the suggestion after all.

Ida's pulse quickened, not in excitement but, to her amazement, with nerves. As if she didn't want him to change his mind. She took her time digesting that.

Instead of being outraged at Cesare's proposition she felt intrigued.

Tempted.

'Forget the mail,' he said brusquely. 'Give it all to Dorotea to package up and I'll have it delivered.'

'I'll write out the address and—'

'I have it.'

Ida frowned. He sounded out of sorts, grumpier than before, though why that should be she had no idea.

'Great. Thanks. I'll get them.'

Cesare shoved his hands in his trouser pockets and watched her go, trying to tamp down his wholly masculine response to her gently swaying hips and the swish of that skirt around her bare legs. The pearlescent gleam of her bare shoulders and the combination of bright, upswept hair revealing a slender neck drove a punch of longing into his gut.

His jaw firmed. It didn't matter what she looked like. She was still the woman who'd helped blackmail him for his money and connections.

Except she hasn't tried to get anything from you in years.

Only because she had Calogero to fall back on until they fell out. And the prospect of a healthy divorce settlement to look forward to.

Cesare dragged his hands from his pockets and opened the French doors, needing fresh air. He stepped outside, breathing in the scents of sunshine on old stonework and freshly mown grass. Of all the exquisite, expensive perfumes his luxury goods company produced, none compared to the scent of home. This place grounded him.

To think he'd almost lost it, along with everything his family had worked for, because of Calogero.

Yet it wasn't relief he felt. His emotions were in turmoil, buffeted by Ida's revelations.

Her fear of her grandfather's henchman evoked sympathy. The way she'd stood up to Cesare appealed too, even as it frustrated him. It felt like drawing blood from a stone, getting information from her.

Why would she want to share with you? She doesn't like you. Just as you don't like her.

And yet…

Cesare frowned as he moved into the garden, feeling the sun's warmth. He tipped up his head. After the miserable cold in London this felt glorious.

Except for the churning in his belly. The knowledge he'd jumped to at least one mistaken conclusion about his soon-to-be ex-wife.

It shouldn't matter that she'd only worked in that strip club to help a friend. It wasn't his business how she earned a living. A woman could choose where she worked.

So why had he almost exploded with fury when he'd found her there, just as his investigators had said? Why had he been determined to drag her out? And why had he teetered on the brink of violence when he saw men eyeing her like a delicacy they wanted to devour?

Sex. That was why. He wanted her. Badly. The fact he'd lusted after her while she flaunted herself like that had infuriated him.

But why?

She was his wife on paper only. She had no place in his life.

For some reason seeing her in that place had taken him

to the brink of civilised behaviour. Discovering she'd been there as a favour to a friend filled him with a relief he had no right to feel, as well as admiration for the way she helped her injured friend.

Now she seemed almost as concerned about returning those clothes as she was about her own predicament.

Ida Montrose—no, Ida Brunetti for the moment—was more complex than he'd imagined. She was doing his head in.

The fact she was a loyal friend and that she'd broken with Calogero didn't negate the way she'd made him a laughing stock, first with the blackmail and then her disappearance.

The fact he wanted her body had nothing to do with any of that.

Yet he was mired in questions, not just about Ida but also about his responses to her. Surely lust and the prospect of a brief affair didn't require so much soul-searching.

But if, in the course of their affair, he was to discover information that would help bring down Calogero faster, so much the better.

Ida might be wary. She might not like him. But, despite her words and frosty looks, she was rubbish at concealing that she wanted him as much as he wanted her.

A warm glow settled in his belly.

Satisfaction. And anticipation.

CHAPTER EIGHT

IDA STOOD ON the long balcony outside her bedroom. The sun had set but there was enough light to see the undulating countryside. Here and there were pinpricks of light from a far-off farmhouse or, on a distant hill, a town.

After London's chill the air felt balmy. Floral scents perfumed the night.

What would it be like living in a place like this? A place both beautiful and abundant. She'd grown to appreciate the extremes of the tiny island where she'd been raised. The white beaches and aquamarine but icy water, the brisk wind that turned so easily into a lashing gale that made you glad to be snug indoors.

Through the recent years in London she'd longed for the countryside. A quiet village rather than the bustle of the city. A place that felt like home, not just a refuge from the dangerous city streets.

She needed to decide on a place to start again. Should she try Liverpool or Birmingham? Somewhere big so she could lose herself in the crowd?

But that hadn't protected her from her grandfather or Cesare. They'd found her eventually.

Should she try for a smaller market town, even a village? But she had to work. Maybe a town.

She supposed it was possible she'd get some money on

her divorce, but most likely her grandfather had manipulated the prenuptial contract so it would be channelled via him. Besides, she wasn't sure she wanted Cesare's money, not after what her family had done to him.

Frustrated, she leaned on the balustrade. It was tranquil and, despite its being Cesare's house, she felt at peace. Maybe it was the quiet. Or the fact he'd left her alone to think. Knowing she was safe, even if her grandfather had guessed her location, made a huge difference.

Yet despite the serenity, Ida couldn't relax.

Because of Cesare's suggestion that they share the wedding night they'd never had.

He had a nerve!

But indignation was no match for other feelings. Fascination. Desire. Temptation.

She was twenty-three and she'd never been with a man.

Apart from those miserable months staying with her grandfather, she'd spent most of her life on a small island. She'd been home-schooled by Kate, her mother's cousin, and later via online courses.

She'd had little to do with men, except for her dreadful grandfather.

Ida had told herself she'd fallen for Cesare's looks and charisma because she was inexperienced. Yet in four years she hadn't wanted a sexual experience with any other man.

From the moment he'd erupted back into her world she'd been fixated on him. Beneath every interaction was the sizzle of awareness. Even now she felt the shivery run of nerves under her skin.

She didn't like him. Yet there was something between them she couldn't deny.

Was it just sexual attraction? She hoped so, given the dangerous romantic dreams she'd woven about him before.

It would be a relief if this was simple chemistry that could be eradicated by a fling.

He knew what he was talking about. He must have had lots of lovers.

Yet to give herself to him…

Ida didn't like putting herself in any man's power. Surely if they had sex, she'd be vulnerable to him?

But he'd admitted to vulnerability too. He'd said he wanted her in Rome.

Ida straightened and turned to walk the length of the long balcony, too keyed up to stay still.

Two things puzzled her: Cesare's kindness, for it *was* kindness, spiriting her away from Bruno, and his confession that he was drawn to her.

Had Cesare altered or just revealed what he'd hidden before?

The man was an enigma. He bothered and teased and fascinated her—

'Can't sleep, Ida?'

The velvety rumble stopped her in her tracks.

Slowly she turned. French doors stood open into a bedroom and a familiar tall figure stood propped against the door jamb.

Her pulse jumped.

Ida couldn't read Cesare's expression. But one glance absorbed his air of lazy masculine power, of intensity beneath the casual stance. His arms were crossed over his bare chest.

A surge of white noise in her ears blanked out the night as she took in that expanse of naked flesh, from straight shoulders all the way down to the narrow girth at his hips where he still wore trousers. His crossed arms emphasised his strength.

She'd sensed it when he was fully clothed but seeing him revealed now, albeit in the shadows, took her breath.

Ida grabbed the balustrade, stone biting her fingers.

'Cesare! I didn't realise…' She wouldn't have walked the length of the balcony if she'd known it led to the master suite.

Would she?

'That's disappointing.' Ida couldn't read his tone. Not amusement but something that she felt as a trickle of heat under her skin. 'I thought you'd decided to join me.'

With the light behind him it was impossible to read Cesare's expression, yet his body told its own tale. He might look relaxed, but the set of his shoulders belied that. As did the tension emanating from him.

Was his heart beating as fast as hers?

Ida wanted to plant her hand on his chest. A tingle ran across her palm as she imagined how it would feel. Would his chest hair be silky soft or crisp?

She swallowed, hands clenching to resist the temptation of him.

'I was just pacing while I make some plans.'

'Ah.' Cesare straightened. 'There was I imagining you thinking about us.'

Ida was about to say there was no *us* but stopped.

Why protest when he was right?

Life had taught her to face problems. Pretending they didn't exist never worked. This *was* a problem. For years Cesare had been there, a weakness she couldn't expunge. Distance hadn't helped, nor had hatred, distress or abstinence.

She drew a breath that felt like a sob.

She'd *tried* to resist him, but it wasn't working. What would it take to be free of this man?

Years of abstinence hadn't cured her. Was it possible his crazy proposition might?

Ida's gaze traced his powerful body. How would it feel to touch him? To stroke him all over, learn the sensations of his body against hers? Discover…?

Was that what this was? A desperation to discover sex?

She'd never had the opportunity for sexual experimentation earlier, and lately she'd been too busy surviving. Perhaps *that* was why now she felt so driven. Ida drew a relieved breath. That was much less scary than the idea that there was something special about Cesare Brunetti.

She should be thinking about transport, accommodation and work. Instead her mind buzzed with awareness of *him*.

Nothing was certain in this life, especially happiness. Joy was rare and fleeting. Maybe it wasn't joy she felt at the prospect of being with him, but it was compelling and as far away from fear as she could get.

Without letting herself think, she walked up to Cesare. He didn't stop her, simply unfolded his arms to give her free access as she planted her hands on his chest.

Excitement shivered through her as she got her answer. Surprisingly soft hair, not coarse, over hot, silky skin and hard muscle. She spread her fingers, splaying her hands, relishing each new sensation.

Cesare's heart thudded beneath her palm, steady but fast.

That pleased her and gave her the confidence to lean in and nuzzle the broad slope of his chest. She pressed her lips there, darted out the tip of her tongue and tasted something new. The dark, sultry tang of Cesare Brunetti.

A shudder racked her from the back of her skull to her toes and everywhere in between.

She'd thought she knew longing. Now she realised how much she had to learn. She'd just opened a Pandora's box of desire. And she wanted more.

Cesare watched Ida stalk across the balcony like a warrior going into battle. Would she argue or even slap him for his provocation?

Nothing prepared him for the impact of her hands across his flesh or the shock of her mouth on him.

His head ricocheted back, his breath an urgent gasp as she seduced him with lips and tongue and the possessive swipe of her exploring hands.

His arms came around her, holding her to him just in case she had any thoughts about retreating.

He doubted she even noticed. She was rubbing her face against him and over the rush of blood in his ears he caught the tiniest sound. Something between a growl and a purr. It came from Ida.

His nostrils flared as his body responded to that innately sexy sound. He planted his feet wide, drawing her against him.

He'd hoped she'd come to him because she wanted him but hadn't truly believed it. Nothing in life was so simple. Especially not his wife.

Cesare stiffened, a jolt of pure hunger driving through his groin as teeth scraped near his collarbone.

'Ida.' He didn't know if it was a warning or a groan of delight. All he knew was that he needed more.

He cradled her cheeks, gently tilting her face up. He saw the gleam of slitted eyes and darkened lips, still open from where she'd nibbled his skin.

Cesare lowered his head, waiting for her response. Could this be a tease? A taunt to bring him to his knees while she demanded some additional divorce settlement?

Once more Ida cut through old expectations with devastating simplicity. She swayed closer, her breasts in that pretty dress against his bare torso, her hips nestling against his groin.

Triumph melded with need and, yes, desperation, turning his body to unyielding hardness. But as he bent his head, inhaling Ida's fresh spring scent, his touch was gentle.

Their lips met and clung and Cesare felt his hands tremble. As if he'd waited so long for this that he couldn't believe it was real.

Her cheeks were soft, her lips too. That made him leash the hammering urge to take her quickly. Instead he wanted to savour every sensation.

Savour Ida.

He swiped his tongue across her open lips then delved further, fascinated by the quick clench of her fingertips where they clung now to his upper arms. Then she relaxed, leaning against him as her tongue briefly touched his.

It was crazy but Cesare felt that brief connection like a thunderbolt passing through his body. He tingled all over as if from an electric shock.

He angled his head for better access, exploring her mouth, losing himself in lush sweetness that tasted faintly of cherries. Their tongues met again, not a darting foray this time but a sliding caress. His eyes closed as, stunned, he registered the extent of his arousal. Just from a kiss!

Ida's hands crept up his shoulders, around his neck and into his hair, tugging him to the edge of pain. The sting only made his senses spark as he deepened their kiss. It was the most flagrantly erotic yet strangely innocent kiss he could remember.

It took him to the edge in seconds. Four years of celibacy took their toll. That had to be the reason this felt like nothing he'd ever experienced.

Cesare dragged air through his nostrils, seeking control. Then Ida rose on her toes, her breasts pushing against his chest as she kissed him deeply.

Thought crumbled beneath that ardent onslaught. Cesare dropped his hands to her hips, holding her high against him, giving back kiss for kiss till he heard it again, that tiny purr of pleasure from the back of her throat.

It galvanised him. Firming his hold, he swung her round and settled her back against the door jamb, stepping in close so she didn't slide down to the floor. Her hands tightened in his hair and then he was helping her lift her legs around his hips.

His hands met soft layers of fabric then smooth, cool skin, and fire ignited.

'Ida.' Her name was a gravel growl in his throat and lower, in his belly where the need for her had been building for so long.

'Cesare.'

Did he hear it or just feel the vibration of her assent through their locked mouths? Either way, nothing had ever sounded so good.

Sweat broke out at the back of his neck as he lifted his hands, dragging them up her slender frame to cup her breasts. They fitted his hands perfectly and, though he longed to tear her free of the fabric, he restrained himself.

Cesare settled for massaging her breasts, finding her nipples through the flimsy fabric and rolling them between his fingers, feeling her body jerk in response and her pelvis thrust towards him.

He lifted his mouth, ignoring her protest, to nuzzle her throat, kissing and nipping and hearing her sighs turn to moans that drove the ache of desire to sharp pain.

His groin felt as if it were in a vice. That one wrong move would undo him.

Cesare shut his eyes and drew a deep breath filled with hyacinths, the rich perfume of warm woman and the beckoning, indefinable scent of arousal.

'I want you, Ida. I need you.'

There was no thought of hiding the truth. Or the fact she'd once been his enemy.

Nothing mattered but *this*.

'Yes, please.'

Please? As if she sought a favour!

His lips curved against her fragrant skin. This would be a mutual favour.

'Hold tight,' he murmured, sliding his arms around her narrow waist and straightening.

It was hard to think when Ida clung to him, when her delicious heat was pressed against his erection. But higher levels of thought weren't required. His body knew what to do, hold her tight and get to his bed as soon as possible. He was barely aware of crossing the threshold but suddenly he was by the bed, illuminated by a single lamp. He turned so that when they fell to the mattress she was on top.

Cesare's eyes shut for a second as he absorbed every detail of delicious sensation.

When he opened them she'd pulled back just enough to look down at him, though their bodies were still plastered together. Desire throbbed through him, and he saw her eyes widen at the twitch of his erection.

That soft green gaze was bewitching. It took a second for him to realise her fixed stare didn't match the message of her eager body.

'What is it?'

'Nothing.' Her pupils dilated as if in surprise. Then she frowned. 'But you need to know I'm not…experienced. I'd rather we went slow.'

Slow? After she'd rocked his world? Her mouth on his flesh, her hands in his hair, her kiss…

And what did she mean by not experienced? He discounted the idea she was a virgin. She'd sashayed up to him with all the confidence of a woman who knew exactly what she wanted.

Maybe she feared he wouldn't take enough time to please her as well as himself. Cesare was about to tell her she didn't need to pretend to innocence. He had every intention of ensuring they both enjoyed this to the full. But he had better things to do than talk.

'I can do slow.' His voice dropped. 'All the better to savour you.'

He watched, fascinated, as colour darkened her cheekbones. And just like that, despite the urgency humming in his blood, *slow* was exactly what he wanted.

CHAPTER NINE

CESARE'S EYES LOOKED almost black, and Ida had no difficulty reading their expression. Anticipation. And something knowing and heated that might have worried her yet instead made her shift against him.

Maybe he hadn't understood. Maybe he didn't realise not experienced meant *no* experience.

But she liked Cesare's heavy-lidded look too much to explain. The last thing she wanted was him changing his mind. If he was happy to go slow, what more could she ask?

Everything about Cesare, from his response to her touch, to his kisses, to the way he'd held her and how his big, bold body felt beneath her right now, confirmed this was exactly what she wanted.

What she needed.

'Aren't you going to kiss me?'

His voice rumbled up from that broad chest beneath her, fascinating her and making her even keener to explore him. She wanted to stroke his firm flesh all over, learn the contours of his body, taste him.

Of course she kissed him again. His kisses were addictive. If she'd known before that a kiss could feel like this...

Ida wondered what he'd say if she revealed she'd never kissed any man but him. But then she was leaning down, lips against his, her tongue reaching out to meet his as he'd taught her, and her mind blanked.

It was the most luscious, decadent thing, lying over Cesare, pressed against his arousal, knowing it was for her.

Her eyes fluttered shut as she gave herself up to a new world of bliss.

Some time later she frowned, belatedly registering something had changed. Even then it took a while to understand her back was on the bed and Cesare was pressed down on her. She gasped against his mouth, wondering at how good that felt.

'Too heavy?' He propped himself up on one elbow, dark hair falling across his brow.

'No.'

But it was too late, he was rolling off her onto his hip. His index finger followed the ribbon running beneath her breasts. His gaze held hers as he traced it up to her shoulder.

'Pretty. So pretty I don't want to tear it. Where's the zip, Ida?'

Something caught in her chest at the idea of Cesare tearing the dress in his urgency. Her pulse thudded once, hard, then she reached for her side.

His hand covered hers. 'Let me.'

Ida lay back and watched him lean over, his hand skimming downwards. The zip sounded incredibly loud then warm fingers touched her hip, her waist, trawling higher.

'So pretty,' he murmured again, as he slipped a finger under first one velvet shoulder strap then another, drawing them down her arms.

But he wasn't looking at the dress. He was staring at her. Then his mouth was on her shoulder, and she was arching towards him.

Cesare's kisses were unhurried and thorough. He moved to her collarbone, to the upper slopes of her breasts and across to her other shoulder, where he nipped at the curve of her neck. Ida's bones turned to liquid.

Her eyes were closed when he pulled back and it took a moment to realise he'd drawn her dress down to her waist. A gentle tug made her lift her hips then she felt the swish of fabric against bare skin as he dragged it off her completely.

Her eyes snapped open. Cesare was surveying her with a curiously shuttered expression. But the throbbing pulse at his temple belied his stillness.

Ida wore a strapless bra and knickers of matching ivory lace. She told herself they were no more revealing than a bikini but the fierce gleam in his eyes told another story. To her surprised delight, she revelled in Cesare's response.

He said something fervent in Italian that curled around her like smoke, feathering her skin and making her shift as an insistent pulse beat between her legs.

'Your turn.'

But he shook his head. 'Not yet. Not if you want us to go slow.'

The way she felt she wasn't sure that slow was an option any longer. But before she could voice that, Cesare lay down beside her and the feel of his hot, bare torso against her stole her breath.

As did his zephyr-light touch, skimming the top of her bra from one side to another, back and forth and back again, making her want more. One finger dipped below the edge of the fabric, sliding across her breast. Her jaw gritted at his teasing and she reached down, towards his belt, only to falter when Cesare pulled the bra cup down and buried his face at her breast.

Was that high, keening note from her? Ida rose off the bed, her hands buried in his hair as she held him to her, afraid he'd stop.

The sensations were incredible. First that exploratory

flick of his tongue that shot lightning through her and now… He drew on her breast and it simultaneously pulled her whole body taut yet made a vital part of her melt.

Nothing had ever felt like this. As if he tapped into a vein of raw need.

She slid against him, rocking her hips, needing to feel him against all of her. Then through the haze of wonder came something new: Cesare's hand slipping deftly under the lace at her hips. There was no hesitation, just an arrow-straight dip straight to the hidden cleft where…

'Cesare!'

She shuddered as hot, bright sensation arced between her breast and his questing fingers.

She'd expected this to be good, but she hadn't *known*.

Ida snapped her eyes open and there was Cesare, his mouth locked around her nipple, his black-as-night eyes hot with passion as he circled then pressed just at the place where sensation centred.

Again Ida lifted off the bed. Lightning forked inside her and she hovered, strung out on a peak of incredible ecstasy until, in a blast of blinding delight, everything else fell away.

The only thing anchoring her to reality was Cesare. The warm weight of him solid and reassuring against her as she soared in a sky full of shattering stars.

Finally Ida became aware of the sound of panting. Swift, shallow breaths and the hard pump of her overworked lungs. She trembled all over. Surely her bones had disintegrated in that white-hot light?

Cesare kissed her breast, a tiny caress, but to her overwrought senses it was too much. She shuddered, echoes of bliss still coursing through her.

Did he understand? The next thing she knew he was lying full length beside her, his arm around her shoulder, holding her close to his collarbone, his other hand rubbing gently between her shoulder blades.

Ida sank into him, trying not to feel overwrought by the roaring rush of ecstasy that had engulfed her.

Would it have felt the same with any other man?

Stupid question when she'd never had the least desire to let any man but Cesare this close.

It dawned on her maybe this whole experience was a dreadful mistake.

Too late now. No time for regrets.

Ida's mouth curved against hot, salty skin. Even reeling from her first sexual experience with a man, she realised that thought was solely so she'd stop worrying and lose herself in what Cesare had to offer.

And he had a lot!

Ida had wanted to explore his body and now he let her, with the proviso that his trousers stayed on and she only touched bare flesh.

She was fascinated by his hands, the sweeping indent of his back, the wide sprawl of his shoulders, and the way he jumped when she rolled him over then sat astride him and nipped tiny scraping kisses down his neck.

He was sensitive just below the shoulder blades, and just above his hip. Ida felt a tiny tremor of response when she kissed him there. Heard his hissed breath when she kissed her way down his chest, her hair trailing over him. She was fascinated by the counterpoint of hot, satiny skin and that smattering of hair that felt so good to the touch. How would it feel against her bare breasts?

This was her opportunity to find out. Tonight, the wedding night they'd never had, she could do what she wanted, secure in the knowledge she could walk away tomorrow and never look back.

A sharp pang sheared through her, making her pause.

'Ida? Is something wrong?'

She slanted a look at Cesare, lying with his hands behind his head, biceps curled in a way that created another tight curl, this time in her pelvis. A sexual response, she assured herself, but something more too. *That* disturbed her.

This was supposed to be a fleeting thing, a chance to satisfy and finally eradicate that edgy feeling of need.

'What could be wrong?'

Ida had been alone so long, depending on no one but herself. This yearning for connection rocked her.

Of all the people in the world, Cesare was the last to want more from her than a single night. She couldn't let her mind stray to impossibilities.

She'd make the most of tonight then move on. There was no other option.

'I can't imagine,' he said and reached out, pulling her to him. He held her for a long moment, liquid dark eyes intent on her. 'You would tell me if there's a problem.'

It was neither a question nor a statement. A command perhaps. There *was* something intrinsically commanding about him, even half-dressed. Especially half-dressed, for there was no mistaking his strength and aura of certainty.

Ida envied him. For years she'd felt weak and worried.

But she didn't feel that way as he flicked her bra undone.

She barely had time to realise what he'd done when his hands and mouth were on her and that glorious conflagration started again, fed by his outrageously extravagant praise.

After that, things blurred again. Another swipe of his hands and her underwear was completely gone. Then Cesare set about exploring her even more thoroughly than she had him.

This man had a sixth sense where her body was concerned. He knew, or quickly discovered, where to touch to make her breath catch and her body burn.

By the time he drew back, reaching for the buckle of his belt, Ida was spent, sprawled boneless on the bed, her body shimmering with pleasure after another exquisite climax.

Even so, the sight of Cesare tugging at his belt then rising and pushing the last of his clothes to the floor made every hormone sit up and take note. Watching him roll on a condom was unbelievably arousing, even for a woman who should be comatose from bliss.

The man was beautiful. His body all symmetry and entrancing planes. Ida's gaze dropped to those heavy thighs and above them a spear of an erection that looked potently impressive.

She thought of their difference in size and about scary stories she'd heard of disastrous first times.

Then Cesare's mouth quirked up at one side, probably because of how she stared, and her tremble of nerves subsided. Theirs might be a temporary alliance, but he'd proven patient and considerate.

Remarkable as it was, *she trusted him*.

Ida met his smile with one of her own and lay back, waiting.

That smile. That body.

Did Ida have any idea how she tested his control, lying there looking so tempting? So outrageously seductive and adorably rumpled?

Adorably? Surely not. Yet there was something about her mix of enthusiasm and almost unconscious allure that made him feel protective as well as aroused.

Taking this slow *had* been the best way. Yet now his capacity for delay was gone. Being with Ida each time she came had only made his own need more desperate.

Cesare nudged her knees wide. Her smile disappeared but she lifted her arms, inviting him down to her, and he couldn't stifle the siren's call any longer.

Her body was soft and accommodating, fragrant and welcoming, and he fitted between her hips as if they were made for each other.

He lifted himself on his elbows, not wanting to squash her, but that left his chest just far enough from hers that her peaked nipples teased him with each breath.

Cesare gritted his jaw, feeling the welded-tight pressure in his groin and thighs, the building heat, and knew he wouldn't last.

Her eyes really were the most amazing colour. They beckoned him to Paradise.

Slipping his palm under her thigh, he raised it so her leg was bent, his aim to make it easier for her to take him. She lifted her other leg and even that slide of silky skin felt far, far too good.

Cesare pushed home.

It was all he'd anticipated and more. Much more. Ida fitted him like a velvet glove, so close he had to shut his eyes and concentrate on not losing himself on the first thrust.

But there was more. A snag. An unexpected sensation that made him try to pause, but it was too late. Even as he registered the sensation it was gone.

He opened his eyes and looked down to find Ida wincing, her eyes screwed tight and…was that perspiration on her brow?

His brain conjured an unthinkable possibility.

Was it possible she'd been innocent as in totally inexperienced?

He was still striving to process that when green eyes met his. They looked foggy. With pain?

He was withdrawing, his mind whirling, when she

grabbed his shoulders and pulled. As if she had the strength to stop him going.

No, it was the determined set of her jaw and the way she hitched first one leg higher around his waist, then the other, that stopped him.

'Don't go now.' Her voice had an unfamiliar raspy edge. 'You promised me a wedding night and I want it all.'

Cesare stared into her flushed face, wondering how badly he'd hurt her. Was she saying that because she felt she owed him or because she really wanted this?

'Don't make me plead, Cesare.'

'I wouldn't dream of it.'

He lifted his hand to her cheek, watched her turn and press a kiss to his palm and felt the tight band around his chest ease. He trailed unsteady fingers to her berry-tipped breast and felt it peak as her pupils dilated and her flush deepened.

Slowly Cesare leaned forward, taking her mouth as his body took hers, gently but steadily, aiming to stir her senses as surely as she stirred his.

But his own arousal was too acute for patience. He slipped his hand between them, teasing her with his fingers while he drove into her with all the control he could muster.

Urgent hands grabbed his shoulders then his skull, and to his relief soon he heard the muffled sound of her ecstasy building, felt her little shudders. If he could just last a little longer...

Cesare moved faster, driven by his own rhythm of need, growing more urgent with each thrust. Then he was swallowing her screams of completion and that shot him over the edge, spilling himself in a desperate, pulsating climax that blanked his mind and undid his body in a cataclysm of pleasure.

Rapture was the word that came to his befuddled brain

much later as they lay together, he on his back with his arms around her, she with her head buried in his neck. He'd always enjoyed sex but that had reached an entirely new level.

Now and then, another little tremor ran through him, and he'd feel her quiver around him in response. Even that felt too acute, too profound.

Four years of abstinence, he told himself when his head finally cleared. That was the explanation. Four years without a woman in his bed. That was why this seemed phenomenal.

In that time his sole focus had been turning the company around from the disasters after his father took over as CEO when Cesare's grandfather died. That and triumphing over Calogero.

Plus, whether from the old-fashioned values instilled by his grandfather, or from stubborn pride, Cesare hadn't wanted to break his vow of fidelity, even to a wife he didn't respect.

And now? She wouldn't be his wife much longer, which was a relief. Yet he was learning she wasn't as he'd imagined her. Not totally at any rate.

He'd jumped to at least one wrong conclusion about Ida. Was it possible there were others?

The idea disturbed him.

Carefully he withdrew from her, settling her on her side and getting to his feet.

For a full minute he stood, watching her. Her eyes were closed and her mouth slightly open as she slept.

She looked delicate, arousing another burst of protectiveness. She also looked exhausted. Not surprising since it seemed she'd never done this before.

Cesare spied a red mark on her breast and another at her throat and lifted his hand to his jaw, finding it ready for a shave. He felt a spiralling drop in his belly. Guilt that he'd grazed her sensitive skin.

He did *not* experience a secret burst of delight and possessiveness at the idea he was her first lover. Or that she carried the mark of his body on hers.

That would be beneath him. It would be uncivilised.

But hadn't Ida always tapped into a vein of something in him that wasn't sophisticated or enlightened? Right from the beginning he'd responded to her with unvarnished emotions that threatened to cloud his judgement.

The fact she'd taken *him* as her first lover stunned, perplexed and delighted him.

Cesare spun away and headed for the bathroom.

When Ida had appeared on the balcony all he'd been able to think about was how much he wanted her.

He'd been wrong to think one brief taste would be enough to satisfy a craving that had built for so long. Especially now.

Even satiated he wanted her.

He had more questions than ever. And he was determined to get answers.

CHAPTER TEN

'I KNOW YOU'RE AWAKE, IDA.'

Ida sighed and burrowed into the pillow. Couldn't he leave her be? He'd got up then stood watching her, and she'd felt vulnerable, trying to make sense of the maelstrom of emotions churning through her.

She didn't feel any more ready to face him now.

Instead of lying here she should have got up immediately and gone to her room. She needed to process every incredible moment they'd shared.

She'd love to think she'd chosen not to leave because she wasn't a coward.

In fact, she hadn't been sure her legs would support her. Her bones felt like jelly and whole swathes of her body seemed to have turned to mush.

Or maybe that was her brain. Because she'd been thinking ridiculous things about Cesare, as if that shocking combination of tenderness and firmly leashed male power as they made love meant something important and personal.

Annoyance at herself and at him for being so contrary and confounding made her frown. She opened her eyes to see him standing, hands on hips, surveying her across the bed.

Hair tousled, jaw darkening, body...well, frankly superb. He was devastating.

So much for assuming sex would cure her attraction.

A warm weight stirred inside. A sensation she should not be feeling after—could it really be three orgasms?

Heat scored her cheeks and she scrambled up to find the top sheet and drag it over her.

At least her arms worked. She still wasn't sure about her legs.

'I'll go soon.'

'No need. I just wondered if you'd like a bath.' He paused. 'In case you're sore.'

Ida drew a slow breath, trying to read his face. She'd told him she wasn't experienced but hadn't been explicit. Had he been disappointed?

The gentle throb between her legs, courtesy of their enthusiastic coupling, told her not to be stupid. Yet she couldn't help wondering.

'What are you thinking, Ida?'

Great. With her pale skin he'd see the flush rising in her throat and cheeks. It was the bane of her life.

'No, thanks. I don't want a bath.'

Still he seemed to be waiting, the muscles around his shoulders and neck standing taut as if something worried him. Could it be the fact she'd given him her virginity?

'I'm not sore. I'm good. Just far too relaxed to move yet.'

Though she'd have to shift soon. She wasn't naïve enough to expect Cesare wanted her to share his bed through the night. He'd specified sex only.

'I'm glad you feel okay.'

He wasn't effusive but maybe she'd guessed right, for the rigid set of his shoulders eased as he drew back the sheet and got in beside her.

That surprised her. She'd thought he'd dress again and expect her to as well.

Instantly every nerve ending sparked. In anticipation?

But he didn't touch her, instead propping himself on one arm, his gaze on her.

'You're not as I remember you, Ida.'

She rolled onto her side to face him, head on the pillow. He really did have the most comfortable bed.

'You said that before. You make it sound like I've changed.' Which she undoubtedly had. 'But you never really knew me.'

'So I'm beginning to realise.'

She waited. Now he'd pepper her with questions about her grandfather, or the strip club, or her supposed role in the blackmail.

Instead the silence stretched so long she felt herself ease further into the mattress, deep-seated lethargy and a sense of peace filling her despite Cesare's watchful stare. Great sex was exhausting as well as exhilarating, she discovered. On top of that she was still worn out from stress and long hours working.

Eventually Cesare reached out and took her hand, drawing it across the sheet towards him.

'What's the problem with your hands?'

She took a moment to register his words. Then she looked to where her fingers threaded through his olive-toned ones. His fingers were long and there was a drift of dark hair on the back of his hand. In contrast her hand was pale, except for the blotches of pink and areas of peeling skin.

Instinctively Ida made to withdraw her hand, but he held it firmly, his thumb stroking a slow rhythm across her knuckles.

Of course he'd noticed her hands. He'd kissed her all over. She'd just been too busy swooning to think about it.

'A reaction to wearing rubber gloves.'

After years of wearing them for work her skin had suddenly become sensitive.

His gaze turned sharp, and she could almost hear his brain whirring, processing that information.

'Is it painful?'

Ida blinked, surprised, though she didn't know why.

'It can be uncomfortable.'

Itchy. And embarrassing, she now discovered. She mightn't be Cesare's wife in the usual sense but part of her was jealous of those beautiful, glamorous women who flocked around him. She hated feeling inferior, though dermatitis was nothing to be ashamed of. Yet she had nothing to prove to him.

What was wrong with her?

'We'll get some ointment for it tomorrow. Dorotea may have some or we'll buy something.'

She'd run out of medicated cream and hadn't had a chance to get more. 'Thank you.'

It was kind of him.

Or was it that he didn't like looking at her damaged hands? Ida tugged and, when he released his grip, slipped her hand beneath the sheet.

She really should go to her own room.

'That's why you wore the black gloves. To hide your hands.'

Ida kept her tone casual though she didn't like talking about it. 'Dermatitis is bad for business.' She wanted Cesare to remember her as sexy and attractive, not the woman with a skin condition.

'And what business were you in that required rubber gloves?'

For a second she thought he was insinuating some sort of kinky sex game. Except Cesare knew now that she was new to sex.

'I'm a cleaner. I clean houses for rich people during the day and offices at night.' Interesting that Cesare's dark eyes didn't look shocked or pitying. In fact, they simply looked warm and attractive. 'Jo was doing some of my night shifts while I filled in for her at the club.'

Cesare's mouth flattened. Did she imagine it?

Ida suppressed a yawn. She was suddenly incredibly tired. She felt as if she was floating. She blamed this soft mattress, the luxury of a truly comfortable bed and knowing she was safe here from Bruno.

True safety was something she hadn't experienced for a long, long time.

'Tell me, Ida.' Cesare's voice was low and soothing. 'How long have you worked as a cleaner?'

She blinked and tried to focus. Why was he interested? On the other hand, what harm could it do to answer?

'Since I went to London. Four years.' She frowned. 'I'm tired. I should go to my room.'

'If you like. Or you could rest here for a bit first.'

That sounded perfect. Even so, it was puzzling. Surely Cesare wanted the privacy of his room now they'd had sex.

Ida was trying to make sense of that when she slipped softly into sleep.

Cesare lay in the darkness staring at the ceiling.

Ida was snuggled under the covers, her hand tucked under the pillow, like a child.

There was something endearing about the way she'd succumbed suddenly to sleep. One moment they'd been talking. The next her eyelids drooped, and she was out for the count.

Cesare wasn't used to sharing his bed. Strange that he didn't find it disturbing now. But he had a lot on his mind.

He'd expected making love with Ida to be memorable—

she'd got under his skin in ways he couldn't explain—yet he hadn't been prepared for their intense passion. For the feelings she engendered in him. And the doubts. She hadn't tried to change his mind about her, yet he was questioning so much.

If Ida had worked the hours she described for any length of time, no wonder she was exhausted.

Why had she been working as a cleaner?

How long had she been hiding from her grandfather?

Cesare had assumed the old man knew where Ida was though he'd claimed not to. He'd probably supported her, laughing up his sleeve as he watched Cesare contend with the far-fetched rumours about his missing wife.

Yet Ida had said she'd worked as a cleaner for four years. It made no sense. She was Calogero's golden charm, his way into the elite society he'd been jealous of all these years. He'd have been delighted with her for marrying Cesare. She had no reason to hide from him.

Cesare needed to get to the bottom of the mystery. Because there *was* a mystery.

Cesare rolled onto his side, watching the woman asleep in his bed.

She was an enigma. Feisty and strong yet vulnerable.

Her virginity had been a total surprise and it altered his view of her.

Lack of sexual experience doesn't mean she was truly an innocent. There was nothing innocent about marrying a man for money and prestige. Or being party to blackmail.

Calogero had made much of his granddaughter's innocence. Maybe that was why she'd still been a virgin, because she knew some men prized that.

The thought stirred nausea.

Yet the woman he'd met yesterday—was it only yesterday?—wasn't the one he remembered.

In London Ida had been angry and abrasive, unimpressed to see him and impatient to end their marriage.

Cesare's thoughts slowed. That had been a blow to his ego. But it didn't explain the compulsion he'd felt, the *need* for her. That predated London.

She'd shown a strength and determination he hadn't noticed before. She'd been open and, as far as he could tell, utterly authentic, both in her dislike of him and later when sharing her body.

Heat beat through his blood at the memory of Ida's soft gasps, that pleased purr and the shocked cries of delight as she'd found her peak. He'd revelled in them all. They'd roused him to a point where pleasure became pain as he tried to keep control.

Cesare had seen Ida's surprise at her own responses and knew the woman in his bed hadn't been playing a game. She'd seemed shocked at her own capacity for pleasure.

Cesare knew he'd finally met the real Ida.

In Rome and before, in her grandfather's home, he'd *felt* her constraint and understood she was careful with her responses to him.

He'd known the woman who'd agreed to marry him was a façade, a construct made to appear as a sweet, appealing fiancée. There'd been a deep reserve about her and the glances she'd shot her grandfather made it clear she took her lead from Calogero.

In London yesterday Cesare had again sensed constraint, and an unwillingness to let him into her world. She'd built walls around herself.

But in Tuscany something had shifted. Had the walls fallen? Or was Ida allowing him carefully curated glimpses of herself, projecting some new image? Was she playing an even deeper game than before? Having seen women string his father along, he knew about female manipulation.

Cesare sighed. He knew better than to think that because Ida surprised him and he liked what he'd discovered, everything had changed.

He'd never let attraction blur caution or common sense. He'd seen the debacle his father had made of his life, seduced by sex, his judgement flawed, the results disastrous.

He needed the truth about Ida. The more he understood, the greater the possibility of uncovering more ammunition against Calogero. But mainly because this felt like unfinished business between him and Ida.

The sheet had fallen low over her shoulder and Cesare pulled it up, brushing the cool flesh of her back. Instantly she rolled closer.

Cesare stilled, then after a moment's hesitation hauled her to him.

It felt surprisingly good, having her snuggle up. He rarely spent the night with a lover, not wanting to raise expectations of permanency.

This wasn't permanent. Even if, for a while longer, his lover was Ida Brunetti, his wife.

Strange how after years of negative thoughts, the idea of this woman bound with him in marriage didn't spark instant rejection.

It had to be because the end was in sight. Divorce papers signed, Calogero's hold on the company gone and the man himself heading towards a criminal trial, though he didn't know it yet.

As Cesare relaxed, drawing in the alluring scent of sated woman and spring flowers, realisation hit.

Having her here wasn't just good for easing his sexual frustration and digging out information on Calogero. It could provide other opportunities. After the difficulties of the last few years, being seen with his wife, albeit for a short time, could be useful.

Cesare smiled as he tucked her closer.

The compulsion he'd felt to possess Ida hadn't *really* been a compulsion. Of course not.

Cesare didn't let lust drive his actions. He wasn't a slave to emotion. He wasn't weak like his father.

He was being pragmatic. Bedding Ida had been beyond his expectations, but his aim was to excise these intense and disturbing urges. It was safer to sate himself with her now in order to distance himself later. To keep head and heart, or at least libido, separate.

Unlike his father, he'd never allow himself to be a slave to emotion or illusions of love. Because he'd experienced the fallout, seen the damage to family and business. Felt the rejection.

It was a trap Cesare would never fall into.

Ida woke to a delicious sense of peace and comfort. She was warm and cosy and...

Her brain jerked into full wakefulness as she realised her cheek rested on sleek, warm skin and that masculine chest hair tickled her hand.

Cesare.

The man she hated.

Except it wasn't hate she felt.

He'd protected her from Bruno.

And made love to her last night until she saw stars.

Despite knowing it was just sex, it had *felt* like making love. Cesare had been gentle as well as eager, breath-stealingly sensual and potent.

'More.' His deep voice was gruff.

'Sorry?' She hadn't even realised he was awake.

'Do that again. I like it.'

Ida hadn't done anything but inadvertently slide her hand across his chest.

Daylight spilled between the open curtains and, tucked against his shoulder, she had a perfect view of his musculature, of the contrast of dark olive skin against pale, and the hard nub of his erect nipple.

A thrill ran through her. Cesare was aroused. She drew her hand back across that wide expanse of muscle and felt him tense.

'I want you, Ida.'

She sucked in air, stunned at the impact of that stark admission. Men had wanted her before, but she'd never been tempted. Until Cesare.

This, whatever it was, felt perilous and profound. An elemental force.

Now you're acting like a besotted virgin, confusing sex with something else.

Ida wasn't looking for anything else.

But she did want more of what they'd shared last night. She'd take all the pleasure she could, hoarding it for the future when life would again be a grim struggle for self-sufficiency, trying to keep out of her grandfather's reach.

She leaned down and licked Cesare's nipple then closed her teeth around it, excited by his hissed exclamation and the way his big body rose against her.

An instant later she found herself above him, his hands at her hips, his bare body wonderful against hers.

Ida raised her head and met brown eyes that had turned so dark they seemed black. But there was light in them and a tortured smile on his face that she read easily. She must have looked that way last night.

Last night Cesare had teased her to the edge of bliss time and again, but she felt nowhere near sated. Time was running out. They'd had their night together. If she wanted more, she needed to take it now.

Pushing herself up on hands and knees, she began to

move down the bed, pausing to swirl her tongue around his navel and feel a shot of adrenaline as Cesare shuddered and groaned. Then she moved lower, fascinated as his erection swelled before her eyes.

Tentatively she touched him, surprised at the combination of incredible softness over such rigidity. His thighs were rock solid, and his body moved with each stroke of her fingertip. He was so incredibly sensitive.

A smug smile curved Ida's mouth, her hair curtaining her face as she bent over him.

One delicate lick of her tongue and she was blown away. All that virile power, straining for her attention. Another stroke then she settled her lips around him.

Cesare rose, lifting her up and pulling her hair away from her face. Looking up, she met coal-dark eyes and heat punched her, rolling down through her body. When he looked at her like that she felt…

'Come here, Ida. I want you.'

She shook her head. She'd only just begun and had so much to discover.

'I promise you can do that later. But now…' She heard the catch in his voice. 'I need you.'

They were only words. They didn't mean anything. Yet something tumbled over inside because he needed her and admitted it. Besides, as fascinating as this was, she wanted him inside her. The empty clenching between her thighs told its own tale.

Soon she was poised above him, knees wide on the bed while he sheathed himself.

'Guide me in, *cara*.'

Cesare's hands went to her breasts as she gripped him and sank down. Sheet lightning blasted through her. The sensations were like last night. That incredible fullness, the friction. But above all, the way he held her gaze with his sultry, hooded stare as he told her how good this felt.

Ida didn't understand Italian, but she knew they were words of praise and encouragement. His hands worshipped her as his body took up a harder, insistent rhythm and she learned to ride him. It was as if they'd been made for this, for the dancing race that grew faster and more urgent with every buck of his hips and every slide of her body.

Until there it came again. The tendrils of fire, the combustion, the white-hot light that caught her just as Cesare called her name and pulled her, shuddering, onto his chest. He wrapped her in his embrace as the world spun and bliss took her, and she felt the hard pump of his orgasm deep within.

Sharing this with Cesare felt elemental. Too profound for words.

Ida just hoped it wasn't addictive.

CHAPTER ELEVEN

THEY BREAKFASTED IN a secluded arbour. The air was warm and scented and before them tranquil gardens stretched towards a landscape of golds and greens, the undulating hills of Tuscany.

Ida had seen the view yesterday but was still entranced. Shifting shadows and colours painted an ever-changing scene. It was even more beautiful than she'd imagined.

Or maybe that was because her blood still fizzed with elation after last night. It had been a revelation. An interlude of glorious joy that cast her grim, difficult world into the shadows, just for a while.

She wished their night together hadn't ended. One night hadn't quenched her desire. If anything, it had taken her awareness of Cesare, her fascination, to a higher level. Her body hummed just from being so close.

But since leaving his bedroom neither had mentioned the night they'd shared. Ida because it felt momentous and far too new for idle conversation.

And Cesare? She couldn't tell what he felt. He was the perfect, solicitous host, but he didn't touch her.

Ida was surprised at how much she wanted him to.

Cesare leaned towards her. 'Coffee?'

Its rich fragrance hit her nostrils like a benediction. In

London her budget was so tight she had only powdered instant.

'Yes, please.' She eyed the basket of pastries warm from the oven. 'This is glorious, thank you.'

'Thank Dorotea. She did all the work.'

That made Ida look at him as he passed her cup.

Cesare had already revealed a considerate side. Yet how many men, especially wealthy men, truly appreciated the work others did for them?

Her view was coloured by her grandfather, who treated staff like automatons rather than people. But interactions with rich clients in London had been the same. They expected her to be invisible as she cleaned. Most saw themselves as innately superior, ever ready to criticise but not praise or appreciate.

But not, it seemed, Cesare.

She thought of how he'd taken time to reassure Jo, who was nervous after her assault. The easy way he'd chatted with staff in the London hotel and on the trip here. He noticed other people. More, he treated them as equals.

Ida liked that.

'I'm lucky to have her,' Cesare added as he passed the basket of baked goods. 'Dorotea takes everything in her stride, is always prepared and is a fantastic cook.'

Ida took a *cornetto*, the Italian version of a croissant, and another pastry. She was starving.

'She's worked for you a long time?'

'Years. Dorotea was my grandfather's housekeeper before I came to live with him as a child.'

'You lived with your grandfather?'

Cesare reached for a pastry. 'He brought me up. I was fortunate to have such a great role model.'

Unlike *her* grandfather, she mused as she bit into light,

flaky pastry. Luckily, she hadn't had to live permanently with the old man. The notion made her skin crawl.

'What's wrong?'

She looked up to see Cesare leaning back in his chair, his indolent posture at odds with that alert gaze. But Ida didn't want to talk about her grandfather.

'I was just surprised. I knew you lost your mother when you were very young, but I hadn't realised your father died when you were a child too.' She'd thought he'd died not long before their wedding.

Cesare's expression blanked and she had the feeling she'd crossed some unseen boundary. Then he shrugged and sipped his coffee.

'He didn't. But he wasn't the paternal type. My father had his own interests and found it easier not to have a kid cramping his style. Plus, he did a lot of travelling for business. He didn't stay in one place long.'

Cesare's posture was relaxed but his eyes, and that edge to his voice, indicated his father's rejection had cut deep.

'I'm sorry. That must have been tough.'

A week ago, she'd never have imagined Cesare sharing anything so personal with her. Or her feeling sympathy for the boy he'd been, shuffled off to be cared for by someone else. It was something they had in common, though their circumstances were very different.

She knew what it was to be wrenched from parents and transplanted into an unfamiliar new world.

He shrugged. 'It worked out well. My grandfather raised me here in Tuscany and I couldn't have asked for a better childhood.'

There was no mistaking Cesare's affection for the man who'd raised him. Ida felt another bond of shared experience.

'My childhood was like that too,' she offered. 'Warm

and happy. My mother was loving and had a great sense of humour. And Dad was patient, always ready to listen and play. He told great bedtime stories too.'

She paused, surprised at her urge to share such memories with Cesare. But this wasn't the cold man who'd turned on her after their wedding.

She'd discovered hidden depths to Cesare. Not just his sensual, passionate nature, but also a level of respect, warmth and understanding that drew her.

'Ah. My *nonno* wasn't quite like that. He wasn't into playtime or stories. But he was patient. He taught me right from wrong, by example as much as anything. Everything I know about honour, family tradition and responsibilities, I learnt from him. And about business.' Cesare's mouth twisted. 'For some reason my father didn't inherit his business savvy. That's why the company became vulnerable to Calogero.'

Ida took her time processing that. It sounded as if Cesare's *nonno* was an admirable man, yet she wondered what it would be like, brought up by someone focused on business and responsibility. Surely a child needed warmth and understanding too? The chance simply to be a child?

Was it telling too that Cesare brought the conversation back again so quickly to the family business?

She suspected that, for all his privilege, his childhood hadn't been as carefree and joyous as hers. That he'd had duty and tradition drummed into him. No wonder he'd been ready to do anything, even give in to blackmail, to save the family business built up over generations.

'*You* didn't go to live with your grandfather.'

Cesare's observation dragged her back to the present. 'You know about that?'

He sipped his coffee then lifted his shoulders in a shrug that was intrinsically Italian yet innately his. 'I hired investigators to find you. They researched where you'd lived before, hoping for leads, and discovered you'd spent years in Scotland, rather than with Calogero in London.'

It was a statement, yet she heard the question.

'And you want to know why.'

Ida's voice flattened. It was one thing to share memories of a happy childhood and a fragile sense of connection. Now she suspected his curiosity was because he wanted to learn more about his enemy, her grandfather, rather than from interest in her personally.

Had she expected a night in Cesare's bed would change things?

Ida swallowed the metallic taste of disappointment.

'Only if you want to tell me, Ida.' Cesare's voice dropped to a low note she'd heard in bed when he'd reined himself in to ensure her pleasure. 'I'm curious about you.'

Ida snapped her gaze up and saw a warmth that contradicted her assumption. Maybe his interest *was* personal.

Something shifted in her chest. Her heart thudded and once more she experienced that phantom sensation from last night. The feeling that together they were on the cusp of something bigger than either of them. Bigger than revenge or family feuds.

Deliberately she looked away, telling herself not to read too much into Cesare's words. They weren't enemies now, but she'd be foolish to think they'd ever share a meaningful relationship as she'd once dreamed.

Her crush on him had dwindled to mere physical attraction.

And if you tell yourself that often enough, you might actually believe it. The man's haunted you for years, even after that dreadful scene in Rome.

'Forget I mentioned it, Ida. Are you ready for another coffee?'

'No, thanks.'

Instead, she took another bite of buttery pastry and almost sighed her pleasure.

She'd learned to appreciate simple delights when they came her way. It was self-defeating to fret over Cesare's feelings for her. Or lack of them. He'd rescued her from Bruno and her grandfather. He'd given her sanctuary and a night to remember. She should be thanking him.

Besides, sitting in the dappled shade, relaxed over this lovely breakfast, Ida felt an ease and wellbeing she hadn't felt in years.

No, she decided. Last night hadn't been a mistake. It had been a gift.

'I didn't live with my grandfather because he didn't want me,' Ida said finally. 'He doesn't care for anyone but himself. My parents had cut off contact with him. I didn't even know he was alive. When they died my mother's cousin Kate took me in and I moved to her in Scotland.'

Cesare saw her wistful expression and hesitated to probe. But his curiosity was too great. Not so much now about Ida's relationship with her grandfather but about Ida herself. The more he discovered the more intrigued he grew.

Though the way she spoke about Calogero, in that cool, tight voice, made him wonder if she'd truly been the old man's willing protege.

The idea made everything inside him still.

'You were happy with her?'

Ida lifted one shoulder. 'Eventually. It took some adjustment, for all of us.'

Surely that was an understatement. She would have been distressed and grieving, torn from the world she'd known.

By contrast it had been a relief for Cesare when he'd come to live here. He'd thrived in a world of structure and stability, knowing his *nonno* cared for him, even if he wasn't demonstrative.

In a funny way Ida's attempt to downplay how hard that time must have been reminded him of his *nonno*, with his reticence and profound integrity.

Cesare watched Ida's gaze turn to the garden and wondered if she saw another landscape entirely. She looked so self-contained. Yet as a child, it must have been a terrifying experience. He couldn't remember his mother and hadn't been heartbroken by his father's death, yet he remembered the pain when his grandfather died.

'*All* of you? Your mother's cousin had a family?'

The investigator's report hadn't mentioned it. Just that she lived in a small community.

'No. Just me.' She caught his stare and went on. 'Kate ran an artists' commune. There were a few women who lived there permanently and others who'd come for a summer or a few weeks.'

'That must have been…interesting.'

Cesare tried to imagine growing up surrounded by artists on an isolated island.

Ida's mouth tucked up at the corner and he felt it like the caress of fingers down his sternum, heat spreading through his chest. He wanted, as he'd wanted from the moment she'd stepped from the house, to gather her close and lose himself in her sweet body.

It took all his determination to keep his distance, not take her back to bed.

It didn't help that her dress was the colour of crushed raspberries and reminded him of her pretty nipples that peaked so easily, begging for his attention. Or that the narrow straps left her shoulders bare.

'It *was* interesting,' she said with another small shrug.

'Kate had been a teacher and home-schooled me. But I learned a lot more than was on the curriculum.'

'You learned from the other artists?'

She hadn't spoken about being an artist. Surely he'd have remembered if she had? But then, he'd been so focused on Calogero and countering his schemes, how much attention had he really paid to Ida before their marriage?

Enough to want her. That had never been in doubt. He'd carried it like a badge of shame because lusting after his enemy's granddaughter was weakness when he needed to be strong.

Cesare didn't feel that way now. Life, his feelings, and above all Ida were far more complex than he'd once imagined. He leaned in, waiting for her answer.

'I'm a competent potter.' She ticked off one finger then another. 'I can spin, weave and make felt. I'm told my lino cuts show real flair, though I'll never make a painter.'

Her wry amusement was deeply appealing, and Cesare felt his mouth twitch in response.

'Plus I have some talent at making jewellery.'

'Is that what you want to do? Make jewellery?'

Her eyes met his, that soft, delicate green bright and clear. 'No. Those women were real artists. I just picked up skills because I had time and opportunity.'

'And there wasn't much else to do on your island?'

Her eyebrows rose as if he'd revealed the pity he felt for a girl wrenched from her home and stuck in such a place.

'It wasn't that bad. I learned German from Traudl and she told the best stories. She was an illustrator and spun tales about dragons and witches and the most amazing places. Peggy had been an accountant and taught me baking and bookkeeping. Beatrice taught me ballet.' Cesare heard the rising inflection of enthusiasm as Ida paused, leaning down to rub her ankle. Then she caught his gaze on her and straightened. 'Zara taught me self-defence.'

This time her smile was more of a grimace and Cesare wondered if Ida had ever needed to use those defensive techniques. His stomach rolled over.

'It sounds like a well-rounded education. Much more varied than mine.' He paused. 'So how did your grandfather fit into your life?'

Ida's expression shuttered. 'He was legally my guardian, though Kate brought me up. The year I turned twelve, he insisted I start visiting him in London. It didn't matter that he was a stranger or that Kate had reservations. He threatened to take me from her if I didn't obey.'

Cesare swore under his breath. A man who'd threaten to take an orphaned child from a place where she'd found sanctuary was barbaric. But that tallied with all he knew of Calogero.

'Didn't you want to see London and meet your grandfather?'

She met his eyes, moving the crumbs of flaky pastry on her plate. 'I can't help you bring him down, you know. I don't have that sort of inside information. So if you're hoping I'll reveal some juicy nugget about his business or his plans, you'll be disappointed.'

Her words sliced deep, leaving Cesare feeling surprisingly guilty.

He took a moment before replying.

'You're right. That was one of the reasons I wanted you to stay. Any information I can get about him is helpful. But…' He held up his hand as she leaned away from him. 'I'm genuinely curious about you. Not because I'm mining for things to use against the old man.'

'That's what you *would* say.'

Reluctantly he nodded. 'True. But in this case my in-

tentions aren't so devious.' He shook his head, hampered
by the long-standing distrust between them. 'It's frustrating that there's nothing I can say that will convince you
to believe me.'

To his surprise Ida laughed. A husky chuckle that rippled
through him like a beckoning hand. 'Believe me, Cesare,
I know the feeling.'

Their eyes met and something blazed between them. He
was tempted to label it desire, but it felt like more. Understanding? Regret? Rueful acceptance?

For the first time in his life his subconscious was out-
pacing logic. His responses to Ida seemed to come from a
deeper, mysterious, visceral level, hitherto untapped.

His grandfather had taught him caution, strategic thinking and good planning. Now instinct threatened to take
over.

It felt dangerous and unprecedented. Yet too powerful
to ignore.

'You're saying I jumped to conclusions about you.'

Ida lifted one shoulder then looked away, biting into
her pastry.

Had he done that? Was the past not as he'd imagined?

Had he let his hatred of Calogero taint his view of Ida?

Certainly the things he'd learned about her in the last day
and a half gave him pause. She surprised him at every turn.

'I'm willing to believe circumstances weren't as black
and white as I thought,' he said, watching her eyes widen.
'I promise to listen to whatever you want to tell me.'

Cesare prided himself on hearing all sides of a dispute
before making a decision. The glaring exception had been
his assessment of Ida's character. The evidence had pointed
to her involvement in Calogero's schemes but had Cesare
had *all* the evidence before he judged her?

He wouldn't bully her about it, however much he wanted

to know. Once, in the flush of fury at being forced into marriage, he might have. But no longer.

'It's your decision, Ida. If you'd rather not talk about it, I'll respect that.'

CHAPTER TWELVE

HE RESPECTED HER right to privacy?

Ida stared. But those espresso-dark eyes were sincere.

She sat back, stunned.

She'd discovered a new side to Cesare in the past two days. He might be strong and decisive, bossy in fact, but not in a way she couldn't handle. Standing up to Cesare actually brought an illicit tingle of excitement. He wasn't like her grandfather, who met opposition with vicious rage.

Ida knew Cesare wanted to discover everything about her relationship with the old man, hoping for details to help bring him down. Yet instead of bullying her he gave her space.

He put her feelings before his need to know. That was a first in her life.

Ida had told herself she didn't care what Cesare thought of her. Even if he did come to accept she wasn't the woman he'd assumed her, what was the point? She'd leave soon and they'd never see each other again.

But it *did* matter. Mattered far more than she'd imagined.

She wasn't some downtrodden woman who worried about how others saw her. She'd learned to be self-sufficient and her recent struggles had reinforced that.

Yet for some reason, she hated the idea of Cesare believing she was in league with her grandfather. If anything, she and Cesare were allied in their disdain for the man.

She licked a lingering crumb from her bottom lip then finished her coffee.

'Of course I was excited to see London. And I was curious to meet my grandfather. The first time.'

Cesare's eyebrows lifted at the words *first time*, but he said nothing.

'He wasn't anything like I expected.' Ida paused, remembering her nervous excitement as a young girl taken to an ostentatiously large house that felt neither warm nor welcoming. 'He wasn't interested in me as a person or in our doing anything together.'

She'd imagined outings to the zoo or the fabled London stores or even to see the crown jewels.

'What was he interested in?'

'Making sure I could pass muster in polite society.' Ida's mouth twisted. 'Checking I wasn't growing up wild. He wanted a demure, presentable granddaughter who knew what cutlery to use at a fancy dinner. Who could hold her own in polite conversation, no matter what the setting.'

'So he did take you out?'

Ida shook her head. 'He employed someone to do that.'

'A nanny?'

She laughed, but to her ears the sound was bitter.

'Never anything so simple. In the beginning it was someone who taught elocution and deportment. He worried I might acquire a Scottish accent.'

'Would that have been so bad?'

'It wasn't what he wanted.'

Ida remembered her second visit, when she'd deliberately adopted a rich Scottish burr. It hadn't lasted a day. He'd thrashed it out of her.

She reached for her coffee, only to find the cup empty.

'I learned to waltz, as well as how to curtsey in a long dress. As I got older I went with art experts to gallery openings and museums and with a chaperone to gala events so I could learn to mingle and not feel overwhelmed. I went to afternoon tea at fancy hotels and had dinner with strangers.'

'He wanted you comfortable at social events.'

'Not all social events. High-society ones.'

She watched that sink in, a frown creasing Cesare's forehead. She thought of stopping there but the flow of memory was too strong and with it came words, tumbling out.

'After every outing he got a detailed report from his expert on how I'd fitted in. Whether I held my own in conversation. How I stood, my posture, whether I'd used the right cutlery or spoken too loudly. If I'd smiled at the right people. Whether I fitted in.'

'And if you didn't?'

Cesare's expression was serious. As if he already understood. Which he probably did, since he knew her grandfather so well.

'I learned it was better not to disappoint him.'

Strange how cathartic it was to share this. As if in doing so she threw off some of the burdens she'd kept to herself so long.

She never spoke of that time. With Kate she'd kept her comments general, knowing the whole truth would upset the woman who'd taken her in. Later, when she'd understood her grandfather's character and that he wouldn't hesitate to follow through with his threats to keep Ida and to harm her cousin, she'd had even more reason not to share her experiences.

'He hurt you?'

Ida met Cesare's blazing stare and read anger there. Not at her, but at her grandfather.

It was so long since someone had wanted to be her champion. Warmth spread through her, curling tendrils of heat that had nothing to do with attraction or desire. She felt *seen*.

'I'd rather not talk about it.'

Cesare's mouth flattened as if he intended to argue. Then he nodded. More proof that he'd abide by her wishes.

Something inside her chest lifted, light with pleasure.

'We weren't close.' Ida repressed a grimace. 'I'd visit London every year and it was both intensive training and an inspection to see if I lived up to his expectations.'

'Of course you did.' At her surprised stare Cesare continued. 'When we met you seemed almost too perfect. Poised and well groomed. You never seemed to find it difficult to make conversation, but you didn't chatter. Whenever we went out you were comfortable and confident.'

Ida remembered it differently. She *had* been nervous because Cesare was the epitome of her girlish yearnings. She'd wanted him to like her, not simply because her grandfather wished it. Cesare was not only tall, dark and handsome but also gravely courteous and with a delicious Italian accent that curled around her heart and made it sing.

She'd fallen for him, building up a fantasy that he cared for her and would sweep her away to a new life far from her grandfather's influence.

'He was grooming you, wasn't he?'

Ida nodded. 'He wanted me to fit into the sort of society that he never mixed with. Yet he didn't want me in boarding school with a set of privileged girls. He thought I might learn bad ways.' And maybe meet boys. 'It wasn't until after we married that I understood his goal. When you explained it all.'

Cesare stared at her, two vertical lines carved down his forehead. But instead of instantly rejecting her words, he seemed to mull them over.

'I didn't know he was blackmailing you. I believed you

when you said it suited you to marry. I thought you wanted a hostess.' Though she should have realised that was wrong. Why choose her when there were so many gorgeous, sophisticated women? 'Plus I leapt at the chance to get away.'

She waited for Cesare to argue. Instead, he seemed to withdraw as if lost in thought.

'My grandfather had become more demanding and restrictive. He even chose the clothes I wore in London. I had to look demure and wear only pale colours because he said they were more *suitable*.'

Suitable for a virgin, though she didn't say that.

He'd threatened dire consequences if she ever tried to date. Because he saw her virginity as an asset to make her attractive to the right bridegroom, his ticket into high society. If the chance to blackmail Cesare hadn't arisen, he'd have pushed her to marry someone else he'd chosen.

'He wasn't your guardian when we met. You were an adult, and he had no legal hold over you. Why were you living with him when I visited?'

'You think he'd let me go just like that? After the years and money he'd invested in me?'

To defy her grandfather would have meant danger for herself and for those she cared about.

'You were scared of him even then?'

A pulse of something throbbed between them. Like a heavy heartbeat, thickening the air. As if once again she and Cesare were linked, not physically like last night, but in shared understanding. She breathed deep, telling herself to stop imagining things.

'Any sane person would be scared of crossing Fausto Calogero.' She broke eye contact and turned towards the glorious view. It felt wrong to discuss the man who was a sinister, threatening presence in her life in this lovely place. 'Can we change the subject? I don't want to talk about him now.'

She wanted to make the most of her time here. All too soon she'd have to face her troubles. Finding a secure place, starting over, staying hidden.

'Of course.' Cesare paused. 'Thank you for telling me.' Then he was on his feet. 'I'll get us some fresh coffee.'

Ida watched him go, following his loose-limbed stride. He was a man easy in his skin. A great lover. Surprisingly caring. Most amazing of all, he'd heard her out without interrupting. He'd *listened*.

Yet why would he believe her when she'd given no hard evidence to back her claims?

She was grateful he was sensitive enough not to push for details about life with her grandfather. It was a time she'd rather forget. She stretched out her legs, rotating her feet to prove the sudden ache in her right ankle was pure imagination, a reminder of her grandfather's brutality.

What did Cesare think of her now? He'd been surprisingly easy to speak to, not even baulking at her explanation that she'd believed he'd wanted to marry her.

But she hadn't been entirely truthful.

She'd let him believe she'd agreed to the marriage because she didn't dare cross Fausto Calogero.

That was true. She'd seen no way to escape her grandfather's control. But she hadn't wanted to defy him when he'd insisted she marry Cesare. She'd *wanted* the wedding. Wanted the man who was, for just a little longer, her husband.

That was one truth she couldn't reveal.

Cesare carried the tray of fresh coffee from the kitchen, relieved to be doing something.

Sitting at the table, watching Ida's expression as she

spoke of how Calogero had planned to use her even from childhood to further his schemes, had been difficult.

He'd wanted to jump up from the table and pace. To curse and berate himself for not considering the possibility that she, too, had been Calogero's victim. That she'd been too scared to defy him.

Cesare stepped out into the sunshine and paused, soaking up the warmth, a counterpoint to the chill in his belly. It had started when Ida spoke of her visits to Calogero but had really taken hold during her silences. When she'd refused to confirm whether Calogero had harmed her. When she'd said no sane person would cross the man.

Given the litany of crimes for which the old man was being investigated, many brutally violent, Cesare knew she'd suffered.

He abhorred the idea of Ida being under his control.

Cesare had no doubt that she told the truth. That haunted look in her eyes had made his skin crawl.

Yet he'd read strength in her composure and a lurking hint of bitter humour that twisted her lips as she skated over things too painful to discuss.

He admired her.

When they'd met, he'd never imagined her to be anything other than his scheming enemy's pampered pet.

Hearing her story had shaken him.

He'd been so committed to his own goals, protecting his extended family and those dependent on the company, he'd not taken time to consider Ida might be an innocent caught up in Calogero's schemes.

Guilt tightened his chest and roiled through his belly. How callous and superior he'd been. How blind!

The coffee cups on the tray Dorotea had provided rattled as he drew in a horrified breath.

All this time he'd prided himself on being decent and

honourable. On having purpose and a plan which was finally bearing fruit as the forces of the law inched closer to arresting Calogero.

But for all his lofty ideals, Cesare suddenly saw himself stripped bare.

He was as flawed as his father, the man he'd despised for so long.

He'd let passion, in his case anger rather than lust, blind him to the truth.

It was even worse than that. His father had let his libido and his weakness for pretty women blind him. He'd allowed gold-diggers to pull the wool over his eyes with fake adoration and words of love.

Cesare had only himself to blame. Only Calogero had made him think Ida was privy to the blackmail scheme. If Cesare had been thinking straight, he'd have taken time to question that. Instead, he'd let fury rule him. Fury not just at the outrageous scheme and the threat to those he cared about. But because the old villain had foisted on him a woman who, despite everything, made him want to forget business and revenge and think only of her.

Letting passion rule his thoughts and actions was against everything he'd learned from his *nonno*. A weakness he'd seen in his father and been determined to avoid.

Cesare grimaced. So much for learning from his father's dire example.

He straightened his shoulders and walked on.

Ida was staring into the distance as if lost in the beauty of the landscape. Or remembering her difficult past.

And he'd added to her pain. The things he'd said in Rome… Shame thickened his throat.

As Cesare approached, he saw she'd crossed one foot over her knee, her fingers rubbing her ankle as if in pain. She'd done that before.

'Have you injured yourself?'

Her gaze darted to his as he put down the tray and took his seat. An instant later she had both feet on the ground.

'Not at all.' She reached for a cup, pausing to inhale the aroma. He guessed it was an excuse not to meet his eyes. 'The coffee here is wonderful. I'll miss it.'

'Then don't go.'

She jumped, spilling coffee on herself. 'Sorry?'

Cesare offered a napkin, but she put the cup down and sucked the hot liquid on her hand.

Something shifted inside him. Not guilt. Desire. He tried to force it away. Surely it was wrong to think about sex with Ida when he'd just discovered how badly he'd treated her.

Weakness for sex had been his father's trademark. Maybe they were more similar than Cesare had thought. This morning was full of disquieting revelations.

'Stay for a while. You're not in a rush to get back, are you?'

Ida surveyed him from under lowered brows. 'But we've had our night together.'

Cesare couldn't help it. Despite the turbulent mix of guilt, regret and shock writhing inside him, he laughed. 'It's going to take more than one night to satisfy either of us, don't you agree?'

He reached over and touched her hand. Instantly awareness stroked through him, lush and warm.

Her eyes met his and he read a matching enthusiasm in those soft green depths. He'd seen that expression last night and earlier this morning when Ida had lost herself to bliss in his arms.

Longing ripped through him.

He wanted her again.

Yet it wasn't just her body he craved. There was something about the way Ida turned to him in the throes of passion. The intriguing combination of strength and vulnerability he'd discovered over the past couple of days. Her proud determination not to be an object of pity.

She deserved better from him.

'I admire you, Ida.'

She looked shocked. 'You do?'

Cesare inclined his head. 'Not many people would have coped with what you've been through. That man dictating your life. The losses you've suffered. Starting over with nothing and no one.'

His skin crawled as he thought about it. He'd contributed to her woes and that shamed him. 'You've faced hardship with grace and dignity.'

She goggled at him as if he'd grown two heads and he couldn't blame her. Not long ago he'd been ready to believe the worst of her.

'You believe me?'

'I do.' Gently he wrapped his fingers around her hand, waiting to see if she'd withdraw. Yet she didn't and he was grateful. 'I acted despicably in Rome. I was so wound up, hating how I'd been manipulated and how powerless I felt, I took out my hatred on you. I never stopped to think that I wasn't the only one he'd forced to do his bidding.'

Cesare's chest rose on a deep sigh as he released her. 'I'm sorry, Ida. If I hadn't been so proud and caught up in my own problems, I wouldn't have treated you that way. You wouldn't have had to run off into the night.'

Pain scraped his throat as he swallowed.

'Thank you.'

He couldn't read her expression. Couldn't tell how she felt about his apology. But she'd accepted it. That was a beginning.

Cesare knew it would take a long time before he felt he'd made it up to her. If he could ever find a way.

'No, thank you for telling me the truth. I realise they're not happy memories.'

Ida shrugged and once more he felt that tug of admiration that she should be so strong after she'd been through so much. Perhaps *because* she'd been through it.

'And I need to be clear.' He held her gaze. 'I'd like you to stay, partly because I want to make up for the mistakes I made before and the way I judged you. I'll also do everything necessary to protect you from Calogero. You'll be safe from him.'

That got a response. A quick blink of stunning green eyes that looked suddenly overbright.

'Thank—'

'Don't thank me! It's the least I can do.' He paused. 'I want to continue what we started last night, for as long as it suits us both. But the invitation to stay and my protection aren't conditional on sex.'

'You said before that you'd wait for me to come to you.'

How arrogant he'd been.

'Stay and have a vacation. With luck it won't be too long before Calogero faces justice for his crimes.'

'Really?' She looked stunned as if she thought her grandfather untouchable. Not surprising given the way he'd controlled her life for so long.

'So I'm told.' If all went to plan, he'd spend the rest of his life behind bars, but Cesare didn't say that. Calogero was cunning and would put up a fight.

'I could show you a little of Tuscany.' The revelation of her past made him want to give her something special. It wasn't much but sharing some of his favourite places might go some way towards lessening his guilt over what had gone before. 'Do you want to see Florence, Siena, San Gimignano?'

'But it will complicate things if we're seen together.

We're getting a divorce. If you're seen with me now…' Her voice sharpened. 'Or is that the idea? To prove I'm alive and well and you didn't dispose of me?'

Right now, that was the last thing on his mind.

The fact Ida had instantly thought of it proved she'd seen too much of how her grandfather's devious mind worked.

And that she didn't fully trust Cesare.

Who could blame her? He had a long way to go to prove himself to her.

Why did it feel vital to do just that?

'I ignore gossip about our marriage.' It had been the only way to cope with so many outrageous stories circulating. At first, they'd wounded his pride, until he decided to focus on saving his business. That left no time for anything else. 'I live my life to suit myself.' He paused to let that sink in. 'I want you to stay. But I see no reason to shut ourselves away here. We have nothing to hide.'

Still, she looked doubtful. Cesare needed another argument because he wasn't ready for Ida to leave.

'Think of it as a holiday. An opportunity to relax and have fun.' She'd had precious little fun.

Ida wavered. He saw it in her eyes.

'And imagine how annoyed your grandfather will be if he discovers you're here with me where he can't get to you. Wouldn't you like, for once, to thumb your nose at the old devil? To do something you want to do, not because you're forced into it?'

Pleasure shot through him at Ida's slow-dawning smile.

And something else, something he preferred not to dwell on. Relief.

CHAPTER THIRTEEN

IDA LEANED BACK in the passenger seat of the open convertible, feeling it cradle her body like an embrace.

As they left the picturesque Tuscan hill town, pealing bells rang out over the low roar of the engine. Late-afternoon sun warmed her shoulders, left bare by her bright summer dress. She snuggled into the deep leather seat and stretched her legs, a pleasant tiredness filling her. She smiled as she flexed her feet. They ached gently from so much walking over quaint cobblestoned streets.

Ida turned to the man beside her and her heart gave a little lurch.

Not simply because he was so charismatic, with his strong features, casual elegance and emphatic air of masculinity. Even the competent way he handled the powerful car was attractive.

Or because last night he'd again taken her to heaven with his lovemaking. Though perhaps that was a tiny part of it.

She felt this profound sense of wellbeing because he'd given her such an incredible, unexpected gift. This glorious day.

She glowed from the joy of it.

'Thank you for today, Cesare. I've enjoyed every minute.'

He turned, dark glasses hiding his eyes, his mouth curving in the tiniest hint of a smile as he turned back at the road. 'I'm glad you liked your first taste of Tuscany.' He paused. 'I'm glad you decided to stay.'

So was she. Incredibly glad.

It was two days since she'd made that decision, yet it felt like a lifetime. As if her old life were a barely remembered nightmare.

That couldn't last. This was a temporary reprieve from Ida's real world. But at least when she returned, she'd have wonderful memories. So wonderful she felt impelled to make him understand.

'I *loved* it. I've never had a day like it.'

'I told you Tuscany is special.'

He didn't understand. He thought she was simply talking about the stunning buildings and pretty vistas. The meandering streets. The cornucopia of produce displayed at the food market.

Ida shook her head. 'The place is lovely, but I meant more than that. It's been a revelation. Not just the architecture and the people. Or even the food.'

She'd adored the food. The lemon *gelato* had tingled on her tongue like a frozen taste of summer. The red wine they'd sampled at a small vineyard had been so rich and full. Their lunch, simple but delicious.

'You've given me…' She searched for the right words, to her chagrin feeling her throat tighten. She didn't *do* emotional.

'Ida? What is it?'

He reached out, his hand squeezing hers.

She felt that immediate rush of pleasure. Was it possible that in just two days she'd become addicted to his touch? It almost felt like Cesare had the power to convince her he could make everything okay.

But life wasn't so simple.

They approached a tight curve in the road and Cesare put his hand back on the steering wheel. Ida told herself she was glad. She felt too much emotion bubbling inside without Cesare's touch befuddling her.

Deliberately she focused on the shadows of dark ochre and plum lengthening across the undulating countryside as the sun dropped.

'It's hard to explain.'

She hesitated, torn between needing to let him know how much today meant and caution at revealing too much.

'Try me. I want to know. I want to understand.'

Ida had spent her life learning to hold in strong feelings, not to share them. Kate was a generation older. She'd cared for Ida and tried her best, but had never been a true confidante, and Ida's grandfather had been the very reason she'd learned to keep her emotions buttoned down.

'Everywhere we went, everything we did, was fun and fascinating. But it's not that. It's the fact you thought about what might appeal and then organised a day that was totally for *me*.'

She heard the tell-tale wobble in her voice and paused.

'Thank you, Cesare. I'll remember today always. It was a lovely gift.'

He'd made her feel special, though she understood his motivations weren't solely about pleasing her.

For the longest time he didn't say anything. Eventually she turned and found him frowning at the road as they swooped down a hill.

Finally, he spoke. The rush of wind past the car must have affected her hearing because he sounded different, his voice hoarse.

'You've never had that before? A time just for you?'

'Not since my parents died.' She stopped. The contrast between her happy childhood and later years was too stark. Even with Kate, Ida had always been conscious that she was an unasked-for burden, though her cousin had never said so. 'Anyway, I want you to know I appreciate it. You've been very generous with your time.'

They could have stayed on Cesare's estate, and she'd have been happy. She adored sex with this man. His tenderness and his urgency, his patient seduction and his outrageously exciting demands. When they weren't making love, she had the run of his pool, his library, the pretty gardens, the cinema room and—

'Usually when women speak about generosity, they mean dates somewhere expensive or extravagant gifts.'

'You mix with the wrong sort of women.' She shot him a challenging stare and saw his tight smile.

'What about tomorrow?'

'Tomorrow? What about it?'

'Don't you want to go out again?'

Ida frowned. 'It's Monday. I thought you'd be working.' He'd already taken time away from his precious company to track her down in Britain. She hadn't wanted to assume he'd take more time out of his schedule.

'I'm delegating. I keep an eye on the business, but I have very good managers now for day-to-day matters. I thought we might go into Florence.'

Her heart leapt. It was somewhere she'd wanted to see for so long. Ever since those forced art-appreciation lessons in London that had unexpectedly turned into a delight, except for the looming threat of her grandfather's displeasure if she didn't learn well enough.

'I'd like that.'

'Excellent.'

Cesare's nod was curt and his smile absent.

Because for him this isn't about pleasure.

She'd forgotten that. She'd let herself be swept away by emotion.

He wants to take you into the city so you'll be seen to-

gether. So word will get back to Fausto. Because Cesare wants to rub his nose in the fact you're together but not on the old man's terms.

Ida rubbed her hands up her bare arms, feeling chilled despite the sun's warmth.

Or was it more than that? Despite Cesare's dismissive words about not listening to gossip, he'd enjoy showing the world that his missing wife was alive and well and spending her days with him.

Of course that was it. Or at least part of his reason for giving up his time to show her around.

Not because she was special. Because there were benefits.

Ida blinked and stared blindly ahead.

What did you expect? You went into this with your eyes open. You don't expect any man to put you first for your sake alone.

For the first time since he'd taken her to his bed, Cesare felt uncomfortable. Deeply uncomfortable.

What Ida had just told him seemed to strip a layer off his skin.

He flattened his mouth and tried to focus on the narrow road. Yet every thought was on the woman beside him.

Ida would hate to think he saw her as a victim. Yet what she'd said pierced deep. Her words hadn't been a bid for sympathy. He'd heard the ache in her voice, her sincerity, and it had dragged him down to earth with an almighty thump.

He'd thought to give her a pleasant day out. He was proud of his home region and wanted her to like it too. But any thought of it as merely a fun outing with his temporary lover had shattered.

It humbled him that something so simple meant so much to her.

Against Ida's past his own troubles had been minuscule. Her gratitude made Cesare aware of all the good things he'd had. A stable home. The love of his *nonno* and extended family even though his father had been a disaster as a parent. Wealth and privilege, access to the best educational opportunities and so much that he'd taken for granted.

Safety.

His *nonno* had been a strict disciplinarian but Cesare had never been in physical danger from him. Unlike Ida, whose fear of Calogero had to stem from his capacity for vicious reprisals.

Cesare's skin chilled at the thought of what Calogero would do if he got his hands on her.

'Here we are.' It was a relief to swing off the road, pausing while the electronic gates opened.

Cesare didn't turn to meet her eyes as he would have earlier today when he'd enjoyed watching her delight in each new experience. And basked in her rare, devastating smiles. At first he'd seen them only in bed, but today, increasingly, he'd watched the curve of her lips and felt entranced.

He hadn't realised how jaded and self-focused he'd been until confronted with her innocent joy.

His breath rushed out and his skin prickled with shame and regret. And deep inside, his determination to bring down her viper of a grandfather glowed white-hot.

They were silent as they entered the villa. Until Dorotea approached with news that there'd been a delivery for Ida.

Cesare followed her into the library. If Calogero had sent some threat…

But Ida smiled as she saw a shabby backpack and a battered cardboard box on the antique desk.

'It's from Jo! But how?'

Already she was opening the backpack. Cesare saw a pair of sneakers and some clothes.

He paused behind her. 'You wanted your parcel delivered to her. My courier returned with your things.'

Even having seen the sparse poverty of that tiny flat, Cesare was stunned by how little Ida owned. He glanced around the room but there was no more luggage.

'Thank you. I never expected you to do that.' Their gazes held and his heartbeat grew ponderous.

'It was nothing.'

She surveyed him for a long time before opening the box and lifting out some books. She ran her fingers over them as if reacquainting herself with old friends. Cesare moved closer, intrigued to know what books Ida treasured when she owned so little.

He saw a cheap photo album and a couple of large folders labelled *Designs*. No fiction titles but a hardcover on art and another on interior design, both battered.

Ida had pulled out her phone and was tapping in a message, presumably to her friend in London.

Cesare, ignoring the fact he had no right to pry, opened one of the folders, discovering neatly handwritten notes, a world of colour and texture, fabrics and furniture design, architecture and—

'Jo says you had someone guard her. Not just at the flat but when she went out.'

Ida looked up from her phone, her expression stunned.

Cesare spread his hands. 'It seemed sensible. Calogero's man could have gone back there to find out more about your plans.' Though he was convinced the old devil now knew precisely where Ida was. 'I didn't want him threatening or hurting her.'

Slowly Ida inclined her head. 'Thank you. I appreciate it.' Her expression remained puzzled.

Had she imagined he'd ignore the danger Calogero presented? Cesare knew the harm he could do. People had died in that factory fire. Others had lost jobs when Brunetti Enterprises hit tough times due to his interference.

Maybe Ida thought Cesare didn't care about anything but getting his revenge on the old man.

That would make him no better than his enemy.

'You haven't mentioned going back to stay with your cousin,' he said, needing suddenly to change the subject.

'That's impossible. Even if I wanted to spend the rest of my life in a remote artists' colony. You worried that Jo might be in danger. The same applies to Kate and her friends. I won't do that to them.'

Ida wasn't the way he'd once imagined her. Neither a gold-digger nor a vamp. Vulnerable yes, and she'd suffered, but she wasn't simply a victim. She was sweet and strong and no pushover.

It was incredible that he'd ever believed she'd tried to claw her way into the aristocracy using his name. Ida was loyal and moved by simple pleasures.

Cesare was drawn by the wonder in her eyes when they made love and when she'd thanked him for their day out. And by her spine of steel.

'What do you want from life, Ida?' Suddenly it was imperative to know. 'What are your plans?'

'Once I'm free of him, you mean?'

There it was again, proof that she lived in the shadow of her grandfather. Not for much longer. Cesare would see her free of him, he swore it.

She didn't answer immediately. Had she lived in hiding so long she hadn't let herself make plans? 'What did you want to be when you were growing up?'

'A dancer. How about you?'

'A fireman,' he replied instantly. 'Funny, I'd forgotten that until now.'

'Let me guess. You wanted to save people?'

'Possibly. But I think it was the lure of driving a big red truck with a loud siren and climbing ladders.'

She laughed and he felt it like ripples under his skin.

'But you didn't have access to a professional dance teacher on your island.'

The sparkle in her eyes dimmed. 'Actually Beatrice, who taught me, had been a prima ballerina. I dreamed of dancing professionally, but I injured my ankle badly.' Abruptly she turned away to repack the books. 'Besides, my grandfather had other plans.'

'I'm sorry.'

She shrugged. 'It doesn't matter. I probably wouldn't have been good enough.'

Perhaps not but Cesare didn't like that she hadn't had a chance to try. 'And now? Interior design?'

Her head lifted sharply then she reached for the folders of what he'd realised were projects.

'Have you worked as a designer?'

She shook her head, her bright hair swishing around her shoulders as she held the folders close. 'As if. I've done a basic online course. That's all. It's hard to get qualifications when you're working all hours to support yourself.'

Ida plonked the folders back into the box, then added the books. Last was the worn photo album. Did it contain pictures of her with her parents?

Compassion filled him for all she'd lost. The opportunities she'd never had. Yet she wasn't after sympathy.

She had to be one of the strongest people he knew.

'How about you, Cesare? If you didn't have your family company, what would you want to be now?'

He leaned his hip against the desk, folding his arms, telling himself not to push her further.

'I have no idea. Since I was a boy I knew I'd work in the family firm. It never occurred to me to do anything else.'

Her eyebrows lifted. 'Really? You had no other driving ambition?'

Perhaps it was that hint of disbelief. Or the feeling he'd short-changed her by not giving an answer when she'd already shared so much. He hated that through most of their dealings she'd had so little agency. Except when they shared their bodies. *Then* there was no power imbalance.

Cesare found himself saying gruffly. 'My one real ambition was *not* to be like my father.'

It was something he'd never admitted, though he was sure his *nonno* had guessed.

Surprisingly he felt no qualms revealing it. The past was the past. Even if his feelings for his *papá* were something he didn't discuss.

Her steady green gaze held his. He saw neither surprise nor judgement there. 'He wasn't a good man?'

Cesare opened his mouth then shut it, forced by her direct question to consider objectively.

'He wasn't a bad man.'

In his younger days Cesare had thought him so. Because he'd been wounded by his *papá's* neglect and lack of interest. Later hurt had morphed into annoyance at how his father's actions had played into their enemy's hands.

'He was weak and selfish. He didn't care about anyone but himself.'

Warmth brushed Cesare's hand and he looked down, surprised to see Ida's fingers sliding across his. Instinctively he captured them.

Her hand fitted his. He noted her chapped skin looked a little better now she'd used the salve Dorotea had provided.

Cesare swallowed. Ida's touch and her silent sympathy felt like a salve on those old wounds that, he now realised, had never healed.

'He hurt you.'

Cesare looked up and read Ida's sympathy. He shook his head. 'I had a wonderful grandfather who loved me. I didn't need my father.'

Ida stepped close, her tantalising scent, like the promise of spring, filtering into his senses. 'Every child deserves the love of its mother and father.'

It hit him then that, while Ida had been orphaned early and struggled since under Calogero's brutality, at least she'd known what it was to have two loving parents. It was there in her quiet confidence, and the concern in those bright eyes.

'He wasn't a brute. He didn't abuse me. He just wasn't interested. He was focused on the woman who was the great love of his life. When she betrayed him or proved herself interested only in money, he'd move on to the next and the next. He had appalling judgement and no time for a child.'

'Maybe he was grieving for your mother.'

Cesare lifted his shoulders. 'Maybe.'

'But that doesn't excuse what he did to you.'

Looking into her grave face, Cesare felt warmth spread through him. Not the potent heat of desire but something steady and comfortable.

Again he shrugged. 'I was okay. I had my grandfather.' Cesare *had* been all right. He'd belonged and been cared for. 'But over time my father grew more unreliable. His work suffered and through it the business. His bad decisions weakened the company, leaving it wide open for Calogero to do his worst.'

Ida frowned.

'What?'

'I know how important Brunetti Enterprises is. Your grandfather drummed that into you, along with your duties and responsibilities. But it's a business. It's not *always* the most important thing. Admitting to pain isn't weakness.'

Ida didn't fully understand. He had a duty not just to

his family but also to the thousands whose livelihoods depended on the company. Yet her words trickled through him, an unexpected truth that he couldn't ignore.

He'd think about it later when he was alone. Because he suddenly felt vulnerable as he hadn't been since boyhood, when he'd brimmed with pain and desolation.

Cesare straightened and took her other hand. He dropped his voice to a suggestive rumble. 'If I'm hurt, will you make me feel better?'

Frustration pinched Ida's face. But when he ran his thumbs slowly across her palms then up her bare arms, she shivered voluptuously.

'You're changing the subject.'

Cesare nuzzled her neck, inhaling sweetness. Now he wasn't thinking of diversions but of a need that was raw and real, the more so for the way she'd dug into his emotions and tried to make them better. As if *he* were the one who needed help.

Instead of annoying him, her sincerity moved him. Not that he'd admit it.

'I have a sudden urge to be close to you,' he murmured. 'For comfort.'

It wasn't a convenient ruse or a teasing invitation. It was, he discovered, the surprising truth.

He wanted the comfort of being with Ida. He needed the intimacy of her body joining with his, her kisses drugging his senses and obliterating the shards of old pain.

He lifted his head and met her quizzical stare. 'Please, Ida.'

What she saw in his face he had no idea. But her expression softened as she planted her palm against his cheek.

'Let's go upstairs,' she whispered.

CHAPTER FOURTEEN

CESARE LISTENED TO his cousin enthuse about the new designer he wanted to bring into the haute couture arm of the company. But his thoughts were metres away with Ida.

She looked stunning. Her full-length halter-neck dress of rich crimson clung, gleaming, to her body. Her hair was up in a seemingly casual twist low at the back of her head, and he couldn't take his eyes off her. Even here, among the glitterati at this exclusive charity event, she stood out.

The elite of Europe was attending this prestigious charity event in the Boboli Gardens beside Florence's Palazzo Pitti, quaffing vintage wine and showing off their finery. None held a candle to Ida.

Six weeks she'd been back in his world and still she stole his breath. When he'd suggested she stay on he'd been thinking in terms of days. Weeks had turned into more than a month, yet he wasn't ready for her to go. And not just because Calogero was still at large.

What did it mean that living with her felt like all the best times of his life rolled into one? Did his years of celibacy and tunnel-visioned focus on work skew his perception? Or was it something else?

'Cesare. Did you hear what I said?'

'Sorry, Francesco. My mind wandered.'

Strange. In the past his mind had been like a steel trap whenever business was discussed.

His cousin laughed. 'I can't blame you. Not with your wife looking so charming.'

'She is, isn't she?'

His wife. Funny how the word didn't disturb Cesare as it had in the days when he couldn't wait to be free of her.

Technically she was his wife *for now*. But for the first time in his life, he was living in the moment. Content to take pleasure in Ida without worrying about the future.

The company was doing well. The management team was focused and energised by new opportunities, and he could step back a little. Calogero hadn't raised his ugly head, though Cesare knew he'd be seething at the fact Ida and Cesare were together while there was no benefit to him. Soon, with luck, the various police investigations into Calogero's crimes would bring results.

When they did would Ida leave straight away?

Cesare gripped his glass tighter, his palm suddenly clammy.

'I'm glad the marriage worked out after all,' Francesco said in a low voice.

Cesare nodded but said nothing. What would he say? That it was only temporary? That what they shared was more like a steamy affair than a marriage? That the divorce papers were already signed?

He drained his glass, vaguely noticing the wine wasn't as smooth as he'd thought.

Ida would return to the UK when it was safe.

Cesare would, in some distant future, find a wife who'd help him carry on the Brunetti line. It would be a sensible, convenient marriage.

Too often he'd seen his father chase the fleeting mirage of romance, confusing lust with love. Seen how it turned him into a fool. Cesare had no intention of following in his footsteps.

Ida laughed at something her companion said, the sound as light as the bubbles in her glass. Her head tipped back, drawing Cesare's gaze from her slender throat to her soft lips and that stunning red-gold hair. She had the colouring of a renaissance angel, but Ida was far more vibrant and alluring.

She held her own in this crowd, as she had at every event they attended. Cesare actually relished attending them with Ida beside him. Instead of networking, Cesare had relaxed and enjoyed the company and the art, since it was mainly performance and other art-related events they chose to attend.

He'd had to smother laughter when some of the worst gossips quizzed Ida about where she'd been since the wedding. She'd dealt with them firmly and with apparent ease, making it clear she didn't fear anything they or the press might say about her. That had garnered respect and, while some regarded her doubtfully, she'd generally been welcomed.

Not that it seemed to matter to Ida. Knowing how she'd struggled these past years and how much of an outsider she must feel, Cesare felt his admiration soar.

He'd been pleased to see signs of a genuine connection between Ida and some of his friends. Like the woman beside her, a talented designer.

The other woman moved away, and Ida turned. Their eyes met with a palpable crackle of connection. Cesare held out his hand to her.

His cousin groaned theatrically. 'Now I've got no hope of keeping your attention.'

Cesare turned to him. 'Serves you right for spending the evening talking business.'

Francesco goggled and Cesare felt almost sorry for him. Once Cesare would have been only too happy to discuss commercial plans at any time. He'd used to attend social events primarily to promote Brunetti Enterprises.

'I'll come to the office tomorrow. You can tell me about it over coffee.'

'I'll look forward to it.' Francesco leaned down to kiss Ida's cheeks as she joined them. 'I don't know what you've done to my starchy cousin, Ida, but he's a changed man. I like it.' He winked and whispered something in her ear before nodding to Cesare and strolling away.

Ida's laughing green eyes surveyed Cesare as he drew her close and draped his arm possessively around her. That felt better. The taut feeling in his chest eased as she nestled closer.

'I like this,' she murmured huskily.

'Good.' His hand slid over her hip and heat built low in his body. 'But it's not enough.'

He didn't give a damn that they were being observed. He wanted her. He wanted a lot more than he could do in this public place. Nevertheless, he found his gaze turning towards the darker corners of the manicured gardens.

Ida slanted him a look that stoked the glowing heat in his belly. 'Maybe we should leave soon. Though Francesco will guess why.'

'Cheeky pup. What did he whisper to you?'

Cesare's voice growled across Ida's sensitive flesh, making her nipples peak. Just as well few guests were clustered in among the lights in this part of the garden.

'Nothing important,' she murmured. 'You know he can't resist teasing.'

'I'm glad you're back with him, Ida. You're good for him.'

That was what Francesco had said, and heaven help her, but the words had struck home.

Because that was how she felt. That Cesare was good for *her*.

She'd blossomed. Not just sexually, though that was a major and wonderful part of what they shared. Ida felt more comfortable in herself, less at odds with the world. At first, she'd thought it was because she wasn't focused on scraping a living or in fear of being found and punished by her grandfather.

But it was more than that.

In Tuscany, with Cesare, she'd begun to feel whole in a way she couldn't remember feeling, except as a child when the world had been simple and happy.

When she'd felt cared for and valued.

Her time with the man who'd all but kidnapped her in London, the man she'd once hoped never to see again, had grown into something unexpected. Something that excited and terrified her in equal measure.

She didn't want to think about it. Whatever this was, however magical it felt, it wouldn't last.

It wouldn't do to get attached.

'We can't leave yet. I'm giving a speech.' Impatience radiated from him as he shot a look at his watch. 'But I'll keep it short, then we can go home.'

Cesare didn't try to conceal the hungry glint in his eyes as his mouth curled into a slow grin.

Home with Cesare. It sounded perfect.

Except it's not your home, is it? You're living in a fool's paradise, letting a couple of days turn into a fortnight. A fortnight into a month. It's six weeks since you arrived, and you've done nothing concrete about moving on.

Because she didn't *want* to move on.

'Ida? What is it?'

Damn the man for being so acutely observant. Sometimes it felt as if he read her as easily as a book.

Ida searched for a distraction, something to break the

spell of Francesco's words and Cesare's magnetism. She looked around, noting there was no one within earshot.

'Will you marry again, Cesare? When this is over?'

His head jerked back, and long fingers dug into her hip. 'Marry?'

'I don't mean straight away.'

Looking into his dark eyes, Ida wished she hadn't asked. Because she'd seen a flash of something unsettling there.

Guilt.

Could it be that Cesare was already planning marriage while having a fling with his soon-to-be ex? She swallowed hard, almost choking on a knot of burning emotion.

But why shouldn't he? This was temporary. Already judicial wheels were grinding their ill-fated marriage into divorce.

Ida made to step away, but he stopped her, his encircling arm like warm steel.

'Why do you ask, Ida? Do *you* have marriage plans?'

Cesare bent so his face was just above hers, his eyes now unreadable. She sensed something new in him, something that reminded her of his fury when they'd met in London.

'Absolutely not!' She paused and hiked her chin higher, ignoring the way it brought her closer to him. 'I don't need a man in my life to make me happy.'

Liar. He makes you happy.

Ida saw Cesare's head jerk back, his jaw flex hard, as if he repudiated her words. But that would imply she'd hurt him.

She digested the idea. Then rejected it. Cesare had made it clear this affair would last only as long as the sparking attraction between them. Which, he'd reiterated, would be transient. Given his greater experience, she had to believe him.

Besides, Ida was no fool. She'd heard Cesare's pain and contempt as he spoke of his unreliable father, consumed by his passion for one beautiful woman after another.

Or had it been a quest for love after the loss of his wife? How much of Cesare's view was shaped by the attitude of the grandfather he'd hero-worshipped?

Not that it mattered. The result was the same. Cesare wasn't a romantic. When he married again, he'd choose someone with a similar background to himself, a suitable CEO's wife. Not a woman like her.

'I can't blame you.' Cesare's words were even, belying the glitter in his eyes. 'The men in your life haven't treated you well.'

Ida put her hand on his arm, feeling the biceps taut beneath the perfect tailoring. 'You've already apologised, Cesare. It's in the past. Let it go.'

She knew he blamed himself for the years she'd struggled since their wedding. But they'd made her stronger and shown her she'd survive the unknown future that seemed so daunting.

A future without Cesare.

Ida's emotions seesawed wildly. She dropped her hand and spun away. 'It's time we joined the others.'

But Cesare's encircling arm held her close. 'Are you trying to tell me you've changed your mind? You've had enough, Ida? Enough of me?'

His gruff words caught the breath in her lungs and a band of heat squeezed her ribs. Without thinking she shook her head. 'No!'

Ida wasn't ready to leave him. Not yet. Her yearning for Cesare was so potent she tasted the plea forming on her tongue, should he try to send her away.

'Excellent. Because I'm not ready for you to go.'

Cesare smiled that slow, devastating smile that turned her legs to overcooked spaghetti. Relief hit like a blast of summer heat, leaving her weak and trembling. Every nerve ending sparked as he raised his hand to her hair, massaging slowly as he drew her closer.

His eyes looked inky black and sinfully inviting and her heartbeat took up a thunderous rhythm. Instinctively she understood she would always respond to that look. Always feel the heady rush of excitement and affection.

But he didn't kiss her. She didn't expect him to. They never kissed in public.

Because every time their lips touched need rose in crescendo, inevitably leading to far greater intimacies. To their being sated and gasping as they shuddered against each other, hands clutching and breaths mingling.

His hold gentled as he brushed his lips across her temple. 'Hold that thought, *tesoro*.'

Then he led her down to the part of the garden crowded with glittering guests. Ida pressed against him, revelling in the feel of his lean body, powerful and reassuring. Reassuring because, far from wanting to leave him, she couldn't imagine being without him.

Are you really so in thrall to this man?

When had her happiness become linked with Cesare?

The alarm ringing in Ida's head drowned out the noise of the party.

Someone bustled over, asking Cesare to follow. Cesare squeezed her hand, assured her he wouldn't be long, and turned away, leaving Ida with her dazed thoughts.

When had the prospect of parting assumed such dreadful proportions?

Ida knew she'd survive without him. But she didn't want merely to survive. Not any more. The time they'd spent together had taught her that she wanted so much more. She wanted happiness. Companionship. Caring. Waking each day to anticipation and delight. Ending each day in Cesare's arms.

Her heart gave a mighty thump that sent shock waves through her.

When had she fallen for her husband? When he'd spirited her to safety, away from her grandfather? When he'd made gentle, passionate, blazingly beautiful love to her? When he'd listened to her story, even putting together the pieces she'd preferred not to describe in detail?

Maybe when he'd apologised for his past behaviour. Or when she'd discovered he'd taken steps to protect her friend Jo. Definitely when he'd organised for her to visit the interior-design offices of the vast Brunetti portfolio, arranging for her to spend a day there so she could ask questions and see the sort of work they did. When he'd talked about her pursuing her interest in design as if that were the most natural thing in the world. And when he'd begun introducing her to his friends.

Contrary to what she'd expected, Cesare hadn't hidden her away. Nor had he deliberately flaunted her publicly, as if needing to prove something to the scandalmongers who'd thrived on the news of her disappearance.

He'd treated her with respect, thoughtfulness and passion. She loved it.

She might never feel totally at ease in Cesare's rarefied world, but she'd met enough of his friends to value them as sincere and caring. Which said a lot about the man himself. He was far from the monster she'd once thought him.

'There you are, cousin.' It was Francesco, his smile wide. 'I've brought some people to meet you. Can't have you standing alone while the great man speaks.'

He winked and Ida felt something roll over in her chest. Because of his kindness. Because in the distance she saw Cesare nod approvingly, making her wonder if he'd instigated this.

Because for the first time in forever Ida felt as if she really *was* with family.

Her throat tightened, her nostrils and the backs of her

eyes prickling. It was an illusion, of course. She didn't belong here. These people weren't her family.

It was just that here, in Cesare's territory, with him and those around him doing so much to make her welcome, Ida's emotions were strangely wobbly.

After her hellish experiences with her grandfather, this acceptance, this kindness, made her feel too much.

So when, just fifteen minutes later, Cesare forged his way through the applauding throng and held out his arm, she stepped close and looped hers through it. Instantly she felt better, as his warmth and lemony cedar scent enveloped her.

'You're sure you're happy to leave?' he murmured.

Ida pressed nearer, surveying him from under veiling lashes, hoping he read only invitation in her eyes.

He was so handsome, so dear, that it almost undid her just to look at him. Ida realised she was storing up memories against the time when they parted.

When the time came it would be almost impossible to leave Cesare and return to her real life far away. In the meantime, it *was* impossible to give up this fragile joy until she absolutely had to. 'Yes, please. I want to be alone with you.'

Cesare stiffened and she saw a pulse throb at his temple. 'Whatever you wish, *tesoro.*'

Then they were sweeping through the gardens, past the crowds, almost oblivious to the faces turned their way, the greetings and invitations to pause. Cesare's pace didn't falter, though he scattered greetings and a few promises to meet up another time, before shepherding her outside, past the clamouring paparazzi and into the car that miraculously appeared before them.

Minutes later they were driving through Florence. Even now its beauty brought a lump to Ida's throat. Would she ever return here, or would it be out of bounds for ever because the city reminded her of Cesare?

Ida was so lost in thought she was surprised to realise the car had stopped and someone had opened the passenger door. 'Cesare?'

But he was climbing out. Ida turned towards her open door and saw they were in front of an elegant hotel, her door held open by a smiling staff member. Then Cesare was there, holding out her hand and drawing her towards the gleaming entrance.

'Why are we here?'

His lips brushed her ear as he drew her inside. She shivered as a ribbon of heat uncoiled within her. 'The villa is too far away. I want you *now*, Ida.'

He lifted his head, his expression questioning. And something more. Something that made elation rise on gossamer wings.

You're imagining things. This is just physical for Cesare.

Yet the look in those dark, serious eyes made her heart judder.

When she managed to catch her breath, her voice was so husky it sounded unfamiliar. 'I feel the same.'

Later Ida couldn't remember crossing the foyer, checking in or getting to their suite.

All she recalled was the feel of Cesare's hand holding hers, the beating excitement in her chest and the glow in his eyes when the door closed behind them and they were finally alone.

Cesare's breathing was harsh in the stillness, the sound matching the heavy thrum of her pulse. Then she was in his arms, and he was striding towards the gilded, beautiful bedroom, his jaw clenched and an expression on his face that twisted her heart in her chest.

Awe, excitement and hope. She felt them all.

Ida was only human. She forgot about the world beyond Cesare's arms. The fact this was temporary. Instead, she listened to her eager heart.

CHAPTER FIFTEEN

IDA WAS IN one of her favourite spots, on a trellis-shaded seat looking across the pool to the gardens and distant hills.

She tried to concentrate on the laptop Cesare had given her, but her mind drifted to their night in Florence.

Their fervour for each other had been even more potent than usual. They'd come together with an urgency that had blown her brain. Yet beneath the speed had been an emotion that made her heart swell.

Later, noting the crescent-shaped marks on Cesare's back where her nails had dug, and seeing the stubble rash of reddened skin on her breasts and belly, Ida had felt a curious mix of satisfaction and tenderness. Despite weeks of passionate encounters, nothing had felt as intimate as last night.

It wasn't just the sex. It was lying entwined on the vast bed, talking sleepily about everything and nothing. It was the laughter and sense of communion. The connection, as if some invisible thread bound them together.

Their intimacy had been about far more than she'd admitted. More than physical arousal. More than feeling safe with Cesare or grateful for his protection and the wonderful time they'd spent together.

In the early hours Cesare had held her to him and asked if she was happy. It hadn't occurred to Ida to be surprised by his question or cautious in responding, not with that sunburst of joy inside her. She'd told him the truth. That she'd never been happier.

For long moments they'd lain there, staring into each other's eyes.

Ida had no words for the feeling that had encompassed her then. Except maybe peace or belonging. Whatever it was, it had felt momentous. Neither had spoken, but finally Cesare had drawn her close and she'd nestled against him, head on his collarbone, their arms wrapped around each other as they fell asleep.

Cesare had brought her to the villa this morning but then turned to drive back to Florence, belatedly remembering a meeting he'd arranged. Ida had secretly been delighted, wondering if their time together was affecting him as well. She sat grinning, reliving every nuance of every word they'd shared.

Had she truly stumbled on a man who saw her for herself? Who really cared about her? Or did her own yearning blind her?

'*Signora.* A phone call for you.' Dorotea stepped through the open doorway, holding out a phone. 'A friend of yours.'

'*Grazie*, Dorotea.'

Ida took the phone. It could only be Jo, though why would her friend call the house instead of Ida's phone? 'Jo! How's it going?'

Silence crackled in her ear. Not the silence of Jo drawing breath but something else. Something that raised the hairs at her nape.

Ida sat straighter, senses alert.

Finally it came. But not the voice of any friend. It was the voice she'd told herself she'd never hear again.

'Hello, Ida,' he croaked. 'Enjoying your romantic tryst with Brunetti?'

She shot to her feet, her heart trying to burst free of her ribcage.

Her instinct was to throw the phone as far as she could, but fear and shock locked her fingers around it. Nausea rose so strong and fast she thought she'd vomit.

Ida swung towards the villa, opening her mouth as if to call back Dorotea.

'Don't even think about it,' her grandfather snarled, the faux gentleness of his first words obliterated by a familiar threatening tone. 'Call anyone and you'll regret it. You're being watched and I'll know if you disobey me.'

The clammy prickle at the back of Ida's neck spread across her whole body. She felt cold and hot at the same time as she turned to survey the garden and distant hills.

Was he here? Just outside the villa? Or one of his henchmen with a telephoto lens? A drone maybe?

Ida swallowed convulsively, her throat tight with terror at the thought of the old man watching her.

She opened her mouth to say something, but no sound came. It was stupid. All she had to do was call out and Dorotea would hear. Cesare's security team wouldn't let anyone on the premises without authority.

Yet logic was no match for fear, ingrained over years.

'That's better. I wouldn't like you doing something rash because there'd be consequences.'

He paused and Ida could hear his cruel smile.

'What do you want?'

'You wouldn't like anything to happen to Brunetti, would you?'

Dread was a blast of glacial air, shutting down her lungs and freezing her skin before seeping in to frost her bones. Ida's chest heaved as she struggled to breathe, her blood rushing in her ears.

At last, she found her voice. 'What are you saying?'

'He just left, didn't he? In that fast car of his, on these narrow roads. So easy to have an accident. A bit of gravel on the road, an unexpected oil slick on a curve. Or maybe a truck's brakes failing at the wrong moment.'

Ida could see it too clearly. Now her blood iced too.

She remembered the malevolence in her grandfather's eyes years before when he'd shoved her down the stairs, leaving her with concussion and a broken ankle. She thought of the people who'd died in the factory fire set on her grandfather's orders. Of the rumours of other crimes.

'I'm listening,' she said, her voice not her own.

'I thought you would be.' He laughed, the sound like bones rattling. 'You thought Brunetti would rescue you, didn't you? As if he'd ever care for a Calogero.'

I'm not a Calogero.

'Or is it the sex you like, you little slut?'

Fortunately something closed down inside Ida then. That same safety mechanism that had come to her rescue in the past when her grandfather started one of his diatribes. She heard the vile words but as if from a distance, so they didn't register. Just the violence behind them.

Ida found herself shaking, great, racking shudders of distress. If he harmed Cesare…

'What do you want?'

There was silence, as if her interruption surprised him.

'I want you here. *Now.* There's a car just beyond the gates. Walk down to it and let yourself out. You know the security code, I'm sure. If anyone asks, you're just going for a stroll.'

Ida shook her head. He really thought he could order her around any more?

'Don't defy me, girl!' His voice turned silky with threat. 'Unless you want your lover to pay. I can arrange it so he doesn't reach his office. Or maybe he'll get there and something unfortunate will happen. A gas explosion maybe.'

Ida's stomach churned with horror. Horror and a certainty her grandfather meant it. He never made empty threats.

She'd defied him by disappearing, ruining his plans. Meanwhile Cesare had somehow manoeuvred him out of the business and Fausto was being investigated by the police.

'Don't hurt him!'

A rusty chuckle filled her ear. 'Well, we'll have to see, won't we? Come to me and I promise he'll be safe for now. I have a new plan and you'll help me. You owe me.'

Ida swayed, bracing herself against the table.

'Don't go inside. Don't talk to anyone. Put the phone down and come to the gate.' He paused. 'If you're not here in seven minutes your lover will pay. That's a promise.'

The line went dead.

She snatched in a breath so sharp it felt as if she'd swallowed a razor. She lifted her head, but her eyes swam so much she couldn't make out anything but bright sunlight.

Ida jumped when the phone clattered onto the table.

She dragged in a breath, then another.

She couldn't go to her grandfather. She *couldn't*!

If she gave herself up to him, she'd never escape again. He'd use her in some new scheme and keep his claws in her for ever. *After* he'd meted out his vengeance for running away and spoiling his plans.

Ida felt hollow inside, except for the crushing weight pressing onto her chest.

Her one dream in all these years was to be free. Finally, after her marriage, she'd achieved that. Each day had felt glorious despite the drab routine of poverty and grinding, poorly paid work. Despite the fear that kept her in hiding.

So you weren't really free, were you? He was still dictating your life, even when he didn't know where you were. Because you lived in fear.

Ida rubbed a hand across aching eyes. She'd fought so hard for self-determination. How could she bear to give that up?

Because the alternative is to allow them to kill the man you love.

Ida slumped, boneless, against the table.

Strangely there was no shock at the revelation she loved Cesare.

It had been at the back of her consciousness for a while now. Even if it hadn't, a moment like this, of life-or-death danger, provided instant clarity.

After a lifetime learning not to trust men, especially wealthy, powerful men, she'd fallen for Cesare Brunetti heart and soul. It felt like the most natural thing in the world.

The most *wonderful* thing in the world. Cesare mightn't love her, but he'd rescued her from that sterile place where her soul had been locked. He'd brought her to life. He'd given her freedom and safety, joy, pleasure and a heady sense of hope.

The thought of him injured, dying...

Ida found herself walking on trembling legs into the garden. The rich scent of jasmine cloyed, turning rancid, as she imagined Cesare's car crumpled under a massive truck. Of his office blown apart by a bomb.

Her breath came in a gasping sob, and she slapped her palm over her mouth, lest Dorotea hear.

Ida forced back her shoulders and stepped onto the grass. With each pace her steps grew firmer.

She refused to allow the blackness that had shadowed her life to injure Cesare more than it had already.

She had no illusions. Fausto would punish her for what she'd done. She knew too that she took a gamble. There was no certainty he'd keep his word. Cesare could still be in danger.

But the alternative, to disobey, *knowing* Cesare would suffer…

Ida quickened her pace. It was a long way to the security gates. She couldn't be late.

'What do you mean, *gone*?'

Cesare scowled at the dark clouds closing in outside his window as he barked into the phone.

'She walked out,' Lorenzo explained. 'Dorotea said she took a call from a friend, a man. Ten minutes later she'd simply disappeared. Didn't even go back into the villa to get her purse.'

'A man? What man?'

None of this made sense. When Cesare had taken Ida back to the villa, she'd talked about relaxing for a while. He'd promised to be back late this afternoon and her slow smile had ratcheted up his libido. As if they hadn't spent last night sating a desire that seemed unquenchable.

'I'm pretty sure it was Fausto Calogero.'

'What?' Cesare's his eyes bulged. 'She'd never go back to him. Not after what he's done.' Cesare had witnessed her distress as she'd described life with Calogero and knew there was more she hadn't shared. His heart had gone out to her.

'Dorotea said it was an older man.'

'Even so—'

'I'm looking at the security film from the gate.'

'And?'

'She wasn't abducted. She typed the code into the keypad.'

Cesare's breath backed up in his lungs. Ida had left of her own volition? Without a word? There had to be more to this.

'She took a car from the garage?'

Maybe Ida was driving to the office, planning to surprise him. He imagined taking her out for a meal. Or locking the door and taking her on the desk.

That had to be it, she was coming here. The sultry look she'd given him earlier had been a clear promise.

'No, boss. She walked through the gates and got into a waiting car.' Lorenzo paused. 'I can send you the film, but I recognise the man. He works for Calogero. He's the one who was looking for her in London.'

Fear ghosted down Cesare's spine.

Bruno. Calogero's enforcer. The man who'd so terrified Ida that she'd leapt at the chance to fly to Tuscany, not even daring to collect her things.

'Send me the film.' He yanked his tie loose and strode to his desk, checking his computer. 'Did you follow them?'

'I didn't know she'd gone until it was too late. But I've got everyone onto it now. And I've put through a call to someone in the police. I hope to have news soon.'

Soon? That wasn't good enough.

But there was no point berating Lorenzo. His team's orders weren't to keep Ida prisoner.

Where had she gone? Above all, why leave with Bruno? Surely Lorenzo was wrong.

Cesare opened the security camera footage.

There was Ida, keying in the code to the gates. They swung wide and she stepped out, skirt fluttering around her legs. His heart hammered. It was the dress with velvet ribbons over her shoulders and beneath her breasts. She looked dainty and alluring, and she showed no hesitation as she walked, not once looking back.

She stopped. Her shoulders rose as if she took a deep

breath. But she only paused a second before approaching a car with tinted windows. The door was open, held by a burly man with a wrestler's physique. Even from a distance Cesare recognised him. The smashed nose, thick neck and impassive face. Not impassive now. The way he looked at Ida churned nausea through Cesare's gut.

But she hadn't baulked.

Ida walked out of the safety of Cesare's home straight to the men she feared. Of her own free will. If Bruno was there, so was Calogero, in the car or waiting elsewhere.

Cesare's head spun.

There was no reason for Ida to do this. He could protect her from her grandfather. He *had* protected her. She was happy with Cesare. She'd told him so and he'd seen it for himself. The way she smiled more, the sound of her laughter, the joy in her eyes.

What had changed?

Maybe nothing had changed.

The insidious voice wove through his thoughts, but he refused to listen.

Cesare hit replay on the security film.

Apart from that instant's pause, when it looked as if Ida gathered herself, there was nothing to indicate hesitation about leaving with the man she'd so feared.

Maybe she hadn't feared him after all. Maybe they were allies, not enemies. Maybe she was playing a long game and you were a fool.

Cesare's breath turned to ash on his tongue.

It was impossible.

He knew the real Ida now. She'd never willingly associate with Calogero or his bruiser.

Again Cesare hit replay. Was that really a momentary pause, or was Ida drawing a breath of relief at being off his property?

Maybe she wanted to go back to her family.

Maybe Calogero wasn't her enemy.

Maybe she spun you lies.

Cesare scowled at the ridiculous idea. And at the searing pain ripping through his belly.

He only had her word for what she'd said about her history.

Maybe Calogero hadn't forced her into compliance.

Maybe she'd been a willing pupil. Learning to scheme and lie.

But Cesare had surprised her in London. She hadn't known he was looking for her.

Unless Calogero's staff had you under surveillance and briefed Ida.

Unless she set you up.

His heart dived. Yet what would she gain? An affair with him wouldn't stop their divorce and she'd signed the papers. The prenup was watertight.

Another scandal? The missing wife returns then disappears again? Cesare frowned. After what he'd already weathered, a bit more gossip meant nothing.

What had she and Calogero to gain?

Ida had been in the villa. She'd had the run of the place, including when he wasn't there. Yet no valuables had gone missing. Ida wasn't a thief.

Cesare's breath fractured and clawing talons scored his windpipe. She'd used his study, often curling up on a sofa there, using the laptop he'd given her. He knew she'd been investigating interior-design courses. Had she been investigating something else too?

Had she hacked into his computer?

He'd broken Calogero's death grip on the company and the old man was about to go down for a range of crimes. But wasn't a cornered animal all the more dangerous?

Had Calogero sent Ida to gather information about the investigations into his crimes, and to locate remaining weaknesses in the Brunetti company?

Cesare turned his back on the screen. He couldn't watch the footage any more.

His heart told him Ida was genuine. That she wasn't a schemer. That she hadn't betrayed him. Yet cold, unemotional logic gave a different perspective.

Cesare had learned in childhood how foolish men could be when in thrall to a beautiful woman. Ida wasn't merely beautiful. She was fascinating, enticing and passionate. She made his blood pump faster and the world seem brighter.

He snatched a breath that didn't fill his cramped lungs.

Had he inherited his father's weakness?

Had he let his libido undermine caution? Had he allowed himself to fall under the spell of a woman who used him to get what she wanted?

Cesare's nape tightened and sweat beaded his brow.

He'd crossed every boundary his *nonno* had taught him. He'd been impulsive. He'd confused business with pleasure, giving emotions free rein. Trusting without demanding proof. His honourable instinct to protect a vulnerable woman had morphed into something more profound and potentially self-destructive.

Had he made the biggest mistake of his life?

CHAPTER SIXTEEN

IDA WOKE HORRIBLY. A headache beat through her skull in time with her hammering pulse and there was something wrong with her mouth.

She lifted her hand to investigate but found something wrong with that too. It took long, befuddled seconds to realise there was something wrapped around her wrists, tying them together. And something around her mouth as well. Panicked, she tried to swallow over the musty taste in her mouth and realised her mouth was filled with fabric, held in place by a gag.

Her eyes snapped open, and she immediately closed them as pain spiked. Cautiously she squinted against the light, inhaling through her nose, fighting rising panic.

Slowly things began to make sense. She lay on her side on a marble floor, its chill leaching into her body. She was in a large sitting room, sombrely and expensively decorated in the style of several centuries ago. She saw gilded antique furniture, dark paintings and heavy velvet curtains partly drawn across tall windows.

Memory surfaced.

Bruno had brought her to this place, a venerable mansion where her grandfather had been waiting.

Convulsively Ida swallowed, fear rising anew as she recalled the scene. Her grandfather had looked far older and more fragile than she remembered. So bad that she'd wondered if he was ill. But his temper hadn't changed.

There'd been sneering triumph and malevolent anticipation in his face as he'd derided her for thinking she could escape him.

He had a use for her, he'd said. First to make Cesare suffer and then as a bargaining chip to get Cesare to call off his investigators. If that didn't work... His voice had turned soft, and Ida's skin had crawled. That was when her grandfather was most dangerous.

He'd peppered her with questions about Cesare, his business and plans. As if Ida would betray Cesare to him!

She'd pleaded ignorance again and again, but that had only infuriated Calogero. For the first time she saw him spooked, fear crossing his jaundiced features as he spoke of someone prying into his affairs. Someone who'd outmanoeuvred his own security.

A flicker of hope had flared. Her grandfather thought it was just Cesare pursuing him. He didn't realise it was the police across several countries. Maybe they were close to an arrest? Cesare had thought so.

Finally, her grandfather's temper had peaked and he'd lashed out, knocking her off her feet. She'd taken a step to save herself but caught her foot in the edge of a carpet and lost her balance.

That explained the pounding skull. It must have connected with the stone floor. Gingerly she lifted her tied hands and discovered a lump on her head. Nausea filled her at that gentle probing, and she had to stop and rest.

While she'd been unconscious someone, Bruno, no doubt, had bound and gagged her. Why? Her grandfather would have people here who'd stop her leaving.

Ida forced herself to lie still and think.

Did she hear voices? Or was it the sound of her pulse?

She scrabbled at the gag but only the tips of her fingers were free of their binding and she couldn't get enough purchase.

Ignoring the screaming pain, she rolled forward, bracing her joined hands and getting onto her knees. Her head swam but she fought it. When her head cleared she was sure of it, there were voices near by. Masculine voices.

Her heart leapt. Was she crazy to imagine that deep tone was Cesare's?

Looking for something to help her up, for her feet were tied too, Ida discovered a spindly-legged sofa and side table beside her. On the table was a glass, a fine goblet with the look of age.

Teetering on her knees, Ida lifted the goblet clumsily in her bound hands. She shot a look towards the door. It was still closed, the voices muffled.

Silently she prayed it wasn't Bruno talking with her grandfather but someone who might help her escape. She had to warn Cesare he was in danger.

'You always were stubborn, Brunetti, just like your grandfather.' Calogero shook his head. 'Why would I kidnap your wife? You can't blame me if she wasn't happy with you.' His eyes flashed maliciously. 'You made a spectacle of yourself driving her away the first time. But to do it twice? You've made yourself a laughing stock.'

His croaky chuckle was like poison dripping on unprotected flesh.

Cesare's skin crawled. Beneath his veneer of calm, he'd never known such violent emotion. It was hard thinking beyond the haze of fury at this man.

'But if she does seek sanctuary here,' the old devil continued, 'in the bosom of her family, I'll take her in and shelter her. If you've maltreated her...'

Cesare stood unmoving, refusing to react to such slander. He wasn't the one who'd treated Ida badly.

He glanced at the stocky man standing in a corner behind where Calogero sat at his oversized desk. Bruno looked every inch the thug Ida had described him. The thought of her at that man's mercy carved a hollow through Cesare's belly.

'Yet Ida was seen leaving my villa with your man.' He nodded at Bruno.

'You astound me.' Calogero swung around in his seat. 'What do you know about this, Bruno?'

'Nothing, boss.' He turned his blank gaze to Cesare. 'Whoever saw it was mistaken. I haven't seen her in years.'

The curl at the corners of his mouth belied his words.

Cesare itched to force the truth from his lying mouth. It might yet come to that, but Cesare suspected violence wouldn't get him far. Calogero would call in reinforcements and Cesare would be overpowered before he could find her.

Frustration rose, but behind it was fear that he was too late. The desperate urge to smash through this pretence vied with cold dread. But revealing his feelings would be disastrous.

Calogero was a vampire, living off others, sucking them dry in his quest for power, riches and recognition.

'Well,' Cesare murmured, flexing constricted shoulders. 'That's unfortunate. I had a proposition for you but if you don't know where she is…' He spread his hands, palms up. 'Never mind. I won't waste any more of your time.'

'What proposition?'

Calogero might be a devious strategist and downright dangerous, but he'd never make a poker player. Those rheumy eyes glistened greedily, and he sat forward, knobbly hands spread on the desk, practically slavering in anticipation.

Cesare met his eyes but didn't speak straight away.

'You want to punish her, don't you? That's why you want her so badly,' the creaky voice continued, and to Cesare's disgust the old man smiled approvingly. 'I can't blame you. A man isn't a man if he can't control his womenfolk.'

Cesare bit back a riposte that a *real* man didn't need to control anyone. But he wasn't here to argue. The stakes were too high.

'Since you have no idea where she is, there's no point discussing it. If she contacts you, call me and we can do business.'

He swung around as if to leave, his heart pummelling his ribcage. If this didn't work...

'Perhaps... Who knows? Maybe I can help you after all. What are you offering?'

Slowly Cesare turned back. Then he drew out the paper his lawyer had drawn up under strenuous protest in the time it had taken Cesare to drive to the address Lorenzo had found.

Calogero sat forward, his spidery body ready to pounce.

Cesare tossed the paper onto the desk and watched him grab it, eyes widening as he read. Then read again. Finally, he sat back. 'This is nothing. Not a contract, just a memorandum of understanding. It's not binding.'

'It will carry weight in a court of law if we both sign it.' Cesare paused, letting that sink in. 'Or if you prefer to wait...' He glanced at his watch, wondering how long before the others arrived. 'My legal team is drawing up the detailed contract now. I didn't give them much time, but I wanted to prove my intentions in the meantime.'

The old man said nothing. Cesare could see the wheels turning in his brain.

'But it's academic,' Cesare continued. 'The offer stands

only if Ida is returned to me. Immediately. Since you don't know her whereabouts...'

Yellowed teeth were bared in a smile that was as eager as it was horrible. 'There may be a way I could help. As a favour to an old friend.'

Cesare checked a contemptuous sneer, merely raising his eyebrows. 'Go on.'

'If I were to find the girl and bring her to you—'

'Not good enough. I want her *now*.'

He drew a fountain pen from his pocket and approached the desk. Calogero licked his lips and looked down at the paper. The man was greedy. He wanted the deal, but he wanted to keep Ida too.

Every muscle in Cesare's body drew taut as he forced himself to hold back.

But it was no good, the need to find Ida was overwhelming. He leaned across the desk, reaching for his nemesis, when a thud made him turn. A door to his left slammed against the wall.

'Ida!'

She was pale, the bright, dishevelled hair tumbling around her shoulders contrasting with her stark pallor. And the bright red stains on her hands.

Cesare's heart plummeted as anger combusted into incandescent rage. What had they done to her?

'Don't sign it!' she gasped. 'Don't give him anything.'

Cesare got to her in a few strides, but Bruno had reached her first. He'd been standing in that corner. He grabbed Ida by the shoulders, shoving her back towards the door.

Cesare acted instinctively. Later he could only recall the feel of a hard muscled shoulder beneath his hand as he swung the bodyguard around. Bruno's massive fist hurtling towards his face. The blocking movement he'd learned all those years ago working in the slums. The sound of bone crunching as Cesare's heel connected with Bruno's knee. And the impact of his knuckles on solid flesh, both fists in quick succession, followed by the gasp of the winded man and the thud as he toppled to the floor.

Then Ida was in Cesare's arms.

He ran his hands over her, checking for more injuries, eyes widening at the bright blood welling from her hands. There were shallow cuts between her fingers and at her wrists. The sight woke a growling beast inside him.

'What did they do to you?'

His throat was so tight he barely got the words out.

Ida buried her face in his chest, hands clenching on his shirt, and he swore his heart stopped. 'You're here! You're really here.'

'Shh, it's all right, Ida.'

He couldn't believe she was safe in his arms. The last couple of hours felt like an eternity in which he'd aged decades. Relief was so sharp it cut his very soul, severing something within that had been bound tight and hard.

In his peripheral vision Cesare saw movement. The old man lifting a phone to his ear, gabbling about help.

Holding Ida close, Cesare crossed to the desk, plucked the phone from Calogero and threw it across the room. It shattered against inlaid marble.

Cesare's breath came as short punches of oxygen.

'You wouldn't harm an old man!'

Cesare surveyed him, cowering in his seat. He wanted to smash Calogero. To make him pay.

Instead, he drew a deep, scouring breath and fought for restraint. His arms settled around Ida, cradling her close, her soft body like a benediction, a lightness in the dark whirlpool of his rage.

Calogero would pay. But Cesare would not lower himself to the villain's standards.

Holding the old man's gaze, he reached for the agreement, crumpled it slowly in his fist and shoved it in his pocket. Then he lifted Ida into his arms and marched to the door. 'It's okay, *cara*. It's over.'

There it was, the sound of sirens and pounding on the street door. The police had been almost ready to haul Calogero in for questioning. Cesare's urgent call had brought that forward.

He took the staircase slowly, conscious of his precious burden.

On the ground floor a number of heavy-set men in suits appeared but didn't try to stop him. Not with police demanding entry. Calogero's thugs were wondering about their future.

Cesare strode through the now open door and didn't look back.

He'd been kindness itself, holding her until the shaking stopped. Sitting with her in the ambulance while a medic checked the bump on her head, gave her a painkiller and saw to the shallow cuts she'd got while sawing through her bonds with broken glass.

Cesare had been everything she could wish for. He'd rescued her when she feared she might never escape. The sound of his voice, the sight of him as she staggered into the room, had almost undone her. He'd dealt with her grandfather and Bruno, the men she'd lived in fear of for so long. He'd even brushed past the police, insisting they wait to question her. Then he'd taken her to his villa, draping his jacket over her shivering shoulders.

Ida should be ecstatic. Instead she felt sick.

For he'd barely spoken. He avoided her eyes as if he couldn't bear to look at her.

She hadn't heard everything her grandfather had said. But Cesare must know she'd chosen to go there.

Did he think she'd thrown in her lot with her grandfather, who'd later turned against her for reasons of his own?

She knew a deep vein of mistrust ran through Cesare. Mistrust of the Calogero family. And of women. She'd heard Cesare's contempt, not just for his father, who he deemed weak, but also for the women he believed had seduced his father.

Did he see her as another mercenary woman out to get what she could? Just as he had when they first met?

The time they'd shared here had been golden with promise and burgeoning love. *For her.*

But for Cesare? Sometimes it had felt as if they hovered on the brink of something wonderful. She'd been almost certain Cesare was opening his heart to her, but he'd never said so.

Perhaps she'd imagined that. Certainly he wasn't loverlike now. He kept his distance and wouldn't meet her eyes.

She'd misinterpreted his passion for the beginnings of love. Though he'd made it clear this was a temporary arrangement.

They were getting divorced! How could she have imagined he felt more?

Ida blinked prickling eyes and turned away from the silent man on the sofa opposite. Night had fallen and outside the underwater lights turned the pool into a shimmering oasis. It was almost too beautiful. She couldn't bear this any more.

She drained her glass of water and made to rise.

'Ida, we need to talk.'

Her head snapped around. Cesare's expression hadn't altered. He still looked as communicative as a statue, his big frame rigid.

She shuddered beneath the silk-lined warmth of his jacket. 'I'm sorry,' she blurted out. 'I did what I had to.'

Her throat closed as she remembered the threat to harm Cesare. Ridiculous that it still upset her now he was safe, yet hot tears flooded her eyes.

'Ida, don't. Please.' His voice was harsh but a beautiful sort of harsh, almost tender. It made the tears come faster because she must be imagining the tenderness. To her dismay he rose and sat beside her.

She groped for a tissue, plunging her hand into the jacket pocket, fingers closing around crumpled paper.

Ida sniffed and withdrew it, bending her head as if fascinated by the paper instead of the man beside her.

A handkerchief appeared before her and she took it with a nod of thanks, dabbing at her eyes. 'Sorry. It's just reaction.'

'Don't apologise.' His voice was harsh. 'I was wrong. You should have a good cry if it makes you feel better.'

But Ida didn't want to weep. She wanted to end this torture, sitting with the man she loved, knowing it was all over. It was obvious he didn't return her feelings. If he thought she'd been in league with her grandfather, he probably despised her.

He'd saved her because he was a decent man. He'd have done the same for anyone.

Ida turned towards him but didn't meet his eyes. 'Did I thank you? I can't remember. It's a bit of a blur.' *Liar.* Today's events were branded on her brain. 'But I appreciate all you've done. And don't worry, as soon as the police have finished with their questions, I'll go.'

Her nervous babble died when a warm hand covered her bare arm. 'I'm sorry, Ida. You must have been terrified.'

'You've got nothing to be sorry for.'

Unthinking, she met Cesare's eyes and then couldn't look away. His expression matched how she felt. Anguished.

She blinked. It couldn't be.

'If you'd felt safe here you wouldn't have gone to him. If you'd believed in me.'

Cesare's mouth compressed to a thin line and Ida saw that flicker of pulse at his temple, something she'd seen in moments of extreme emotion. She stared at his drawn features. Was it possible he felt *guilty*?

She shifted and instantly his hand dropped.

'*You're* not responsible, Cesare.'

'No?' His lips curled. 'If you felt you could trust me, you'd have come to me instead of going to him when he demanded it. I thought you *knew* I'd protect you. Hadn't I made that clear?'

He didn't wait for an answer. 'It's my fault you don't trust me. It's because of how I treated you before, isn't it? Because of my prejudice.' He yanked his tie lower, dragging his collar undone as if it were too tight. 'I failed you.'

Agog, Ida digested Cesare's words. He wasn't berating her for being in league with her grandfather. He blamed himself for her leaving!

'What hold did he have over you, Ida? How did he force you to go without even telling me?'

Ida stared, still unable to believe what she'd heard. When she spoke her voice seemed to come from far away. 'You don't think I was working with him?'

Cesare's head jerked back. 'Working with him? You were terrified of him.'

Ida's heart galloped and she felt light-headed. She licked suddenly dry lips. 'You believe I was a victim?'

He looked down at the bandages on her hands, his expression truly ferocious. 'Believe? I know it.' Then his eyes held hers, his gaze searching. 'What did he threaten, Ida? How did he get you there?'

It was so unexpected, to have this powerful man who'd once lived and breathed mistrust, believing her without question. As if their early history and his prejudices meant nothing.

Because he believes in you.

Could it be true?

A squall of emotions tumbled through her. Amazement, joy and disbelief so strong she felt like crying and laughing at once. Her shoulders shook but her eyes were dry and staring.

Now she saw something in his dark gaze that hijacked the breath from her lungs. Something strong and tender. Something like the yearning she felt.

Cesare's hands were gentle on her upper arms. 'You're safe now. He can't hurt you, truly. With the evidence against him across two countries there's no way he'll be bailed. I suspect he'll spend the rest of his life behind bars.'

Ida swallowed, trying to find words as her heart swelled. 'Cesare.' It was a whisper, barely louder than her pulse, and he leaned closer. 'You...trust me?'

For so long she'd been entangled in a world of duplicity and sham, of threats, fear and mistrust. She'd told herself again and again that Cesare's attentions were the fleeting product of lust. But this felt *real.*

'Absolutely.' He lifted one bandaged hand and carefully pressed his lips to a patch of bare skin. 'When I heard you'd gone I died a thousand deaths, imagining what might happen to you.'

Ida hung on his words yet still couldn't quite take them in. Almost as if she wanted him to recant and admit he'd doubted her. 'But I wasn't kidnapped. I walked straight out.'

'I saw the film and it almost broke my heart.' Another

kiss to her fingers, more fervent than the last, sending a shaft of heat through her chilled body. 'Everything I'd learned about manipulation told me you'd played me for a fool.'

His hand tightened as she made to draw back. 'But my heart knew better. It told me the only way you'd go to him was because you'd been forced. What was it? Did he threaten your cousin in Scotland?'

Ida looked into that proud, concerned, dear face and wondered how she'd doubted him. What she saw there overwhelmed her. This time when she blinked back tears, they were tears of joy.

'It's okay. We can talk later. You need rest.'

'No! What I need is you, Cesare. Only you.' She turned her hand to grip his and lift it to her mouth, inhaling that unique scent of cedar, citrus and hot, delectable male that she'd become addicted to. She kissed his hand, tasting the salty essence of him.

Long fingers threaded through her hair, gently massaging her scalp and drawing her closer. She wanted to sink against him but he was right. They needed to talk.

'He threatened to harm you. Either a car accident on the drive into Florence or an explosion at the office.' Ida felt Cesare stiffen. 'He told me I was being watched and that if I made an attempt to talk to anyone, or send a message, you'd pay. I believed him.'

Silence but for Cesare's ragged breathing. Finally he spoke, his voice hoarse. 'You walked into danger for *my* sake?'

She lifted her shoulders. 'I couldn't bear the thought of him harming you.'

Cesare drew their joined hands against his wide chest, so she felt his drumming heart. 'You're the bravest woman I know.'

Ida shook her head. 'Not brave. Just desperate.'

Heat flared in that liquid dark gaze, tugging at her heart.

'I knew you were remarkable,' he murmured. 'Right from the beginning there was something about you that made me weak for you. But I never guessed the half of how amazing you are.' His expression was full of admiration and something so powerfully tender that Ida's soul soared. 'I don't understand what I've done to deserve such incredible loyalty. Such sacrifice.'

To Ida's amazement Cesare's deep voice wobbled on the last word before his jaw clamped tight.

'After what you've done for me? You gave me hope in dark times. You gave me…'

Her words faded as she struggled to explain how he'd turned her life around, giving her not merely security but happiness such as she'd never known and a renewed determination not simply to hide from her grandfather, but also to build a positive future.

'I didn't give anything you didn't deserve.' Still holding her hand to his chest, Cesare skimmed his knuckles along her cheek and a seam of longing opened up in her heart. 'Even when we married and I told myself it was just sexual desire I felt, I *knew* you were important to me, Ida. Maybe that's why I reacted so badly. I didn't want to be vulnerable.'

Cesare grimaced. 'Learning the truth, learning about *you*, has made me question everything I was so sure I knew. The old mantra of duty over passion, strategy and success instead of love, none of that worked any more.'

His palm cupped her face. 'You mean so much to me. I love you, Ida.'

Shock made her stiffen and instantly Cesare released her, his mouth flattening.

'It's too early, I know. I shouldn't have blurted that out. Blame it on shock.' In one swift movement he was on his feet, stalking away then spinning on his heel to look back at her, his chest expanding on a huge breath. 'I only realised what this feeling was today, when I thought I'd lost you. But you've had enough for now. This can wait.'

'No, it can't!' Ida didn't feel tired now. There was enough energy sparking through her to light up a whole city. 'I just wasn't expecting—'

'I know it's hard to believe after the way I behaved. I've got a lot of catching up to do.'

He was flagellating himself over the past when none of that mattered. Ida's hands curled in her lap and something crackled. She glanced down to see a paper on her lap, smoothed flat by her restless hands.

And then she didn't hear anything else Cesare said.

There was a roaring in her ears like a high-speed train and she shook all over as if from its vibration.

'Cesare?' Her voice when it came was thin and high. 'You were going to do this? For me?' When she lifted her head, she looked into eyes so intent she felt his stare as a tangible, stroking caress. 'You were going to give him a controlling share of Brunetti Enterprises?'

Even reading the words in black and white, it seemed impossible.

'If it meant getting you back.'

'Cesare, you couldn't! It's your family firm. The thing you worked for and loved all your life. It's tradition and history and family.'

Ida knew those were as vital to him as the blood flowing in his veins. His pride in his family's achievements, his concern for those dependent on the company and his focus on innovation and success were part of him.

Yet he didn't say it had been a ploy to trick her grandfather. Instead, a slow smile edged the corners of his mouth.

Not a confident grin. For remarkably, Cesare looked anything but self-assured.

'I've found something I love more.'

Ida's hand went to her throat where her heart thrashed as if trying to escape.

'I still want what's best for the company. I'll still do all I can to protect it and nurture it, but I've learned that a business is just that. It's not my life and I don't want it to be. Given a choice between saving you and the company, it had to be you.'

He went on, seemingly oblivious to her shock. 'Even after you signed the divorce papers I couldn't bring myself to give them to my lawyer. They're sitting in my desk drawer.' He read her stunned expression and nodded. 'Yes, even then, *tesoro*. Though I didn't understand why. I just knew I suddenly wasn't ready to end our marriage and I needed to know why.'

Cesare paced towards her and with every step the glow in his eyes dissolved the last vestiges of doubt. 'My priorities have shifted. I'd rather have love.' His voice was whisky and gravel and utterly compelling because she heard the raw ache there. It matched the sweet shaft of pleasure-pain inside her. Again Ida saw that vein throb at his temple. 'If you give me a chance. With time…'

Remarkably Cesare seemed to run out of steam, as if the persuasive words he'd once wielded so easily were now beyond him. He lifted his shoulders and spread his hands as if inviting her to take a chance on him.

Inviting.

Not demanding.

Not cornering her so she had no choice.

Not putting his desires above her own.

Once Ida had thought him similar to her grandfather, ruthless and self-focused. She'd been wrong.

Cesare looked almost as vulnerable as she felt.

Ida felt the flutter of paper against her leg as she rose, eyes locked on Cesare's.

'You trust me.' Her voice was a wisp of air. 'You care for me.' Her words were firmer now. 'You make me feel worthy of love.' Something she hadn't experienced for so long. 'I can't tell you how much that means.'

'You don't need to explain, Ida. You make me feel the same.'

'I've never in my life felt as good as I do with you, Cesare.' There, she'd admitted it, the truth she'd shied from for weeks. 'Because I love you too. I've loved you such a long time, even when I tried not to.'

Suddenly his arms were around her, tender but firm. Those dark eyes that looked to Ida like paradise gleamed overbright. The smile curling the corners of his mouth made her heart want to fly.

'Does that mean you'll take a chance with me, Ida?'

She shook her head. 'It's not taking a chance, my love.' How wonderful it felt to say those words. 'I believe in you. I believe in *us*. I've never been more certain of anything as I am that we're meant for each other.'

Cesare smiled down at her, letting all he felt show. Then, because words were superfluous, he drew her close and proved in other ways exactly how precious she was to him.

EPILOGUE

'HAVE I TOLD you how gorgeous you look, *tesoro*?'

In the full-length mirror Ida saw Cesare approach, looking too scrumptious and tempting for a woman expecting a houseful of guests in a few minutes. She'd like to drag that formal black jacket from his wide shoulders, tug the silk bow tie undone and have her wicked way with him.

From Cesare's smug expression he read her thoughts. Not surprising, since they were so attuned.

'You've mentioned it once or twice.' She grinned as he stopped behind her. 'But I don't object to repetition.'

He bent and kissed that sensitive spot at the base of her neck that made her skin tingle and butterflies swarm deep inside.

'That dress looks magnificent on you.' His teeth skimmed her flesh and she shuddered as delicious sensations shot through her. 'But you look wonderful no matter how you dress. Or even if you don't dress.' Cesare made a sound at the back of his throat, a soft, purring growl of approval that liquefied her knees. '*Especially* if you don't dress.'

Ida leaned back against her husband, letting him take her weight.

In the mirror she saw a woman in a form-fitting lace dress of seafoam-green that matched her eyes. A woman wearing such a look of such dazed delight Ida knew she needed time to make herself presentable before their guests arrived.

But then Cesare met her gaze in the mirror, sliding his arms around her to rest his broad palms on the tiny swell of her abdomen, and suddenly Ida didn't care about the guests. Not the renowned interior designer who'd just offered Ida a part-time job. Or even Kate and Jo, who'd flown in for the anniversary party, arriving on the same flight as Francesco, who was driving them here to the villa now.

'Happy?' Ida asked, her voice husky.

'It's impossible to explain how much.' He stroked his hand over the spot where their first child nestled. 'You changed my whole life, Ida. You know that, don't you?'

'You changed mine too.' And she didn't just mean because her grandfather and his thugs were behind bars. 'Sometimes I can't believe how lucky I am.'

'It's more than luck, my love. You deserve all the happiness in the world.'

'So do you. You're the best man I know.'

The world blurred as Cesare spun her around and drew her tight against him, his head lowering.

'I've just put on my lipstick!'

Too late. His mouth was on hers in a kiss so full of love and just-controlled passion that Ida didn't even try to resist.

Finally, Cesare lifted his head and frowned. 'I hear a car.' He sighed. 'You've just got time to refresh your lipstick.'

Ida breathed deep, inhaling the familiar scent of this man she adored.

'Some things are more important than lipstick. I've decided on a more natural look for tonight. Besides, Dorotea will answer the door and take their coats.'

'Which gives us another few minutes.'

He pulled her to him, and Ida laughed with pure delight.

Her instinct when they'd met all those years ago had proved correct. Marriage to Cesare Brunetti was everything she'd hoped for and so much more.

* * * * *

COMING SOON!

We really hope you enjoyed reading this book.
If you're looking for more romance, be sure to
head to the shops when new books are
available on

Thursday 10th November

To see which titles are coming soon, please visit
millsandboon.co.uk/nextmonth

MILLS & BOON®

Coming next month

WEDDING NIGHT WITH THE WRONG BILLIONAIRE
Dani Collins

"It's just us here." The words slipped out of her, impetuous. Desperate.

A distant part of her urged her to show some sense. She knew Micah would never forgive her for so much as getting in Remy's car, but they had had something in Paris. It had been interrupted and the not knowing what could have been had left her with an ache of yearning that had stalled her in some way. If she couldn't have Remy then it didn't matter who she married. They were all the same because they weren't him.

"No one would know."

"This would only be today. An hour. We couldn't tell anyone. Ever. If Hunter found out—"

"If Micah found out," she echoed with a catch in her voice. "I don't care about any of that, Remy. I really don't."

"After this, it goes back to the way it was, like we didn't even know one another. Is that really what you want?" His face twisted with conflict.

"No," she confessed with a chasm opening in her chest. "But I'll take it."

He closed his eyes, swearing as he fell back against the door with a defeated thump.

"Come here, then."

Continue reading
WEDDING NIGHT WITH THE WRONG BILLIONAIRE
Dani Collins

Available next month
www.millsandboon.co.uk

LET'S TALK
Romance

For exclusive extracts, competitions
and special offers, find us online: